"OKAY, I BELIEVE YOU. LET'S SEE THE PERIMETER. . . ."

Karl Wolf switched from LI to sensor feed, and his faceplate lit up with a dozen blinking red dots. The unexpected sight made him forget his Terranglic. *"Mein Gott!"*

Each one of those red lights was a sensor reporting movement by man-sized bodies pushing through the jungle. There might be a dozen moving targets out there—or even more.

Wolf hit his commlink button. "Alert! Alert! Movement outside the camp!" He didn't have time to repeat the warning before the whine of kinetic energy rifles erupted from the brush. He grabbed Antonelli by the web gear and pulled him down beside him. "Keep your head down, kid!" he said harshly, switching his faceplate back to LI vision again before groping for his pistol. "And let 'em have it!"

COHORT OF THE DAMNED

If you and/or a friend would like to receive the *ROC Advance*, a bimonthly newsletter featuring all the newest and hottest ROC books and authors, on a complimentary basis, please fill out this form and return it to:

ROC Books/Penguin USA
375 Hudson Street
New York, NY 10014

Your Address

Name _____

Street _____ Apt. # _____

City _____ State _____ Zip _____

Friend's Address

Name _____

Street _____ Apt. # _____

City _____ State _____ Zip _____

THE FIFTH
FOREIGN LEGION
Cohort of
the Damned

Andrew Keith

A ROC BOOK

ROC
Published by the Penguin Group
Penguin Books USA Inc., 375 Hudson Street,
New York, New York 10014, U.S.A.
Penguin Books Ltd, 27 Wrights Lane,
London W8 5TZ, England
Penguin Books Australia Ltd, Ringwood,
Victoria, Australia
Penguin Books Canada Ltd, 10 Alcorn Avenue,
Toronto, Ontario, Canada M4V 3B2
Penguin Books (N.Z.) Ltd, 182-190 Wairau Road,
Auckland 10, New Zealand

Penguin Books Ltd, Registered Offices:
Harmondsworth, Middlesex, England

First published by Roc, An imprint of New American Library,
a division of Penguin Books USA Inc.

First Printing, February, 1993
10 9 8 7 6 5 4 3 2 1

To the legion of the lost ones,
to the cohort of the damned

—Rudyard Kipling
Gentlemen Rankers, 1892

Prologue

Beau Soleil: Distance from Sol 94 light years . . . Spectral class G2V; radius 1.0 Sol; mass 1.0 Sol; luminosity 1.01 Sol. Stellar Effective Temperature 5800° K . . . Seven planets, including one habitable world, Beau Soleil III, designated Devereaux . . .

III Devereaux: Orbital radius 0.96 AUs; eccentricity .0068; period 0.94 solar years (343.6 std. days) . . . No natural satellites . . .

Planetary mass 0.9 Terra; density 0.95 Terra (5.225 g/cc); surface gravity 0.93 G. Radius 6265.2 kilometers; circumference 39,365.49 kilometers . . . Total surface area 493,263,949.23 square kilometers . . .

Hydrographic percentage 64 percent . . . Mean atmospheric pressure 0.85 atm; composition oxygen/nitrogen. Oxygen content 23 percent . . .

Planetary axial tilt 21 degrees 39 feet 17.6 inches. Rotation period 28 hours, 18 minutes, 14.2 seconds . . .

Planetography: Devereaux is a familiar Terra-type world, offering few surprises . . . There are three major continents as well as a significant chain of islands which together roughly equal the smallest continent in land surface area. . . .

Temperatures and climatic zones are within Terrestrial norms, though overall conditions tend to be slightly warmer and more arid than in equivalent Terran zones. The most noteworthy terrain features are the Archipel d'Aurore, the massive island chain extending through the tropical band of the planet's eastern hemisphere, and the Great Desert which dominates much of Devereaux's largest continent . . .

Although a diversity of native life forms is found on Devereaux, there is no native sapient life . . . of some interest to planetary ecologists is the impact of three successive waves of colonization over a five-thousand year period on the planetary biosphere . . . the native biochemistry is basically compatible with Terran life forms, and transplanted Terran species have flourished. . . .

People: Population 378,000,000; Urbanization 45 percent . . . Ethnic Groups: Gwyrran 96 percent, Human (primarily French) 3 percent, Other 1 percent . . . *Languages:* Terranglic, French, Gwyrran dialects . . . *Religions:* Universal Church of Gwyrr 93 percent, Catholic 5 percent, Other 2 percent . . . *Capital:* Villastre; *Major Cities:* Villastre (18,206,963), Ile de Havre (12,658,419), Premier d'Atterissage (10,743,072) . . . *Port Facilities:* Haut Port geosynch orbital spaceport, 5 planetary spaceports . . .

Government: Type: Commonwealth Trust . . . *Head of Government:* Governor Guillaume Gerard . . . *Local Divisions:* 5 . . . *Defense Budget as Percentage of GDP:* 2.2 percent . . . Military Manpower 6 percent . . .

Economy: *Resources and Industries:* Natural Agricultural Products, Ores, Radioactives, Petrochemicals, Processed Agroproducts, Alloys, Agro Byproducts, Light Manufacturing, High-Tech Systems . . . *Exports:* Processed Agricultural Products, Agro Byproducts, Light Manufactured Goods . . . *Imports:* Gems and Crystals, Heavy Manufactured Goods, Electronics . . . Arable Land 15 percent (26,636,251 sq. kms.) . . . *Labor Force:* Agricultural 38 percent, Industrial 29 percent, Service 25 percent, Resource Extraction 8 percent . . .

Finance: *Currency:* Commonwealth Sol . . . Gross Domestic Product 737,100,000,000 sols . . . Per Capita Income 1500 Sols . . .

History: Originally settled by Gwyrran colonists under the auspices of the Semti Conclave approximately 5,000 years ago, the planet now known as Devereaux formed an important center for trade, exploration, and military operations for the Conclave for many centuries. A series of devastating plagues and famines drastically reduced the Gwyrran colony during the period from roughly 1800–2200 A.D. and left no more than 15 percent of the predisaster population alive . . . the survivors, known today as Wynsarrysa (from the Gwyrran phrase best translated as "The Lost"), suffered technological and sociological devolution, slipping back to a largely preindustrial level . . . These changes were apparently viewed favorably by the Semti, who made no effort to relieve conditions during or after the plagues began . . .

Around the middle of the 24th Century humans arrived on Devereaux following the discovery of the planet by the survey ship CARTIER. The initial survey mistook the Gwyrran population for a native sophont race, and permission to colonize was granted by the Imperial Minister for Colonial Affairs in 2364 . . . As a prime colony world Devereaux was settled primarily by French and Western European stock, both from Terra proper and from the established colony worlds of Ys and Concorde. . . . Roughly two million human settlers arrived before the disintegration of the French Empire heralded the beginning of the Shadow Centuries and the loss of Terran interstellar travel.

It was during this period that the Semti Conclave renewed contact with Devereaux, establishing a new Gwyrran colony on the planet. The humans, cut off from Terra and not fully self-sufficient, welcomed Semti hegemony and became willing subjects of the Conclave. . . .

Devereaux was one of several flashpoint worlds along the Conclave frontier which helped trigger the Semti War. With the emergence of a Terran Commonwealth presence in the sector, human settlers on Devereaux appealed to their own species for assistance against what was perceived as the intolerable excesses of the Semti/Gwyrran government . . . Commonwealth forces intervened and established the Fourth Foreign Legion headquarters on Devereaux to furnish protection for human colonists against the Gwyrran locals and the possibility of Semti intervention. During the Semti War this Legion garrison was destroyed during the Semti occupation of the planet, but bought valuable time for the Commonwealth by delaying the progress of the enemy attack through a determined resistance effort. . . .

Since the Semti War Devereaux has been a Trust, ruled by a local-born human Governor and sending Observers to the Commonwealth Assembly. A growing cadre of humans with Citizen status form the solid core of the urban population, supported by Gwyrrans of the last Semti colonization effort who have retained a high-tech, industrial orientation. Most of the Wynsarrysa prefer rural lives and serve as labor on farms and plantations. Some remain hostile to the human presence and roam the wilderness areas in war bands, making their livelihood through raiding settlements or operating overland caravan routes between remote settlements.

The planet is most notable for its continued connection with the Commonwealth's Fifth Foreign Legion. The Legion's primary headquarters and training facilities are located on the planet, and Legion garrisons continue to provide protection for the population against disaffected elements—primarily Wynsarrysa, who continue to pose a threat to the security of the colony.

—Excerpted from *Leclerc's Guide to the Commonwealth*
Volume V: The Cis-Conclave Frontier
34th Edition, published 2848 A.D.

Chapter 1

We are the wounded from every war, the world's
damned ones.

—from *Adieu vielle Europe*
Marching Song
French Foreign Legion

A laser bolt struck the wall bare centimeters from *Leutnant* Wolfgang Alaric Hauser von Semenanjung Burat, burning into the tough duraplast. The scorching heat of the pulse, the acrid tang of burning plastic, the hoarse shouts of his men sent adrenaline surging through his veins, and his grip on his CAR-22 laser pistol tightened as Hauser shot desperate glances left and right, seeking a way out.

He had never imagined combat would be so terrifying, never, in fact, envisioned that he might find himself in a battle at all. A commission in Laut Besar's Sky Guards was the accepted career for a young Uro aristocrat, but no one thought that they might actually face combat. It was unthinkable. . . .

But now the unthinkable had become all too real.

"This way, *Tuan*!" *Sersan Peloten* Radiah Suartana shouted. The Indomay NCO held an enemy rocket launcher in his hands, the Ubrenfar weapon large and awkward even for Suartana's massive frame. He braced himself against the wall and raised the cumbersome weapon, unleashing an explosive-tipped projectile in the direction of the advancing Ubrenfar assault troops, completely at ease in the low gravity despite the launcher's powerful recoil. "Over here!"

Another laser bolt sizzled past his head. Hauser rolled sideways, squeezing the trigger of his laser pistol for a blind shot. Then he pushed off in a powerful leap toward the *sersan*'s position near a bend in the corridor. Telok, the inner moon of Laut Besar, was little more than an oversized planetoid, its low gravity almost unnoticeable.

He was grateful for hours of practice in the port's low-G gymnasium. It was almost second nature to turn in the air and land beside the *sersan,* absorbing the inertia of his jump with no more effort than if he'd been playing a game of airhockey with his friends from the BOQ block. They used a handrail to pull themselves around the corner and through a pair of massive armored doors, clear of the Ubrenfar field of fire.

Hauser scanned the inside of the chamber. It was one of the warehouses servicing Docking Bay Five, long and wide with a high ceiling hung with handling machinery and a catwalk running around the entire room three meters off the floor. In the port's weak gravity, terms like "ceiling" and "floor" had little meaning, but the warehouse floor could be magnetized to hold cargo modules in place and allow workers with steelloy boots to operate without the distracting effects of low-G. The power was off at the moment, but restraining nets held the scattered cargomods in place. They would provide cover, at least, if his men had to fight the Ubrenfars here.

The warehouse was also a junction for a number of different corridors, including one that led to the airlock doors of the docking bay. Inside, the frigate *Surapat* was still taking on refugees from the rest of the Telok port complex. She was the last ship in port, the last hope of escape. The other docking bays had already been overrun by the Ubrenfar assault troops who had infiltrated Telok aboard an unarmed freighter, boiling out of the hold and overwhelming every group of defenders they had encountered.

Sensors had picked up the main Ubrenfar battle fleet soon after the fighting began. Within four hours that fleet would arrive, cutting off all hope of escape for anyone who managed to survive the initial onslaught.

Hauser's wristpiece buzzed insistently. He touched a stud and watched as the small terminal screen glowed, swirled with color, and then resolved into the grim features of Major Erich Neubeck von Lembah Terang.

"Leutnant," the major said crisply. "Your status?"

"We have been forced back to Warehouse 5-C, *Herr Major,"* he said. "Contact with the enemy temporarily broken. I have twenty men, from miscellaneous units. Mostly light weapons, one captured rocket launcher. Not enough to make a stand.''

Neubeck frowned. ''You're going to have to try, *Leutnant*,'' he said. ''I need you to hold that position for at least fifteen minutes more, longer if possible. It's critical.''

''*Herr Major . . .*'' Hauser stopped, swallowed, looked around the warehouse again. ''The men here aren't a coherent unit . . . some of them aren't even soldiers! We have no combat armor. Ammo is running low, and morale is poor at best. I don't know how long these men can hold against a determined attack. Can you send some reinforcements?''

The major pursed his lips. ''I'll see what I can do, Hauser. But that position has to be held. Do your best.''

''Yes, sir,'' Hauser responded. ''But without some steady troops here I don't know how good our best will be.''

The screen had already gone dead.

Hauser glanced across at Suartana. The *sersan* seemed to read his thoughts. ''We can hold the scalies for a while, *Tuan*,'' he said. ''But not forever.''

''You heard the man, *Sersan*. We defend the warehouse.''

He jumped back to the center of the chamber in a single low-G bound as Suartana shouted orders. He hoped Neubeck would be as good as his word. These Indomay defenders wouldn't be able to stand up to a major attack for long, not discouraged and disorganized as they were now. If this position was as critical as Major von Lembah Terang maintained, it would have to be secured by better men than these. . . .

''We'll be ready to lift in twelve minutes, *Herr Major*. I'll hold the count as long as possible, but I've got nearly three hundred men to think of.''

Major Erich Neubeck von Lembah Terang let out a ragged sigh and nodded. ''I understand, *Herr Kapitan*. The refugees have to come first.'' He glanced around Telok's Master Fire Direction Center, with its banks of control consoles and computer terminals. It was crowded with Sky

Guards working feverishly to complete the job Neubeck had set them. They might be able to finish in time. . . .

On the monitor screen dominating one wall of the FDC, the image of the captain of the frigate *Surapat* looked relieved. He was a Uro aristocrat, of course—officers of all the military services on Laut Besar were Uros—but he came from a minor family from one of the poorest districts on the western side of the continent of Malaya Besar. The prospect of arguing with a member of the powerful, well-connected Neubeck family would have been daunting at best. "I will keep you appraised, *Herr Major*," he said.

Before the captain could cut the connection, Neubeck interrupted. "A moment, *Kapitan*. Have you been identifying your passengers?"

"The list isn't complete," the captain told him. "But we're doing our best with it."

"Is Walther Neubeck von Lembah Terang aboard? An *oberleutnant* in the Fourth Sky Guards?"

There was a pause. "Yes . . . yes, he's on the list, *Herr Major*."

Neubeck tried not to betray his relief at the captain's words. "Very good. Neubeck clear." He shut off the commlink and leaned back in his chair.

At least his brother would win clear of this hell. That was some consolation.

Oberleutnant Wilhelm Stoph appeared beside him. "Third Squad just reported in, sir," he said. "Corridor twelve is sealed off now. Do you want the squad to join the demo work?"

Neubeck frowned at his subordinate, weighing his options. He had promised to find more men for *Leutnant* Hauser. The warehouse the *leutnant*'s ad hoc force had fallen back to controlled the only remaining route into the Fire Direction Center . . . and the only line of retreat Neubeck's men could use to reach the *Surapat*. Hauser had sounded unsure of himself, uncertain if his men could keep that route secure.

On the other hand, the most urgent task at this point was to make sure that the Fire Direction Center couldn't be used to turn Telok's two linnax railguns against the owners. Refugee ships were lifting clear of Laut Besar as quickly as they could load up. If the railguns fell into Ubrenfar hands those ships would never escape . . . and there was the further danger that the guns might be turned against targets on the planetary surface. With defeat looming near, Neubeck had to take those railguns off line at all costs, and the more men he set on the demolition job the quicker they would finish.

Hauser would have to make do with what he had. Neubeck nodded curtly to Stoph. "Do it," he said. He undid the safety harness that held him close to the control chair and stood up carefully in the low gravity, then dropped the faceplate on his vacuum armor and checked the seals. "Let's get this over with and get the hell out of here."

Sersan Radiah Suartana pushed back his uniform cap to wipe the sweat from his forehead, then stared down at his hand. The gesture was an uncomfortable reminder of how ill-equipped the Sky Guards were. The soldiers were still clad in their Class One uniforms, designed for smart, parade-ground looks rather than combat use, while the three civilians who had attached themselves to the unit were wearing technicians' coveralls. At the very least Suartana wished they had been wearing duraweave battledress, with combat helmets and plates of chest and back armor. Or, better yet, fully armored vacuum gear . . .

But the fighting on Telok had erupted without warning, and none of the soldiers on duty in the military spaceport complex had been ready for it. They'd lost a lot of men already today to wounds even ordinary combat fatigues would have prevented. Now the men of *Leutnant* Hauser's ad hoc unit were sure to lose more. Against Ubrenfar commandos in full armor the humans were seriously overmatched.

The *sersan* darted a glance at Hauser. The Uro officer was gripping a cargo net with one hand, while the other clung tight to his laser pistol. He had a grim, determined look on his face and seemed completely oblivious to the rest of the men, Indomays all, crouching behind the improvised cargomod barricades or perched high on the catwalk watching the entry, waiting for the Ubrenfars to come.

Suartana frowned. Hauser had paid little attention to the defensive preparations. He seemed totally withdrawn into himself, a man already defeated. The men could sense his mood, too. They knew he had no faith in them, and now they had precious little faith left in themselves either.

He had known Hauser since the young aristocrat was a baby. The family was one of the best known on Java Baru, Laut Besar's smaller continent, and it had been his honor to serve three generations of the clan. Hauser's grandfather had been a member of the Chamber of Delegates; his father and uncle had both staked out promising political careers. Now young Wolfgang Hauser had struck out on his own, the first of his prominent line to join the military. The *Leutnant*'s sharp, fox-faced features reminded Suartana of Karl Hauser, Wolfgang's father. He would have been proud of his son. Too bad that hunting accident had carried him away.

Too bad in more ways than one. Since Karl Hauser's death his older brother, the Graff von Semenanjung Burat, had tightened his grasp on the family holdings. A firm proponent of Laut Besar's Aristo-Conservative Party, Rupert Hauser had resisted every move toward political reform the government had undertaken. Despite his faction's resistance, the Indomays were starting to make progress toward equality, but it was slow going. Suartana had watched the Graff's nephew grow up believing in the superiority of Uros over Indomays. That was something the boy's father wouldn't have been proud of, he thought. The young officer's stubborn arrogance seemed stronger than ever now that he had earned his Sky Guards commission. And with that exalted feeling of Uro superiority came an equal tendency to denigrate the Indomay class.

And when Hauser, a Uro, was almost paralyzed with fear, he couldn't believe his inferiors capable of anything. . . .

"I hear them," one of the *koprals*—Suartana thought his name was Lubis—said in Terranglic. "They're coming. Get ready, men." He looked nervous, but determined.

The man had every right to be nervous. *"Selamat, saudara."* Suartana said in Indomay. "Good fortune, brother." The Uros used mostly German when speaking among themselves, while the lower classes preferred the traditional tongue from the early days of the colony. Everyone spoke Terranglic, though, and it was largely replacing Indomay as the primary language of Laut Besar.

Sometimes Suartana regretted that, but most of the books and technical chips that the Indomays needed to better themselves were in Terranglic.

The *kopral*'s grip on his weapon tightened. "*Kembali,*" he said. "I return it."

He looked at Hauser. "The men are ready, *Tuan,*" he said. *As ready as they'll ever be,* he added to himself.

Then the doors erupted in a storm of fire and smoke.

Half-seen figures loomed through the swirling smoke around the doors, hulking dinosaur shapes encased in full vacuum armor. Hauser fired his pistol, and an instant later the rest of the defenders joined in with a ragged volley of fire from their ill-assorted collection of weapons. Laser beams and the needle-thin rounds from FE-FEK/24 combat rifles chopped through the billowing cloud, but only one of the massive, two-meter tall Ubrenfars fell. Their armor protected them from most of the damage the human defenders could mete out.

The Ubrenfars fanned out, moving fast in the low gravity despite their bulk and their clumsy, forward-leaning postures. They were highly trained assault troops, specialists in space combat situations. More than a match for the Indomay defenders, most of whom had never heard a shot fired in anger before today.

He forced the thought from his mind. The men in his command weren't the best, but they were still *men.* They should be more than a match for mere ales, no matter how well trained or well equipped. He'd grown up believing in the natural order of things, the inherent superiority of Uro over Indomay, human over alien. All he had to do was rally his men to put up a solid defense. The Ubrenfars would surely give way. . . .

"Pour it on!" he shouted. "Fire!"

The defenders kept up a steady stream of fire, and another of the Ubrenfars went down with the faceplate of its vacc helmet smashed, the face beyond a bloody pulp. Someone gave a hoarse cheer in Indomay. "*Ure!*"

Then one of the Ubrenfars raised a rocket launcher, a twin to the massive weapon Suartana had scavenged earlier. A rocket streaked from the tube, trailing flame, tearing into a stack of cargomods near the center of the warehouse. The warhead tore through the improvised barricade, and a gout of fire and whirling debris erupted from the other side. The three men using the cargomods for cover spun away, hurled bodily across the chamber by the force of the explosion in the weak gravity field. Hauser saw the body of the senior *kopral* hit the far wall and bounce. The man's face had been burned away. One of the other soldiers was dead, too. The third was gaping at the stump of his forearm, eyes wide with shock. Then a laser shot bored straight through his chest, and the eyes glazed over. The man hadn't screamed, had hardly seemed to understand what was happening to him.

Swallowing sour bile, Hauser tried hard to stay in control.

"Got one!" a rifleman on the catwalk above Hauser's position shouted. He was waving his FEK in triumph. "Got one of the scaly bastards!"

Then a whole barrage of laser fire from the assault troops probed the human positions. Four rapid pulses of raw energy sliced into the soldier on the catwalk, nearly cutting his torso in half. Unlike the other men, he had time to scream.

Wolfgang Hauser knew he'd hear those screams for the rest of his life.

Something *whooshed* from the doorway. The rocket struck the wall near Hauser's position and exploded in a fury of light and sound. Smoke billowed and fragments careened off the walls like bullets. Pain stabbed through Hauser's leg, and he looked down to see blood oozing from a gash in his thigh. Someone was moaning nearby.

He scrambled for fresh cover, with *Sersan* Suartana close behind him. As the smoke cleared, Hauser could see the shattered bodies of four more of his men sprawled nearby. The rest of the defenders were wavering, their fire slacking off as they hunkered down behind the cargomods.

Eight dead in seconds, out of a scant twenty. And they'd taken only three of the enemy with them. . . .

Hauser grabbed Suartana's massive shoulder. "We can't hold them! We've got to pull back! If we can seal the corridor behind us . . . get to the frigate . . . !"

"What about our orders, *Tuan*?" Suartana asked. "Major Neubeck said—"

"Damn what Neubeck said!" Hauser exploded. The major had promised him more men, then let him down. . . .

He fought down the waves of fear and anger, trying to regain at least a semblance of composure. Suartana was right. He couldn't just abandon this position without checking in with Neubeck first. But if the major didn't send help right away the defenders in the warehouse would be overwhelmed, and Hauser's first responsibility had to be to the men in his outnumbered unit.

Hunkering down behind the cover of stacked cargo-mods, Hauser activated the communications function of his wristpiece computer. As the screen began to glow he raised his arm to speak into the sound pickup.

A laser bolt sizzled through the air less than a meter to his left, and he flinched from the crackling, the stench of ozone in the air. With or without support from Neubeck, he wasn't sure how much longer he could face the Ubrenfar attack.

"Just hang on for a few more minutes, Hauser," Erich Neubeck said, frowning at the wall screen. "We're almost finished up here."

The young *leutnant* hesitated, and opened his mouth to speak. An explosion went off nearby, and the picture on Neubeck's screen jumped wildly as Hauser moved, the vision pickup following the motion of his arms. Against a backdrop of whining FEK fire and crackling flames, someone was screaming.

Hauser's voice cracked as he shouted orders. "*Kopral!* Have somebody see to that man!" There was a short pause. "Damn it, Suartana, too many of the scalies are leaking through! Can't you *do* something?"

The edge in that voice worried Neubeck more than anything else. The kid was cracking under the pressure. . . .

"Major, my men can't hold this position without immediate reinforcement," Hauser went on, speaking into his wristpiece again. "Where are the men you said you were sending me?"

"I need them here," Neubeck shot back. "For God's sake, man, we're all shorthanded! You've got to try to tough it out with the men you've got!"

More combat sounds filtered through the commlink. "What I've got is a handful of men who can't hold any longer,'' Hauser said tightly. ''We can't do it! We just can't!''

''Hauser, I'm ordering you to—''

But the *leutnant* wasn't listening. ''Pull back!'' he shouted. ''Pull back now, Suartana! Regroup at the corridor head!''

The channel went dead without warning.

If those men in the warehouse fell back now, Neubeck's troops in the Fire Direction Center would be cut off. They'd have to act fast if they wanted to retrieve the situation.

''Stoph!'' he shouted. ''Tell one section to open up a retreat route through the warehouse! If you can get there in time to keep that bastard Hauser from falling back we might still get out of this!''

The *oberleutnant* saluted and hurried off, shouting orders and checking the charge level on his laser pistol as he trotted toward the door. Other men joined him, trading demo packs for rifles.

When the airtight door slid open, Neubeck thought he could hear the distant echoes of combat drifting up the corridor from the warehouse.

Sending Stoph and his men would slow the demolitions work, and any delay now could be fatal. But they had to try to win through the Ubrenfar lines.

Deep down, though, Neubeck knew it was probably too late to try. . . .

Chapter 2

Hope no longer existed. Still, no one thought of
surrender.

—Corporal Louis Maine
Report on the Battle of Camerone
French Foreign Legion, 1863

"Pull back!" Hauser shouted. "Pull back now, Suartana!
Regroup at the corridor head!" He cut power to the wristpiece commlink function. "Now, damn it!"

Neubeck had promised men to stiffen his meager defense force, but he had been lying all along. There never
had been any reinforcements. The major had no right to
expect Hauser to sacrifice his entire command to carry out
impossible orders. . . .

And he wasn't about to listen to any more screaming
casualties on Neubeck's behalf.

Suartana hesitated a moment, staring deep into Hauser's
eyes. Then the big *sersan* gave a single curt nod. "Ujo!
Yahia!" he called. "Maintain fire but keep your heads
down! The rest of you fall back!"

It didn't take much encouragement to get the troops
moving toward the door at the far end of the chamber. The
two soldiers the *sersan* had singled out kept firing, covering the retreat. The others were leaping for the safety of
the corridor that led to the docking bay. The Ubrenfars
picked off several men as they broke cover.

Hauser checked the charge of his laser pistol and rolled
to the edge of the debris they'd taken shelter behind, ignoring the throbbing pain in his leg. He clenched his teeth,
determined not to give in to fear, to hold here until all his
men were safe. Leveling the CAR-22, he squeezed off a
shot.

Suartana pulled him back. The *sersan* crouched beside

him, clutching the captured rocket launcher. "Get clear, *Tuan*!" he said. "I'll hold the bastards . . . for as long as I can." He fired as if to emphasize the words, and an explosion erupted in the doorway, smashing into the mass of Ubrenfars still pouring into the warehouse.

Hauser hesitated, unwilling to abandon the Indomay, but knowing there was little enough he could do to help him, either. Finally he nodded tightly. "I'm . . . I'm sorry, Suartana. . . ."

"Go, *Tuan*! Go!"

Ignoring his wounded leg, Hauser pushed off, leaping toward the rear doors. Suartana's rocket attack had forced the Ubrenfars to keep their heads down, and the trio of shots fired in his direction all went wide.

As he used his good leg to absorb the shock of the jump against the wall beside the door, *Serdadu* Yahia joined him, his FEK trailing behind him as he leapt with the receiver empty. The soldier slapped the pressure plate to open the doors just as an Ubrenfar rapid-pulse laser punched a half dozen neat holes through his lower torso. Hauser shoved the body away in horror and dived through the doors. A hundred meters further on, the five surviving men from his shattered command were clustered around the airlock that led into the docking bay.

He looked back into the warehouse. Despite Suartana's rocket fire, more Ubrenfars were pouring into the chamber now that the volume of defensive fire had slackened. Some of the assault troops were already breaking off to bound toward the corridor that led off toward the Fire Direction Center. That would be their principal objective, of course. Control of the linnax railguns would ensure control of any ship traffic trying to move to or from orbit. . . .

And Neubeck's men were up there, cut off now. Hauser swallowed, realizing for the first time the wider implications of what he had done by ordering the retreat. More than just his own little command had been riding on what happened here, but he had focused entirely on his own men instead of seeing the wider picture. But it was too late now. He didn't have enough men to counterattack successfully even if he could have found it in himself to give the orders for what was sure to be a suicide attack.

Hauser swiveled his head in response to another explosion. Suartana was maintaining his lonely defense, but now the *sersan* had only two more rockets. After that, there would be nothing left to hold back the enemy tide. . . .

"That's the last of them, *Tuan*. All charges in place and ready to detonate."

Erich Neubeck accepted the detonator from the Indomay *sersan* and verified the program entered into its chip memory. One coded sequence to arm the mechanism, then a single touch of the activator stud would be enough to trigger all the charges in a set sequence.

He nodded, satisfied, and clipped the device to the belt of his vacuum suit. At least they had carried out their mission. There wouldn't be much left of the Fire Direction Center once the explosives were set off. It wasn't only the controls that had been mined. Soldiers in vacuum suits had also used the access shaft that led from the FDC alongside the number one railgun and out to the surface of Telok to plant charges that would disable the linnax system itself. Even if the Ubrenfars managed to jury-rig a new control system, at least this gun would be unusable . . . more if the other sabotage teams had carried out their jobs.

The difficult job was finally done. All that remained now was to find a way out . . .

A muffled explosion rumbled in the corridor outside the airtight door. Neubeck leapt across the room, shouting to the other soldiers to join him. Stoph and his men hadn't been out there for very long, and it sounded like they'd run into resistance already.

Damn Hauser for letting the invaders through!

He hit the control button and the door slid open, letting in a tumult of combat sounds. A laser beam crackled past the door, and somewhere down the corridor there were hoarse shouts and an inhuman cry that must have been a wounded Ubrenfar.

Neubeck hesitated before plunging out into the corridor, and in that moment he heard Stoph's voice calling out. "Retreat! Retreat back to Fire Control! We can't do anything else here!"

The major gestured to a pair of Indomays armed with RG-12 grenade launchers. The men dived through the door to take up positions on either side of the corridor. One of them fired a rocket-propelled projectile, aiming high, and it leapt from the barrel with a *whoosh* of burning propellants.

Soldiers hurried up the corridor, taking full advantage of the light gravity to cover the distance quickly. One stopped at the door and turned to fire his FEK back down the passage, but it only chattered uselessly on an empty magazine. The Indomay cursed luridly and ejected the clip as he rolled into the Fire Direction Center. Then he threw the weapon violently against the far wall as he realized he was out of ammunition.

A trio of men landed together, awkwardly, two Indomays with slung rifles supporting Stoph between them. The *oberleutnant* was bleeding from half a dozen wounds, and one arm dangled uselessly. Pale and wild-eyed, Stoph stumbled through the door. Neubeck caught him and guided him to one of the control chairs.

"It's . . . no good, sir," the Uro gasped. "They were already in the corridor. Too many . . . too well armored. I couldn't break through . . . couldn't . . ."

"Easy, Stoph," Neubeck said quietly. "You did everything you could."

The *oberleutnant* coughed. "Trapped up here . . . no way to get back to the docking bay now . . ."

"*Tuan!*" an Indomay shouted. "That's the last of them! What do we do now?"

"Lay down a heavy barrage of grenades and then get those two inside. Seal the doors. That's all we can do, for now."

An Indomay *kopral* in Sky Guard full-dress uniform pointed to the entrance to the maintenance shaft beside the wall screen on the other side of the room. "Some of you could still get away, *Tuan*," the soldier said. "The ones in suits. Out the access shaft to the surface, then across to the docking bay. It's only about two hundred meters. . . ."

Neubeck bit his lip. He had ten men, including himself, who could use that escape route, twenty-five more who could not. It galled him to even think about abandoning them to their fate, but the alternative was to stand in place and die a useless death.

At least he could send the rest of the troops with vacc suits out. A few might survive this deathtrap that way . . .

Stoph grabbed his arm. "Take the ones you can, sir,"

he said, coughing again. "I can stay in charge here . . . until the scalies come." He looked significantly at the detonator hanging from Neubeck's belt.

Neubeck hesitated. It didn't make sense to throw his own life away with the rest, but honor was important to a Uro, particularly a Uro Sky Guard officer. He didn't want to be seen to abandon his proper place, to run away from death. That could dishonor the proud name of the Neubecks von Lembah Terang.

"Please, sir," Stoph insisted. "Please . . . let me do this. . . ."

Reluctantly, Neubeck nodded. This time the honor belonged to Wilhelm Stoph.

"Throw me a rifle!" Hauser shouted. It was too late to do anything about the Ubrenfars heading for the Fire Direction Center, but he was damned if he would abandon Suartana to his fate.

A green light flashed above the airlock doors as the mechanism cycled, and the massive doors rumbled open. One of the Indomays looked from the airlock to Hauser and back again. Then he grabbed an FEK from one of the others and bounded back up the corridor, leaving the other four men to pass through the heavy doors.

The soldier thrust his extra rifle into Hauser's hands and crouched beside him at the doorway. Turning to look over his shoulder, Hauser shouted instructions. "Get to the *Surapat*!" he ordered. "Warn them the Ubrenfars could break through any time!"

One of the Indomays acknowledged the order with a wave of his rifle. The doors ground together, shutting with a clang that had the ring of grim finality.

"Suartana!" Hauser shouted, turning back to search the chamber for the massive figure of the *sersan*. "Here, man! Get back here now!"

The big man gave no outward sign of having heard the call. He lifted the rocket launcher to his shoulder again, bracing his body against a cargomod. The rocket streaked straight into the smoke and debris from his earlier shots. Then he turned and jumped, covering the distance in one easy bound. Hauser and the Indomay *serdadu* beside him laid down a heavy covering fire, but despite that the other soldier in the rearguard, Ujo, went down as he sprinted for the safety of the corridor.

As the *sersan* scrambled through the doors, Hauser hit the pressure plate above his shoulder to close them. They'd hold no longer against Ubrenfar weapons than the ones that had led into the warehouse, but at least the defenders would have a few moments of comparative safety.

If they could wreck the airlock controls on this side, the Ubrenfars would be stalled until they could bring up something heavier than rockets. Those doors were proof against almost any portable weapon. . . .

Hauser pointed to a small sphere dangling from the belt of the Indomay trooper. "You've got a grenade," he said. "I want it rigged on the control panel there. Before we cycle through. We'll pull the pin before we go and let it wreck the panel before the scalies try to follow us."

"Yes, *Tuan*," the soldier acknowledged crisply. He crossed to the panel, unhooking the grenade. Despite the horror of the fight, the man still had some spirit left.

Knowing how close to the edge he was himself, Hauser wondered how much more the Indomay could take. He watched the man return to the airlock and begin to rig the makeshift demolition charge. He and Suartana fell back slowly, keeping their eyes and weapons trained on the warehouse doors.

Behind them, Hauser heard the doors grinding open. At almost the same instant the warehouse doors burst open in a roar of smoke and searing flame.

"Pull the pin! Let's go!" Hauser snapped.

The soldier at the panel started to respond, but his reply turned into a throaty gurgle as a laser beam slashed out of the smoke cloud and caught him in the back of the neck. He sagged slowly to the floor.

Suartana fired his last rocket with an Indomay curse, then flung the launcher aside. Diving past the dead *serdadu,* Hauser grasped the pin on the grenade and yanked it out. He was grinning as he turned back for the airlock door. . . .

And a searing heat scorched his side. He smelled burning flesh and realized it was his own. Hauser gasped, staggered, feeling dizzy with pain and a sudden, overwhelming fatigue.

Huge hands closed over his shoulders, pulling him

through the airlock door. The door seemed to take forever to slide shut. As it slowly cut off his view up the corridor, Hauser saw Suartana's last rocket detonate just as a pair of Ubrenfars trotted out of the smoke.

Before he passed out, Hauser heard their inhuman cries, but they were drowned out by the memory of his own men screaming as they died.

His last thought, before blackness claimed him, was the hope that he would never have to wake up and face that memory again.

Oberleutnant Wilhelm Stoph shifted in the control chair and winced at the searing pain that lanced through his chest and arm. The makeshift Sky Guard unit hadn't included any medics, and the only first aid kit anyone had carried was near the end of the corridor now, overrun together with its dead owner by the Ubrenfar assault. He couldn't find relief in painkillers . . . but Stoph knew he wouldn't have to fight the pain much longer.

The access hatch to the maintenance shaft was open, and the troops wearing pressure suits were starting through. The major hung back until the last, his face hard to see inside the plashield helmet, but his body language making his reluctance to abandon the other defenders plain. Stoph held up the detonator with his good hand, and the helmet inclined in an exaggerated nod. Then Neubeck straightened to attention and snapped off a salute before turning to follow the others through. A pair of unsuited Indomays sealed the hatch behind him.

Outside the other door, something clanged loudly against the wall, and every eye inside the Fire Direction Center focused on the entrance.

"Get set, men," Stoph said quietly. He gestured to one of them. "You . . . give me a hand."

The soldier helped him across the room to a better position, shielded from the door by a bank of sensor monitors.

"Thanks," he told the Indomay. As the soldier started to move away, he gripped the man's sleeve. "No," he said. "Stay here. If I'm hit, make sure you set off the charges."

The man nodded and unslung his rifle, checking the magazine. Neubeck had urged the defenders to draw the Ubrenfars into a fight at the end, so that there might be a concentration of them in the FDC when the explosives went off. It was only a gesture at this point, but all they had left now was gestures. Dignity. Honor. Stoph would take as many of the enemy with him now that his time had come.

He checked the detonator again, then entered the code sequence to arm it into the keypad. A red light glowed above the activator stud.

They waited.

He didn't know if seconds were passing, or minutes . . . or even hours. It seemed like an eternity of tension and pain and fear.

More clanging sounds echoed through the door. Stoph summoned his strength to speak. "They're going to blow the door," he said, his voice a dry croak that somehow still sounded loud in the still room. "Get set . . ."

The door burst inward in a shower of arcing debris. Thick smoke obscured everything, but he could hear the heavy-booted feet of the attackers as they poured into the room.

"Fire! Fire! Pour it on!" His shouted order trailed off into a spasmodic cough, but the Indomays obeyed. FEKs whined, their gauss fields hurtling high-velocity slivers of metal into the smoke on full auto fire. The alien cries he had heard out in the corridor before broke out again, louder this time, a cacophony of wailing and hooting that might have been pain or anger or sheer blood lust.

But the attackers wore combat armor, and the heavy firing produced comparatively few casualties. Saurian shapes broke from the swirling smoke, their combat lasers pulsing as they sought out targets. A panel nearby exploded from a direct hit, and the men behind it were down. Another Indomay rolled out from behind a stanchion near the door, firing as he scrambled for better cover, but an Ubrenfar cut him in half with rapid-pulse shots from its laser rifle.

A massive shape vaulted over the panel Stoph was crouching behind. The Indomay who had helped him twisted to one side and tried to fire, but the attacker was too fast. The man's head disappeared in a red haze as the Ubrenfar found its mark.

Stoph stared up at the alien for what seemed an endless moment. The Ubrenfar shifted its aim to cover him.

With a last smile of triumph, Stoph jabbed the detonator stud . . .

And his world disappeared in fire and smoke and thunder.

* * *

"Keep together, men," Neubeck said into the microphone of his suit commlink. "It's not much further."

Behind him the nine suited figures moved slowly, awkward in the narrow confines of the access shaft. It was necessary for the soldiers to make use of handholds spaced along the wall to pull themselves toward the surface. The temptation to leap against the weak gravity was offset by an awareness of how easy it would be to tear a suit or break a faceplate on an unexpected projection. Galling as their slow pace was, it was the safest course. Since passing through a safety hatch near the bottom of the tube they had been in a vacuum, where any mistake could be instantly fatal.

He reached the top of the shaft. Looping one arm over a handhold, Neubeck worked the hatch controls to open it up. Blue-green light reflected from Laut Besar blazed bright overhead as Neubeck scrambled out of the tube and bent over to help the next man up.

Somewhere behind them, there was a distant rumble.

"Move it! Move it! Get clear!" he shouted over the commlink. The soldiers hastened to obey as the rippling explosions at the far end of the shaft spread and intensified.

All but one of them made it out before the shock wave erupted from down below. Fragments of the airlock hatch hurtled like bullets straight up the shaft, and one of them tore a two-centimeter hole through the unlucky man's stomach. The body twitched for a moment, then fell back, drifting very slowly down the deep access shaft.

Another man lost, along with everyone in the FDC. Neubeck swallowed sour bile and bit back a curse. "Come on, men. The docking bay is that way . . . just beyond those rocks over that way. Let's move out."

As they started forward in ground-eating bounds, Neubeck thought again of *Leutnant* Hauser. If the man hadn't run from the warehouse fighting, they might have saved most of Neubeck's unlucky command instead of this pitiful handful of survivors.

He hoped the Ubrenfars hadn't killed Hauser during the *Leutnant*'s retreat. Neubeck wanted to confront the man himself some day . . . so that Hauser would know in full measure the price of his cowardice.

Chapter 3

I felt that I had thrown away my birthright. I was
a despicable renegade.
> —Legionnaire Frederic Martyn
> French Foreign Legion, 1889

The carriership loomed large in the observation lounge
viewport, a vast, spindly web of metal that blotted out half
the sky. Only a handful of the separate docking modules
held ships, and most of them were battered and battle-
scarred from running fights with the Ubrenfar Navy. It was
a miracle any of them had eluded the invasion fleet.

Wolfgang Hauser was one of the dozens of refugees
crowded into the lounge to watch as the passenger liner
eased closer to the Commonwealth carriership SOLO-
MON. Just over a week had passed since *Surapat* had
blasted clear of the Telok port complex. Hauser had spent
most of that time in the frigate's sick bay, sharing limited
regen facilities with the scores of other wounded aboard.
The doctors had told the dramatic story of how Suartana
had brought him through the airlock and aboard ship with
only minutes to spare before she sealed up for launch, but
Hauser hadn't felt much like thanking the Indomay. The
painful memory of the desperate fighting in the warehouse
on Telok still burned within.

Perhaps it would have been better if Suartana had left
him for the Ubrenfars, he told himself bitterly as the slow,
stately dance of the docking continued outside. Thanks to
his mistakes, a lot of good men had died back there. He
had no business being alive. . . .

He thrust the thought from his mind and tried to concentrate on the activity on the screen. Hauser had never
traveled beyond Telok's orbit, and this was his first encounter with one of the huge carrierships that were the

heart and soul of all interstellar travel. Under other circumstances he would have been totally absorbed by the excitement, but today he found it hard to feel anything but regrets.

It seemed wrong to be here, fleeing Laut Besar's star system and the invaders who had occupied his homeworld. But he'd been given little choice in the matter.

Surapat had fled from Telok to Danton, the cold, dreary planet-sized moon of Barras, the huge superjovian world occupying the outermost orbit of the star system. Perpetually locked with one face toward its brown dwarf primary, Danton was a world of fire and ice, heated by the faint radiation of Barras on one side, but bitterly cold across the face away from the giant planet. Still, Danton was considered marginally habitable, and the Terran Commonwealth had leased the world from the government of Laut Besar as the site for a scientific research station and the system terminal, Systerm Liberty, from which visiting carrierships were serviced.

The commonwealth science station on Danton had transformed in a matter of days into a huge refugee camp crammed with fugitives from the fall of Laut Besar, while a handful of surviving Besaran ships and military units, including the frigate, remained on active duty . . . but only under the protective umbrella of Commonwealth forces. Even the Ubrenfars would hesitate to stir up a direct confrontation with the Terrans. Decades of minor clashes and border disputes had made both sides wary.

But how long the Commonwealth would continue to extend protection was still unknown. Once the nearest regional Governor got involved, anything could happen. If he decided that protecting Laut Besar's refugees wasn't worth the risk of war with the Ubrenfars, Danton wouldn't survive as a safe haven any longer. . . .

The world was fast becoming an armed camp, and as quickly as ships could gather in the refugees they were being shipped out by way of Systerm Liberty to the waiting SOLOMON. The carriership had dropped out of irrational space during the first week of the crisis, a lucky coincidence for the fugitives from the Ubrenfar invasion. Laut Besar wasn't on any regularly scheduled carriership routes and frequently went months without receiving a visit from one of the huge FTL transports. SOLOMON had made the short side trip from the nearby Commonwealth world of Robespierre, and the commander of the military contingent attached to the carriership, Brigadier Nachman Shalev, had taken stock of the situation quickly and deployed his troops to Danton on his own initiative. Three regiments of Commonwealth colonial troops seemed little enough to challenge the Ubrenfar invasion force, even with the help of the reorganizing Besaran units which had escaped the fall of their homeworld. But as long as higher authority within the Commonwealth didn't overrule Shalev, those units on Danton would at least make the Ubrenfar commanders pause before escalating their incursion into a full-scale confrontation with Humanity.

Hauser had still been carried on the sick list when *Surapat* dropped him off with the rest of the refugees at the systerm, and the authorities had ordered him transferred to the liner *Freiheit Stern* rather than allowing him to stay with the military units assembling on Danton. He hadn't been given any other options, but that didn't help salve his conscience much. He was abandoning Laut Besar, just as the military and the core of the government had left the planet to the tender mercies of the Ubrenfars.

The most disturbing part of it all was the sense of relief he had felt at the news. Hauser had never thought of himself as anything but a patriot . . . until now.

On the wall-sized viewscreen a carriership docking cradle dominated the scene now as the liner maneuvered closer. Long seconds later, there was an almost imperceptible jar as the ship made contact. The liner's hull echoed with the clangs of boarding tubes and support conduits hooking up, turning the ship into an integral part of the vast carriership complex.

The wall screen went blank for a moment. Then it displayed the nebula-and-starship logo of the Commonwealth Merchant Service. A pleasant, well-modulated voice, a shade too even to be human, began to speak. "I am SOLOMON. Welcome aboard. Your cabin terminals are now integrated into my database, and you may feel free to question me at need. Passengers are invited to leave the ship to visit other docking modules, but please allow one hour for final docking checks before you debark." There was a short pause while the carriership's enormous artificial intelligence attended to some other duty . . . or more likely a whole host of duties. Hauser had heard about the sentient computers that piloted the huge interstellar transports, but he had never expected to meet one of them. Only an intelligent computer could handle the myriad computations necessary to maintain a Reynier-Kessler irrational field.

Carrierships by themselves were impressive enough, massing millions of metric tons of interstellar drives, a-i computer networks, and support systems. But the carriership proper was really only a framework in which a host of smaller vessels took passage from star to star. This trip SOLOMON, which was referred to by the masculine pronoun "he" instead of the more traditional "she" of classic naval usage, would be running light. He would be carrying no more than twenty assorted liners, freighters, and transports, all of them filled with refugees from Laut Besar. Most of the ships he had brought into the system—warships and military transports, for the most part—were staying behind in support of the deployment on Danton. A strictly commercial operator would have been screaming over the waste, but like all carrierships SOLOMON was a part of the Terran Commonwealth's Naval Reserve Fleet, subject to activation at need. The SOLOMON computer, technically classed as an intelligent being, was now carried as a warrant officer in the Commonwealth Navy for the duration of the ship's service.

The voice of the computer resumed smoothly. "We will shortly be departing from Danton orbital space. As we have been assigned two yard tugs, the maneuver will be made under constant acceleration, and we will reach the Reynier Limit in just under six hours. Throughout that time, escort will be maintained by the Commonwealth Navy. Please do not be concerned for your security or safety during the departure operation."

Hauser let out a low whistle at that. Carrierships were designed for deep space operations, with low power thrusters for minor course corrections but no large-scale normal-space drives. Operating between systerms at the fringes of inhabited star systems, there was rarely a need for anything beyond a slow but steady progress in a minimum-fuel solar orbit to carry the carriership and its docked craft beyond the Reynier Gravity Limit that inhibited use of the interstellar drive. SOLOMON was being treated differ-

ently now, though, assigned a pair of tugs to maintain
constant boost and greatly reduce the transit time between
Systerm Liberty and the transition to irrational space.

Plainly, Brigadier Shalev wasn't planning on wasting any
more time than absolutely necessary. The faster SOLO-
MON left Danton behind, the quicker he would reach
neighboring Robespierre for another shipment of Commonwealth troops and ships.

"Screens will be reactivated when the departure maneuver commences," the computer went on. "Thank you for
your attention."

The voice went silent and the logo faded from the
screen. There was a long silence in the crowded passenger
lounge as the refugees considered SOLOMON's words.
Hauser looked around one last time and then pushed his
way through the door and into the corridor outside.

The disturbing feelings associated with leaving Laut Besar were getting to him again more than ever. He needed
solitude, the privacy of the suite he shared with *Sersan*
Suartana, to consider those feelings more closely.

Wolfgang Alaric Hauser von Semenanjung Burat felt like
a coward. That was something he would have to come to
terms with somehow if he ever expected to hold his head
up among his peers again.

"The departure of this latest contingent of troops and
ships underscores the importance of Laut Besar to the
Commonwealth," the reporter on the trideoscreen was
saying. She was an attractive woman with a strange, lilting
accent and blond hair cut in a style Hauser thought too
mannish, but that was in line with her very presence an-
choring a news broadcast. On Laut Besar Uro women lived
pampered, sheltered lives, and rarely worked at any of the
male-oriented aristo careers. Indomay women were a different matter, of course.

Hauser wasn't sure he approved of a society that allowed
Uro women to be thrust into the public eye.

But he was no longer on Laut Besar, and standards here
were different. Since SOLOMON had arrived at the systerm on the fringes of the Soleil Fraternité star system,
Freiheit Stern had been on her own again, shaping her
course for Robespierre along with the rest of the ships
which had taken passage on the carriership. The trideo

broadcasts from Robespierre gave the new arrivals a chance to get a glimpse of their destination before they had to face the problems of direct interaction with a strange culture.

It was ironic that the normal-space trip from the outermost world of the system to Robespierre would take longer than the three-day Reynier-Kessler irrational drive voyage from Soleil Liberté.

The reporter on the trideo was still talking. "Among the units included in the most recent draft of reinforcements for Operation Cordon is an ad hoc battalion of the famous—some would perhaps say notorious—Fifth Foreign Legion. The battalion includes three light infantry companies, including the unit commanded by Captain Colin Fraser which served in the high-profile Legion operations on Hanuman and Polypheme over the last two years." On the screen, the reporter was replaced by a scene of smartly-dressed soldiers in khaki dress uniforms with blue cummerbunds and red epaulets marching at a slow pace down a crowded city street.

The reporter continued her voice-over commentary. "This will actually mark the second time the Fifth Foreign Legion has been called upon to intervene in Besaran affairs. The first occurred sixty-two years ago, when the Besaran aristocracy called upon the Commonwealth to help put down a massive insurrection by the lower class which threatened to oust the established government in favor of a popular democratic movement. Many people both then and now have criticized the government for taking this stand in favor of a ruling class which has been characterized as greedy, self-serving, and repressive, but the Commonwealth's commercial interest in the onnesium supplies on Laut Besar has always outweighed any anti-aristocratic or prodemocracy sentiments."

"Trideo off," Hauser said with a snort. The three-dimensional image faded as the monitor switched off, leaving Hauser to stare at the blank imaging tank with a lingering feeling of disgust.

It was obvious that the media on Robespierre knew next to nothing about Laut Besar, even though the planets were the closest of neighbors as interstellar communities went. The distorted view of Besaran society these people held made it sound as if the Ubrenfars were actually justified somehow in their decision to launch the unprovoked invasion of Hauser's homeworld.

In a way, he supposed, that attitude was inevitable, no matter how wrong it might have been. Laut Besar had been settled under the provisions of the French Empire's notorious Clearance Edicts, drawing involuntary colonists from Terra's Southeast Asia region and putting them down on the new world with a minimum of outside support. Those Clearance Edicts had ended up sparking the collapse of the Empire, galvanizing resistance to Paris instead of siphoning off the malcontents as the Imperial government had intended, and within half a century of being settled, Laut Besar had been virtually abandoned. The war that had brought down the Empire led into the era known later as the Shadow Centuries, when interstellar contact among Terra's colonies had all but broken down. Like so many of the planets settled through involuntary colonization, Laut Besar had fared poorly during that time. The colony had all but failed by the time the next wave of Terrestrial exploration rediscovered the planet, and the Indomays who had survived had lost most of their technology and civilization in the process.

They didn't really understand the situation here on Robespierre even today. It had been a prime colony, not a dumping ground for Terra's excess population, and though they had lost interstellar travel and were forced to fall back entirely on local resources, the French-descended inhabitants of Robespierre had never really fallen on hard times like their neighbors on Laut Besar. If they had seen what the first Uros had found among the Indomays, they might have comprehended the forces that had led to the development of modern Besaran society.

The Terran Commonwealth had ultimately emerged from the Shadow Centuries to reclaim Terra's sphere of influence, and the first survey mission to revisit Laut Besar had found the Indomays on the verge of complete collapse. But they had found something else of critical importance, a discovery that had put Laut Besar on the star charts in a way no one could have predicted. When the Imperial surveys had first mapped the planet they had noted the presence of large quantities of onnesium, a rare element which existed in an island of stability beyond the short-lived radioactives on the periodic table. At the time it had merely been a curiosity, the apparent result of a mammoth asteroidal strike which had crippled the planetary ecology and reshaped the face of the world in an earlier age.

But in the interim between the first and second surveys, onnesium had become important, vitally important, and the deposits on Laut Besar boosted the planet into interstellar prominence. Onnesium had become the principal element used in plating the field coils of Reynier-Kessler interstellar drives. Interstellar travel was possible without onnesium, using the technology of pre-Commonwealth times, but those early drives had been primitive and inefficient compared to the new models that made use of onnesium plating. Since it was still comparatively scarce, any large deposits merited exploitation and development. Laut Besar's plight had aroused sympathy but little action . . . until the critical commercial value of a viable settlement there had emerged. Then, suddenly, everyone was interested in assisting the Indomay "lost colony."

Specialists in mining and industry had come to the planet from the Commonwealth courtesy of Lebensraum Bergbau und Ingenieurwesen Korporation, a resource exploitation company. They reintroduced advanced technology to Laut Besar and helped the Indomays recover from the long years of isolation and decline, and in the process managed to gain long-term control over the major onnesium deposits and, just as importantly, the new factory complexes and other industries they were bringing to the world. The Indomays had lacked the knowledge and the assets to do any of this for themselves, but they'd been more than happy to share in the prosperity the Uros were bringing. That had laid the groundwork for the development of the Besaran class system, especially after the corporation relocated its main offices to Laut Besar and began to encourage large-scale Uro immigration. The Uros, few in numbers but in possession of the sophisticated skills needed to make Laut Besar rich, had slowly transformed into an aristocracy ruling over the more numerous but less advanced Indomays who had preceded them.

Then came the Semti War, when Mankind faced its most formidable opponents in a full-scale interstellar conflict. It was at the height of the war that the Uros on Laut Besar decided to sever their political connection with the Commonwealth, not out of disloyalty but rather in the hope of gaining a better deal with a Terran government already notorious for colonial exploitation on the most unfair terms. With the need for onnesium more urgent than ever because of the war, the Terrans had been willing to recognize the Besaran Declaration of Sovereignty, providing the supply pipelines stayed open. After the war the Uros had skillfully played the Commonwealth against the other emergent interstellar power of the postwar era, the Ubrenfars, who had quietly occupied a habitable world in the third system of the trio of stars that contained Laut Besar and Robespierre several decades before. Each interstellar government was eager to support a neutral and fully independent Laut Besar if the alternative was losing access to the onnesium. But the Commonwealth had always regarded the Besarans with suspicion and no little disdain for their secession, and the growth of the aristocratic society on the neutral world had only added fuel to the fire among Commonwealth citizens who regarded democracy as the only reasonable form of government.

Hauser, like most Besaran aristos, had no real quarrel with the principles of democracy . . . but conditions on Laut Besar hadn't been right for a completely open government by all the people. The Indomays were slowly learning the intricacies of modern civilization, and some day they'd be ready for full participation. But not yet. Not for many years to come.

Now, though, everything had changed. One or more of the semiindependent Ubrenfar warclans had evidently decided to risk Commonwealth intervention in order to win total control of Laut Besaran onnesium. The Commonwealth was sure to rally behind the legitimate Besaran government. They had sent assistance in the past, and they were doing so now. But after a hundred years of talking about the inequities of "greedy, self-serving aristocrats" who "exploited their Indomay compatriots," the Commonwealth news media might be slow to break old stereotypes and recognize that the Besarans were their allies, the victims rather than the villains of this particular drama.

Thinking about Commonwealth misconceptions, Hauser found his own personal doubts had vanished. He loved his planet, his culture, his people . . . and these things deserved to be defended, whether it was against the slurs of outsiders on Robespierre or the guns of Ubrenfar invaders.

Wolfgang Hauser would go home again some day, go home to fight. No other course made sense.

Chapter 4

A sense of honor is a wonderful thing for an officer
or a civilian, but I'd rather see a legionnaire with
a sense of self-preservation any day.
                              —Colonel Alexandre Villiers
                              Third Foreign Legion, 2397

The walls surrounding the Besaran consul-general's huge
country estate were made of stone, built with modern technology in a style that predated human spaceflight. They
looked out of place here on Robespierre, a full Member-
World of the Terran Commonwealth with all the high-tech
trappings of modern life that political status implied.

Those walls served no real purpose beyond their impressive, anachronistic appearance. For true security there
would be a whole host of detectors and sophisticated in-
truder deterrent systems scattered around the perimeter.
But the high stone walls and brooding iron-wrought gate
gave the compound an atmosphere of aristocratic splendor
that made the estate a small slice of far-off Laut Besar.
The homeworld was three light-years away, but looking at
this compound, Wolfgang Alaric Hauser von Semenanjung
Burat couldn't help but feel a little bit homesick. The place
looked like the Hauser family's seat on Java Baru and was
a bitter reminder that he wasn't likely to see that home
again any time soon.

With a high-pitched whine of revving turbofans, the
hired floatcar set down a few meters from the gate. Hauser
touched the small ident disk adhering to the base of his
neck and pressed it against the scanplate of the computer
terminal mounted in front of him. The vehicle's on-board
computer processed the transaction, shifting twenty-two
sols ten from the Commonwealth account of the von Semenanjung Burat family to Transport Capitale and record-

ing the time, date, place, and nature of the business in its
own files and in the tiny chip inside the ident disk itself.

The scanplate flashed green, and the computer's synthe-
sized voice said "Thank you, sir." The passenger doors
swung upward with a sigh, and Hauser and Suartana
stepped out of the automated vehicle. When its sensors
detected that they were clear, the computer closed the
doors and the floatcar lifted on its magnetic suspension
cushion, hovering a meter and a half above the ground.
The turbofans kicked in, raising a cloud of dust as the car
sped back in the direction of Cite Capitale.

Hauser watched it all with an expression of mild distaste. Like any civilized world Laut Besar made extensive
use of computer technology in all avenues of life, but there
was something faintly obscene about the preponderance of
totally automated systems on Robespierre. Here virtually
every job was conducted by computer-control equipment,
with little room for human involvement.

The high-tech base left the populace little useful work
to perform, a whole planet of idlers. Cheap fusion power
and the nearly inexhaustible resources of an interstellar
society had left their mark on society as a whole, and the
inhabitants of the rich worlds of the Commonwealth able
to take full advantage of these high-tech blessings had no
need to work in order to survive, though some still found
activity more bearable than enforced idleness. Some found
jobs in the areas that still required human intervention,
like government service or supervisory and executive positions in business. Others turned their attention to creative
pursuits. But for many there was no incentive to do anything productive with their lives. The population of a full
Member World received universal Commonwealth Citizenship and thus were eligible for the basic living wage of
the ever-present Citizen's dole. It was a microcosm of
conditions on decadent Terra, and the whole idea made
Hauser cringe.

At least on Laut Besar wealth and technology had not
completely ruined society. Onnesium deposits had made
the planet wealthy even beyond Commonwealth member
worlds like Robespierre, and the Uro aristocrats who controlled the extraction and sale of the mineral were very
rich individuals indeed. But they were still expected to
work, by the force of custom and family honor if not for

economic incentives, and work they did, managing family estates and business concerns, filling government posts, serving as officers in the Sky Guards, the Navy, or the Planetary Defense Force.

And the Indomays, whom the Uros had rescued from certain economic and social collapse by the introduction of high-tech industry and onnesium mining a hundred years back, they were expected to work as well. The Uros had avoided the pitfalls of the welfare state so evident on worlds like Robespierre. Wasn't it wiser to let the lower classes earn their living as workers, farmers, drivers, or whatever instead of subjecting them to the demoralizing, debilitating influence of the monthly dole?

Laut Besar enjoyed access to the same level of technology as the Commonwealth worlds, but by restricting the uses of that technology the planet had been able to preserve a social structure closer to that of the various Commonwealth Colonies, where the number of true Citizens was small and most men still had to work if they wanted to survive and prosper. That gave Laut Besaran society a vigor that was lacking on worlds such as Robespierre, and it was the preservation of their unique culture that had led the Uro ruling class to resist many Commonwealth attempts, some quite strongly made, to bring Laut Besar into the mainstream of Terra's interstellar empire.

Despite the problems—the ongoing balancing act between guaranteeing the Indomays their basic human rights without creating total chaos by giving them more political or economic power than they were prepared to handle, for instance—the Besaran system had worked just fine. Until now.

Now that the Ubrenfars were entrenched on Laut Besar, it was going to take Commonwealth assistance to free the planet. Even if liberation was achieved it was possible that the Besaran debt to the Commonwealth would be too large to permit the leadership to ignore a new request for Laut Besar to join. One way or another, the homeworld would never be the same again. . . .

Hauser shook off his gloomy thoughts and turned toward the gate. During the past week, as *Freiheit Stern* had made the crossing from the systerm to Robespierre, Hauser had spent a lot of time considering his options. He had shied away from committing himself to the cause of Liberation at first. It would have been easy enough to resign his commission and sit out his exile in luxury. The von Semenanjung Burat mining and shipping interests had amassed a sizable account balance here on Robespierre, unaffected by the Ubrenfar occupation of the homeworld. Plenty of other Uros had already opted for that course of action, and Hauser's meager skills surely wouldn't be missed even if there really was a counterattack against the invaders.

But much as he feared the prospect of facing combat again, and especially the thought of leading others into danger, Hauser was more afraid of giving in to that fear. Unless he tried again, he would always have to live with his failure on Telok and the recurrent dreams where he heard dying men screaming in agony. At least by returning to duty he would have the chance to redeem that failure, to prove himself. In the end, that argument had carried the day.

His Sky Guard staff post was gone, of course, and in the confused state of things among the refugees there was no clear-cut organization, no solid chain of command to report to any longer. Lacking any better options, Hauser had decided to seek out the Free Laut Besaran Regiment forming among the refugees here on Robespierre. All the media reports had featured the unit's call for volunteers to serve under *Oberst* von Padang Tengah, the hero of the campaign against the Indomay rebellion on Java Baru a decade ago. The newscasts had indicated that there were still plenty of openings for junior officers.

The *oberst* had arranged to quarter and train his recruits here, on the extensive country estate reserved for the use of the Besaran consul-general and chief commercial representative. So Hauser had left his luxurious hotel suite in the capital, with *Sersan* Suartana in tow, to see if he could arrange a posting. He only hoped there were as many vacancies as the reports indicated.

Unfortunately the Hausers, prominent as they were in homeworld politics, had few connections in the military establishment, and that could be a handicap. Both the Sky Guard and the PDF establishments relied heavily on patronage for the placement of qualified officers. Hauser had obtained his staff position through a *feldmarshall* who had owed his uncle a favor, but there were precious few other connections available for him to call on now. It was dif-

ferent for a well-connected military family like the Neubecks von Lembah Terang, who could get preferment
anywhere they applied.

Hauser felt a momentary burst of anger that he couldn't
use his links to his mother's family. *Oberst* von Padang
Tengah was a distant connection of the Wrangel family,
and should have been a useful ally. But the scandal of
Hilda Wrangel-Hauser's mental breakdown and bizarre
suicide had opened a huge gulf between the two families.
There had even been a pair of duels in the wake of the
incident, and now neither clan would even acknowledge
the existence of the other in public. There would be no
help from that quarter . . . in fact, the *oberst* might actually block his application if he was close enough to the
main branch of the Wrangels to care about the old feud.

He would just have to hope that the manpower shortages
were real, that he could win a slot in the regiment even
without a patron to speak on his behalf.

The gate was closed and locked, but he spotted the adjacent intercom system and buzzed for attention. A moment later the speaker squawked an interrogative.

"Applicant for the FLB regiment," Hauser responded.
"Uro. Active commission in the Sky Guard as *leutnant*."

There was a short pause. Then the gate swung slowly
open and the speaker came on again. "Please wait in the
gatehouse. Transportation has been dispatched." He
couldn't tell if the voice belonged to a person or to another
computer.

Minutes passed before a civilian model floatcar, hastily
repainted in a camouflage scheme and bearing the Free
Laut Besaran *binatanganas*-head crest on each door, appeared and settled to the ground outside the gatehouse.
This vehicle wasn't automated, at least. An Indomay bearing *kopral*'s stripes was driving, and a *serdadu* rode alongside him. Both saluted smartly as Hauser climbed into the
car. Suartana sat with him, maintaining a respectful silence.

The estate proved to be even larger than Hauser had first
envisioned, a sprawling compound given over mostly to
rolling hills and unspoiled woodland. Purchased from the
government of Robespierre soon after the inception of the
lucrative onnesium trade, the land was classified as a foreign embassy and thus technically Laut Besaran soil. It

included a small shuttle port with control, repair, and warehouse facilities, all highly automated in Robespierran fashion, plus the Inner Sanctum, where the Residence, business officers, and servants' and workers' quarters were located.

The block of apartments that had formerly housed the serving staff had been turned over to the regimental headquarters staff for the duration of their stay on Robespierre, while the landscape was dotted with makeshift housing. Not all of the latter was military, though. There were large numbers of Indomay refugees living on the estate now. Unlike the Uros, most of the Indomays lacked the wherewithal to support themselves, except for those like Suartana directly attached to a Uro's personal "tail." There was no work for refugees here, and as non-Citizens they couldn't even qualify for the Commonwealth's dole. Government relief measures were still being debated. In the meantime the consul-general had invited the refugees to stay on the estate grounds, and was purchasing food and other supplies for them out of government discretionary funds.

Still, the precarious position of the refugees made it certain that there would be no shortage of recruits for the regiment's enlisted ranks. Their pay, at least, would be guaranteed for the foreseeable future.

The floatcar grounded outside the Residence, and the *kopral* pointed toward a doorway flanked by a pair of smartly dressed sentries. "Officers' recruitment is through there, *Tuan,*" the noncom said. "First door on the left after you leave Reception. Go straight through if there's no one at the front desk."

"Terima kasih," Hauser replied. "Thank you." The two Indomays looked surprised and more than a little pleased at his use of their own phrase. It was a courtesy his father had always insisted on, though one rarely seen among Uros today. But Karl Hauser had been a progressive politician whose chief platform had been the advancement of Uro rights. Wolfgang Alaric Hauser had never paid much attention to the politics of the Indomay rights question, but he had always tried to live up to his father's insistence that the Indomay people, lower class or not, deserved to be treated with dignity.

The reception room was empty of either visitors or staff,

so Hauser took the NCO's advice and led the way down
the corridor to the indicated doorway. It was standing
open, and inside he could see the makeshift office furnishings that had replaced some Residence staff members'
quarters. A Uro wearing a naval *leutnant*'s uniform and a
regen cast on one leg sat in front of a desk. Behind it three
more officers, all Sky Guards, were ranged in a row, questioning the man.

It took Hauser several seconds to realize that he knew
two of the men.

The younger man, wearing an *oberleutnant*'s insignia,
had been a classmate of his at the Academy, never a close
friend but at least an old acquaintance . . . Walther Neubeck von Lembah Terang. And next to him was his brother,
Major Erich Neubeck. Hauser had seen his frowning features last on a commlink screen during the fight on Telok.

He hadn't given any real thought to what might have
happened to the major after things went sour back
there. . . .

Just then Erich Neubeck looked up and caught sight of
Hauser. Anger twisted his handsome features into a dark
frown. "Hauser!" He managed to turn the bald name into
a venomous snarl. "What are *you* doing here?"

Hauser stepped back, taken by surprise by the hatred
and contempt in the major's tones. "I—this is a mistake.
I didn't mean to disturb you gentlemen." He strove to
keep his voice even, to maintain the polite forms even in
the face of the older man's obvious fury. The aristocracy
of Laut Besar placed a premium on keeping up a public
mask of civility even under the most stressful conditions.

Major Neubeck stood, a flowing, catlike movement.
"Not so fast, *Leutnant* Hauser," he said firmly. "I asked
you a question. Why are you here?"

"Maybe he wanted to apply for a position in the regiment," Neubeck's brother interjected. Unlike his brother,
he sounded more amused than angry, but there was a razor-
sharp edge hidden under his light tone. "That would be a
real laugh, wouldn't it, Erich?"

The major's blue eyes were cold. "Not funny to me,
little brother," he said. "There's no place in this outfit for
a man who would disobey orders and desert his post."

The words stung, but Hauser fought down his rising anger. Both of the Neubecks were being openly scornful,

without making any pretense of civility. That kind of treatment implied that Hauser wasn't a real gentleman, that he wasn't within the bounds of polite society. Hauser had always had trouble keeping control of his emotions. His temper had always been short, his sense of honor touchy at best, but this time he was determined to stay calm. He couldn't let the Neubeck brothers goad him into an outburst he'd regret later.

"We retreated because we couldn't hold that position against the scalies," he said, trying to sound reasonable. "Because *you* didn't send the reinforcements you promised. That wasn't a matter of disobedience or desertion. We simply couldn't hold the position without proper support, and your men weren't there to help."

"The men I sent ran into Ubrenfars in the passage *your men* were supposed to be securing," Neubeck shot back. "Thanks to you, all but a handful of my people were killed."

"You made it out," Hauser said. Everything the major accused him of was a distortion of the truth . . . but it struck just close enough to home to hurt. "I was one of the last men out of the warehouse. How is it *you* escaped if so many of your men were killed?"

Neubeck looked as if he'd been struck. "You . . . you dare to suggest . . ." He took a step toward Hauser. "I won't take that kind of talk from a damned coward like you, Hauser!"

All of Hauser's anger and frustration came to the surface at once. He had tried, really tired, to keep from losing his temper, but this was more than he could take. There was no way he could stand there and let Neubeck call him a coward, not in front of other Uros. His honor had been insulted publicly, and there was only one way a Uro gentleman could react to that.

"Coward is it?" Hauser grated. "Coward? Take that back, Neubeck, or by God I'll . . ."

"You'll what?" the major taunted. "There's nothing a gutless softsnake like you can do to me, von Lembah Terang. Nothing!"

"I said retract it, Neubeck . . . unless you'd rather meet me with steel."

The major laughed coldly. "A duel? A puppy like you would challenge me to a duel? Did you hear that, brother?"

The younger Neubeck followed his brother's lead. "Maybe he's never seen you fence, Erich," he said, grinning. "He wouldn't last five minutes in a fight with you."

"Last?" Major Neubeck laughed again. "He doesn't have the guts to *show up* for a duel. He'll run again, just like he did on Telok."

"You think so, Neubeck?" Hauser said quietly. "You really think so? You'll see differently soon enough." He turned away, pushing past Suartana and striding down the hall briskly with the Neubecks' laughter echoing in his ears.

Erich Neubeck was a well-known duelist back on the homeworld, and Hauser knew he didn't have much hope of winning a fight. But this was a question of courage and honor, not of skill, and he was determined to prove to the two brothers that he was no coward.

At the same time, perhaps he could prove his courage to himself as well.

Chapter 5

> The old legionnaires were made of quite different
> stuff and were in it for reasons ranging from man-
> slaughter to unrequited love.
> —Legionnaire David King
> French Foreign Legion, 1914

Hauser returned the Indomay sentry's crisp salute and strode through the high-arched double doors into the courtyard. Suartana stayed close behind him, rigid, precise, his attitude never deviating from perfect correctness toward his Uro superior yet somehow managing to convey a faint hint of disapproval at the same time. Their booted feet clattered on the cobblestones as they crossed the open space within the walled garden.

There were already five figures waiting by the fountain in the center of the courtyard. The two Neubeck brothers and the major's Indomay attendant barely acknowledged Hauser's arrival with narrow-eyed glances. Another Uro, wearing a Besaran naval officer's uniform with the insignia of the medical corps, was plainly the doctor required by the formalities. The fifth, also a Uro but clad in exquisitely tailored civilian clothes, was Freidrich Doenitz von Pulau Irian, Laut Besar's consul-general and chief commercial representative on Robespierre and owner of the estate. He was the neutral party here, the man responsible for overseeing the final arrangements for the duel.

"Ah, *Freiherr* von Semenanjung Burat," Doenitz said cordially, stepping forward with his hand extended. "I wish we could have met under more . . . congenial circumstances. I knew your father quite well before his unfortunate accident."

Hauser took the proffered hand. "He spoke well of you, *Freiherr*," he replied. "My uncle, as well."

The consul-general gestured toward the Neubecks. "A sad business, this," he said softly. "At a time like this, with the Homeworld overrun, shouldn't you save your anger for the Ubrenfars? We need all our young officers if we are to regain our homes."

Shrugging, Hauser half turned from the diplomat. "This is a matter of honor, *Freiherr*. Surely you don't expect me to disgrace my family's name?"

Doenitz shook his head sadly. "There are many kinds of disgrace, young man," he said in the same low voice. "I only hope you can choose between them." He walked back toward the others, leaving Hauser to his own thoughts.

Custom had dictated every move in the intricate dance of the dueling code. Hauser had made the challenge in anger, but the outburst had been in front of other Uros, witnesses of power and substance. With no graceful way out, the only face-saving choice was to follow through with the affair. Suartana had delivered the formal challenge to Neubeck's Indomay retainer, who in turn had presented the major's acceptance. Time, place, weapons, all had been arranged with scrupulous regard for tradition.

Now it was out of the question to even consider backing down. Neubeck had been a champion fencer at the Sky Guard Academy, so his choice of sabers had been no real surprise. His reputation made it all the harder for Hauser to stop the duel. That would look too much like the very cowardice Neubeck had accused him of, and Hauser would never be able to mix with his peers again if the label of "coward" clung to him any longer.

Duels were rarely pursued to the death. He would fight Neubeck to prove his courage, and even though he would probably lose, his honor would remain intact.

"Gentlemen," Doenitz called suddenly. "It is time."

Hauser stalked toward the fountain slowly, acutely aware of everything around him. Suartana loomed over his left shoulder, tense, a coiled spring as tightly bound by tradition as Hauser himself. The Indomay had tried to talk him out of the fight. Now, caught between his promise to the family to protect Hauser from harm and the strict rules of the duel, Suartana had the look of a rembot caught in a program loop, unable to choose one course of action over another.

"I will ask you both one more time," the diplomat said in even, measured tones. "Won't you settle this matter without shedding blood?"

Woodenly, Hauser stepped forward. His voice sounded like it belonged to someone else, some actor playing a trideo role. "He has already called me a coward. Why should I give him further reason to make the claim?"

"If you'd stood on Telok we wouldn't have to be here, Hauser," the major said harshly. He spat eloquently, a contemptuous gesture that had no place in polite society. "But you won't stand up to my blade now any more than you did to the Ubrenfars then. You don't have the guts for it. So let's get this charade over with now."

Doenitz looked grim. "Very well, *gentlemen.*" He made the word sound like an obscenity. "Weapons will be sabers. Select them, if you please."

At Hauser's gesture Suartana moved forward, and Neubeck's Indomay joined him. That, too, was custom. If the Uro principals showed too much interest in the weapons selection it would be an implied criticism of the neutral arbiter's impartiality. While Doenitz was clearly no dedicated duelist himself, that would be an affront to honor even he wouldn't have been able to overlook.

Suartana returned with the saber. It was heavier than Hauser had expected, with a wide, slightly curved blade honed to a razor-sharp edge. Long before the age of spaceflight weapons like this one had played major roles in Terran battles, but now they were anachronisms. Officers carried swords as part of their dress uniforms, but by and large they were strictly for show.

But on some worlds, including Laut Besar, dueling was an accepted social custom, a challenge of courage, manhood. There were few tests of personal bravery better than facing an opponent armed with cold steel.

Hauser tested the balance of the blade, made a few quick practice cuts, and gave a satisfied nod. It was Besaran manufacture, a genuine Kohl saber from the famous swordmakers of Djakarta Baru. A fine weapon, elegant and deadly.

"If you please, gentlemen," Doenitz said. "This engagement shall be to first blood—"

"What?" Major Neubeck's voice was an angry whipcrack in the still morning air. "I specified a fight to *angenehm aufgeben.* Is this more of your damned dodging, Hauser?''

He opened his mouth to make an angry denial, but Doenitz answered first. "Will your honor not be satisfied by drawing blood, Major? I really do feel that . . .''

"Angenehm aufgeben," Neubeck said, cutting him off.

Doenitz looked at Hauser.

"Angenehm aufgeben," he echoed flatly. Much as he appreciated the old diplomat's gesture on his behalf, Hauser couldn't help but feel angry at the interference. Now it looked as if he had been trying to save himself by altering the agreed-upon conditions of the fight.

The terms of the fight to *angenehm aufgeben*—"acceptable surrender"—required the duel to go on until both parties agreed to end it. A ruthless duelist could press the battle to the death, though that was a fairly rare result. But it did give Neubeck the chance to thoroughly humiliate his opponent, perhaps wound him seriously, before accepting a surrender, rather than simply going through the form of a quick engagement to first blood that would satisfy most questions of honor.

Hauser knew he wasn't a match for Neubeck in a prolonged duel. But he was willing to accept the humiliation of an unbalanced fight if it would prove once and for all that he wasn't a coward who would run from personal danger.

"The fight is to *angenehm aufgeben,*" Doenitz conceded. "It will continue until one party yields and the other accepts the surrender. Gentlemen, take your places . . . *anfangen!*"

As the diplomat stepped back, Hauser dropped into the proper fencing stance. He had fought saber back at the Academy, well enough to be on the first-string fencing team in his last year. But he was nowhere near Neubeck's skill level.

And there was a vast difference between Academy matches, with blunt-edged weapons and heavy protective padding and electronic scoring, when compared with the reality of facing an armed man in actual, lethal combat.

Neubeck's blade flicked back and forth in tiny, neat strokes, beating against Hauser's saber, probing, testing reactions. The major's fencing style was a reflection of the man himself. Controlled and precise, he refused to commit himself to an attack until he had taken the measure of his opponent.

Such a careful style was kilometers away from the crowd-pleasing swashbuckling antics so dear to the hearts of the spectators in Academy tournaments, but in the long run it was exactly the kind of fighting that won the match.

Or the kill.

Hauser beat his opponent's blade aside and lunged suddenly, trying to take control of the tempo of the duel. If he allowed Major Neubeck to stick to the slow, deliberate pace he was building, the major's greater experience and talent would be sure to carry the day. But if he was thrown off his preferred speed, particularly now while both of them were still fresh, then anything might happen. Hauser needed every advantage he could get. Neubeck was seven years older, but the younger man couldn't count on any advantage in stamina. The major was trim and fit . . .

And agile. Neubeck danced back from the attack, dodging Hauser's hasty stroke easily. An unpleasant smile showed just what he thought of his younger opponent's tactics.

Suddenly the major exploded into action himself, and Hauser recoiled under a flurry of quick cuts and thrusts which took all of his ability to hold off. There was no room here for parry and riposte, nothing but hasty blocks and retreats that left the initiative squarely with Neubeck.

The man's final slash was a fraction too fast for him to deflect, and Hauser stifled a cry as steel bit deep into his right arm just above the elbow.

Neubeck stepped back, still on guard, still sneering. "Too much for you, Hauser?" he asked, voice dripping sarcasm. "If you throw away your sword and run, I probably wouldn't bother to chase you. Running away should come easily enough to you." He wasn't even breathing hard.

But Hauser didn't have the wind to talk and fight. He just shook his head and tried to ignore the warm, wet, sticky trickle of blood running down his sword arm.

The major renewed his attack abruptly, leading with the beat-beat-*beat* of a double disengage that turned into a whistling cut aimed at Hauser's neck. Again he managed to block the attack, but this time Neubeck didn't break off once the block was made. He bore down against Hauser's blade with his full weight until they stood corps à corps, glaring at each other over crossed steel.

They held the pose for what seemed like an eternity before Hauser twisted suddenly to the left. Neubeck recovered his stance with the speed of a cat, but not before Hauser managed to score a hit of his own, a shallow cut across his opponent's thigh. It wasn't much, especially when set against Hauser's bleeding arm, but it was a hit.

Knowing that the man wasn't invulnerable after all was as important to Hauser at that point as the wound itself.

Neubeck backed away, keeping his guard up and regarding Hauser with a new look that might have been grudging respect. They touched blades again tentatively, the initial flurry of aggression now replaced by caution.

Now Hauser led off with a foot-stomping attack, but the distraction didn't break Neubeck's concentration for so much as an instant. He parried Hauser's thrust easily, almost casually, and riposted in a smooth, flowing motion. Giving ground, Hauser blocked three quick slashes, then parried a fourth and counterattacked. But it was useless, and in seconds he was falling back again, thoroughly outmatched. He skipped back out of reach as Neubeck stepped into a classic lunging attack, a move more common to foil or epee fencing than saber, but still effective. The major grimaced as he took his weight on the injured right leg, and he was slower than usual recovering to the guard position.

Not that it was much of an advantage, especially now that Hauser's arm was starting to give him just as much trouble. Each block and parry made it throb, and he was having trouble controlling the blade as the hilt grew slippery with his blood.

On Neubeck's next attack the saber went flying from his grasp when he tried to parry. The cut landed on his right forearm this time, not deep but painful. Hauser threw himself sideways, hitting the ground in a roll that brought him up on one knee beside his sword. He scooped it up in his left hand, and shifted immediately into a block against a fierce slash aimed at his head. As Neubeck dropped back, he rose awkwardly and dropped into the guard position, still using the left hand.

The major was smiling again, no doubt thinking that his opponent would be handicapped fighting with his off hand.

Few people knew that Hauser was ambidextrous. He had rarely fought left-handed at the Academy, but he had practiced often enough in the *Ortwaffen* on the Hauser estate under the harsh eye of Otto Roehiyat, the half-breed *anteilzucht* fencing instructor, who, like Suartana, had served three generations of the Hauser family.

Now he finally had an advantage of sorts. Fighting a left-handed fencer was almost always unsettling for fighters used to right-handed opponents. Neubeck's experience might actually work against him for a change.

No . . . he actually had *three* advantages. The major's overconfidence, and his injured leg, would both be valuable allies if Hauser could only make them work for him. For the first time he began to believe that he might have a real chance to win this duel.

But his right arm was still throbbing painfully. Advantages or not, he couldn't keep this up indefinitely.

Neubeck renewed the fighting without warning, catching Hauser by surprise. He fell back before the major's assault, almost tripping as he stepped off the cobblestone pavement into a flower bed. As he parried a whole string of fast strikes, Hauser cursed inwardly. Apparently the only one who was suffering from overconfidence right now was Wolfgang Hauser.

He rallied and counterattacked, less graceful than the major but fierce enough to make the man recoil. Back on firm footing, he decided not to press the offensive. At this juncture he needed to bide his time and stay in control. Conservative fencing was the need here, not a rash gesture that could throw away his hard-won advantages. Roehiyat had told him repeatedly that his two most dangerous shortcomings as a fencer were his impatience and his short temper, and he could still remember how he had lost the championship bout during his last year at the Academy by letting blind range take over where reason and caution should have held sway. It was almost as if he were reliving those times again instead of facing Neubeck. Hauser told himself that this time around he wouldn't make the same mistake. . . .

Their contact again broken off, the two duelists faced each other for a long moment. The older man was sweating and short of breath now, but he still seemed to be holding up better to the exertion than Hauser. Neubeck was regarding him with a narrow-eyed look of concentration, calculation, assessment. Perhaps he was actually feeling some concern for the first time in the fighting. At the very least he had learned to treat Hauser with some caution.

Hauser lunged forward once more, driving, slashing, forcing the tempo, trying to make Neubeck use his wounded leg as much as possible. The major did give ground at first, but suddenly changed tactics to meet a savage cut with a solid stop-thrust. Again their sabers locked, standing close enough together for Hauser to feel his opponent's hot breath on his cheek.

Neubeck shifted his weight suddenly, twisting his blade to bear down hard on Hauser's sword. He tried to counter the unexpected maneuver . . . and his saber flew free from his grasp like a live thing. It spun in the air as if in slow motion, catching the morning sunlight. The sword clattered on the cobblestones five meters away, too far this time for Hauser to dive for it.

Hauser looked down at the point of the major's saber, bare centimeters from his throat.

"Do you yield?" Neubeck asked coldly.

"Yield," he agreed, almost choking on the single word.

The blade remained poised for long seconds, as if Neubeck were debating whether or not to renew the attack on his disarmed opponent. Then the major lowered the sword with a careless shrug and turned away. "Surrender accepted," he said gruffly. He stalked back toward his brother, handing the sword to his Indomay attendant without another word. It was as if he had dismissed the duel from his mind already.

Hauser picked up his saber, grinding his teeth in frustration and anger. For all the advantages, all of his self-deluding hopes, he had still lost the fight to Neubeck. And now the man wasn't even following through with the accepted forms that would be accorded to any gentleman after the conclusion of an affair of honor.

Freidrich Doenitz was glaring at the Neubecks, obviously just as concerned that proper customs should prevail. He stepped forward, darting a glance at Hauser before returning his attention to the major and his brother, then clearing his throat noisily. "Ah . . . *Freiherr* von Lembah

Terang . . . you will surely acknowledge now that *Freiherr* von Semenanjung Burat is no coward . . . ?''

There was a long moment of utter stillness in the court-yard. Then Neubeck looked up at Hauser and Doenitz and laughed, a cruel, callous sound. "I suppose the puppy's not a coward," he responded, laughing again. "Too stu-pid to be a coward. He's soft in the head . . . just like his mother."

Coming on top of the pent-up anger and frustration from the duel, the words and the cold laughter were more than Hauser could take. Something inside him snapped. "Damn you, Neubeck!" he shouted, pushing past Doenitz to get at the man. "You'll pay for that!"

Hot fury consumed him, made him lash out at his enemy in an outburst of hatred. Half blinded by a red haze of raw emotion, he was hardly aware of the weapon in his hand, hardly aware of anything except the overpowering need to strike out.

The jarring impact of his saber sinking deep into flesh sobered him instantly.

Too late.

Neubeck staggered back, almost jerking the sword out of Hauser's hands before the blade came free. The major sagged to the ground with blood pouring freely from the ugly gash in his neck. The saber had sliced deep through the neck and throat, almost to the bone, and Neubeck's head, half severed, hung at an impossible angle.

There was a moment of stunned silence, broken by the navy doctor. The man dropped to one knee beside Neu-beck's stricken form, raising his left arm to speak urgently into his wristpiece computer terminal. "Ambulance to the Doenitz estate. Now!"

Hauser could do nothing but stare at the tableau. His sword slipped from nerveless fingers and clattered on the stonework again unheeded. Then Doenitz and Suartana were there, urging him toward the Residence. Unresisting, he let them lead him.

At the door he paused as Neubeck's brother spoke for the first time. "This isn't over, Hauser," the *oberleutnant* said harshly. "You'll pay! You hear me, you dirty mur-derer? You'll pay!"

Chapter 6

A good legionnaire is a man who needs to find
something in the Legion. If he has a past he wants
to forget and needs a lifeline to cling to, and providing he is in good physical condition, he will
have the right motivation to succeed with us.
                                        —Colonel R. Forcin
                              French Foreign Legion, 1984

The study in the consul-general's Residence was decorated
in dark paneling, a quiet, somber room that suited Hauser's bitter mood. He sat in a straight-backed chair at the
richly inlaid *kajudjati* desk Doenitz had brought to Robespierre from Laut Besar, holding his head in both hands
and staring unseeing into the glossy, polished hardwood
desktop.

He could sense Suartana hovering nearby, but ignored
the Indomay. The *sersan* had tried to attend to his injured
arm, but Hauser had waved him away. Neither had spoken
for a long time now, and the silence of the study had been
broken only by the brief flurry of noise in the courtyard as
the ambulance had arrived to pick up Erich Neubeck.

Long minutes passed before Doenitz came in. Hauser
looked up at him hopefully, but the consul-general shook
his head. "It's no good, Wolf," he said slowly. "It took
too long. There's no hope of reviving him now."

The words knocked down the last hope Hauser had been
holding on to. Medical technology on a world as sophisticated as Robespierre could work miracles, and even a
mortal wound like Neubeck's might have been treated at a
high-tech hospital facility. But without a regen capsule on
hand to keep the body on life support until the ambulance
arrived there had never been much hope of that. Now there
was no hope at all. Erich Neubeck was dead.

"What about . . . his brother?" Hauser asked, turning away from Doenitz.

"He left with the body. But he's more determined to even the score than he was when you left. They were . . . a close family."

Hauser nodded. "What'll he do? A challenge? Or is there some legal action he can bring instead?"

"Neubeck provoked the whole thing," Doenitz replied. "A Uro court would find in your favor, since the man so obviously flouted the conventions. You satisfied the demands of honor and yet he continued to insult you."

"Unfortunately, this isn't Laut Besar and there are no Uro courts available," Hauser pointed out grimly. "I've seen how they feel about the Besaran aristocracy around here."

"The offense took place on Besaran soil," the consul-general pointed out. "Robespierre has no jurisdiction . . . but there's no organized homeworld civil authority that Neubeck could turn to. He might argue that it's a matter for a military court. That would mean the *Oberst* von Padang Tengah."

"Who is married, if I remember correctly, to a Neubeck," Hauser finished the thought glumly.

"It's more likely he'll issue a challenge of his own," Doenitz went on. "And he's nowhere near as good with a saber as his brother. You could probably beat him."

Suartana cleared his throat. "You might beat him, *Tuan,* but you know that wouldn't be the end of it."

"Yeah." Hauser slumped in the chair. "There must be a dozen Neubeck connections in the regimental mess alone . . . including the *oberst.*"

"Nor would von Padang Tengah be too happy if you kept fighting his officers. You know the Neubecks will turn this into an outright blood feud. All duels to the death . . . not just an agreed capitulation. So either you die in a duel, or you keep killing off officers until the *oberst* decides that military court is in order."

"Always assuming that *Freiherr* Neubeck sticks to the proprieties," Suartana added hesitantly. Indomays were usually careful to avoid questioning Uro honor, but the *sersan's* words were blunt even if his tone was not. "If he's really out for revenge he might just round up a few of his men and ambush you somewhere."

"He's an honorable man," Hauser said, but he made the admonishment more from habit than conviction. "But the alternatives don't sound too good . . ." He trailed off. Inwardly he was cursing the hot temper that had made him strike Erich Neubeck down. It was a betrayal of everything he believed in. Hauser had cut off more than a man's life in that courtyard. Honor, reputation, both his and the Hauser family's, had died on the cobblestones alongside the major.

"I warned you," Doenitz said. "You were worried about the disgrace of cowardice, but what you've ended up with is . . . worse. Infinitely worse."

Hauser turned in the chair and met the old man's eyes. "What do you suggest, *Freiherr* Doenitz?" he asked softly. "What would you do in my situation?"

The consul-general's dark eyes were sad. "There's nothing left for you here, Wolfgang. Home, family . . . those are gone already. If you stay and fight for your name, you only condemn yourself to death, and I hate to see anyone throw away a life to no good purpose."

"What's the alternative?" Hauser asked.

"Leave Robespierre. Turn your back on all this . . . and find something to do with your life. That's my advice."

"Just . . . abandon my honor? My family's good name? I don't know if I could do that." The idea went against everything that Wolfgang Hauser had been brought up to believe.

"Your other choice is to stay and die. It's that simple. It doesn't matter if you die fighting some pointless duel, or if you're condemned by a court martial, or if a gang of hired thugs attacks you in a dark alley some night. In the end, you'll die unless you leave . . . and leave quickly."

"The von Lembah Terang money gives the Neubecks a long reach, *Tuan* Doenitz," Suartana commented. "How safe would it be to stay in the Commonwealth?"

Doenitz looked thoughtful. "That's a good point, Suartana. A very good point." He was quiet for a long moment. "There's one option you might consider, Wolfgang," he went on at length. "But it's a drastic one."

"It sounds like anything I do will be a drastic measure," Hauser said. "What is it?"

The diplomat didn't answer right away. When he did, his voice was soft. "There is a place where people can

run from their problems, where they can take on a whole
new identity if they wish. It's a Commonwealth military
unit, but it accepts anyone who can measure up to its standards. They're tough, but you have what it takes, I think
. . . if you want to try.''

"The Fifth Foreign Legion," Hauser said slowly.

It was one of the best-known military formations in the
Terran sphere, a unit which carried on a romantic tradition
that stretched back through centuries of human endeavor.
The Fifth Foreign Legion had been called an elite fighting
force and a haven for the worst social outcasts in the Commonwealth, and such was the power of the myth surrounding it that no one could really say which description was
more apt.

But the Legion was certainly known as a safe haven,
where recruits could vanish into the anonymity of a military life. Legion recruiters didn't care if a man was wanted
for a long list of crimes, as long as he had the potential to
be a good soldier. And they were supposed to protect their
own, no matter what.

Wolfgang Alaric Hauser von Semenanjung Burat would
never have considered joining the Legion . . . but the man
who had killed Erich Neubeck and forever stained his name
and honor would fit in perfectly among the other flotsam
of human space. The thought that he might somehow ex-
piate his dishonor among such men was seductive.

"Do you really think they'll take me?" Hauser asked.

"Well, it takes more than a strong back to be a soldier,"
Doenitz said. "But you've already had military training at
the Academy. If anything, your background as an officer
puts you ahead of most of the recruits they take in. You
could get tapped as an NCO if they think you're leadership
material.''

Hauser shrugged. "After Telok I'm not sure what kind
of leader I'd make," he said somberly. "But that doesn't
really matter, I guess." He paused, frowning at Doenitz
for a long moment. "You sound sure of yourself, *Freiherr.*
Have you dealt with the Legion before?''

Doenitz shook his head. "Not me, no. But I had a
brother once, Wolfgang . . . he joined the Legion a long
time ago, after a quarrel with our father. He . . . never
came back. But the last holo I had from him was full of
stories about Legion life. He said it was a harder life than

he'd ever imagined, but also the most rewarding." The diplomat looked away for a long moment, then turned his sad eyes back on Hauser. "I was proud of him, Wolfgang. People said he turned his back on our way of life, but I was proud of him. Do you understand?"

Hauser nodded slowly. "I think I do, *Freiherr.* I hope you can be as proud of me . . . even after what I did today."

For the first time since the end of the duel he felt as if he had a future. He would join the Fifth Foreign Legion, and he would prove himself the only way he still could, now that his old life was closed to him. And maybe he could make this one old man proud.

"Name?"

"Wolfgang Hauser von Semenanjung Burat."

"God, what a mouthful," the NCO at the computer terminal commented wryly. His stripes identified him as a *sersan*, but Hauser had already learned that rank titles were different in the Legion from the ones he was used to at home. "You expect us to call you that, kid?"

"Wolfgang Hauser will do, sir," Hauser said quietly. He spoke slowly, carefully. It had been a long time since he'd used Terranglic, and he hadn't taken a chip course to brush up on the language for years.

"Not 'sir,' " the man told him. "Sergeant. You reserve 'sir' for officers, politicians, journalists, and other scum." He entered Hauser's name. "Are you a Commonwealth citizen?"

"No. I'm from Laut Besar."

"Ah . . . one of the refugees." The sergeant looked at him. "Look, son, far be it from me to turn away a recruit. Lord knows we can always use fresh meat. But if you're enlisting with the idea of fighting the Ubrenfars, stick with the Besaran army they're putting together out in the country. There's no guarantee the Commonwealth'll even get involved, and even less that you'd get a posting to your systerm after Basic. Any good card player knows not to play against the odds, see?"

Hauser shrugged. "I wasn't counting on anything, Sergeant. And I have my reasons for preferring your Legion . . ."

The sergeant gave him a knowing look. "Like that,

huh?'' He grinned. "Well, whatever it is you've done, the Legion'll look after you. We'll protect your identity . . . you don't have to tell anyone anything more about your past than you want to, once you're in. But we'll need a complete history before we can process you.''

"Whatever you want, Sergeant,'' Hauser said. Despite the commitment he'd made to himself at the consul-general's Residence, part of him still felt empty, as if he was just going through the motions.

Consul-General Doenitz had handled all of the arrangements once Hauser had made up his mind to enlist. The diplomat had placed a call to the Legion's Robespierre recruiting office, arranging for a floatcar to pick Hauser up at the estate. It had arrived a little more than an hour later, giving Hauser time to make arrangements to have his meager personal effects picked up from his hotel in the capital. Nothing he had left there had any particular value or usefulness, and anyway Doenitz had said the Legion wouldn't let him take much of a personal kit, but he needed to wrap up the loose ends in his life. It was almost a symbolic gesture, closing out his past life to clear the way for his Legion career.

But there was one loose end he hadn't known how to wrap up. Radiah Suartana had insisted on accompanying Hauser into the Legion, and despite all of Hauser's protests and orders the Indomay had bluntly refused to be put off. Even after it was pointed out that the Legion might not let them stay together the big *sersan* had remained set in his intentions. He had been told to watch over Hauser by the family he had served for years, and he would not give up that charge under any circumstances.

In a way Suartana's stubbornness was comforting. A part of Hauser recoiled from the idea of this complete break with his past, and the unswerving loyalty of the Indomay, despite everything that had happened, was something Hauser could draw strength from as he faced the most difficult moment in his life.

The Legion floatcar had been piloted by a tough-looking, scar-faced man wearing the insignia of a *kopral,* but he was a Uro—of Old Terran European stock, at least—and he told Hauser and Suartana to address him as "corporal.'' He was plainly a long-service veteran, with close-cropped hair beginning to go gray. Each of his five hash marks indicated completion of a five-year hitch in the Legion, and in response to a question from Doenitz he indicated that his sixth term was nearly over. Most legionnaires on recruiting duty were approaching their retirements, and this man was no exception.

For all his long military experience, the corporal was good at dealing with civilians. He was polite to Doenitz, brisk and businesslike toward Hauser and Suartana. They had surrendered their ident disks to the noncom, then followed him to the floatcar for the hour's trip to the Commonwealth military installation on the fringes of Robespierre's principal spaceport.

The Legion occupied its own compound within the larger complex, a building surrounded by a high chain-link fence topped by barbed wire. Over the single gate was the inscription *Legio Patria Nostra*—"The Legion is our country"—one of the many unofficial mottoes of the Fifth Foreign Legion. The two would-be recruits were escorted to a waiting room outside an office on the first floor, where the corporal left them to take their ident disks inside. Hauser spent the time examining his surroundings.

It was a spare, Spartan room with few furnishings, white walls contrasting with tile floors colored red. Holopics and paintings depicting legionnaires in a variety of situations and environments hung on the walls. Looking at scenes of combat on far-off worlds had brought back the remembered horror of the fighting on Telok, and Hauser had nearly elected to back out at the last minute. Yet there was something compelling about those images, too, something that touched him on a deep level of his soul where romance and adventure reigned supreme. They made Hauser feel as if he were poised on the brink of something large and mysterious which he simply had to explore, no matter what the consequences might be.

He hadn't been given much time to debate the question, though. The corporal had emerged from the inner office, pointed at Hauser, and jerked his head toward the door. The NCO had knocked sharply as Hauser approached, and a voice inside had growled "Enter!"

So now he was inside, seated on a hard chair looking across a broad, cluttered desk at the sharpest and most alert man Hauser had ever encountered. Like the corporal, the recruiting sergeant was an aging veteran with short, grizzled hair and an air of tough competence. His sleeves were rolled up to reveal well-muscled arms covered by intricate tattoos, and his chest was decorated with three rows of colored campaign ribbons and the space-helmeted death's head insignia of the Legion's elite assault troops.

"You'd be surprised how many people try to join up thinking they can get a billet without any kind of background check," the sergeant went on amiably. "We'll take damn near anyone who meets our requirements, but even the Legion has some standards!" He laughed as if he'd made a brilliant bon mot, then checked his compboard and asked another question. "Date of birth? In standard reckoning, please, no local calendars."

Hauser had to use his wristpiece to translate Besaran dates to the Terran Commonwealth's system. The questioning continued from there as the sergeant led him through the list of questions. He answered each one as truthfully as possible, and the sergeant seemed satisfied even after Hauser recounted the story of the duel and Neubeck's death. After half an hour he leaned back in his chair. "All right, Hauser. The crime, or whatever you'd call it on Laut Besar, occurred out of the Commonwealth's jurisdiction, and anyway it probably wouldn't change anything if you'd murdered a man in the middle of the capital. What matters to us is your qualifications . . . and your aptitude. You'll be given scholastic, physical, and psych tests, and you'll have time to record your personal history in more detail. I'd also suggest you chip Terranglic. You're pretty good, but you'll be expected to understand and obey orders promptly, so you'd best be comfortable with it."

Hauser raised an eyebrow. "Does that mean I'm in, ah, Sergeant? A legionnaire?"

"Hell, no!" the sergeant said with another laugh. "You are now a Probationary Engaged Volunteer. That means you're under military discipline, but we haven't made up our minds about keeping you. Pass your evaluations and you can drop the 'probationary' . . . but you won't be a legionnaire unless you get through Basic Training first."

"I see . . ."

"Don't worry, Hauser. You can back out as long as you're still under Probationary status. A lot of guys pull out as soon as they sober up and realize what five years in the Legion really mean."

"I won't back out, Sergeant," he said flatly.

The recruiter smiled. "Think it over, Hauser. It's a damned dirty job, you know. We're not one of the glamour regiments, y'know. The Legion's been getting the short end since before Mankind had spaceflight. If you don't die in some worthless skirmish on a frontier world helping some politician or corporation carry out some half-assed policy, then you'll probably get a dose of the bug and go nuts . . . maybe you'll try to desert, and get caught and sent to the penal battalions. Or maybe you'll pull it off and end up stuck on some dead-end frontier world without a way off planet."

"You make it sound like you don't want me," Hauser said.

The sergeant gave a shrug. "Throw your life away any way you want, kid. Just keep in mind that the Legion isn't about glory, or romance, or adventure, or any of that crap you might come across in a vidmag. When you join the Fifth Foreign Legion, kid, you're giving us everything . . . body, mind, and soul. The Legion looks after its own, and we'll expect you to be there for your buddies the way they'll be there for you. And if you survive your hitch, you'll get citizenship, a stake on some new colony planet . . . and the knowledge that you were part of something special. The Legion's tough, Hauser . . . but if you're the right man for the job you'll find out there's no going back. Think about whether you want to make the commitment . . . and *why*." He turned away. "That's all, Hauser. You'll spend the night in the barracks room here, then we'll shuttle you and our other recruits up to the transport *Bir Hakeim* tomorrow morning. Recruits take Basic on Devereaux, at the main Legion depot, so unless you flunk out on your tests en route that's where you'll end up in about ten weeks. After that . . . well, that's up to you and your drill sergeant." The sergeant gave him a lopsided smile. "And may God have mercy on your soul. Now wait outside again until I've finished with the other applicant. Then someone will show you to your quarters. Dismissed."

Hauser left the recruiter's office with an unexpected jumble of impressions and ideas whirling through his mind.

The Legion sounded far more complicated than it had seemed when he'd first decided to join.

Chapter 7

There will be formed a Legion composed of Foreigners. This Legion will take the name of Foreign
Legion.

> —Article 1 of the Royal Ordinance
> establishing the French Foreign Legion
> 10 March 1831

A different corporal had the task of escorting Hauser and
Suartana from the sergeant's office to a barracks room on
the second floor. The door slid smoothly open as the noncom approached, and from inside came a swirl of narcostick smoke and chatter in half a dozen different languages.
There were perhaps thirty people in the room, some sitting
around a small square table playing cards, the rest lying
in three-tiered bunk beds. All of them stood as the corporal entered the room.

He jabbed a finger at the closest man. "You," he said
flatly. "Show these men their beds and let them know
what's expected of them."

The man gave a broad, pleasant smile. "Aye, Corporal,"
he answered. He spoke Terranglic with a lilting accent
Hauser couldn't place. It was nothing like the French-
influenced tongue he'd heard in use here on Robespierre.
"Dinna worry. I'll see to the laddies."

Apparently satisfied with this, the corporal left without
another word, leaving Hauser and Suartana standing just
inside the door, taking in their temporary home in silence.

They were still wearing the formal Besaran day clothes
they'd worn for the duel, and were the only ones in the
room in civilian garb. The others wore plain gray shipsuits, the simple coveralls that were standard for spaceship
crews. Lightweight and comfortable, they would convert
easily to pressure suits with the addition of gloves, boots,

and a bubble helmet. No doubt they'd been issued so the recruits would be ready for the shuttle flight the sergeant had mentioned.

For the moment, though, they made Hauser feel uncomfortable. He knew he stood out from the crowd, and that was never a good thing even among social equals. With such a diverse mix of backgrounds represented among the people in the barracks, he would have preferred more anonymity.

"So, fresh meat for the Legion machine, eh?" the man appointed to look after them was still smiling. He was slightly built, with reddish brown hair and fine-sculpted features. The hand he extended to Hauser was soft and delicate, almost feminine. "The name is MacDuff. Robert Bruce MacDuff, Younger of Glenhaven. If you're a civilized man, ye'll ken that to be on Caledon."

Hauser answered his smile as he took the hand. "Then I'm afraid I'll have to own to being a barbarian," he said. "I've never heard of Caledon, much less of Glenhaven. My name's Hauser. This is Suartana."

MacDuff flashed his easy smile at the Indomay, but something in Suartana's stolid stance and expression kept him from offering his hand in that direction. Instead, he turned and pointed. "We've still got a few free bunks left. The accommodations are not precisely up to the standards recommended by Harker Travel Guides, but they're tolerable. A mite drab, but ye'll see worse, no doubt, if you stay in the Legion."

They followed him down the double line of bunks. MacDuff paused once to tap impatiently on the end of one of them. "Here, Carlssen, why don't you see if you can round up kits for our two new gentlemen of fortune, eh? They'll probably be ready in a minute or two."

The blond man in the bunk shrugged and nodded amiably. "Sure, Mac," he said, rolling out of the bunk.

MacDuff grinned at Carlssen's retreating back. "Poor laddie made the mistake of drawing tae an inside straight last night. He's working off his debt in a few wee favors." He looked at Hauser. "And do you play cards at all, lad?"

Hauser shook his head. "Sorry, not me. I decided a long time ago that you can't call it gambling if you always lose."

The Caledonian laughed. "A man who kens his ain limits. I like that.'' He pointed. ''One of those bunks will do for you and your quiet friend.''

He started in the direction MacDuff had indicated, then stopped at the sight of a short nonhuman figure lying on the lowest bunk in the tier. He turned toward MacDuff and gestured toward some empty bunks on the opposite side of the aisle. ''How about those, instead?''

MacDuff studied him for a long moment with a poker face, then shrugged. ''Suit yourself, laddie.''

Hauser nodded to Suartana, who sat on the bottom bunk without speaking. Checking the mattress on the middle bed, Hauser tried to ignore the feeling that the little alien on the other side was watching his every move.

Nonhumans made him nervous. The few aliens who lived on Laut Besar permanently knew their place in society, but since arriving on Robespierre Hauser had been thrown together with all too many who seemed to regard themselves as the equals of the humans they traveled among. It was an aspect of Commonwealth culture Hauser had never really been aware of. Back home the natural order of things was clear. Uros might be far above Indomays on the social scale, but any human, even the poorest Indomay peasant, came ahead of the things.

He thought of the Ubrenfars and shuddered. Mankind had made a sorry mistake leaving their worlds alone after the fall of the Semti Conclave. The attack on Laut Besar only proved how wrong it was to allow alien races free access to space. . . .

Did the Legion really accept aliens as regular soldiers? Or would they be assigned to segregated units once the selection process was completed? He hoped that would be the case. Soldiers had to know they could rely on each other, and he could never bring himself to trust a nonhuman.

Just then the recruit named Carlssen appeared, carrying two compact bundles. He passed one to Suartana, offered the other to Hauser, then headed back to his bunk without a word. He was tall and pale, with hair so blond it was nearly white, and younger than Hauser had thought when he saw him the first time. Shy, too, from the looks of it, completely unlike the brash Caledonian, MacDuff.

He had wondered if he would fit in among the ''typical'' prospective legionnaires, but now Hauser was beginning to wonder if there was any one type who *was* typical. So far he'd seen an alien, a shy teenager, and an enigmatic gambler with the composure of an aristocrat. In that mix, maybe he and Suartana with their military backgrounds were the closest to how he'd always pictured legionnaires.

Hauser laid out the shoulder bag on his bunk and opened it up. It was small but well stocked, with two of the gray shipsuits and a single set of hostile environment accessories to go with them, plus work boots, undergarments, and a personal kit that included grooming supplies and a small first aid pouch. He opened the bottle of antibeard lotion and wrinkled his nose. It was a cheap brand, the kind of thing Indomays might have bought at one of the teeming floating markets of Kota Delta back home. He replaced the cap hastily and checked the bag again, coming up with a small, cubical chip library.

The touchpad on the end accessed the index chip. Holding it to the side of his head just behind the left ear, Hauser closed his eyes and "saw" a catalog listing each of the tiny computerized books in the library. There were courses in Terranglic, Legion history, military protocol and procedures, and a variety of basic academic subjects. A careful thought brought up another, similar mental vision, this one a recommended study program. He knew there would be other information in the index program as well, such as a simple orientation covering various ships so that he could find his way around the transport they were embarking aboard in the morning. For now he wasn't interested in exploring the chips further, so he cleared his mind and lowered the box.

One of the listed chips, though, was important to him. This was his ident disk, which hadn't been returned to him before. He removed the disk carefully from its slot in the box and frowned. It wasn't the one he'd worn before. This one didn't bear the familiar Hauser family crest.

Unlike the adchips in the library, the ident disk was meant to be accessed through a computer terminal. He spoke a soft-voiced command to his wristpiece, then watched the data scroll across the small screen. This disk identified him only by a serial number, and the credit balance recorded there was only five hundred sols, the enlistment bounty awarded to all new Commonwealth recruits. He frowned for a moment, then shrugged. He'd heard they made new recruits break with their pasts completely when they joined the Legion. If he ever needed access to his own credit balance or personal history again, he could get a new ident disk through Doenitz. Hauser touched the adhesive disk to its accustomed place on his neck, then started to strip off his civilian clothes.

MacDuff was still lounging against stacked bunks nearby. He cleared his throat and jerked his head toward the back of the barracks room. "If you want tae preserve your modesty, lad, you may want to change somewhere else."

Following the gesture, Hauser finally noticed the woman lying in one of the bunks, staring straight up at the mattress above her. She was dressed in the same garb as the other recruits and seemed oblivious to the rest of the room.

Hauser hadn't thought that the military career was open to women in the Commonwealth. No woman on Laut Besar—at least no Uro woman—would dream of joining any of the services. Thinking of the newscaster he'd seen on the trip in, he realized he probably should have made the connection. Women on these worlds didn't lead the same sheltered lives they did back on Laut Besar.

He shrugged again. "Doesn't look like she's taking much of an interest," he said, trying to sound nonchalant. He went ahead changing, though he turned away and stepped behind the bunks for some added privacy. There were a lot of things he was going to have to get used to, it seemed, before he'd be able to fit in to this new life.

As he closed up the coverall, he looked up at MacDuff. "Look, thanks for all the help. I'm going to need all the help I can get steering around all the cultural differences around here."

The Caledonian nodded. "Dinna fash yourself, lad. It's a big Commonwealth. Room for all kinds."

"Yeah." Hauser thought of the alien and the woman. That was already more "kinds" than he'd expected. "So what kind are you, Robert Bruce MacDuff? You look and sound like a gentleman, not a soldier. So how do you come to be in the Legion?"

"I'm not the only one who looks more like an aristocrat than a soldier," MacDuff replied. "But—"

"Excuse me," a quiet, diffident voice interrupted him. The alien had stood up and come up beside MacDuff.

Short, bald, wearing a coverall that had been cut down to size and tailored to expose the ruff of quills at the alien's neck, the humanoid figure was almost a parody of humanity. "It is generally considered to be very poor manners in the Legion to ask about another's past. Such information may be volunteered, but should never be a subject for questioning."

"This is a private conversation, ale," Hauser said harshly. "And among *humans* it's considered bad manners to interrupt someone who is talking or push yourself into the company of your betters."

The alien's quills moved as if they were being stirred by a summer breeze, but the expression on its face was unreadable. MacDuff took a step back, as if startled or shocked. "Look, Myaighee, don't worry about it," he told the little alien. "I don't care who knows my story. But thanks for the reminder."

Myaighee continued to study Hauser's face for several long seconds. Then it turned away and walked back to its bunk.

"Take some well-meant advice, lad," MacDuff added quietly to Hauser. "Ye'll nae get sae far around here with that kind of attitude. Whatever it may be like where you're from, here there is equality between species."

Hauser bit back an angry retort and nodded. "Yeah . . . okay," he said. "Sorry if I gave offense, MacDuff. Like I said, I'm new in these parts."

The Caledonian let out a careful breath, then grinned. "Aye, and anyway we strayed from a subject of much greater importance. Namely myself! You were asking how I come to be in such princely surroundings."

He nodded and gave an encouraging grin.

"Truth is, lad, my auld feether owns half the land in Glenhaven, and I was aince destined for a career as a banker. But cards and dice have always been my weakness, and while I'm more than a match for any honest gambler ye care tae set against me, even I canna beat the house when the games are rigged. After I ran through two trust funds and all the money I'd saved from my . . . other sources of income, the auld man cut me off cold. Said I had to reform before I could be trusted with high finance again." MacDuff paused. "I had been considering the military life already, but with some more decent outfit like the Caledonian Watch. Unfortunately, one of the gents who claimed I still owed him money sent some laddies with more muscles than brains to collect the debt. I'm afraid we had a wee tulzie, and one of the braw lads happened tae end up on the wrong end of my needler. Rather than stay around tae argue the differences between self-defense and manslaughter with the compols, I felt a tour in the Foreign Legion might be just the sort of change of pace I was looking for. For my health, you'll understand.''

Hauser studied the Caledonian. His expression hadn't changed, but there was a faint twinkle in his hazel eyes that suggested the man wasn't completely serious.

He didn't know if the story was true or not, but there was something about MacDuff that made him instantly likable, and Hauser decided he wanted the man for a friend.

Nonetheless, he resolved never to underestimate the slight, inoffensive-looking Caledonian. For along with that humorous twinkle, Hauser had seen something else in those eyes. Something dangerous.

Bright and cheery, the shuttle terminal was a place of gleaming duraplast and cheap, gaudy furnishings. It was a civilian area temporarily appropriated for military use, and the thirty-four recruits in their matching shipsuits looked out of place in a lounge that should have been thronged with colorfully garbed tourists.

But all the regular military terminals were tied up with last-minute, feverish preparations to load troops and supplies outbound for a rendezvous with SOLOMON and the voyage to Soleil Liberté, and the draft of recruits setting out for Devereaux weren't high enough on the priority list to warrant interfering with the logistical nightmare of supporting Brigadier Shalev's expeditionary force. So instead they had been brought here to wait for a shuttle that would carry them to the *Bir Hakeim*, a transport lighter scheduled for an overhaul at Lebensraum's orbital shipyards. Since the transport was heading in something approximating the right direction, it would carry the recruits from Robespierre until they met up with another ship bound for Devereaux.

Hauser leaned back in one of the molded chairs and studied the other recruits. Actually, only a few of them came from Robespierre. Aside from Suartana, there were two Indomays from Laut Besar. Hauser knew the type, poor, desperate men, probably on the run after breaking faith with a Uro employer or landholder. Most were like MacDuff, though, drifters from a score of worlds who had signed up for the Legion for one reason or another and who had been moved from one world to another following the vagaries of available shipping.

There was one group of recruits, though, who held themselves aloof from the others. MacDuff had told him that they had all been sent to the recruiting office from a regular Legion outfit, where they had already been serving as legionnaires for some time. Apparently the Legion did a lot of local recruiting, but regulations required that they all pass through the official training course on Devereaux at some point before they could proceed with their military careers. Both the woman he had seen in the barracks—her name was Katrina Voskovich, but beyond that and the bare fact of her Legion experience Hauser hadn't learned much about her—and the alien Myaighee numbered in this group.

He saw the two talking together in the far corner of the lounge, Voskovich nodding vigorously at something the short humanoid was telling her. Hauser wondered how they had come to join the Fifth Foreign Legion in the first place.

"Out of my way, aristo," a deep, gravelly voice growled. Hauser looked up, startled, taking in the sight of an oversized recruit he'd heard referred to as Crater, presumably from his scarred, pockmarked face . . . or perhaps from what he did to other people's faces, judging from his bullying tone. "I want to sit here, and you're in the way."

Before Hauser could react, Suartana was there, looming behind Crater and reaching out to touch the man's beefy shoulder. Crater jerked away and spun to face the Indomay, but stepped back as he looked into Suartana's grim face. "Don't make trouble," Suartana said quietly. "It wouldn't be smart. Got it?"

"What's going on here?" a new voice broke in. A legionnaire in camouflaged fatigues and sergeant's stripes had appeared behind the two glowering giants at the entrance to the shuttle boarding tube.

Suartana smiled gently at him. "Nothing at all, Sergeant," the Indomay said. "I'm afraid I was clumsy and bumped into my friend here. He was startled."

"Yeah," Crater said, with a sidelong look at Suartana. "Startled."

The sergeant studied them for a long moment, then nodded. As he moved off, MacDuff's slender form settled into the chair beside Hauser. "Pretty good setup ye've got there, laddie. I never thought to bring my ain bodyguard into the Legion with me." He was grinning, silently daring Hauser to deny it. But Hauser was still watching the sergeant, who had still been within earshot as the Caledonian spoke. The noncom's eyes narrowed as he looked at Hauser, and he jotted a note down on his compboard.

"All right, you nubes, listen up!" the sergeant shouted. "I'm Sergeant D'Angelo, and I'm in charge of your little tour group while you're enjoying the good life on the old Beer Hatch. Shuttle's ready for boarding. Line up, single file, and get aboard. Let's mag it!"

Hauser, MacDuff, and Suartana were near the end of the line. As they filed through the extendible boarding tube into the passenger compartment of the shuttle, another Legion NCO, a corporal this time, directed them into acceleration chairs. Gesturing with a stun baton that hummed faintly, the noncom placed Hauser into the seat next to the woman.

When the last of the recruits was strapped in, Sergeant D'Angelo sealed up the lock and faced them. He was another old veteran, like the legionnaires at the recruiting station, but he was easily the fittest man aboard. "For the benefit of you newcomers, I'm supposed to start exposing you to the Legion. Maybe one in five of you will actually make it in, but from here on we're going to pretend you've all got a shot." He glanced at his wristpiece. "In just under six minutes we'll be boosting for orbit. The transport lighter *Bir Hakeim* will be taking us on the next leg of our trip to Devereaux."

He paused before continuing. "The transports used by the Legion are operated by the CSN, but they are procured using Legion funds and are devoted exclusively to Legion missions, because the Legion is considered a part of the Colonial Army instead of being counted among the Regulars. Every other Colonial Army formation is supported by its own planetary navy, but even though the Legion calls Devereaux home it isn't officially associated with any individual planetary government. So even though you're headed for a navy ship, it's really part of the Legion, as much a part of the service as any of our units. That may not mean much to you now, but those of you who make it through Basic will understand some day. Legionnaires have no home except the Legion . . . and ships like the *Bir Hakeim* are part of that home. After you've been shot up in a tough op on some godforsaken planet somewhere you might appreciate it.''

D'Angelo's eyes roved over the recruits slowly. ''Legion transports are named for the places legionnaires have shed blood for the Contract. *Bir Hakeim* was a battle fought on Old Terra long before they had spaceships. Like a lot of Legion battles it was an uneven match between a small force from the French Foreign Legion—the original outfit we trace our descent from—and the forces of a nation-state called Nazi Germany commanded by a general named Rommel. The computer library aboard the ship has a full account of the battle. While you're aboard, chip it. That's not a suggestion . . . that's an order.''

There was a murmur from some of the recruits, quickly stilled at the corporal's shout of ''Silence!''

''Before boosting to a rendezvous with any Legion transport, it is customary to remember the heroes who helped give that vessel its name. MacDuff . . . the names inscribed under the colors in the ship's auditorium, please.''

MacDuff's voice piped up from near the rear of the compartment. ''Koenig, Pierre. Amilakvari, Dmitri. Messmer . . .''

The whole ritual struck Hauser as foolish, and the sound of the Caledonian faithfully reciting names of people long dead whose memories remained alive only in the traditions of these outcasts from the Legion made him smile. Then he chuckled. These legionnaires seemed to set more store in the past than the present. Would they be expected to ride animals into battle next?

Sudden pain lanced through his arm and shoulder as the corporal lashed out with the stun baton he'd used to direct traffic earlier. The man glared down at him. ''Quiet, nube,'' he growled.

''Messmer, Pierre,'' MacDuff resumed after faltering for a moment. ''Travers, Susan. And the other officers and men of the Thirteenth DBLE, First Free French Brigade.''

"We will remember them," D'Angelo said quietly, his eyes resting thoughtfully on Hauser. He turned away a moment later and started strapping himself into an empty seat.

Hauser was still rubbing his throbbing shoulder as the shuttle lifted. He had learned an important lesson about the Fifth Foreign Legion already. . . .

They took their traditions and customs seriously here. And he would have to learn to do the same, if he intended to get along in this strange new life he'd chosen.

Chapter 8

You're like in a cage. There's people from all over the world there. There's a lot of fights because there's no discipline. All you're doing is waiting. Waiting to get that red band that says you're clear. I think that if you can get through Aubange you can get through a lot.

—an anonymous legionnaire
French Foreign Legion, 1984

Bir Hakeim had been designed to transport a full company of legionnaires plus support troops and all the equipment needed to conduct independent operations on a remote planet. Carrying less than forty recruits plus a handful of NCOs heading back to the depot on Devereaux for one last assignment before they retired from the Legion, the transport had barely a quarter of the available troop berths filled. The accommodations should have seemed luxurious, but the recruits weren't given a chance to enjoy that luxury.

The noncoms seemed determined to make sure that there were no idle hands among their charges. Recruit labor was put to work in a variety of menial tasks, everything from chipping old paint to cleaning latrines to donning pressure suits and working on structural repairs that would have been done when the ship reached the shipyard anyway. There was little consistency to the schedule, and Hauser doubted that it was intended to do anything more than occupy idle hands.

Hauser, Suartana, and seven other brand-new recruits who had joined up on Robespierre were spared these work details during the first leg of the journey, but this didn't mean they had any leisure time. They were kept busy with a seemingly endless battery of tests supervised by the transport's Navy doctor. After they rendezvoused with the carriership ARISTOTLE and shifted to Reynier-Kessler drive for the interstellar voyage out from Soleil Egalité, much of the testing was taken over by the computer itself.

The tests ran the gamut from physicals to academic quizzes to psychological profiles. Hauser had never realized just how carefully new recruits for the Legion were screened. Given their reputation for taking any outcast, they seemed surprisingly concerned with picking and choosing their new soldiers.

The criteria used to select suitable recruits was hard to follow. The NCOs seemed impressed by Hauser's past military training and academic preparation, for instance, but they acted just as interested in a tough little Robespierran peasant named Lauriston whose only evident qualification was superb physical fitness and a calm, phlegmatic manner that no amount of testing could shake. On the other hand the big recruit named Crater, whom Hauser had picked as a stereotypical legionnaire, was bounced by the time ARISTOTLE reached Mecca Gideed, the first stop on the long voyage to Devereaux. Rumor had it that Crater was pronounced too psychologically unstable to make acceptable Legion material. Apparently even the Legion drew the line at taking in people who enjoyed violence too much.

One of the Indomays left the transport at the same time, down-checked due to medical problems, but a draft of new recruits joined up, and the process went on as ARISTOTLE set a course for another colony world, Bonaparte.

Hauser had completed all the required testing sessions, but a final verdict on his acceptability still hadn't been handed down. Recruits who had been passed for Basic received a red shoulder band to wear with their shipsuits, but even after the stopover at Bonaparte Hauser still hadn't received that final stamp of approval, and he was growing concerned. They hadn't failed him yet . . . but neither had they taken him in. When Suartana earned his red band and started full-time duty with the rest of the recruits on work details, Hauser couldn't help but feel ashamed. Additional tests were scheduled. Some were obviously intended to verify his academic and military knowledge, and these didn't worry him. But he recognized others as new psych exams, and those were disturbing. Hauser had never considered himself a candidate for a down-check based on instability. . . .

Yet when *Bir Hakeim* separated from ARISTOTLE at Bonaparte's systerm to pick up another carriership heading for Lebensraum, Hauser received orders to transfer along with the rest of the recruits to a new, larger transport, the *Kolwezi,* which was joining up with ARISTOTLE to complete the trip to Devereaux. *Kolwezi* carried another, larger contingent of recruits, a few of whom were reportedly from Terra itself. There were also more noncoms, but despite the additional supervision less time could be devoted to individuals. When the carriership left the star system behind, Hauser still didn't have his red armband, but he was assigned to many of the same work details as the others while the NCOs and ARISTOTLE reviewed his case further. It gave him time to get to know the others in his bunkroom a little better.

At first most of the recruits were strangers, but as time went on Hauser got to know many of them as individuals. Some, like MacDuff, were friendly from the start. MacDuff's background was enough like his own for the two of them to hit it off right from the start, though the young Caledonian's outgoing personality stood out in startling contrast to Hauser's own reserve. Addicted to games of chance of every variety, and a natural master of scams and cons, MacDuff didn't act like any aristocrat Hauser had ever seen, but there was something about the man's inborn assurance and easy leadership that made it plain he'd been accustomed to money and power from birth.

Not everyone was as approachable to Hauser, and he found it took a special effort on his own part to win any sort of acceptance among them. Some found his manner too reserved for their taste, and for some reason they found his unwillingness to make friends with the alien Myaighee as grounds for resentment.

Hauser didn't exactly dislike the alien, but he did find its presence disturbing. As the one recruit who had more than a year's worth of actual Legion experience, Myaighee was in a strange position that left Hauser feeling uncertain and confused. How much weight was he supposed to give to that experience? He wasn't sure how nonhumans were supposed to be treated in Commonwealth society.

Plainly they were regarded with more respect than would

have been the case back on Laut Besar. It particularly bothered him when the alien tried to impose its own values on him, such as in their first encounter in the barracks on Robespierre. He saw others having similar problems relating to the ale from time to time, but somehow no one else seemed to elicit the same reactions he did.

After the recruits had transferred to *Kolwezi,* for instance, Myaighee had a run-in with one of the NCO's who had been in charge of the recruit contingent already on board the new transport. The little nonhuman had corrected Chief-Sergeant Colby when the noncom referred to Myaighee as "he." The proper word, so the alien insisted, was "ky," a gender-neutral term used on its homeworld of Hanuman. Myaighee's species was hermaphroditic, and concepts of "male" and "female" didn't apply. Colby had hardly listened to the explanation, and went right on calling Myaighee "he." So did almost everyone else, except a few of the recruits who had been with the ale from the very start.

Chief among these was the woman, Katrina Voskovich. Short, dark-haired, and quite a bit different from the Uro women Hauser was used to in both looks and attitude, Voskovich was a fierce partisan of Myaighee's and hence kept her distance from Hauser. He learned a little bit about her through MacDuff, who seemed to be able to find out anything about anyone. She had been an electronics technician employed by a large corporation with interests on Polypheme, a backwater world where a Legion company had fought a desperate campaign against hostile natives. When it was over, the company's hold on the planet had all but collapsed even though the legionnaires had won the war. Voskovich had actually been involved in some of the fighting together with other volunteers from the ranks of the corporate employees, and had chosen to enlist in the Legion rather than remain in her old job. Unlike Myaighee, she didn't have all that much experience, but she shared the alien's high opinion of their unit, Captain Colin Fraser's Bravo Company.

Few of the others really stood out. Young Carlssen and the tough little peasant Lauriston were both friendly with MacDuff, and seemed to like Hauser well enough. Suartana, of course, remained a rock he could always rely on, though as time went on he saw less and less of the Indomay, apparently on the orders of the chief-sergeant. According to one rumor that went around the bunkroom, Suartana was a big reason for the delay in passing Hauser's application to the Legion. He was regarded as a symbol of Hauser's aristocratic background, and apparently the aristocracy was viewed with some distrust by the legionnaires. They seemed to feel that Hauser was too soft to make a good soldier, though his other qualifications were excellent.

At least he still had a chance of earning a place in the Legion. He resolved to work harder and hope for the best.

Legionnaire Third Class Myaighee sat cross-legged on a mat in the center of the gymnasium and tried to picture home. Following the advice of Corporal Rostov, kys lance leader from bravo Company, Myaighee had saved up a large stock of synthol and offered it to the Navy CPO in charge of Environmental Systems maintenance aboard the transport in exchange for permission to use the variable-climate training compartment when it wasn't needed for other purposes. As Rostov had suggested, the exchange had been welcomed enthusiastically. The cli-control system allowed the user to set the chamber to virtually any combination of atmosphere, pressure, temperature, and humidity, but nothing could bring back the sights or sounds of nighttime in the jungle or the hubbub of a village market.

The world humans called Hanuman was far away, and Myaighee had not been home in over a year. Ky missed the jungles, the friends and family left behind, and knew ky was not likely to see any of them again.

Feelings like these had stayed comfortably far away when ky was serving in Colin Fraser's Legion company. During the desperate fight on Polypheme ky had never felt lonely. There were friends enough within the ranks of the Legion, friends like Corporal Rostov and Legionnaire Grant and the female-human Kelly, who had been a Navy officer before becoming a Legion combat engineer. Kelly had been kys first friend, the one human who had taken an interest in Myaighee during the horrible days of the company's retreat from Dryienjaiyeel. Ky—no, "she" was the word for a female-human—had helped Myaighee see that giving up home did not necessarily mean giving up life itself.

After Polypheme the company had been ordered to Devereaux, and Myaighee had accepted the assignment to recruit training with the thought that kys friends would be close at hand. But en route the crisis on Laut Besar had erupted, and the company had been diverted on reaching Robespierre. But the draft of recruits had been sent on to finish their training.

Now Myaighee's friends were in the thick of another crisis, and Myaighee wished ky could face it with them.

A few other recent recruits had been shipped out with Myaighee, but none with kys seniority. Katrina Voskovich, a civilian technician who had helped the legionnaires on Polypheme, seemed friendly enough, but Myaighee barely knew that female-human. There were complete strangers among the recruits who were more like friends than that one.

So many strangers . . . such a strange place . . .

Loneliness could do strange things. There had been the alien from Polypheme, Oomour, a native scout from a primitive nomadic culture. Oomour's entire clan had been wiped out, and the scout had adopted the Legion as his new home. But the cramped confines of a transport lighter had been too much for a being accustomed to ranging the seas of his native world unhindered, and Oomour had committed suicide long before the legionnaires reached Robespierre. Corporal Rostov had given Myaighee a piece of the rope Oomour had used to bind his gill-slits closed, claiming it would bring good luck. Myaighee still had it, but couldn't see how it could be lucky to carry the ill-omened object.

All the cursed thing did was remind Myaighee of how much ky had in common with Oomour. Both aliens from backward cultures in a place shaped and dominated by humans. Both far from home, struggling to adjust to new ways . . .

Most humans didn't even try to recognize Myaighee as an individual. Insisting on treating ky as a male-human instead of a hermaphrodite of the *kyendyp*, for instance, that was something kys old lancemates would never have done. Despite Myaighee's best efforts to educate the other recruits, ky was almost always referred to by male-human pronouns.

And humans like Volunteer Hauser seemed to actively

despise Myaighee. Ky had known human scorn before, back on Hanuman before becoming a legionnaire, but ky had always assumed it was because they were so advanced and the *kyendyp* so obviously backward. Here there was no such standard for comparison. If anything, Myaighee should have commanded respect because ky had been part of Bravo Company. Unlike the other recruits, Myaighee already held the rank of Legionnaire Third Class, already had a right to wear the coveted white kepi. But all these things didn't change the sense of scorn ky felt when some humans were near.

It made Myaighee wonder if ky had been right to leave the jungles of home behind in pursuit of an intangible *something* ky had sensed in the Fifth Foreign Legion.

The door to the gymnasium slid open with a sigh and a sudden blast of cool, dry air. Myaighee looked up, saw the slender, fair-complexioned figure of Hauser in the doorway.

"Allmächtiger Gott!" The recruit's words were in a language Myaighee didn't know, by ky recognized a human's cursing when ky heard it. "What's with the sauna?"

Myaighee felt kys neck ruff rippling in confusion, but knew few humans could understand the emotional content. "I do not understand some of your words," ky said mildly.

"Why is it so goddamned hot in here?" Hauser said, a look of exasperation crossing his alien features.

"Ah, the heat." Myaighee mimicked a human shrug. "These settings make the air much like my homeland on Hanuman."

Hauser mopped his forehead with his sleeve. "Then God save me from getting posted there," he said.

"If you wish to use the room, I will leave. I was almost finished in any case."

"Finished? You were sitting on the floor staring at the walls. What was that, some weird ritual the ales do back on your planet?"

Myaighee stood slowly. "I try to spend my free time remembering my home," ky said slowly. "It has been a long time since I saw it last. Remembering helps . . . relax me."

The human shrugged. "Hell, what you do when Chief-Sergeant Colby isn't looking over our shoulder is your business," he said. "But I can't figure why you'd leave your own kind and try to mix with humans in the first place.''

Kys ruff bristled. "Are you, then, among your own people? You do not fit in as you would like to, true?''

The shot seemed to hit home, and Hauser fell silent. Myaighee crossed to the cli-control panel and cut the settings back to their Terran-standard norms. Then ky turned to Hauser, who was still staring at Myaighee. "If you wish, perhaps you would like to learn the relaxation technique I was using when you came in.'' Ky paused. "Actually, it is a 'weird ritual' native to a planet called Pacifica, and I learned it from the human who was my company's Exec.''

Myaighee pushed past the tall, lanky human into the cool air of the corridor outside. Ky didn't feel any less lonely, but at least there was satisfaction in knowing that the humans kys people had once thought of as demons or gods were, in fact, not that much different from ky after all.

"Fall in! Fall in, you straks! Move it! Move it!''

Wolfgang Hauser unstrapped the seat harness and shoved his way into the ragged double line of recruits forming up in the center aisle of the shuttle passenger compartment. A trio of corporals in Legion battledress moved through the motley group, shouting orders and curses and laying about freely with their stun batons as they tried to enforce order. From time to time they used their fists instead. Hauser obeyed the bellowed commands and tried to keep from drawing attention to himself. Three months in transit had taught him the value of remaining unobtrusive. Gradually order emerged from chaos as recruits shouldered bags or grabbed suitcases and found their places in line.

The shuttle grounded with a sharp lurch that nearly bowled over the recruits and set the noncoms to lashing out all over again. Over fifty would-be soldiers in a cramped, ancient landing craft took a lot of controlling, but these legionnaires knew how to do the job.

Colby, the burly chief sergeant in charge of the passenger compartment, ran a cold eye over the recruits and then slapped the switch beside the stern loading ramp. With a groan of long-used machinery the doors swung open and the ramp dropped slowly to the ground, letting in a blast of hot, dry air that made Hauser's skin prickle. The fierce

glare from outside was brighter, more intense than the familiar orange glow of Soleil Liberté or the muted artificial
lighting of the ships that had been his home for nearly
three months now, and he had to blink back tears as the
corporals prodded the line into motion down the ramp and
out onto the planet surface.

Chief-Sergeant Colby stopped at the foot of the ramp,
facing a gate in the duracrete berm that surrounded the
shuttle pad. A guard dressed in full Legion parade uniform—white kepi, khaki trousers and jacket with archaic
red-and-green epaulets, green tie and blue cummerbund—
took two brisk steps forward, his rifle coming to port arms.
Behind the man, flanking the gate, two flags fluttered in
the hot wind, one the stars-and-globe of the Terran Commonwealth, the other a tricolor emblazoned with the V
emblem of the Fifth Foreign Legion. Colby saluted each
flag crisply. "Recruit detail to enter the post," he rasped.

The guard gave a sharp rifle salute in return. "Detail
may enter. Major Hunter welcomes you."

"Devereaux shall not fall again," the chief sergeant responded. The grim, almost fanatic note in their voices
fascinated and repelled at the same time. Like the old-
fashioned legionnaire's uniform, the ritual was part of the
tradition of the Fifth Foreign Legion. Hauser had studied
some of the background en route, but the reality made him
shiver despite the desert heat.

The gate slid open as the guard stepped aside to let the
recruits pass through. Fort Hunter was the main training
depot for the Fifth Foreign Legion, standing near the town
of Villastre near the edge of the Great Desert on Devereaux. Near the present military base, over a hundred years
ago, Commandant Thomas Hunter of the Fourth Foreign
Legion had led a ragtag band of legionnaires in a desperate
raid against terrible odds as part of a prolonged resistance
to alien invaders. The legionnaires had perished almost to
a man, but their sacrifice had helped buy valuable time for
the Commonwealth in their bitter war against the Semti
Conclave. When the Fifth Foreign Legion was established
out of the ashes of the Fourth, Hunter and the fighting on
Devereaux had formed a key part in the deliberately cultivated mystique of the new organization.

Hauser could still remember the stun-lashing he'd received after scoffing at Legion tradition that first time in

the shuttle leaving Robespierre, but even that beating hadn't completely driven home the genuine seriousness with which the legionnaires regarded their unit and its history.

As the recruits shuffled slowly through the gate, he realized that he still had a lot to learn. The long voyage to Devereaux was over. Now the training would begin.

He was still a little bit surprised at having made it all the way to Devereaux. His red arm band had finally been awarded a few days out from Bonaparte, after a final round of evaluations supervised by Chief-Sergeant Colby, who had come all the way out from Terra on *Kolwezi*. A few words from Suartana had helped Hauser pass those last tests. Once he'd realized how much he was hurting his own cause, he had made a conscious effort to tone down his stiff-necked pride. Colby had inadvertently helped him get a grip on himself by insisting that Hauser demonstrate his proficiency with the saber in a practice fight in one of the training compartments. The match—against Colby himself, a tough bulldog of a man—had reminded Hauser vividly of the duel with Neubeck and the way his short temper and touchy sense of honor had forced him to seek refuge in the Legion.

The fight had helped another way, too. Apparently Commonwealth standards of swordsmanship were a lot lower than Laut Besar's, because Hauser actually managed to impress the NCO with his prowess with a blade. Few people on *Kolwezi* had succeeded in impressing Colby at anything.

Fifty-five recruits had boarded the shuttle in orbit over Devereaux, the candidates deemed acceptable after the selection procedure. Suartana was the only other Besaran left. The other two Indomays hadn't made it, the one because of his medical problem and the other for some unknown failing only the Legion understood.

Somehow, Hauser had made it through the tests, though he'd come close to failing more than once. Chief-Sergeant Colby had been brutally direct in summing up his future with the Legion. "You've got the education and the intellect to be an officer," he'd said harshly. "But you'll have to shake off that goddamned snob routine and learn how to take orders if you're gonna make it as a marchman. I'm passing you . . . but instructors at Fort Hunter might not be so charitable. Just watch yourself!''

Something in the sergeant's words had given Hauser pause. The Fifth Foreign Legion was widely regarded with scorn by more spit-and-polish units both inside the Commonwealth and beyond its borders. Despite the hard-fighting reputation of the unit, the Legion was known as a refuge for the misfits, the malcontents, and the no-hopers who couldn't make it anywhere else. But Colby's tones had held nothing but haughty pride and superiority, as if Hauser was in danger of not measuring up to the Legion.

Since that interview, winning the acceptance of men like Colby had suddenly become very important to Wolfgang Hauser.

Chapter 9

> The curious thing was that the regiment, which
> formed a compact unit because of an esprit de corps
> which bordered on fanaticism, was composed of
> the most diverse elements.
> —Legionnaire Charles-Jules Zede
> *Souvenirs of My Life*
> French Foreign Legion

It took half an hour for Hauser and the others to reach the
actual grounds of Fort Hunter's Recruit Training Center,
a huge, semi-independent compound surrounded by its
own security fence and linked to the main fort by a maglev
tube network. Nothing in the orientation sessions had prepared Hauser for the full scope of the Legion facilities,
and in answer to another recruit's comments on the subject
Colby had just laughed and pointed out that there were
several other Legion bases scattered around Devereaux just
as large if not quite so important. Devereaux was the Legion's headquarters and administration center, the planet
every legionnaire called home regardless of where duty
might take the individual unit. A large percentage of the
civilian population on Devereaux directly supported Legion activities, from the food processing workers who produced their rations to the factory technicians who turned
out munitions and other supplies to the prostitutes, male
and female, who worked the off-base brothels. And there
were no small number of former legionnaires on the planet
as well, veterans who had chosen to invest their stake in
this adopted home planet rather than seeking a post-Legion
life on some other developing world.

Colby formed the recruits up into a double line outside
the tube station and led them at a trot across the RTC
compound toward the cluster of large buildings near the

center of the complex. Hauser was surprised to note that the structures at the very hub of this fort-within-a-fort were not barracks or administration buildings, but rather an imposing museum which faced a monument across a reflecting pool. The familiar slogan *Legio Patria Nostra*, in two-meter tall letters, frowned down from above the entrance to the museum. Without breaking stride, Colby informed the jogging recruits that the museum was devoted to the history of the Legion and its four predecessors, while the other structure was reputed to be an exact replica of the original Monument aux Morts—the Monument to the Dead, a raised globe guarded by four stern-faced soldiers of the old French Foreign Legion. In the days before Mankind had left Mother Terra, such a monument had stood, first in the old Legion's headquarters in the colony of Algiers, later in a camp in southern France. The original had been destroyed in the fighting that ended the Second French Empire, defended to the last by the Third Foreign Legion. This replica, though, carried the tradition down across the centuries. It wasn't an exact duplicate, though. At the four corners of this monument were modern additions, further statues depicting soldiers of each of the four Legions that had followed the original.

Finally Colby signaled a halt outside of a long, low building near the edge of the central sprawl. The sign outside the door proclaimed that they had arrived at Hut 4, Processing.

"All right, you slugs!" Colby shouted. "You're ready for the final stage of processing, starting now. First order of business is to file inside that building in an orderly fashion. When you get inside, stow your luggage in the bins by the door. Make sure they've been tagged with your assigned serial numbers. If you don't have 'em tagged, you won't get 'em back!"

The sergeant paused, glaring fiercely. "Next item. Once you've stowed your luggage, peel down to your underwear. Keep your clothes with you until you're told otherwise. You may want to make sure any personal effects you want saved get stowed in your bags. That includes wristpieces, pictures or holocubes, and other mementos. Keep your ident disks on you until someone says different. When you've done all that, your troubles are over. All you have to do after that is wait. Listen for the last two digits of

your serial number to be called. Keep the noise down so
everyone can hear their numbers called. Think you straks
can handle all that?''

A ragged chorus of voices answered him. Colby exchanged a weary glance with one of the corporals and then
shrugged. "Right, then get moving! Now!''

Hauser was one of the last ones inside, and he found
that even the straightforward instructions Colby had issued
had produced chaos among the recruits. Voices were raised
in noisy complaints or questions, and several recruits had
simply found a corner and sat down to wait, fully dressed
and with luggage close at hand. Others were wrestling with
bags too large for the bins.

Here and there Hauser caught sight of a few who had
managed to get everything right, but even a few of these
were generating their share of disorder. A pretty blond
woman unzipping her shipsuit was the object of comments
from a small male audience led by a dark, good-looking
kid who looked even younger than Swede Carlssen . . .
certainly too young to be a legionnaire recruit. ''*Si! Si!
Spogliarello!*'' he said with a whistle. Then, in Terranglic
with a thick accent Hauser couldn't identify, he continued.
''Take it off!''

''Quiet!'' A new voice bellowed, cutting through the
hubbub with the quality of a spacecraft launching with
booster assistance. ''I said QUIET!''

The room fell silent as a squat, stocky man with a bullet
head emphasized by his short haircut strode from the inner
door. Though physically almost the opposite of the massive Chief-Sergeant Colby, the newcomer had the same air
of self-assured competence Hauser would have recognized
even if the man's uniform had not been marked with a
sergeant's stripes.

''That's better,'' the man said in a voice only slightly
less penetrating. ''I am Gunnery Sergeant Ortega, and I'm
in charge, heaven help me, of your recruit training. I do
not like noise, and I do not like disorder. Right now, that
means I do not like you. Let's see if you can improve my
opinion of you straks before I get you out on a parade
ground somewhere. Now go about your business in an orderly manner. If you have a question or need assistance,
raise your hand and wait for me to help you. I'll get to
everyone in time, so be patient and we'll make this as

painless as possible." He turned his glittering stare on the dark-haired youngster who had been voicing his approval of the blonde and raised his stun baton under the youth's chin. It wasn't switched on, but the sergeant's thumb was less than a centimeter from the power button. "As for you, lover-boy . . ." he said in a low, dangerous voice. "What's your name?"

"Antonelli, *signore* . . . sir," the kid replied. Despite the menace of the baton his voice was cocky.

"You address me as 'sergeant' when you talk, boy," Ortega said, his voice a whipcrack. "Now listen to me, Antonelli. The whores in town'll be glad enough at all the things you can do—if you really can, that is. Save the enthusiasm for them and leave her the hell alone. Got it?" He didn't wait for an answer.

Hauser's bag was small, all he needed for the small kit he'd collected en route. He double-checked the label to see that the serial number was clear, opened it up long enough to transfer his wristpiece computer and a few odds and ends from his pockets inside, then sealed it and tossed the bag into a bin. He stripped off his clothes quickly and cast around in search of a place to sit.

He looked for MacDuff, but the Caledonian was surrounded by a mob of other recruits already, including the hannie Myaighee. Hauser didn't care to mix with the ale again. He had tried to soften his resentment of the nonhuman after hearing Suartana's advice on trying to adopt more Commonwealth-oriented attitudes, but that didn't mean he liked the bald-headed little monkey any better. So far it had stayed away from him, and he didn't intend for things to change now.

Instead, he finally found a cold metal chair next to another recruit, a big, raw-boned man with auburn hair and a collection of scars on his chest. A tattoo on one arm showed a crest of some kind, together with the words "Third Assault Marines" and the slogan "Death Strikes From Orbit." Hauser hoped his own appearance wouldn't stand out too much among the rough characters in the waiting room. Most of the skin displayed carried scars or tattoos of some kind, though there were others who looked more like Hauser than the big man next to him.

There was little conversation under the watchful eye of the sergeant. Periodically, someone would call out a number from the inner door, and another recruit would leave. Then it was Hauser's turn.

"Number forty-eight! Forty-eight!" There was a pause. "Serial number 50-987-5648!"

Hauser suddenly realized the call was for him and stood up with a jerk.

"Waiting for a goddamned engraved invitation?" Sergeant Ortega asked him harshly. The NCO lashed out with a stun baton, and Hauser's forearm tingled and burned as the blow landed. "Mag it, strak!"

As he crossed the waiting room, Hauser knew he was taking the last steps in his journey. He found himself hoping, too late, that his decision really had been the right one.

At the door, he was called upon to surrender his ident disk. Then the processing began, a seemingly interminable job that lasted more than four hours and left Hauser weary, discouraged, and less sure of himself than ever.

Despite weeks of preparation in transit, it seemed as if Hauser was starting from scratch. There was a fresh physical examination, with another long look at the lingering traces of his wounding and regen treatment. A psych team questioned him yet again, concentrating on his familiarity with chip training procedures. Then came a haircut, a sonic shower, vaccinations against various bacteriological and viral threats, and the injection of a five-year birth control agent. Legionnaires contracted for a term of five years and gave up all right to formally sanctioned marriages or any chance of children. In the Fifth Foreign Legion, personal ties were always frowned upon.

Through it all, the officers, noncoms, and civilians remained completely impersonal. The recruits had numbers and were never referred to by name. Hauser had never felt so completely removed from his aristocratic background. It rankled to be referred to by an ident number instead of a name, but somehow he held his tongue and avoided further trouble.

He had thought he'd be drawing a Legion uniform, but instead ended up in secondhand coveralls and boots a size too large. The explanation offered by a bored noncom at the supply counter was that uniforms and kits would not be issued until training actually began, perhaps as much as another two weeks off. ARISTOTLE had brought only about half of the recruits who would comprise Hauser's training company. More would arrive to fill out the unit when the carriership PETRONIUS arrived in-system. Meanwhile he and the other recruits would wear these secondhand clothes. It was another Legion tradition. The new recruit made a clean break with his past. A fresh start. Though they would be allowed some personal effects, there was something symbolic in having the new arrivals start out this way, wearing used clothing as anonymous as the identification numbers and nearly as impersonal.

The process ended in a small office in the administration building, a large structure which faced the Monument aux Morts and the museum along the broad extent of the road the legionnaires referred to as "The Sacred Way." Room 2312 was windowless, with the wall behind the desk dominated by the Legion colors. A woman with captain's bars gestured to the lone chair beside the desk as Hauser was shown in.

She consulted her wristpiece. "Number 50-987-5648. Hauser von Semenanjung Burat, Wolfgang Alaric."

"Yes, Captain," he responded. It was a relief to hear his name used at last.

"Good, good. Needless to say, you've been accepted for a five-year enlistment in the Foreign Legion. You are aware that you may take this enlistment under a pseudonym, a *nomme de guerre,* as the French used to call it?"

He nodded slowly. That, of course, explained the pointed avoidance of using names throughout the processing. From the time their ident disks had been taken, the recruits had been in a sort of limbo. Anyone who wanted to could take new names upon entering the Legion, to make the break with the past complete.

"It is not required that you change your name," the captain went on. "In some cases it is essential, such as when we accept a recruit with a criminal record. The change of identity, which includes issuance of complete records—birth certificate, passports, everything—the change is designed to protect the Legion and the legionnaire alike. If you were wanted for murder on Caledon and we got a query regarding Wolfgang Hauser, we could honestly say there was no such person, and produce complete records to prove it. That's been a basic building block of the Legion for hundreds of years."

She looked at him with a smile. "That doesn't apply to you, though. However, a lot of legionnaires choose to change their names just for the tradition, the romance, the sense of adventure . . . and frankly we encourage the change because it helps cement the new beginning you're making with us. Have you given any thought to a *nomme de guerre*?''

Hauser shrugged. "Not really, Captain," he said slowly. "I suppose a change might be a good idea. Even if I'm not considered a criminal, there's a few Besarans who might not be too pleased to know that I'm here."

She nodded. "The possibility had occurred to us, based on the background information you gave the testers aboard *Kolwezi*. Mind you, the Legion looks after its own, no matter what your name might be. But you could save yourself, and us, a lot of trouble. What name shall we enter you under, then? Or would you prefer we give you some random identity selected by computer?"

He looked away. The Hausers had always been known as the "Wolves of the West," after their holdings on Java Baru's Western Peninsula. His given name, Wolfgang, echoed the old nickname. . . .

And his father, Karl Hauser, had always called him "Little Wolf."

"Legion tradition or not, I don't like the idea of completely breaking with my past. My father's memory, at least." He spoke more to himself than to the captain. "I'd like the name Karl Wolf, Captain."

She touched some keys on her wristpiece. "Karl Wolf. Very good. The name is now entered on your ident disk and in our files. You are now Engaged Volunteer Karl Wolf. Welcome to the Fifth Foreign Legion."

The man who now called himself Karl Wolf leaned back in his bunk and stared at the tattered mattress slung above him. He barely noticed the noise made by the other recruits crowded into the transients' barracks. For the moment he was too wrapped up in the gloomy knowledge that they faced yet another delay before the training would begin. It seemed that boredom was more likely to claim his life than any enemy on the field of battle.

After finishing in Room 2312 he'd been ordered to the barracks building. The assignment was temporary, until the new training company was fully assembled and settled into standard quarters. Twenty men shared this dormitory, mostly others from Wolf's batch of new arrivals. There were a handful, though, who had been in residence for over a month already, some of the holdovers from the last training company which had formed at Fort Hunter. Wolf hoped he wouldn't end up like them, forced to wait for yet another batch of new recruits to be assembled.

His bag had arrived ahead of him. There had been a few moments of worry over that, but the seals had been untouched and the contents all accounted for.

"This my bunk up here?" a gentle, lilting voice broke into Wolf's private world. He turned his head to see the big redhead from the processing hut looking down at him, holding what looked like a military-issue kitbag in his beefy hands. The voice reminded him of MacDuff, and was completely at odds with the man's powerful build and hard eyes, and Wolf wasn't sure which to go by. He'd heard of bullies in situations like this forcing weaker men out of choice spots . . . like lower bunks.

Wolf raised himself on his elbows. "I figured we were supposed to sleep wherever they tossed our stuff, but I haven't seen any sign that we're actually assigned anywhere," he told the big man in his most reasonable voice.

The redhead nodded. "That's what I thought. They did the same thing at . . ." He trailed off. "At another military base I heard about once."

The tattoo with the Assault Marine crest was hidden by the man's coverall sleeve, but Wolf's eyes strayed to the forearm anyway. When he met the recruit's level gaze again he saw a tiny smile. "That's my story and I'm sticking with it," the redhead said in a quiet voice. "Look, boyo, I mass about twice what you do, and this bunk looks like it was part of the base they had here back when this fellow Hunter was stationed here. Would you rather sleep in the upper or run the risk of having me fall through and smother you in your sleep? Doesn't matter to me."

Wolf grinned back. "Put that way, I'm inclined to be generous," he said, sticking out his hand as he swung his feet to the floor. "The name's . . . uh, Wolf. Karl Wolf." He had almost forgotten his *nomme de guerre*.

"Tom Callo—Tom Kern," the other responded, taking

his hand in a powerful grip. "The names take some getting used to, don't they?"

Nodding, Wolf relinquished the bunk. He was surprised to find himself warming to this man even though he was obviously nothing at all like the people he'd been friendly with back home. There was something about Kern that made him almost instantly likable despite his fearsome appearance.

Kern didn't sit down immediately. Instead he turned to the drab gray locker beside the bunks and started emptying his kitbag, staying well clear of Wolf's meager possessions. That done, he dropped the bag into the bottom of the locker and stripped off his coverall, hanging it neatly. In fact all his motions were precise and careful, further confirmation that he had plenty of experience living out of a military kit or a barracks locker.

A recruit stirred on the upper bunk next to them. It was Antonelli, the dark-haired kid who had been making trouble in the waiting room. "Hey, Red," he said easily, a trace of accent overlaying his Terranglic. He pointed to the tattoo. "You a *veterano*, man? Why would an Assault Marine end up in a jerk-ass outfit like the Foreign Legion, huh?"

Kern shot him an angry look, but didn't answer the boy.

"Hey, come on, Red," Antonelli persisted. "We're supposed to be *compagni* . . . comrades in arms, now!"

"Quiet, there!" The kid's bantering tones were cut off by the harsh voice of Gunnery Sergeant Ortega. The NCO had come up behind the youngster as he was talking. Now he was peering up at the kid with an expression of supreme distaste. "Everybody, on their feet! At attention!" His stun baton lashed out to prod the kid, who scrambled out of his bunk hastily. The other recruits were falling into line beside their bunks, shaken out of their complaisance by the sergeant's penetrating shout.

"All right, stand easy," the sergeant growled. He surveyed the bunkroom with a withering look. "You lot will be spending two to three weeks in these transient quarters until the rest of your training company arrives. Until then, technically, you aren't even part of the Legion, because your contracts don't start until the company is formed."

He looked straight at Wolf. "That means you still have a few days to back out if you want to. A five-year com-

mitment to the Legion might sound exciting or adventur-
ous back home, but I'm here to tell you it's nothing of the
sort. It's not like some holovid or dreamchip scenario
where the stalwart heroes fight it out on some sanitary field
of honor, then go back to swap yarns over a bottle somewhere. Legion life is month after month of duty so boring
it'll drive you crazy, followed by a few days or hours when
you're too busy trying to save your ass to realize that you're
really in one of those exciting battles you heard about back
when you were a civilian. Think about it . . . Five years
of whatever duty we think suits your qualifications. That's
what's waiting for you even if you manage to make it
through Basic.''

Antonelli spoke up. ''Uh, Sergeant, what happens if we
wash out of the training?'' He managed to look brash and
nervous at the same time.

Ortega glared at him. ''There are just four ways out of
the Legion once the contract is in force. You can wash out
of Basic, or resign if you decide you can't take it. Pass
Basic and your options get slimmer. Then you can complete five years' service and get your H-and-F stamp on
your discharge papers, or you can take the Last March or
get yourself wounded bad enough to pull a medical out,
or you can desert. I wouldn't recommend deserting. We
don't like deserters, and you won't like what we do to you
if we catch you trying.''

There was a stir in the barracks room, but no more questions. ''In short, just remember one little rule and you'll
get alone fine. Stay out of trouble. As long as you obey
orders and don't go screwing up we'll all be one happy
family.'' Ortega looked around the room. ''Just because
you're not official doesn't mean you get a vacation. You'll
work until PETRONIUS brings the rest of the company in.
That starts tomorrow. Lights out is at 2300 hours tonight,
with reveille at 0430. Keep in mind that you've got a
27-hour rotation period here, and set chronometers accord-
ingly.'' He paused again. ''Dismissed.''

Wolf followed the sergeant's stocky form with wary eyes.
The noncom made him nervous. Ortega seemed to look
straight at him every time he spoke of people not measuring up. It reminded him of Colby, of the recruiting sergeant back on Robespierre. It was as if they all expected

him to fail. Was he really too soft to be a part of the Fifth Foreign Legion?

A sign on the wall caught Wolf's eye: YOU LEGIONNAIRES ARE SOLDIERS IN ORDER TO DIE, AND I AM SENDING YOU WHERE YOU CAN DIE. The sign attributed the words to a General Negrier of the old French Foreign Legion. The quote had been uttered over a thousand years ago, and it was still part and parcel of the unit's tradition.

That said more about the Legion than anything Ortega or any other legionnaire had put into words.

Chapter 10

It takes an iron hand to bend such diverse elements
into the same mold.
                    —Comte Pierre de Castellanne
                    French Foreign Legion, 1845

"All right, you straks, ten-HUT!"

The recruits had been milling around the parade grounds
on their own for the better part of an hour, and the sudden
shout caught most of them by surprise. Wolf found a spot
in the second row as they formed up into three lines in an
approximation of military attention. One hundred twenty
men, women, and nonhumans stood sweating in Devereaux's afternoon sunlight, assembled for their first official
muster as Training Company Odintsev. They still looked
more like a motley assortment of convicts than a military
unit, with their secondhand coveralls and sloppy, unmili-
tary bearing, but from this moment the process of turning
them into legionnaires would begin.

The arrival of the transport *Sevastopol* had ended three
long weeks of boredom. It hadn't come a moment too soon
as far as Wolf was concerned. Ortega had decided he was
best suited for latrine duty, and five days of scrubbing out
the facilities with a toothbrush and a pile of rags was
enough to make almost any other duty sound attractive.

The shuttle from *Sevastopol* had touched down shortly
before noon, and while the new batch of recruits was going through the processing routine, Wolf and the others
had been drawing their Legion kits and getting ready for
the changeover from boredom to Basic. Almost everything
he'd need for the next five years was stowed in the bulky
kitbag beside him—shoes, boots, five grades of uniform
from duraweave battledress up to the khaki shirt and trousers of full dress, a canteen and mess kit, and other ac-

coutrements, including the white kepi that was the Legion's
unique badge of office. None of them would be allowed to
don the sacred headgear until they had convinced their
instructors that they really were Legion material.

Those instructors were standing in a cluster behind the
stocky figure of Gunnery Sergeant Ortega. Unlike the recruits, they wore comfortable gear for Devereaux's mid-
afternoon heat, shorts and T-shirts in khaki and green with
the Legion motto *Legio Patria Nostra* emblazoned in bright
scarlet letters across their chests. The casual rig revealed
that Ortega had a tattoo on his forearm even gaudier than
Kern's, a skull and crossbones with the motto "Living by
chance, soldiering by choice, killing for fun" running under the picture.

A pair of stiff figures emerged from the administration
building behind the noncoms and crossed the street at a
leisurely pace. They wore crisp khaki uniforms and black
kepis, and the one in the lead had *hauptmann*'s—no, captain's—bars. Behind him was a woman wearing a lieutenant's insignia. Gunnery Sergeant Ortega saluted, and the
captain returned the gesture casually.

"I am Captain Dmitri Odintsev," he said, raising his
voice to make himself heard over the whining turbofans of
a passing MSV cargo carrier. "Today you will begin your
Basic Training as members of Training Company Odintsev. I expect good things from the recruits under my command. My units have won the Training Company
Commendation three terms running, and I intend to make
it a fourth time with your help. You will find the work here
hard, and not all of you will finish the process. That is
only to be expected. Even the ones who wash out of Legion training should hold their heads up high, because as
long as you give us your best you will know that you've
been part of something special, something ordinary soldiers will never understand. Regardless of what some people claim, the Fifth Foreign Legion is a good outfit . . .
the *best* outfit . . . and for those of you who do measure
up I can promise that you'll find a home for life."

Odintsev paused. "As Company Commander, most of
my duties are strictly administrative, and the same goes
for Lieutenant DuChateau, my Exec." His gesture took in
the woman beside him. "Most of your training will be
directly supervised by Gunnery Sergeant Ortega and the

rest of the Training Company's noncommissioned officers. In addition, some of you may be assigned instructor duties in areas where you have demonstrated particular proficiency. However, even though the lieutenant and I won't be directly involved in day-to-day training, we're still available if you need us. The Legion looks after its own, and even though you aren't full legionnaires yet rest assured that I take care of my recruits . . . for good or for ill.

"Most of the academic work you do in Basic will consist of chip education coupled with practical applications classes," the captain continued. "Part of your screening included tests on your tolerance for chip learning, so none of you need to be concerned by any stories you might have heard about some people being unable to handle chip learning. You should, though, keep in mind that training through direct mind-computer links may be faster and easier than any other form of education, but will still vary in quality according to your individual aptitudes and desire to learn. Don't expect to retain everything perfectly just because you review a chip on a subject. You may have to repeat a chip several times before you fully understand the material."

He paused again before continuing. "The purpose of applications classes is to put some of what you learn from adchips into actual practice. You will find that you'll retain information much better when you do it, as opposed to merely studying it. Your progress will be monitored, and where necessary you may be assigned extra course loads or the assistance of a tutor to help you. Do not be discouraged by any problems you may have. I've known old legionnaires from Neusachsen and Beaumont who never learned Terranglic well enough to shed their native accents, even after years in the Legion and plenty of chip instruction. They muddle through. So will most of you."

The captain moved on to other topics, touching a number of subjects briefly. "Now as far as the overall training program goes," he said at last, "I'll lay out what you can look forward to in the months ahead. For the next three weeks you will undergo your initial indoctrination here at Fort Hunter. This will consist of physical conditioning, courses in military discipline and etiquette, Legion background, singing, first aid, basic weapons familiarization, and so on. At the end of that period you will have two more weeks at Hunter in intensive training with Legion equipment, including weapons, some vehicles, and your combat helmet and battledress capabilities.

"Following this will be a series of two-week courses designed to familiarize you with various environments and to give you actual field experience. Fort Kessel in the Nordemont mountain range, Fort Marchand in the jungles of the Archipel d'Aurore, Fort Souriban in the deep desert, and the orbital station of Fort Gsell will each serve in turn as your home base during the appropriate stages of training. As Christmas falls within this period, many of you will also be participating in extracurricular activities related to the holiday, and training will be interrupted for a week around Christmas so that the entire training battalion can celebrate together here at Hunter. The final two weeks of your basic training will consist of a series of tests to determine your fitness to graduate the course and receive the white kepi of the legionnaire."

He studied the recruits for a long moment. "That's all I have to say for now . . . except for one more thing. Welcome to the Fifth Foreign Legion." He smiled, then turned toward Ortega. "All right, Gunnery Sergeant, they're all yours." They exchanged salutes again, and the two officers headed back for the admin building.

Ortega waited until they were inside before raising his voice again. "Let's get a few things straight right now," he shouted. "Captain Odintsev is listed as Training Company Commander, but you'll find that you'll see a hell of a lot more of me than you will of the officers. When you address me you will salute and call me 'Sergeant.' Do you understand?"

There were sprinkled replies, a ragged and discordant chorus. Wolf didn't join in. Behind Ortega the other noncoms were fanning out to move through the ragged formation, dressing the lines and frowning at the recruits.

"Do you understand?" Ortega repeated, sounding menacing.

More soldiers answered, but it was still a dispirited response. Wolf chuckled . . . until the numbing shock of a stun baton across his shoulders made him gasp. Other recruits were getting similar treatment up and down the line from the corporals moving among the ranks.

"We'll keep this up until you get it right," Ortega announced loudly. "You will salute and say 'Sergeant' when addressing me. The proper answer to any question asked of you is 'Yes, Sergeant' or 'No, Sergeant,' DO YOU UNDERSTAND?"

This time Wolf joined in the chorus, all too aware of the hovering noncom near him. "YES, SERGEANT!"

Ortega nodded, a quick, curt gesture. "You straks . . . no, that's an insult to every damned strak that ever jumped into the Mistfloor Gorge. You lot aren't straks . . . and you certainly aren't men, so you must be the lowest form of life. Nubes. Newbies. Recruits. You nubes are the best of a bad lot, the sorry-assed few the processors couldn't get rid of any other way. So now you'll spend fifteen weeks finishing your basic training here and elsewhere . . . unless you screw up first, and I'm sure most of you will! While you're here you'll learn how to be a legionnaire, but odds are none of you will ever be fit to breathe the same air as a real legionnaire. By the time it's over every last one of you'll be wishing you had just signed up for Hell, 'cause pitchforks and eternal flames would be comfortable compared to what you'll be doing!"

He paused, looking them over slowly, contemptuously. "For the rest of the day you'll be settling in to your permanent quarters. The company will be divided into four platoons of thirty recruits each, and each platoon will be assigned to one barracks building. Those of you who've been with us for a while will be glad to hear you'll be getting more locker space and semiprivate cubicles. After we've divvied you up by platoons, sections, and lances, you'll spend the afternoon getting squared away. Evening mess is at 1800 hours. After that you'll have two hours of free time, with retreat and lights out at 2100. Reveille is at 0300 hours."

Ortega checked the tiny screen of his wristpiece computer. "In addition to myself, twelve NCOs are responsible for the bulk of your training, though you'll also be given specialized lectures by other officers and noncoms as necessary. You will obey these men at all times. If you have a problem, you go through the chain of command. That means you see the corporal in charge of your section first, and if he thinks it's worthwhile you see the sergeant in charge of your platoon. Heaven help you if they think it has to be brought to me . . . or if you bother me with some damned complaint without seeing them first!'' Ortega gave a savage little smile and made a gesture to the NCOs nearest him. ''All right. Tell 'em off by lances and sections and get 'em moving. This isn't some strakking picnic!'' He turned on his heel and stalked off.

One of the noncoms took Ortega's place. ''First Platoon!'' he bellowed. A corporal took over with a shout of ''First Section. Alpha Lance!'' He recited five names, including Suartana's, then added, ''Form up over here. Now!''

The process seemed to go on interminably. There were a few mutterings in the ranks until the corporal who had hit Wolf lashed out a few times with his stun baton. Then the other recruits were quiet.

First Platoon was filled out, and the sergeant in charge was leading them away at a trot. After a few minutes more Wolf saw the corporal with the well-used stun baton stepping clear of the ranks.

''Second Platoon, Second Section, Delta Lance! When I call your names fall in behind me. Antonelli, Mario! Kern, Thomas! Myaighee! Scott, Lisa! Wolf, Karl!'' He paused before starting in on Echo Lance.

As the corporal continued assembling his section, Wolf studied the recruits beside him. He knew Myaighee, of course, along with Kern and Antonelli from his transient barracks room. The redhead was friendly and good-natured; the young Italian's brash manner made him unpopular, but for all that there was something about the kid that would have been engaging if he hadn't been trying so hard to play the role of the cocky tough guy.

The last member of the group was the same blond girl Antonelli had been admiring in the processing hut that day. She was tall and slender, and moved with a catlike grace. Her short hair and worn coverall couldn't hide the fact that she had once been used to power or money. Like MacDuff, she looked like an aristo. He wondered what her background was, what had led her to join the Legion.

The corporal finished calling names, and a tall, rugged sergeant with a face scarred beyond the ability of reconstructive surgery to repair bellowed for Second Platoon to follow him. They struck out at a brisk trot, following First Platoon through a gate into a fenced-off compound containing several buildings and a large central parade ground. They stopped outside a building labeled Barracks 18, where the two sections separated and were called to order by their respective corporals.

"All right, you miserable nubes, stand easy and listen up!" the NCO told them. "I am Corporal Stefan Vanyek, and until you put on the kepi or wash out of training the second section of this platoon is under my authority. For the next fifteen weeks you'll be answerable to God, two sergeants, and me . . . but not necessarily in that order! When I say jump, you'd better ask how high. Screw up and I'll be all over you like scales on an Ubrenfar. Got it?"

"Yes, Corporal!" the section members answered in unison.

"Good! Now . . . each of you has four lancemates. Think of your lance as your family. You'll train together, march together, eat together, sleep together, and God willing fight together for as long as you're here. Got it?"

"Yes, Corporal!"

Beside him, Antonelli smirked at Wolf and jerked his head at the blond woman. "Sleep together, huh," he whispered. "Hey, man, maybe this ain't gonna be so bad!"

Vanyek whirled and stalked toward them. "Who said that?" he demanded, looking at Wolf. No one answered.

"All right, nubes. Delta Lance, take a lap around the parade ground. Mag it!"

They fell out of ranks and started running. Antonelli set a brisk pace, and pulled out ahead almost at once with the girl following close behind. Wolf noticed Kern and the hannie holding back, choosing a steady ground-eating trot over Antonelli's faster gait. Though he wasn't sure about the alien's reasons—perhaps those short legs just couldn't manage anything better—Wolf decided Kern probably knew what he was doing and fell into step beside the big man. Although they weren't pushing themselves particularly hard, they were soon drenched in sweat, and the dry, hot air seared Wolf's throat before he had rounded the last corner of the field.

The run completed, they fell back into the line and Vanyek resumed his harangue.

"Next time one of you nubes mouths off in ranks you'll get a real punishment, not just a warning." He paused. "As I was saying, the lance is everything. Your best friends, your family. One of you screws up, the whole lance screws up. Keep it in mind.''

A shuttle roared overhead, drowning out the sounds of Fort Hunter. Vanyek waited until it was gone, then continued. ''One recruit from each lance will be appointed as lance leader. The lance leader is responsible for discipline and all actions of the lance. You will obey your lance leader's orders except as overridden by higher authority.''

He looked at Wolf's lance with an expression of distaste that Wolf was coming to recognize as the standard look of the NCO instructors at Fort Hunter. As Vanyek called up information on his 'piece, Wolf suppressed a smile. Kern's military background and aptitude would make him the obvious choice for lance leader, and that would suit Wolf well enough. Or perhaps his own education and Academy training would count for something, as Doenitz had suggested back on Robespierre. Although he had disclaimed any desire for a leadership role, he wouldn't shirk the responsibility if it was offered. . . .

''Delta Lance,'' Vanyek mused. ''Hmm . . . you, the ale. Your file says you've already had Legion combat experience?''

The alien nodded, a completely human gesture. ''Yes, Corporal. With Captain Fraser's company on Hanuman and Polypheme—''

''Did I ask for a service history, nube?'' The corporal cut the alien off short. His gaze swept over the rest of the lance. ''When the Legion recruits locally, during a campaign, there isn't always time for the regular training process. Myaighee here is an example. He has served in two campaigns already. Since you have combat experience, Myaighee, you'll be the designated lance leader for Delta Lance. Understood?''

''Yes, Corporal,'' the alien replied.

''But—'' Wolf burst out. He stopped himself.

''What is it, nube?'' Vanyek asked sharply.

''Uh . . . nothing, Corporal. Nothing . . .''

Vanyek gave him a long, speculative look. ''I've seen your file, Wolf. It says you think you're better than most people. Is that so, nube?''

''No, Corporal,'' Wolf responded crisply.

''Ah . . . well, then that means you think the psych tester lied about you. Right?''

''No, Corporal,'' he repeated.

Vanyek snorted and gave Wolf a brief touch of the stun baton on low power, making the muscles in his arm jerk spasmodically. "Get something straight, nube. And the rest of you trash. If you've got any hangups about an ale as lance leader, you'd better swallow them double quick! We don't worry about how many arms you have or whether you hatched from an egg or whatever. Anyway, all nubes are the lowest form of life, so trifling differences aren't gonna bother you. You got it, nubes?"

"Yes, Corporal," they all responded.

Vanyek shoved his stun baton under Wolf's chin. "What about you, nube? You got any problems taking orders from a hannie?"

"No, Corporal. None." Wolf swallowed, uncomfortably aware of how the man's words were hitting home. He'd heard about Myaighee's Legion experience back on the *Kolwezi,* but he'd assumed a nonhuman would never have a shot as a leader at any level.

"You think you could lead this lance better'n Myaighee, nube?" Vanyek persisted.

"No, Corporal!" he replied quickly . . . perhaps too quickly. Vanyek regarded him for a long minute before finally nodding. "Myaighee, Delta Lance." He moved down the line. "Now, Echo Lance . . . hmmm . . ."

Wolf's attention wandered as the corporal moved to the next group of recruits. It seemed the Legion wasn't making any allowances for the differences between people, between whole cultures, even though it drew manpower from across the Terran sphere and beyond. He had expected to find differences, of course. His ancestors had emigrated to Laut Besar largely to get away from some of the stricter aspects of the Commonwealth, and in just over a hundred years the two cultures had diverged. Now he was expected to adapt, and with people like Vanyek pushing him it just made the job all the more difficult.

He glanced at Myaighee. Did the hannie find it hard to understand human ways? Of course the alien had already been exposed to the Legion before coming here. Alone of the recruits in Training Company Odintsev, Myaighee wore the insignia of a Third Class Legionnaire. He—Wolf refused to use the alien word *ky*—was already a veteran, and would probably go back to his old unit no matter what.

That was as galling as the hannie's sudden promotion to lance leader.

Wolf felt his jaw tighten. He'd adapt to these Legion ways, all right . . . if only to see how Vanyek and Ortega reacted. If that meant treating an alien as an equal, even a superior, so be it.

A few moments later, Vanyek was finished with the lance leader assignments, and the section followed him into the barracks building. It was designed to hold an entire platoon of thirty men, with quarters on the ground floor and a basement gymnasium and exercise area underneath reached by a flight of stairs and an airlock arrangement. The exercise room, Vanyek explained, could be set for a variety of different environmental conditions, much like the training compartments in the transports.

The quarters block was divided lengthwise, with one section occupying each side of the main floor. Each lance shared a room with five semiprivate cubicles and a common room. At one end, near the only outside door, the Section NCO had an office and private room. The other end contained another office/quarters suite, slightly larger, for use by the platoon NCO, Sergeant Konrad, plus a large communal latrine and shower room that was shared by the entire platoon.

Delta Lance had the quarters adjacent to the shower. Initially, Wolf was inclined to grumble about the arrangement, especially when several First Section recruits started using the showers and he realized how much noise they could make. But Kern only smiled and pointed out that he'd be a lot happier with the arrangements when everyone in the building was eager for a shower and Delta Lance would have the advantage in getting there first.

The quarters themselves were comfortable enough, far superior to the transient's bunkroom. Each cubicle had a cot, a small writing desk and computer terminal, and an individual locker, with a lightweight folding door that could give at least the illusion of privacy. The common area at the center of the room was as Spartan as the cubicles, with no more furnishings than a table and some chairs.

Compared to his private room at the Sky Guard Academy it was appalling, but judging from other aspects of Legion life, Wolf felt lucky to have such good quarters.

As he unpacked his kitbag, the memory of Vanyek's words kept coming back. They were determined that he would fail, that he couldn't handle life in the Legion. And maybe they were right.

Chapter 11

The Legion is a moral paradise but a physical hell.
—attributed to an unknown colonel
of the French Foreign Legion

"All I'm saying is that some of these guys are pretty damned free with their stun batons, that's all," Wolf said.

The recruits had finished their evening meal and were back in barracks, enjoying their last night of comparative freedom. Everything they'd heard since arriving on Devereaux suggested that Basic was going to be tough, but at least they had one more evening of calm before the storm.

Wolf was sitting at the table in the common area with Kern and Lisa Scott. Myaighee had closed himself off in his cubicle with an adchip on leadership principles, while Antonelli was perched on his bunk watching the others and absently shuffling a deck of cards.

The conversation had started after Sergeant Konrad had finished up his inspection. He hadn't found any faults with Delta Lance, but there had been some excitement a few minutes later after he handed out extra duty to everyone in Echo Lance as punishment for one recruit's sloppy locker. When the sergeant left, Volunteer Lauriston had taken it on himself to chastise the offender, a small recruit with features like an Indomay, named Kochu Burundai. The resulting fight had been quickly broken up by Konrad and Corporal Vanyek, but not without some heavy-handed use of stun batons.

Hauser had seen a lot of that sort of thing, both here at Fort Hunter and back aboard the two transports, and it still grated. On Laut Besar even Indomays didn't get that sort of treatment, yet in the "enlightened" Commonwealth no one could make a move without worrying about being subjected to a stun-lashing.

Tom Kern didn't seem particularly shocked, though. "It's rough, I'll give you that. But they've got their reasons. You'll find the military always has a pretty good motive for whatever it does, even if it doesn't look that way to an outsider."

Volunteer Scott laughed. "I can't buy that one, Kern," she said, raising an eyebrow at the big ex-Marine. "You can't tell me that anybody in his right mind would have put together this lance."

"She's got you there, Tom," Hauser chimed in. "Look what they decided would make a compatible unit. We're not exactly a typical bunch, are we?"

Kern shrugged. "I've seen stranger."

"Sure. A deserter from the Marines—"

"I never told you that!" Kern shot back, sounding more amused than annoyed. During the time they'd spent together in the transients' barracks waiting for the company to form, Hauser had picked up plenty of clues about the backgrounds of some of the other recruits, including Kern and Antonelli.

"Okay, okay, a Marine veteran, then," he amended. "Then there's a street kid who was sentenced to the Legion against his will." He darted a glance at Antonelli, who flashed a cocky grin. "An ale that doesn't know what sex it is. I'm the token aristocrat with the shady past, I guess . . . and of course there's our mystery guest here."

Lisa Scott looked away, blushing faintly. She was close-lipped about her past, and so far no one had breached Legion tradition to interrogate her. That didn't stop her new lancemates from speculating, though.

"Not exactly the ideal outfit," he concluded. "How in hell did anybody come up with a team like us? Somebody program the master computer to pull practical jokes?"

"They're supposed to match psych profiles," Kern said. "And yes, scoff if you will, the pair of you, but they really do know what they want. You've had military experience, haven't you, Wolf?" At his nod, Kern went on. "Well, so have Myaighee and I. I'd guess you haven't, Scott . . . and I know Antonelli there hasn't. They try to pair up novices with people who've had some kind of training. And mixing social background is supposed to get us used to interacting without thinking about status and all that shit."

"They sure don't take background into account in the

training, do they?'' Wolf commented. "Hell, that guy they nailed for a messy locker never even saw running water until he went on board *Kolwezi* . . . !''

"Yeah, I know,'' Kern replied. "I heard that Burundai was a herder on Ulan-Tala before he signed up. They reverted to a nomad culture during the Shadow Centuries, but they weren't as lucky as your bunch. They never had anything worthwhile to attract new settlers to yank them back into a modern frame of mind. That's the whole problem with the Legion. Regular outfits have the glamour and get the best recruits, while the Colonials are mostly drawn from common backgrounds. But in the Legion they're getting recruits in from everywhere, from Terra to Ulan-Tala and anything in between. That's the reason for the tough physical discipline.''

"Come again?'' Lisa Scott asked.

Kern spread his hands and looked at the tabletop, but his mind seemed light-years away. "The theory is that the instructors can give lectures until Sol goes nova, but some of them might never understand what we're telling them. Would you really want to explain to that herdsman why civilized people use a latrine instead of a convenient bush? Multiply that by a hundred and twenty, because every last recruit comes from a different background and culture with different ideas of what conduct to call proper. It's a hell of a lot easier to get people to accept a single standard of behavior by showing them a good, selfish reason for it—keeping their precious skins intact—than it would be to individually overcome each recruit's lifetime of social training.''

"And here I thought Vanyek just liked to make people twitch,'' Wolf said dryly. "How'd you pick up so much on what makes these people tick, Kern?''

The big redhead looked away for a long moment. "I was a DI in the third . . . for a while.'' He paused. "I'd rather not think about that now, though.''

As the conversation died away, Antonelli rolled out of his bunk and approached the table, still practicing a one-handed shuffle that would have made Robert MacDuff envious. "Hey, let's knock off the heavy philosophy and have some fun,'' he said. "Come on, it's our first night, and it's free time. What d'ya say we play some cards, huh?''

"No thanks,'' Wolf replied automatically. He stood up.

"I think I'll emulate our great leader and chip something until they call lights out."

"I just thought maybe you'd like to sit in on a game or something, you know?" Antonelli put the cards on the table and tapped the deck.

"Thanks anyway." He still wasn't sure what he thought of Antonelli. The kid tried hard to make others like him, but he had a knack for saying the wrong things. Like his comment on the parade ground, or the way he'd acted the day they'd processed in.

"Just trying to be sociable." Antonelli turned away. "How 'bout you, Red?"

"Not for me, mate," Kern said, affably enough.

Antonelli sat down at the table. "Man, what a bunch of killjoys they stuck me with," he complained. "Come on, just a coupla hands, okay?"

Kern shook his head slowly. "Maybe after we get our first pay slip, all right? I used up my whole advance before we even got off the transport, and gambling's no good without stakes."

From his cubicle, Wolf watched Antonelli shrug and look across at Lisa Scott. "You'll play, won't you, honey?" Antonelli said loudly. "I'll bet we can think of some stakes worth playing for, huh?"

She didn't answer. Instead, she crossed to her locker, took out a towel, then headed for the door. A few moments later the sound of running water confirmed her destination.

Antonelli leered again. "Hey, maybe she's got the right idea. Maybe I'll just clean up, too. . . ." He got up and followed her.

Wolf rolled out of his cot. "Maybe we'd better help out Scott . . ."

"Better wait and see if the lady needs any help, boyo," Kern advised. "Could be old Mario's in for a surprise or two from that one."

Before he could respond there was a shout from the shower room, then a string of curses in hoarse tones barely recognizable as Antonelli's. Wolf raced for the door with Kern close behind. Myaighee joined them as they ran down the hall to the showers.

Antonelli was backed against the wall next to the door clutching his left arm. Blood seeped through his fingers and dripped to the tile floor. "She cut me! The bitch cut me!"

Lisa Scott took a step toward the bleeding man. She made no effort to cover her nude body, and the knife in her hand, held at the ready, never wavered. "I'll cut you worse if you come near me again," she said in a soft, dangerous voice. "And in some place a lot more painful than your arm. Depend on it."

"What's going on in here? Get out of the way!" Corporal Vanyek's strident tones broke through a babble of voices from the corridor, where members of the other lances were gathering in response to the commotion. "Out of my way, I said!"

The corporal brushed past Wolf and took in the scene with a single glance. "All right, back to your quarters. Now! Mag it!" He halted Wolf and the other members of Alpha Lance. "Not you straks."

He turned away, toward Lisa, then suddenly whirled around and slammed a fist into Antonelli's stomach. The recruit doubled over, gasping, and Vanyek hit him again, this time in the face.

"You stupid bastard," Vanyek said, almost in a monotone. "You strak-faced piece of ghoul shit." For emphasis he struck again, then signaled for Wolf and Kern to pull the injured man to his feet. "The Legion wasn't set up so you could party with female legionnaires, Antonelli. You got that?"

Antonelli nodded weakly, and Vanyek hit him again. "I don't think you're hearing me, nube! I don't know how it is in whatever sewer you grew up in, but in the Legion there's no distinctions drawn between men and women. None! That means there'll be female soldiers in your units, here and out in the field. But they weren't put there as playthings for the likes of you." He raised his fist as if to strike again, then seemed to think better of it. The recruit was barely conscious as it was. "Now get this, nube, and get it good. You can screw whoever or whatever you like, whenever you like, on your own time. We've got whorehouses to take care of the troops outside the fort. If some legionnaire is crazy enough to want you, that's fine, too, but you better make sure we're talking consenting partners here. You get me, nube?"

He nodded, gasped out, "Yes, Corporal!"

Vanyek smiled coldly. "Good . . . because you try a stunt like this again, and I'll personally make sure that whatever the woman leaves intact gets carved up anyway."

"Yes, Corporal," Antonelli repeated weakly.

The corporal turned his angry eyes on Lisa. "You, nube. You made it clear that you didn't want anything to do with him before you pulled the knife."

She met his eyes without flinching. "Yes, Corporal. Several times today, and again when he came in here."

He frowned at her. "And you brought that thing in here with you. You always take a knife into the showers, nube?"

Flushing she gave a grim nod. "Yes, Corporal," she repeated. "I do. Since I was seventeen. I have a right to defend myself."

Vanyek was suddenly a blur of motion, his hand snaking out to chop at the wrist of her knife hand as he stepped past her guard. The knife clattered on the wet tile floor as the corporal gave the naked girl a backhanded slap that sent her reeling. "Get this straight, nube," he roared. "You don't have any rights while you're here! None! And you certainly don't have the right to go carving up members of your own unit! How did you get that knife into the barracks in the first place?"

She rubbed the red spot on her face where he had hit her. "It was in my bag. There's a hidden compartment . . ."

"So you just smuggled yourself a weapon onto the base," he finished. He spat for emphasis.

"No one said anything about forbidding weapons, Corporal," she said quietly. "And I never intended to do anything but protect myself . . ."

"Shut up!" he bellowed, raising his hand as if to strike her again. Then he dropped it and went on in lower tones. "We'll go to your quarters and have a look through the rest of your things, just to make sure you haven't brought in any other little surprises."

Vanyek bent down and retrieved the fallen knife. "This weapon is confiscated, and if I catch you with another one I just might decide to use it myself." He tucked it into the top of his boot. "I could have you and Antonelli both on your way out of here, but I'm going to recommend leniency. This time, that is. The Legion doesn't like to waste recruits in barracks knifings. And there are good reasons why we don't like our recruits running around with weapons unless we give them to you. Get the picture?''

She nodded tightly, but didn't answer. Vanyek ignored the silence and went on. ''I'm putting you down for twenty hours extra duty in an unarmed combat class, starting tomorrow. Use what you learn to discourage any other rutting straks you run across, and save the cutlery for the enemy.''

Swallowing, she found her voice at last. ''Yes, Corporal.''

Vanyek fixed Myaighee with a harsh look. ''I don't want any more trouble out of either of these two again, you hear me? Next time your whole lance draws punishment.''

''Yes, Corporal,'' the hannie said, the quills of his neck ruff twitching. Wolf had heard that those spines moved in response to strong emotion.

''Antonelli, you get two hours a night extra duty starting tonight, and until I decide otherwise. You can draw a toothbrush and clean the shithouse after you wrap up your arm. Let's get going!''

Vanyek slammed the door open and led the way back to their barracks room, with Myaighee following. Kern and Wolf got on either side of Antonelli, supporting his stumbling figure. As they left the shower room, Wolf saw Lisa Scott rub her jaw once before turning to pick up her clothes. She trailed behind them, drying herself with a towel, and stood aside as Vanyek went through her locker.

Finally satisfied that she wasn't hiding any other weapons, Vanyek favored them with a last savage glare. ''All right. That's enough excitement for one night. Patch up that strak's arm and send him to my office. The rest of you . . . lights out in ten minutes!''

Myaighee had already broken open a medical kit hanging on the wall near the door, and with Kern's help the alien started bandaging Antonelli's wound. Wolf looked at them for a moment, then headed for his own cubicle. Next door, Lisa Scott started to close the screen, caught his eye, and shrugged.

''Not much point in modesty anymore, is there?'' she said with a sardonic smile. But she closed the screen anyway without waiting for Wolf to reply.

He stretched out on his cot, then picked up the adchip he had been about to study before the trouble began. He frowned at it for a moment, then put it down. After everything that had happened, he doubted he could get into a chip lecture before the call for lights out sounded. Reluctantly, he leaned back, listening to Antonelli cursing while Kern and Myaighee applied the bandage.

Wolf wondered, again, what he had gotten himself into by joining the Fifth Foreign Legion.

It was quiet in the barracks building now, half an hour after the PA order for lights out. Engaged Volunteer Mario Antonelli wiped the sweat from his forehead with his sleeve and winced as the motion set his arm to throbbing again. It was all so damned unfair . . . !

Having the bitch pull a knife on him had been bad enough, but then Corporal Vanyek had beat him until he could hardly move. Now the noncom expected him to spend two hours on his hands and knees cleaning toilets. Vanyek had left little doubt that another beating, worse than before, would follow if the work wasn't done to the corporal's satisfaction.

"This shit is crazy," he muttered aloud. "*Pazzo*. God-damned judge . . ."

Antonelli had never intended to join the military, much less a hard-luck outfit like the Fifth Foreign Legion. But here he was, against his will, with no hope now of escaping.

He had been born in Rome, on Terra, and at the age of fifteen he'd become a full Citizen with all the rights and privileges that went with that simple title. A hundred and fifty nations on Terra and a score or so major world governments extended Commonwealth Citizenship to their entire populace automatically. In theory it meant the right to vote in Commonwealth elections, and the Citizen was supposed to have precedence over Colonials and other non-Citizens in all things, from the chance to own Colonial land to the best seats on shuttles or floatbuses.

In practice, though, most Citizens on Terra didn't give a damn about any of it. The one thing the vast majority of the beeswarm billions of the Mother World's overcrowded cities cared about was the Citizen's dole. With cheap fusion power, artificially intelligent computers, synthetic foods, and the wealth of an interstellar empire to draw on, nobody on Terra had to hold down a job to survive. The dole took care of basic needs. If a Citizen wanted more, there were opportunities he could take advantage of, all the way up to emigration to some frontier world where Citizenship carried real power.

But like so many of his kind, Antonelli had been perfectly willing to accept state-sponsored housing and the minimum dole rather than exerting himself to find some kind of use or meaning to his existence. Instead he'd drifted casually into a life of petty crime and dissipation, mostly out of boredom and because it was the only way to rebel against a cold, impersonal society. He'd run with I Paladini Blanci, the White Knights, a gang of like-minded youths, none of them really violent or dangerous characters, but they acted tough and expected him to do the same.

Then he'd stolen a floatcar and gone on a joyride among the rezplexes outside of Rome on a dare from some of the Knights . . . and the compols arrested him and the judge sentenced him to a term in the service. And not just any service—the Fifth Foreign Legion. His Citizenship was suspended, and only by completing a five-year term of enlistment would he get it back again. Otherwise he'd be sent to one of the Colonial Army penal battalions, and when his term was up there would be no more dole, no more state housing . . . nothing.

He hadn't really thought much about being a Citizen until the judge had taken the title away.

But for a time the idea had seemed exciting, like anything but punishment. A chance to get off Terra, get away from endless mobs of people, find adventure on distant planets . . . he'd leapt at the chance. The Legion had a murky reputation back home as a haven for all the cast-off scum of a hundred worlds, but at the same time there was a romance about the lonely life of the soldiers who guarded distant frontiers that had made him dream of coming home covered in glory.

He had even told his parents that he had volunteered. His mother had cried, but old Sergeant-Major Enrico Antonelli had beamed with pride. The old man was getting on in years, and the artificial heart they'd put in him after the fighting on Horizon was giving him trouble these days, but when he thought the son of his old age was finally going to follow in his footsteps there had been no doubt of his feelings. Antonelli had shipped off Terra feeling good for the first time in a long, long time.

Now he was in the Legion, and the glory had vanished like a mirage in the desert. Why couldn't he fit in here? He'd tried to put up the same tough image that had won him respect with the Knights, but he'd been rebuffed at every turn. The corporals and sergeants were worse than compols, and then the girl . . .

In the crowd he ran with back home, any girl would have understood him. He had been showing his appreciation for a good-looking woman, that was all. Sure, if she'd been interested they could have had some fun, but he hadn't planned to force her or anything. Antonelli didn't need to use force to get a girl. It had all been in fun, the kind of macho horseplay all the Paladini Blanci went in for. He'd intended it to break the ice with the legionnaires, nothing else.

Until the bitch had pulled the knife and slashed his arm. Now he was branded a rapist, and the noncoms would come down twice as hard as before. And he was off on the wrong foot with his lance, with the whole outfit in fact. He would have to work twice as hard to be accepted now.

Antonelli bit his lip and leaned forward to start scrubbing again, favoring the bruises where Vanyek had hit him in the stomach. He couldn't afford to fail with the Legion, not if he wanted to win his Citizenship back. Not if he wanted to see that same look in his father's eye the next time he went home.

He *had* to make it work.

Chapter 12

You have to be tough with recruits. We get very
hard men coming into the Legion, and hard men
expect hard treatment. That's why they join the
Legion.

—A drill instructor
French Foreign Legion, 1984

"Reveille! Reveille! Come on, you nubes, up! Up!"

The numbing shock of a stun baton between his shoulder blades made Wolf scramble out of his cot, groggy and barely able to remember where he was. The attention was entirely impersonal, though. Corporal Vanyek was already moving on to prod Volunteer Scott into wakefulness. Across the common room Wolf saw Antonelli, face and torso mottled with the bruises of the beating in the shower room, leaning against his locker door and fumbling with his clothes.

"Come on, people, what are you waiting for?" Vanyek demanded. "Let's get with it! Assembly on the parade ground in five minutes. Wear your sweats, 'cause that's what you're gonna be doing out there! Mag it! Mag it!"

Wolf groped in his locker for his clothes and dressed, still trying to clear his head. By the time he was done, Kern and Myaighee were helping Antonelli, and the whole lance poured out of the building at the same time. They formed up alongside the rest of the platoon, shivering in the cold predawn wind that blew off the Great Desert. The other platoons of the training company poured out of adjacent buildings.

Sergeant Horst Konrad blew a whistle and trotted into view, looking too fresh, too alert. "What a sorry bunch of nubes!" he shouted. "When reveille sounds you people had better mag it out here on FTL, or I'll know the reason why! Now all of you drop and give me fifty!''

He pushed them through a grueling series of calisthenic exercises, with frequent repetitions when anyone failed to perform to his satisfaction. Wolf kept expecting to see Vanyek or one of the other noncoms wielding their ubiquitous stun batons among the sweating, straining recruits, but they were nowhere to be seen.

Finally it ended and they were back in line, standing stiffly at attention. ''All right, you nubes!'' Konrad said brusquely. ''Chow line forms in ten minutes. Change to fatigues before you eat, and police the barracks! Go!''

Wolf and the rest of the lance trotted back into the barracks, only to find their room a complete shambles. While they had been exercising, someone had dumped the contents of their lockers on the floor and overturned all the cots. Wolf discovered that his uniforms had been thoroughly soaked in the scented antibeard lotion he'd purchased at the base exchange a few days before. Judging from the noise coming from elsewhere in the building, the other lances had found similar scenes waiting for them as well.

''Cristo!'' Antonelli moaned, righting his cot and sitting on it with an air of hopelessness. ''Why the hell did they do this? As if we don't have enough grief already!''

''What's the matter, nube?'' Vanyek's mocking voice came from the doorway. ''You want your mother to come and clean up for you?'' The corporal's cold blue eyes fixed on Wolf, and he gave an exaggerated sniff. ''Fancy perfume. Too good for the common soldiers, I'd say, but just right for a fancy aristo. Smells expensive. Was it expensive, Aristo?'' He didn't wait for an answer. ''There's no servants in the Legion to keep you fine aristocrats from getting your hands dirty. You'd better get this mess cleaned up and get changed in a hurry if you want to have any breakfast!'' He spat eloquently and moved on, leaving the recruits staring at the mess in dismay.

Myaighee broke the spell. ''Kern, you and Antonelli get the cots in order.'' The alien's nose wrinkled. ''Wolf, see if you can find a set of fatigues that isn't too wet. Scott and I will start folding clothes and putting the lockers in order, yes?''

Wolf had to suppress the urge to tell the hannie to mind

its own business. Myaighee was his lance leader, and if Vanyek or Konrad found out he'd disobeyed the alien's orders there might be trouble. And, after all, Myaighee had told him to do exactly what he would have done anyway. . . .

It took nearly twenty minutes to restore order from the chaos and lay out each locker in the exact order prescribed by the Legion. By the time they reached the mess hall, they had only ten minutes left to go through the chow line and get a few bites to eat. The strong smell of antibeard lotion made several other recruits make comments about his taste in perfume, but Wolf wasn't the only one in the company who'd been given the treatment. Volunteer Kochu Burundai, the nomad from Ulan-Tala, had found all of his uniforms laying in a pool of water in the showers. He promptly received the nickname "Soak" and was the butt of at least as many jokes as Wolf.

Then Konrad was blowing his whistle again and shouting orders. Wolf gulped down a bitter cup of Ysan tea and joined the race for the parade ground.

Once outside, the sergeant set them to running, leading them at a brisk pace across the camp and out into the rugged desert beyond. Konrad and the other noncoms didn't seem to find it a strain, but the recruits, already tired and hungry, were hard-pressed to keep up. Corporals with stun batons helped the laggards find a second wind, though. Somehow Wolf forced himself to keep going, though it took every ounce of willpower. He saw Vanyek darting looks in his direction from time to time, but he was determined not to give the corporal the satisfaction of seeing him fail.

Antonelli wasn't so fortunate. After what Wolf estimated was five kilometers the recruit stumbled and fell, and Vanyek's stun baton couldn't get him moving again. The unit kept going. As other stragglers fell by the wayside, a medical van on screeching turbofans skimmed by, stopping to gather in the casualties.

Eventually, the torment was over, and they were back on the parade ground gasping and panting. Wolf's uniform, still smelling faintly of antibeard now thoroughly mixed with sweat, was making him itch, and the long run had almost done him in. But he had made it, seen it through, and that was what was important. Konrad dismissed them with curt orders to shower, change into fresh fatigues, and assemble in ten minutes.

When Wolf stumbled back onto the parade ground, Vanyek gave him a quick cuff and a jolt from his stun baton for being the last man back from the showers. Antonelli and the other stragglers were back in ranks now, looking dejected. Wolf thought he could detect a few fresh bruises on the battered youngster's face.

He wasn't sure what to expect next after the hard pace of the morning workout. Incredibly, what followed was two hours of singing practice under Konrad's stern tutelage.

"You nubes will learn the songs of the Legion," the sergeant told them harshly. "You will practice until you can sing any song, any time, to my satisfaction!"

He started with the words to "Devereaux Lament," a slow, sad ballad of the Fourth Foreign Legion and Hunter's last battle against the Ubrenfar and Semti forces more than a hundred years back. Shouting the words a line at a time, making the recruits repeat them back over and over, Konrad looked like some mad choir master with his crisp fatigues and close-cropped head. Wolf almost laughed, until he saw Lisa Scott chuckle and then gasp as Vanyek used his stun baton on her.

It seemed absurd, but one of the lectures he'd chipped aboard *Kolwezi* had discussed the importance of singing in Legion training. Songs helped transmit the spirit and mystique of the Legion, and singing bound the recruits together on a basic, very human level. Like so many other aspects of the training program, it was one of the old, solid traditions that went back almost to the beginnings of Legion history.

Once he got past the seeming silliness of it all, Wolf had to admit he enjoyed the interlude.

Unfortunately, after two hours it was time to parade for lunch, which meant falling in to ranks again, going through another round of calisthenics, and then trotting off after Konrad, singing "Devereaux Lament," to the mess hall. They had more time for this meal, but there was still precious little chance for relaxation before the training started up again.

That first day set the pace for the next three weeks of Basic. Mornings were spent in physical training, exercising, marching, running, singing. After the noon mess call, the platoon usually shifted to academics in the lecture halls of the admin building, where the recruits went over material from individual training chips and had a chance to do practical, hands-on work that reinforced the chip courses. The period following the evening meal was supposed to be set aside to give them time to study chips or relax, though Wolf soon discovered that this "free time" was frequently taken up by extra duty imposed at the whim of Vanyek, Konrad, or Sergeant Baram, Konrad's deputy.

This standard pattern was by no means a constant, though. Some days the morning march turned into an all-day excursion, and during the second week the whole company covered fifty long desert kilometers on foot, then made camp overnight and returned the next day. It was hard work, far harder than anything Wolf had experienced in the Sky Guard Academy, and as the days passed, he found himself wondering more and more if the noncoms who had doubted his ability to measure up might have known what they were talking about after all.

Still, he kept on trying. During that first overnight march, he managed to stick with the column all day, though there were others who fell behind. Two days later, Wolf was pleasantly surprised to find himself selected to give instruction to the rest of the platoon in saber fighting, and for at least an hour a day he could feel that even Vanyek and Konrad had to respect him a little bit.

Throughout these early weeks, the drills and lectures were only a part of the overall training process, though if it hadn't been for Kern's observations Wolf might never have noticed the deeper significance of the work. The Legion program started with the assumption that every recruit was completely inexperienced not just in military matters but even in many of the accepted norms of education and proper social behavior. At first it seemed a waste of time and effort, but as time went on Wolf could see how the recruits absorbed the lessons that made the Legion a common denominator for all of them. Rich in tradition, the Fifth Foreign Legion was almost a culture apart, as far removed from Antonelli's origins on the streets of Rome as it was from Wolf's aristocratic Besaran heritage. Though Wolf remained cynical about the whole process, he watched men like Burundai latch on to their new "culture" eagerly, and understood how the Legion could breed the fanaticism he had seen in some of the noncoms' eyes.

On a purely military level, it was probably right to approach the training in such a stolid, step-by-painful-step way. Out of his training company of one hundred and twenty recruits, forty-eight admitted to prior military service, but there was a wide gap between Wolf's Sky Guard background and the experience of Engaged Volunteer Hosni Mayzar, a twenty-year veteran of the Commonwealth's crack Centauri Rangers who was leader of Second Platoon's Echo Lance. And the ones with no military background at all had to learn even the simplest of things from the ground up. Those with some soldiering experience were expected to help the others along, whether they were giving formal instruction like Wolf's saber training, or just passing along advice and useful tips as Kern seemed to do for his lancemates almost daily. The "veterans" didn't get a break from the training routine just because they already understood something, though. They were expected to relearn the military trade the Legion way.

Like so much in the Legion, it made sense when viewed dispassionately, but it was damned hard to deal with the Legion's ruthless but often painfully slow approach to turning the recruits into soldiers.

As the end of the first phase of the training program drew near, the recruits in Wolf's lance were beginning to draw together into a solid, close-knit unit. Wolf grudgingly gave much of the credit to Myaighee, the hannie. He—no one in Fort Hunter bothered with the alien term "ky"—didn't seem likely as lance leader, but somehow Myaighee did the job without losing the soft-spoken, diffident manner that was the little being's most noticeable characteristic. Although he came from a background entirely unlike anything the human members of the lance could comprehend, Myaighee seemed to understand the Legion and its ways better than any of them. Perhaps that came with experience. Myaighee had started out as a servant employed by Terrans on Hanuman, his home planet, but during a rising by his people against the human population, he had thrown his lot in with the offworlders and ended up joining a column of legionnaires marching across hostile jungles to the safety of the main Terran enclave. In the course of the campaign the alien had helped the legionnaires on more than one occasion, and when it was all over he had chosen to stay with the unit rather than return to the home he had left behind. Another campaign on Hanuman, and one on the watery world of Polypheme, had followed.

Wolf still had trouble accepting Myaighee as a superior, or even as an equal . . . but surely once they were in the field the natural order of things would assert itself and the nonhuman members of the legion would find the proper place. After all, according to the background chips less than ten percent of the Fifth Foreign Legion was made up of nonhumans.

Mario Antonelli was still the odd man out in the lance, but the young man's brash, cocksure attitude had softened under Legion discipline. Antonelli's background typified everything the Uro aristocracy of Laut Besar objected to in the Commonwealth. Convicted of some minor offense— no one in the lance knew what he'd done, and the Legion tradition of asking no questions about a man's past kept it that way—Antonelli had been sentenced to serve a hitch in the Legion, one of a handful in the training company who hadn't volunteered.

Strangely, it was Myaighee who got along best with the moody youngster. The alien claimed that one of his lancemates from his old outfit had come from a similar sort of background, and encouraged him to devote his free time to wood-carving and other hobbies with surprisingly good results. In training he tried hard and seemed determined to succeed, but he frequently ran afoul of Vanyek and Konrad through carelessness. Wolf found it hard to show much sympathy to a man from such a completely foreign social strata, and Lisa Scott continued to treat Antonelli with disdain. Nor did the Italian seem particularly interested in overcoming their low opinions. Everything he did seemed focused on the bare effort to hang on no matter what the Legion threw at him.

On the other hand, everyone found Tom Kern easy to talk to but hard to know. The big redhead was a quiet man. He never spoke of his past or his reasons for joining the Legion. He spent most of his free time alone. He knew a great deal about the training process and occasionally let slip comments about his past as a drill instructor. Most of the recruits figured him for a deserter who had sought out the anonymity of the Legion to ply the only trade he knew.

Whether the speculation was true or not, Kern was the ideal lancemate. Though he rarely sought out the companionship of others, he was always willing to put aside his own problems and share an hour in spinning a yarn or playing cards, and on the parade ground his consistently cheerful, solid competence was valuable to the entire lance. Academics gave him more than his fair share of problems, but Wolf had started as his tutor early on and they were making good progress. And though Kern in his way was as far removed in background and social standing as Antonelli, Wolf regarded him as something more than just another member of the unit. He was no substitute for the faithful Suartana, whose posting to First Platoon kept him well out of Wolf's orbit, but he was as close as Wolf expected to find in the Legion.

The fifth member of the lance was altogether more of a puzzle. Lisa Scott's background was even more mysterious than Kern's. No one had an inkling of why she had joined the Foreign Legion or where she had come from, but Wolf thought he recognized in her the quality of another aristo. She was not from Laut Besar, of course, but she plainly came from a good bloodline and had enjoyed the same kind of wealth and good education he'd received. But she was a startling contrast to the pampered, protected daughters of the Uro aristocracy he'd known on Laut Besar. Self-assured, independent, and as tough as any of the men in the training company, she should have seemed as alien as Myaighee in Wolf's eyes, but somehow the qualities he would have found repugnant in a woman of his homeworld seemed ideal for Lisa Scott.

He might have sought a closer relationship with her, but the memory of that unwavering knife and her cold blue eyes in the confrontation with Antonelli made Wolf cautious. She remained completely aloof from all the recruits, male, female, and alien alike, a loner who did her job but seemed unable or unwilling to lower her barriers and let anyone else get close.

He could sympathize with the feeling. The more he saw of these people who had chosen the Legion life the more Wolf wondered at his own choice. Sometimes he felt like more of an alien than Myaighee. It was a feeling he wasn't sure he liked . . . but the alternative, becoming a part of all this, scared him even more.

"All right, next up! Antonelli! Let's go! Let's go! We could spend your whole strakking enlistment waiting for you to get moving! Go!"

Wolf suppressed a smile as Antonelli stumbled on his way to the weapons rack at the front of the Barracks 18 exercise room. For all of his tough talk, the youngster couldn't manage to keep his cool in the face of one of Sergeant Konrad's badgering tirades. The sergeant came from Lebensraum, where most of the Besaran Uros had originated, and his uncompromising drive for perfection never failed to remind Wolf of his own grandfather. Konrad was no aristocrat, but he would have been right at home supervising an onnesium mine or running an industrial complex on Laut Besar .. at least, on Laut Besar before the Ubrenfars came.

Antonelli selected a saber and stepped onto the strip facing Wolf. Saluting the Italian with his blade, Wolf dropped into the guard position.

"I want you to try the disengage I showed you earlier," he said. "Remember that the idea behind the disengage attack is to mislead your enemy, to make him parry a false blow and leave himself open to your real strike. Do you understand?"

The youngster nodded a little uncertainly and dropped into guard stance without a blade salute. Wolf frowned, then dismissed the slip. Antonelli had enough trouble with the practical end of saber fighting without further confusing him by insisting on precise adherence to the proper forms. Later Wolf would have to go over the etiquette of dueling.

For just an instant Wolf looked over his blade at Neubeck, not Antonelli, and knew a moment's revulsion. The feel of the sword in his hand kept bringing back bitter memories of that day on Robespierre. He fought back the feeling and nodded. "Begin."

Antonelli beat his blade once, a brief tap lacking authority. His second beat, on the same side of the blade, was a little firmer, and Wolf nodded in encouragement. The younger recruit screwed up his face in concentration and struck Wolf's blade a third time, then twisted his wrist to the left to make the disengage attack. Wolf parried the blow and stepped back, lowering his saber.

"All right," he said with another nod. "Now that one wasn't too bad, but you need to work on your technique. You've been chipping too many swashbucklers, kid, and you've got a tendency to make your attacks a little too wild. Keep your attacks precise and controlled. That's the way to win the point."

The younger recruit nodded, but Wolf wasn't sure how much he actually understood. Before he had a chance to go on, though, he was interrupted by Sergeant Konrad. "Right! Platoon . . . muster on the parade ground for calisthenics! Move! Move! Move!"

The order caught Wolf by surprise. He had thought they'd have another half hour or so of fencing. But Konrad was nothing if not unpredictable, and he shrugged and headed for the weapons rack to put his saber away.

Konrad intercepted him as the rest of the recruits filed out of the exercise room at a trot. "You, nube," he said, his voice harsh. "You are a good fencer."

The sergeant rarely paid a compliment without balancing it with something scathing, and Wolf halted in midmotion at the words. "Thank you, sergeant," he said tentatively.

"A good fencer . . . but the Legion doesn't want good fencers." Konrad picked up a saber and hefted it in his hand. "We are not training recruits to fight saber in the Commonwealth Games, nube. Or to fight in duels between aristos, either. Do you know why we train our legionnaires to fight with blades, nube?"

"Uh . . . I *thought* I did, Sergeant," Wolf replied. "It speeds the reflexes, sharpens perception . . ."

"Nein! Nein!" Once again Wolf was reminded of his grandfather as Konrad lapsed into the German of Wolfgang Hauser's youth. "We fight with swords because some day we may have to use them in battle, nube! Many times our garrisons are on primitive planets where the sword is a major weapon. The Wynsarrysa outlaws right here on Devereaux use blades, for instance, when they can't take anything better from settlers. So we learn enough that a legionnaire can fight with whatever weapons come to hand. *That* is why we learn saber . . . and knife fighting, and

hand-to-hand combat, and all the rest. Do you understand that?''

"Yes, Sergeant," Wolf replied slowly. He still wasn't sure why Konrad had decided to point all this out to him, but he was learning from experience to be careful in dealing with the man.

"When you train my men," Konrad went on, "I want you to stop worrying so much about proper forms and good technique. I want my legionnaires to know how to defend themselves with a blade, not how to score points in a match. Understand me?''

"Yes, Sergeant," Wolf repeated.

"Good. Keep one thing in mind, nube, and we'll get along just fine. In the Legion, we fight to win. Not for any other reason. We fight to win.''

Konrad turned away abruptly. "Now move it, nube, or I'll have you on report!''

Chapter 13

There are many, too many, who join the Legion with no sort of qualification for a soldier's life, and these men do no good to themselves or to France by enlisting.

—A Legion recruiting officer
French Foreign Legion, 1889

"Look sharp! Look sharp! It could come at us from anywhere!"

Wolf hunkered lower behind the protective bulk of a rock outcropping and blanked his mind to access the interface chip that controlled his combat helmet. The tiny computer could translate thought into orders that could govern a variety of helmet functions, from communications to vision settings to tactical data displays, though it was far less complex than a conventional adchip or computer implant. An ordinary soldier not only didn't need full-scale computer access, but in fact would be handicapped by having too much information available at times when survival depended on combat instincts rather than sophisticated data retrieval. But the combat helmet was a versatile tool he was finally beginning to master.

He called up a sensor map on the inside of the helmet's faceplate. Superimposed on the computer-generated topographic chart, five green triangles showed how he and his four lancemates were spread out over the barren ground in a loose skirmish line. He took careful note of their positions to avoid any chance of mistaking one of them for the hostiles who would be trying to penetrate the defensive zone sometime in the next few minutes.

"Look sharp, people," Kern repeated, voice gruff. Despite his experience, he sounded as much on edge as any of them.

Wolf switched off the map and raised his faceplate to get an eyeball view of his surroundings. The Legion combat helmet was an amazingly versatile piece of equipment, fitted with a computer-coordinated sensor system that could generate a wide range of different displays, including maps, optical sighting, passive and active infrared, light-intensification, and electronic magnification and image enhancement, but none of them was a completely satisfactory replacement for the human eye and brain. He still trusted his own senses best.

Motion to his left attracted Wolf's attention, but it was Lisa Scott running a zigzag course to reach a gully that would give her a better view of the battlefield. The lance was fitted out as a heavy weapons unit, and she was acting as a spotter.

He shifted the bulky tube of the Fafnir missile launcher in his hands. It was a versatile weapon that packed a powerful punch, its programmable targeting system equally effective at seeking out and destroying any specific target type, ground or air. But he didn't care much for the job of Fafnir gunner. The notion of having only five warheads and a pistol to fall back on when his ammo was used up made him appreciate the standard-issue FE-FEK battle rifle with its hundred-round magazine of mylar-coated plastic needles and the 1cm autogrenade launcher. *That* was a weapon that could keep a soldier in a firefight. . . .

But for now he had the Fafnir, and the tacdata briefing had reported the likely opposition would be small, fast-moving Ubrenfar attack pods which wouldn't be vulnerable to ordinary small arms fire. That put most of the burden on Wolf and Antonelli, who was carrying the unit's onager plasma gun.

"Motion! Motion bearing three-two-three degrees!" Kern called out.

"Gunner ready!" Myaighee chimed in.

Wolf swung to face the indicated stretch of terrain. It was dominated by a series of low, undulating ridges that could mask the approach of an enemy.

The on-board fire-and-forget tracking system on the Fafnir could be programmed to discriminate an Ubrenfar attack pod—or almost any other type of vehicle, aircraft, or installation the Legion expected to come up against—and attack it at long range, unhampered by considerations of intervening terrain or line-of sight. Wolf opened his mouth to request a "weapons free" order from Myaighee, then bit back the question. Over and over again during weapons training he'd been given stun-lashings by Vanyek and other instructors for trying to tell the lance leader how to do his job. That was a mistake he wouldn't dare to make again.

Anyway, it might not *be* an attack pod. Without visual confirmation he might just be throwing away a missile to no purpose. Better to play it safe . . .

At that moment, as if to taunt him over his decision, the attack pod darted into view from behind the cover of the ridge at lightning speed. The flattened sphere paused, suspended on magrep fields as its turret sensors swiveled in search of a target. Wolf gritted his teeth and fought the urge to open fire with his Fafnir. Doctrine required him to give the onager gunner first crack at a target. The Fafnir's limited ammo supply could be a drawback in a firefight. But the *fusil d'onage* Antonelli was carrying, on the other hand, was good for twenty high-powered shots and could be recharged from any fusion power source. When the target was in plain line of sight, the onager had priority.

But the onager wasn't firing, and the attack pod was starting to move once again.

"Fire, damn it!" The angry voice was loud in Wolf's ear. "Fire the goddamned onager! Fire *something*, for Tophet's sake!"

The Ubrenfar vehicle was gathering speed, closing on his position. Wolf's fingers danced over the Fafnir's programing keys, feeding in the target type information the fire-and-forget missile needed to lock on and attack.

Suddenly a bolt of raw energy surged across the open field as Antonelli opened fire at last. A clump of scrub a good fifty meters to the left of the target vanished in the searing fury of the onager bolt. The attack pod shot off at an angle on powerful fusion airjets, disappearing behind another low ridge line. Wolf squeezed the trigger on the Fafnir, watching the missile streak skyward and then arc down.

There was a flash before the warhead was even below the masking terrain. A moment later the attack pod was in sight again, its weapons trained precisely on Wolf's fox-hole.

Then the image flickered and faded out as the holographic projector creating the illusion cut out.

"You're dead, Stinky!" Vanyek shouted from behind him. "No more perfume for you, ever, and all thanks to Lover-boy!"

"Ah, shit, man," Antonelli said, clambering out of his own foxhole and pulling off the heavy-duty combat helmet that covered his face. "If he'd started shooting before the machine broke cover that *bastardo* never would've come close."

Wolf didn't respond. For three days now Vanyek's section had been training with support weapons, with each lance in turn acting the part of a heavy weapons unit on the firing range. The standard doctrine for engagements like this one had been drummed into them over and over, but Antonelli seemed unable or unwilling to comprehend the role each weapon was supposed to play in combat.

"Get your sorry asses down here," Vanyek snapped. "Now!"

Wolf checked the Fafnir's safety and trotted back from the firing line to the trench where Vanyek and the other recruits waited. It took longer for Antonelli to cross the distance, hampered as he was by the bulky onager and the full body armor required to protect him from the weapon's deadly, scorching backblast. As the Italian appeared at the lip of the trench and started to climb down, Vanyek swore and darted toward him.

"Christ Almighty!" the corporal said. His hand reached up to yank the power cord connecting the weapon to Antonelli's ConRig harness assembly. A red light on top of the onager went out. "You strakking idiot, you didn't safe your weapon! You could've fried everybody, damn it!"

Antonelli blanched and stammered his response. "I-I'm s-s-sorry . . ."

"Sorry doesn't cut it, you stupid bastard!" Vanyek shouted, thrusting his face a few centimeters from the Italian's. "Never, ever leave the firing line without safing your weapon, for God's sake! Now get out of that armor. You're done for the day."

As Kern and Scott moved forward to help Antonelli start to unstrap his armor, Vanyek turned away to address the section as a whole. "All right! Critique! What did these two straks do wrong out there? Myaighee!"

The hannie shot an apologetic glance at Antonelli before he replied. "Volunteer Antonelli should, by doctrine, have engaged the target as soon as it was in plain sight. The Fafnir must be preserved as a weapon of last recourse, except as specified otherwise by higher authority."

"True enough," Vanyek said. "Mayzar?"

The leader of Echo lance answered briskly. "When he did fire the onager, Antonelli overcompensated on the aim. The onager is more responsive than it looks, because the ConRig slaves the tracking system to the operator's eye movements." He sounded like he was reciting from the instruction chip. "As a result, his shot was too wide to do any good, and there was no opportunity for a second attempt."

Vanyek gave him a curt nod. Mayzar had spent more than his share of time trying to get the hang of the tricky ConRig system. Although he was one of the most experienced soldiers in the recruit company, his time with the Centauri Rangers had stressed other skills than heavy weaponry, and he was sadly out of practice. It was no wonder he could quote the chip instructions verbatim. He'd gone over them often enough.

"Who else noticed mistakes?"

None of the other recruits answered. After a long pause, the corporal turned to face Wolf. "All right, here's a few. Wolf waited to program his target type until he had visual verification of the pod even though he knew that was what we were going to be up against . . ."

"But—" Wolf bit off the rest of his protest too late. He grunted as Vanyek slapped his arm with the stun baton.

"It takes no longer to reprogram a Fafnir than it does to program from scratch," Vanyek went on as if nothing had happened. "If your intel briefings say you're up against a specific weapons system you should be ready to handle it. Just make sure you're also ready to handle surprises quickly as they arise. Preprogramming the Fafnir might have given you the edge to hit the bastard while he was still scurrying for cover."

He let the point sink in for a moment before jabbing his baton at Kern. "And you, nube. Where were you in all this?"

The redhead looked glum. "I should have laid down sustained fire as soon as the pod came into view, Corporal," he said. The big ex-Marine looked down at the MEK he still cradled in his hands. It was a larger, heavier version of the FEK with a bigger magazine and larger-caliber ammo, useful for antipersonnel and general suppression fire.

"That's right," Vanyek said with a sarcastic edge to his voice. "Your fire might have caused the bad guys to hesitate even if you couldn't penetrate their armor. The mix of weapons in your lance is designed to be mutually supporting, and you weren't pulling your share. Why not?"

Kern looked embarrassed. "I guess I knew that the simulation wouldn't be diverted that way, Corporal," he admitted slowly. "So I didn't want to waste the ammo."

Vanyek looked at him with an expression that mingled disappointment and distaste for a long moment. "We'll give you some time to think about that doing a few laps around the range in place of lunch," he said at last. He raised his voice. "I expect you all to treat every exercise exactly like the real thing. You understand me?"

The corporal glared at the recruits. "Next point. Myaighee, you're the lance leader. Why weren't you taking charge?"

The hannie looked back at Vanyek, neck ruff stiffening. "I understood this to be an exercise for the gunners, Corporal," he said slowly.

"The lance is a unit, damn it!" Vanyek shot back. "You should know that by now! In the field it would have been your job to encourage your gunners . . . and to give the order releasing the Fafnir sooner. You said it yourself: higher authority is supposed to decide when to override doctrine. Your job! Nobody fired until I said something, and they don't issue instructors in your battlefield supplies!"

There were some chuckles from the rest of the section. Wolf started to smile, not so much at the corporal's joke as at the satisfaction of seeing Myaighee taken down a peg or two. Because of the hannie's past Legion experience the little alien had always come across as a cut above the rest of the recruits. And although Wolf had come to admire his skill in handling the disparate characters in the lance, he still found it hard to accept a nonhuman as a superior. Now that the hannie had made a mistake, maybe attitudes would be changing. . . .

"And you can wipe that grin off your face, Stinky," Vanyek said sharply, jerking Wolf out of his reverie with a quick brush of his stun baton. "Just because you didn't have orders is no reason to sit still and do nothing!"

He replied without thinking. "But doctrine . . ."

Vanyek jabbed him in the stomach with the stun baton, and he doubled over in pain as the muscles of his stomach and diaphragm went into spasm. "Doctrine is no excuse for stupidity, nube," the corporal told him. He stepped back, raising his voice for the benefit of the others. "When are you straks gonna get it through your heads that this is combat training? Kill or be killed, that's the name of the game. Out on the battlefield you have to think for yourself. If you stick to one set of rules and freeze up when you can't find some tenet of doctrine to cover your ass you're gonna end up dead . . . maybe take a bunch of your buddies out with you, too. So you use doctrine, but you use your own initiative, too. If you see that something's not going the way it's supposed to—and that pretty much describes any battle you'll ever be in—then you have to adapt. Act. Don't just sit still and wait to get killed."

Lisa Scott raised a diffident hand. "Corporal?"

"What is it, Scott?" Vanyek's voice was almost gentle, now. She was the only one of the five who hadn't drawn his ire.

"If we're supposed to think for ourselves, why drum the by-the-book doctrine into us?"

The corporal gave a thin-lipped smile. "Because the rest of the army, not having the benefit of seeing screwups like you, still believes in a perfect world," he said quietly. "It's true that under textbook conditions it would be best to take out an attack pod with an onager and save the Fafnirs for better targets. And we'd rather see you try it that way because Fafnir warheads are expensive and we don't want to waste them . . . nor do we want to use up all our shots the first time the bad guys show up, and end up with nothing but rocks to throw at them later on. So we teach you to give the onagers a chance at the easy targets first."

Vanyek's voice became harder. "But at the same time you've got to learn to really put yourself into a fight. It won't be a practice exercise when you're out in the field. Mistakes will kill people. So you've got to learn to judge when to play it by the book, and when to throw the book aside and make it up as you go along.''

Wolf was still feeling the effects of the stun baton, but the corporal's words struck a familiar chord. He remembered the battle in the corridors on Telok, the moment when he'd panicked. Maybe if he had shown more initiative then, instead of giving in to appearances, things might have gone differently. Not just the battle, but everything that had followed. The quarrel with Neubeck . . . the duel . . . his flight from Robespierre . . .

The pain of that battle was still like a raw nerve, but he forced himself to think about it. His lack of sound judgment in that fight had convinced him. He would never be a leader of men.

Now he was beginning to realize that it could keep him from being a soldier as well. . . .

Mario Antonelli listened to the corporal's systematic critique of the lance with a sinking feeling of failure and despair. *Nothing* he did ever seemed to come out right. Somehow he'd avoided washing out of training so far, but he was making no more than a barely passing mark. Sooner or later he wouldn't even manage that, and then it would all be over.

Why couldn't he deal with the training better? Why couldn't he fit in here?

All the talk about the legionnaires being a family, helping out each other, that had been a big lie. No one had offered *him* any help. If you weren't a perfect little rembot who snapped to on command, you were beat up, and nobody lifted a finger to save you. They all said they cared. "The Legion takes care of its own" was how they kept putting it, but it wasn't so. He was an outcast, would always remain an outcast among these people who always demanded more than he was able to give.

Sometimes he thought it would be better to just give up, leave the Legion and serve out his sentence with a penal battalion. At least then he wouldn't have to face the constant pressure, the continual bullying from the instructors and the unspoken amusement of his lancemates.

But if he didn't make it with the Legion, he'd lose that look of pride he'd finally kindled in his father's eyes. The old man probably wouldn't survive the shock if he found out his son had been consigned to a penal battalion.

The sharp pain of a stun baton across his shoulder blades made him jump. "You want to get with the program, nube?" Vanyek bellowed into his face. "Or am I boring you?"

"N-no, Corporal!" he said, snapping to attention.

The NCO struck him again, but the shock setting was lower and just made his shoulder and neck tingle. "What you did out there was bad enough," he growled. "But ignoring the range safety regs is a screw-up you don't make twice in *my* unit. You get me, nube?"

"Y-yes, Corporal." The reply was anything but crisp.

Vanyek hefted the baton in one hand as if contemplating the best place to apply it, then lowered the wand and turned away from the Italian.

"All right, that's enough for this morning," Vanyek said at last. "We'll try another drill this afternoon. Get your gear, fall out, and head for the mess hall."

The recruits looked surprised. By rights he should have kept them on the firing line for at least another quarter hour, and after what had happened none of them would have been shocked if he'd kept them longer . . .

As Antonelli started to bend over to round up his equipment Vanyek stopped him with the baton, its power turned all the way off this time. "Not you, Antonelli. You stay here. We still have some things to talk about." He turned away again. "And you, Kern, you start your laps. I'll let you know when to stop!"

The redhead nodded and moved off at a trot, leaving the others to round up his MEK and combat helmet. When everyone was gone Vanyek spoke again, his tone quiet and almost sympathetic.

"Listen to me, Antonelli," he said slowly. "And listen good. I know the training is tough, and I also know that you've been trying as hard as anyone. But you're still making mistakes—stupid mistakes—that you should have stopped making the first week of training. Normally I'd work you over for a while with this." He hefted the stun baton for emphasis. "You'd have a few aches and pains to remind you to do better, and we'd move on. But I've done that enough to know that it isn't gonna help this time. The question is, what *will* get you motivated?"

Antonelli didn't answer, didn't know how to answer.

The corporal looked at him for a long time in silence, then shook his head. "I just don't know. I really expected you to snap in and start showing some skill, kid. Your kind usually do well in the Legion. But it's clear you're heading straight for an unsatisfactory mark on your training record. That means you struggle on for days or weeks longer, with noncoms using you for a punching bag and poking these glorified joy buzzers at you until you do something really dumb and get sent to the penal battalions . . . or you might not do anything spectacular and still wind up doing hard labor because your performance just isn't up to specs. Maybe you ought to just drop it now and save yourself the grief."

"No!" Antonelli said, pulling back. "No! I can cut it . . . I *have* to!"

"It's not that big a deal, kid. Penal battalions are no picnic, but it's not really as tough as the Legion in some ways. You won't get your Citizenship back, but . . ."

Antonelli shook his head violently. "Let me keep trying, man! Please!" He hesitated. "*I miel genitore* . . . my parents, my whole family . . . they don't know I was sentenced. They think I volunteered. And they were proud of me. . . ."

"That won't help you much if you pull an unsat rating, kid," he said gently.

"It will kill *mio babbo*, my father, if I don't make it," Antonelli went on as if he hadn't heard. "It'll kill him. I've gotta keep trying. . . ."

"I can't force you to put in for the penal battalions, kid," Vanyek said reluctantly. "If you won't go voluntarily, you'll have to earn yourself a trip there. Which is what you'll do if you don't buckle down and show some improvement pretty damned quick. What'll your parents think if you keep screwing up the way you did today, huh, kid?"

The recruit didn't answer.

"All right," Vanyek told him. "You've had your warning. Just remember that you're about a centimeter shy of an unsat already, so you'd better get your act together. You'll pull two hours a night extra duty on the indoor weapons range for the rest of this training phase. By the time you're through I expect you to take that onager and use it to light a narcostick a klick away without hitting the guy who's smoking it. Think you can handle that, nube?''

"Y-yes, Corporal," Antonelli responded, pulling himself to attention. There was a long pause. "And . . . *grazie*. Thanks."

"Don't thank me, nube," Vanyek told him. "Not until you pass. Now . . . what shall we have you do to learn about range safety? Maybe what you need is some exercise with your buddy Red, hmm?"

Antonelli followed his gesture and saw Kern rounding the far end of the practice range. He suppressed a groan and started to run, but inwardly he was elated. He had a second chance . . . and he would work twice as hard this time to make it work.

Chapter 14

As for myself, my tongue was down at least to my feet, but I kept going, knowing what awaited stragglers.

—Legionnaire Eugene Amiable
Mexican Campaign
French Foreign Legion, 1863–1867

"Engaged Volunteer Wolf. Four weeks' service. Delta Lance, Second Platoon, Training Company Odintsev. At your orders, Sergeant!"

As he went through the ritual recitation of name and unit, Wolf drew himself up to rigid attention beside the door to his cubicle. In thirty-four days the recruits had become accustomed to the routine. Twice each day, just before breakfast and before evening lights out, the NCOs held an inspection of the recruit quarters. A noncom in a bad mood could find plenty of things wrong during inspection. Even if the lockers and bunks were flawless, like as not Corporal Vanyek would tip a recruit's belongings on the floor and then punish the luckless trainee and the rest of the lance as well. One night Vanyek had rescheduled evening roll call four times before finally letting them turn in at 2600 hours.

This morning, though, Gunnery Sergeant Ortega was conducting the inspection in person. Wolf hoped the senior NCO would be satisfied with what he saw.

Ortega prodded the contents of Wolf's locker with his stun baton and gave a reluctant nod. "Better, nube. Better," he said grudgingly. He started to turn away, then looked back at Wolf. "But I can still smell your perfume. Ten push-ups, nube."

Ten push-ups, after the calisthenics program the Legion

had put him through, was little enough. Wolf dropped to the floor . . .

And Corporal Vanyek stepped nimbly onto his back. "Begin, nube," he ordered harshly.

Wolf strained to lift the extra weight. Somehow, he got through the exercise as Ortega moved to the next cubicle. He was surprised when Vanyek held out a hand to help him up.

It was somehow typical of the training regimen, he thought as he snapped back to attention. Just when it seemed as if the instructors had finally gone too far, pushing a recruit beyond the limits of endurance, some little gesture like this one put everything back into perspective.

The company had spent a full two weeks at drills like the one with the simulated Ubrenfar pod, learning how to handle all sorts of special Legion-issue equipment. By the time it was all done with, Wolf knew how to handle a Fafnir or an onager, an MEK or a laser sniper's rifle, all in addition to the basic FEK. The recruits had learned all the useful functions of their combat helmets and had discovered the effectiveness of the climate-controlled, chameleon-weave battledress fatigues in constant practice maneuvers. They had even been exposed to some of the more exotic gear in the Legion arsenal, like the Galahad antipersonnel mine and the complex C^3 communications backpacks. The program finished up with exposure to the APCs and AFVs that made up the Legion's mechanized arm. Some of what they learned was intended only as an introduction, since many of the more advanced systems were properly the realm of Legion specialists who had completed their first five-year hitch and gone on to advanced training, but the recruits learned enough to get by with virtually anything they might encounter in the field. Between chip instruction and practical experience the recruits developed their skills quickly, though their progress was far from uniform. Wolf found his efforts drawing grudging approval from Vanyek and the other NCOs by the time it was over, but it was Kern, and more surprisingly Lisa Scott, who earned most of the praise in the lance. Kern was a natural with virtually all heavy weapons, especially the onager, while the blond woman showed a genuine flair for handling mag-rep armored vehicles.

Antonelli, on the other hand, continued to struggle. Although Kern, at Corporal Vanyek's direct order, devoted an hour of free time each night to extra tutoring, the Italian's performance was still barely up to the minimum he needed to stay in Basic. That put him under even more pressure than the rest of the recruits. Wolf could wash out of the training, even choose to resign voluntarily, and would be no worse off than when he'd started. But if Antonelli failed, he would end up sweating out his five years in a penal battalion with no hope of seeing his Citizenship restored. Even after his sentence was finished he'd still be paying the penalty for his petty crime, cut off from the easy life of the dole and without any worthwhile skills to help him make a fresh start.

His case drew sympathy from the other recruits, and even some of the instructors seemed concerned for him, but all the goodwill in the world couldn't make up for the simple fact that Antonelli wasn't cut out for the soldier's life. Five weeks of training had already seen twenty recruits dropped from the company, and it was clear to everyone that Antonelli wasn't far from joining them.

More and more, Wolf was beginning to feel a certain kinship for the youngster. Though he was doing far better than Antonelli in training, deep down Wolf was still an outsider. The rituals that bound the Legion together didn't reach him the way they did many of the others, and he was still conscious of the gulf that separated him culturally, socially, and intellectually from the rank and file around him. Sometimes the only thing that kept him going was pride. He was still determined to prove the doubters wrong and see the thing through, despite everything. But the knowledge that he didn't face the dilemma that hovered over Antonelli tempted him sometimes.

Now they were finished with weapons and equipment orientation. Tomorrow the recruits would move on to a new phase of their training. For the past five weeks Basic had concentrated on teaching the essentials of soldiering, and as Captain Odintsev had pointed out during one of his infrequent appearances at morning assembly a few days earlier, the recruits were now at a point that would have qualified them for active service in any of the armies of Terra before the days of starflight. But they were only a third of the way through the Legion's course, and what remained was a far more difficult curriculum than what had gone before.

He was roused from his reverie by Gunnery Sergeant Ortega. "You straks might be worth keeping after all," he growled. "At least until we get some real legionnaires in here. Right, then, listen up! Tomorrow you begin the next phase of training, the first of a series of two-week tours for intensive specialized training in multienviron operations. Your first assignment is to the Archipel d'Aurore for practice in jungle and amphibious warfare ops and advanced recon."

The soldier of the Commonwealth was expected to serve on a variety of different worlds, each as complex and diverse as Laut Besar or Old Terra. There was no way to prepare the recruits for every possibility, but according to the training chips this phase of Basic was designed to get them accustomed to as many different environments and situations as possible. As Kern had put it in a late-night bull session, the purpose of the multiple-environ portion of the program wasn't so much to prepare them to serve in the specific conditions they would be exposed to, but rather to make the would-be soldiers aware of the range and diversity of their possible duty stations . . . and to drive home the simple but often overlooked fact that every new environment possessed its own unique properties, its own tactical realities. And its own individual dangers.

"For the rest of the day you'll be getting ready to move out," Ortega continued with the faint smile the recruits had come to associate with trouble on the horizon. "But I don't want any of you to get the idea that you'll be short of work to do. Corporal . . . ?"

Vanyek consulted his compboard. "Delta Lance . . . you'll be getting a workout down at the shuttle bay, loading platoon equipment onto the transport."

"In addition, you will be responsible for packing up your own kits and policing the barracks here," Ortega went on smoothly. "And each of you will be expected to draw the background chip on Fort Marchand to get acquainted with your new duty station before you leave the base tomorrow morning. Any questions?"

There were none. Ortega smiled again and checked his wristpiece. "Ah, yes. I almost forgot. Antonelli!"

"Yes, Sergeant!"

"Starting tonight, you will spend one hour of each free period working on a special project."

"Yes, Sergeant!" Antonelli was learning that it was best to stick to the safe response, though he still forgot and talked back sometimes in the heat of drills or practice sessions. Wolf wondered, though, how the young Italian would handle yet another extra assignment. He was already spending most of his free time trying to keep up with his studies, and it was a rare week that didn't see him pulling nighttime punishment details as well.

The sergeant smiled coldly. "Good attitude, nube," he commented. Shifting his glance to take in the others, he went on. "Christmas comes in just under five weeks. One of our regular ways of observing the holiday is to hold competitions in the construction of cribs, Nativity scenes. Since you've shown special aptitude working with your hands, Antonelli, I thought you'd be a good candidate for your platoon's team. Volunteer Mayzar is in charge of the proceedings. Report to him in the repbay tonight. The work will continue when you get settled into your new duty station, and up until the Christmas training break. Understood?"

"Yes, Sergeant!" Antonelli's expression didn't reveal if he was happy or unhappy with this added duty. Nor did anyone seem to find it odd that Volunteer Hosni Mayzar, a native of Mecca Gideed where over ninety percent of the population was made up of Moslem extremists, was in charge of preparing a Christian Nativity scene. Just as everyone attended Sunday services with a Catholic chaplain, so the entire unit was expected to follow the Legion line when it came to holidays and observances.

"If any of the rest of you can carry a tune, Corporal Vanyek will be in charge of the holiday music program," Ortega went on. "You're expected to teach the other singers at least one carol from your native culture . . . if, of course, your culture observes Christmas." His eye rested on Myaighee, and it looked like he was trying to hide the ghost of a smile. Maybe even fanatics like Ortega realized the irony of some of their actions, at that.

"All right, that's enough small talk. Fall in on the parade ground for the march to the mess hall. Mag it!"

Wolf thought he heard Kern humming some old Irish carol as they headed out the door.

Perhaps, he thought with a twinge of uncertainty, perhaps the Legion knew more than he did about involving recruits in the life of the unit.

The preparations that day took as much time and effort as a long training session, but eventually the work was done and Wolf and the others could tumble into their bunks for some much-needed rest. Reveille came an hour early the next morning, and all four platoons of the training company traveled by maglev tube to the shuttle port.

At Sergeant Konrad's order Second Platoon filed aboard the TH-19 Pegasus hypersonic transport at Docking Bay Eight. Wolf already knew the sleek craft's lines all too well from the loading duty the previous day. The Pegasus was an old shuttle design, no longer used much in front-line duty except by the Legion. It could reach any point on a Terrestrial-type planet in less than an hour, and performed ground-to-orbit service as well, but the design definitely emphasized rugged efficiency over comfort. Wolf stowed his field pack under the bench seat between Kern and Lisa Scott, then strapped in, but it was a long time before the shuttle received clearance to take off.

He spent the time reviewing the background on their new base, knowing they'd probably be quizzed by some of the NCOs before the trip was over. The Archipel d'Aurore was a scattering of large islands to the east of the primary continent which stretched in a loose arc right across the planet's broad equatorial zone. Instead of the dry barrens around Fort Hunter, the recruits would now be coping with the tropical heat and humidity of a region popularly referred to by older legionnaires as the Devil's Cauldron.

Although most of the islands were covered by dense jungle, they were far from uninhabited. The Archipel d'Aurore was the source of one of Devereaux's most important exports, the sap of the *arbebaril,* and plantations raising the stubby, multitrunked trees dotted the island chain. The Legion outpost where Second Platoon would receive its jungle warfare training had been founded on the largest of the islands—actually more of a small continent—to protect the plantations. Its role in the training process was only secondary. For the first time the recruits would be facing actual field conditions.

That might mean a certain amount of danger. Although

the region around Fort Hunter was thoroughly settled, civilized, the same couldn't be said of the eastern island chain. Like most of the backwater areas of the planet, the Archipel d'Aurore was home to large numbers of Wynsarrysa, and many of them were hostile to the human colonists on Devereaux.

The Wynsarrysa were the original inhabitants of the world, not native to the planet but descendants of a Gwyrran colony planted there nearly a thousand years before the first visit by Terrans. The Gwyrrans had been a key client race in the old Semti Conclave, which had exercised rigorous control over its subjects in everything from interstellar movement to technology to social organization until they were finally overcome by vigorous, unpredictable humans.

Devereaux had been a major point of contention in the Semti War. The Gwyrrans—massive, ponderous, slow-thinking, but with a reputation as warriors that nearly matched the Ubrenfars—had proven unable to make their settlement flourish, and the colonists had lapsed into a state of barbarism which the calculating Semti had found entirely to their liking. When Terran explorers had first arrived, they found the locals to be few in number and too primitive to be a significant factor in planetary development, and promptly planted a human colony on the primary continent.

The new Devereaux colony had suffered during the war. The Semti, with their Gwyrran combat auxiliaries, reoccupied the planet and set out to put an end to human resistance. The struggle had seen the end of the Fourth Foreign Legion, which had been assigned to protect the world. Commandant Hunter's band of guerrillas were the last to resist, but in the end they'd fallen almost to a man . . . but they had won the Commonwealth valuable time to organize a counterthrust that ultimately destroyed the artificial world that had formed the heart and soul of the Conclave.

The Wynsarrysa had flourished again for the brief months of the Semti occupation, only to be disarmed and dispossessed by the new waves of human colonists who arrived after the fighting was over. Most had been absorbed into society, but there were a stubborn few who refused to bow to the new masters. They continued an uneven guerrilla struggle, raiding settlements and living a marginal, outlaw existence. And the Fifth Foreign Legion remained on Devereaux to keep them in check, guarding the inhabited regions of the planet from outposts like Fort Marchand.

That meant that the recruits would be training in an area that could erupt into violence at any time. The dense jungles of the archipelago region were especially favorable to the rebels, who could use the cover to dodge orbital and aerial drone reconnaissance efforts. That meant that even though the Wynsarrysa were no match for legionnaires in a stand-up fight, anyone who strayed too far from the fort or straggled during a march would be fair game for guerrillas. The orientation chip had made that point abundantly clear.

As he'd expected, the assistant platoon leader, Sergeant Baram, spent most of the time they were in the air barking out names and questions about Fort Marchand, the Archipel d'Aurore, and the conditions they could expect to encounter in the region. The trip took less than half an hour, but it seemed three times as long in the face of Baram's relentless interrogation. Fortunately, the one question that came Wolf's way, regarding Chief-Sergeant Guy Marchand's role in the last stand on Deveraux, was one he could answer. Antonelli was less fortunate, and earned himself another five hours of extra duty for failing to remember the percentage of the planetary export revenue attributable to *arbebaril* sap.

At last they grounded and the questioning ended. As Wolf and his lancemates filed down from the shuttle, he was struck first by the heat, so different from the arid climate around Fort Hunter. It had been hot there at the edge of the Great Desert, but this heat lay over everything like a heavy, soaking blanket. His first deep breath of outside air made him sputter and cough.

The other thing he noticed was Fort Marchand itself.

It was a compact base surrounded by a perimeter fence dotted by prefab watch towers and presumably ringed by sensors and, perhaps, mines. The shuttle had grounded in the northwest corner of the compound, inside the fence, which helped drive home the danger of the region. Usually shuttle bays were kept at a discreet distance from inhabited areas in case of an engine failure, but that wasn't the case here.

Looking around, Wolf couldn't help but draw the comparisons with Fort Hunter. This was no ceremonial headquarters and training center. There was a functional feel to the camp . . . and to the grim-faced legionnaires who stood watch over the perimeter.

Fort Marchand was part of the real world.

"All right, you nubes!" Corporal Vanyek barked. "Enough gawking! Mag it! Mag it!"

They trotted across the parade ground, full kits hitched high on their backs, urged on by the noncoms. The block of transient barracks that served as the compound's training center was cramped, and their new quarters made the facilities back at Fort Hunter look positively luxurious by comparison. But there wasn't much time for grumbling. Less than fifteen minutes was allowed for stowing gear before the platoon was assembled in front of the building to sweat at attention while Konrad addressed them in ponderous, heavy-accented tones.

"Welcome to the Legion!" he began. "Up until now you nubes have lived the good life and thought it was hell. Now we'll show you how legionnaires really live every day of their lives. You'll soon think back to the easy days at Fort Hunter and feel wistful for the good life, I assure you." He waved his stun baton, a gesture that took in the entire compound. "Fort Marchand is a real Legion post manned by real legionnaires, and you nubes will do well to stay out from underfoot except as your duties require. Remember that these men have jobs to do, and in the field the smallest disruption can cost lives.

"There have been reports of Wynsarrysa activity in this area in the last several weeks," Konrad continued harshly, his gaze wandering over the ranks freely now. "It is probably nothing significant, and it will not interrupt the training schedule . . . but you must all be constantly aware of the fact that out here things are not the same as they were in Fort Hunter. Out here you must behave as if you were really in the field, where a mistake can be deadly not just to you but to all of your comrades." The sergeant's eyes seemed to be resting on Wolf. "Do not let your guard down. Not even for a moment. Because the legionnaire who lowers his guard is a dead man."

Chapter 15

. . . brutal and undisciplined, but ready to encounter anything.

—Legionnaire Clemens Lamping
French Foreign Legion, 1840

"Join the Legion, they say. Adventure. Excitement. Why the hell did I ever listen to that shit?"

Wolf smiled as the other legionnaire, a massive, shaven-headed black from Uhuru, spat expansively without missing a beat in his grumbling commentary. Volunteer Otema Banda had raised discontent to an art form, but somehow never seemed to run afoul of the NCO instructors.

"Ah, but just think what you would've missed by not signing up, laddie." That was Robert Bruce MacDuff, Banda's lancemate. "Why, who would have believed you could stuff ten healthy soldiers into such a small space and expect them not merely to survive, but in fact to fight like demons when they emerge? Mind you, it's my theory that anyone would go out and defy death in battle knowing that the alternative is climbing back into one of these floating coffins!"

Laughter filled the compartment. Ten recruits from two of Second Platoon's lances were crowded into the back of the M-786 Sandray armored personnel carrier, and although it was supposed to carry twelve plus a crew of two in "ordinary field use," the vehicle was by no means spacious. Even though the platoon was getting used to the routine of recon exercises after more than a week at Fort Marchand, no one claimed to find the confining ride in a Sandray comfortable.

Today's mission was a typical one-vehicle, two-lance patrol. Wolf and the rest of Myaighee's Deltas were equipped as a heavy weapons lance again, with Antonelli carrying the onager and Wolf the Fafnir launcher just as they had before. They were accompanied by Charlie Lance, from the platoon's first section, and for a change Corporal Vanyek wasn't supervising the exercise. This time they were under the orders of the assistant platoon leader, Sergeant Baram. Vanyek was conducting a separate exercise with Echo and Foxtrot lances somewhere else in the far-flung Archipel d'Aurore, and Wolf for one was glad to be out from under his stern eye for a change.

It was the first time in weeks that Wolf had been thrown together with Robert Bruce MacDuff, and that was another welcome break in the routine. Though they were members of the same platoon, they rarely saw one another. Most of the time exercises were performed by individual lances, or sometimes by sections, and it was only since the start of the second phase that they had started to work in two-lance groups like this one. By the end of their stay at Fort Marchand they were supposed to be into full-platoon operations, which would be considerably more complex.

For the moment, though, the chance to renew the acquaintance with MacDuff was enough of a boost to Wolf's morale to let him put aside concerns for the future. The young Caledonian, irreverent and carefree as ever, seemed to have adapted well to the training program.

The Sandray lurched, throwing Wolf sideways against Lisa Scott. He straightened up quickly, but not before she elbowed him just under the chest plate. It was just typical recruit horseplay, nothing serious, but it was a hard enough jab to make him grunt. That brought a laugh from some of the other recruits.

"Goddamned student drivers," he said, bracing himself with one hand on a strap beside his head. The contingent acting as the platoon's transport unit was drawn from veteran legionnaires who were going through advanced training as vehicle crews, and some of them still hadn't learned how to control their responsive charges. The APC rode on magnetic suspension fields, moving under the thrust of powerful turbofans, but sudden shifts in direction were just as violent for the passengers as anything an old-fashioned groundcar would have caused. Wolf noticed that Antonelli, the full body armor that went with his onager complete except for helmet, gauntlets, and power pack, was looking distinctly pale at the uneven motion. He'd earned himself a hundred push-ups two days earlier after throwing up during one exercise, and Wolf hoped the younger recruit wasn't going to be sick again today.

At least the exercise wasn't likely to offer any surprises. These practice recon runs went down pretty much the same way each time. The Sandray carried two lances out to some remote island, the troops practiced quick deployment under simulated combat conditions, and then proceeded to conduct reconnaissance and attack exercises in a variety of different terrain conditions. The tacdata briefing chip for today's mission had indicated they'd be focusing on movement through marshes and thick secondary jungle, and that didn't sound like it would offer any unusual complications. Wolf was beginning to get an old hand's tolerance for the repeated exercises.

The Sandray skewed sideways at high speed, an even more violent motion than before, and recruits around the rear compartment cursed and held on.

"Listen up, back there," Sergeant Menachem Baram's voice crackled in Wolf's headphones. He was in the cab up front, with the driver, occupying the seat that would normally have been reserved for a gunner for the Sandray's kinetic energy cannon. "We're diverting to check out a possible trouble spot. When you get the order to dismount, do it fast and clean. This won't just be another exercise. So don't screw it up!"

The channel went dead, and for a moment everything in the troop compartment was quiet. Then Banda spat again. "Yeah. Right. I guess they think we'll jump through hoops for them if they peddle this 'not just another exercise' shit. Bastards just don't give up."

"I'm not so sure," Kern said softly from his seat beside Wolf's. He had flipped his helmet's faceplate down. "Take a look at the feed from the forward cameras."

Wolf fumbled for a moment getting his own faceplate down and patched into the Sandray's video system. Suddenly he was gazing across a broad expanse of ocean at a humpbacked island swelling noticeably as the APC sped toward it. Most of the visible land was covered by a dark tangle of jungle. Numbers scrolled along the bottom of the view, readouts of the vehicle's speed, course, and precise location, but he paid only minimal attention to any of them.

It was the black smear of smoke coiling above the island that held Wolf's attention. He let out a low whistle. "I don't like the looks of that," he said somberly.

"Me, neither," Lisa Scott said, her voice muffled by her own helmet. "From the grid coordinates, that would have to be the Ile de Mouton, wouldn't it?"

Wolf checked the numbers unreeling across the lower left-hand corner of the display and tried to match them in his mind to the area map they'd been studying for the past week, but he wasn't sure enough to verify her conclusion. She was better at map work than he was, and he suspected that her excellent memory was the product of a computer implant in her brain. Frustrated, he cut the feed and raised the faceplate.

"Ye've got that right, lass," Macduff said a moment later. He flipped his own faceplate up. "Right there on the map . . . not very large, but there's a plantation marked on the northeast side. It just calls the place Savary's here."

"It could just be a fire," Katrina Voskovich, another member of Charlie Lance, spoke up. Like Myaighee, she had come to training from Colin Fraser's Legion company, but she didn't carry herself like a veteran. Her tone was more hopeful than convinced. "The briefings said that *arbebaril* sap is flammable . . ."

"Yeah . . . but the fire could've been set, too." Kern snapped his faceplate up again. So did Scott. "By rebels. We'd better figure on hostiles in the neighborhood. If it turns out it was caused by a careless foreman with a narcostick, then we get a pleasant surprise. But it's better to be ready for the worst."

"Like the man said, it isn't just an exercise this time," Engaged Volunteer Yeh Chen, acting lance leader of Charlie Lance, said. He was a small Oriental whose talent in hand-to-hand fighting was a legend in Second Platoon, and Wolf had heard him described as completely unflappable. But he sounded tense and preternaturally alert now.

No one else spoke as the APC continued on its way. Each of the recruits checked over weapons and field kits, actions they'd performed hundreds of times under the cold eyes of their instructors but which seemed somehow different, more urgent, now that the drills had become terrifyingly real.

Even Antonelli seemed to have his mind completely on

the job for a change. Kern and Myaighee were helping him into the last of his onager armor, finishing up by settling the heavy helmet over his swarthy features. Unlike the standard combat helmets the rest of them wore, Antonelli's didn't have a movable faceplate. It covered his whole head and fastened to the collar of his chest armor, providing a sealed environment that was proof against any atmosphere as well as the incredible heat generated by the plasma rifle he carried. With the addition of air tanks to replace the filter intakes at the rear of the helmet Antonelli could have worn the same garb in vacuum.

The Italian checked the power connections on the onager and powered it up just long enough to confirm it was fully charged, then safed the weapon and sat down again on the bench. The extra practice he'd been putting in, Wolf thought, was paying off now.

Wolf checked his Fafnir just as carefully, but not without a wistful glance at the FEKs most of the other recruits were carrying. The Wynsarrysa guerrillas didn't have access to the kind of heavy equipment the missile launcher was designed to counter, and it was likely he'd have little to do in the event of a firefight. The thought reminded him to check his FE-PLF rocket pistol, the backup weapon he would use in case of a close-in threat. The laser sniper's rifle MacDuff was carrying would have suited him far better.

Approaching target," Baram reported from the driver's cab. "We've got fires and heavy smoke around the OZ, so go to Echo Charlie Three and set your vision circuits to Image Enhance."

"Echo Charlie Three, Image Enhance." Myaighee, as the ranking recruit lance leader, repeated the orders back. Environmental Condition Three called for lowered faceplates and the attachment of a breathing filter across the lower portion of the combat helmet, while image enhancement would use computer processing to improve the quality of helmet-mounted video cameras using normal light and magnification settings.

Wolf unhooked the filter attachment from his web gear and snapped it into place, taking a few deep breaths to make sure it was working properly. Then he dropped the faceplate into place, turned on the cameras, and switched to the image enhancement mode. The image flickered, but in the well-lit compartment there was nothing for the computer to interpret and the view didn't change noticeably. All around him the others were going through the same drill. They were ready.

Or at least as ready as they could be . . .

The whine of the turbofans rose in pitch as the Sandray slid crabwise around some obstacle. Then the vehicle halted suddenly and grounded with an abrupt jar. "By lances, deploy!" Baram shouted over the comm circuit. "Standard dispersal and perimeter! Mag Out!"

The rear door was dropping as he spoke, and Voskovich and one of her lancemates, whose name was Owens, were already on their feet and moving before the ramp reached the ground. FEKs at the ready, they scrambled out and took up crouching positions on either side of the Sandray. Yeh Chen and Banda followed moments later, to take their places as the first two fanned out further. MacDuff, his laser sniper's rifle cradled in his hands, was next out.

Then it was time for the Deltas to go. "Delta Lance, move out," Myaighee ordered calmly.

Antonelli, with the heaviest firepower, followed MacDuff, moving more slowly than the other recruits but secure in the knowledge that there were few weapons on Devereaux outside of Legion arsenals that could have penetrated his combat armor. He was followed by Myaighee and Scott. Kern, carrying the bulky MEK, and Wolf with his Fafnir, dismounted last.

He dropped to one knee beside Scott at the base of the ramp and scanned the terrain cautiously. The computer chip in his helmet needed a few seconds to fully interpret the smoke-obscured surroundings, but it slowly began to fill in the details as he looked. The effect was like having a haze slowly lifted under the morning sun.

It was a scene from hell.

The plantation consisted of a broad clearing holding five prefab colonial buildings surrounded by orderly rows of multitrunked barrel trees. At a guess, Wolf estimated it would have housed twenty or thirty people, and given the Commonwealth's tendency to use rembots for manual labor instead of lower-class workers that would have been about right for a midsized Devereaux plantation.

Not one of the buildings was intact now. The two-story manor building directly in front of Wolf and Scott was

burning fiercely, and most of the doors and windows had
been shattered. He thought he could identify the pockmark
cratering on the wall around the main door as the scars
from a wild barrage of 1cm grenades fired from an FEK
on the full-auto setting. Off to the left the blackest roil of
smoke came from a windowless building that looked like
a storehouse, where there were probably tanks of sap still
smoldering.

But the real horror had nothing to do with the buildings.
Eight bodies lay between the recruits and the manor house,
and the sight of them made Wolf turn his head away for a
moment before he could force himself to study them ob-
jectively.

From the look of it none of them had been killed there.
They had been dragged from other parts of the compound,
stripped, and laid out with arms and legs spread-eagled. Even
from a range of twenty meters Wolf could see that the bodies
had been mutilated as well.

Bile rose in his throat.

"Report!" Baram's voice was sharp, jerking Wolf back
to reality. The savages who had done all this might still be
somewhere near. He focused his attention on a thorough
scan of the surrounding jungle as Yeh Chen's recruits made
their observations in the order they had debarked.

"Charlie Two," Owens said. "No sign of life. Just
burning buildings and . . . bodies."

"Charlie Five." That was Katrina Voskovich. She
sounded sick. "That's all I see. Nothing moving. Nothing
alive."

The others had the same negative reports. Even
MacDuff's usually jaunty manner was distinctly subdued,
and Antonelli didn't speak at all when his turn came.

Myaighee, on the other hand, was matter-of-fact, stepping smoothly into the awkward silence left by Antonelli.
"Delta Leader. I see nothing in motion. Two groups of
casualties, one north of the Sandray, one southwest. Eight
bodies in each. All buildings showing smoke, but fires
seem to have died out. My estimate is that it has been
several hours since this area was attacked."

The rest of the Deltas added nothing significant. Antonelli, when he finally managed to make his report, was
barely able to speak, and Lisa Scott broke off halfway

through, gagging. Wolf was last. "Delta Four," he said harshly. "I concur. Whoever was here is gone now."

"An observation based, no doubt, on your vast experience," Baram said sarcastically. He appeared in the rear door, in full kit with an FEK held at the ready. "Reassuring as Volunteer Wolf's opinions may be, I want this area searched. Thoroughly. Charlie Lance will carry out the recon in pairs, while Delta maintains overwatch from here. MacDuff, you're with me. Myaighee, you take your orders from Legionnaire Yancey. Understood?"

There was a chorus of acknowledgements. As Baram and the five recruits from Charlie Lance split up and moved cautiously away from the APC, Legionnaire Second Class Yancey spoke up. "Wolf, Scott, take a closer look at the casualties," the Sandray driver ordered. "Helmet cameras on relay. I'll record from here. The rest of you maintain watch. Mag it!"

Wolf handed his Fafnir to Kern and drew his rocket pistol. While Scott stood watch with her FEK, he moved cautiously to the first line of bodies and dropped to one knee beside one of them.

"Booby traps," the blonde said curtly.

He nodded, remembering a lecture Gunnery Sergeant Ortega had given early in Basic regarding the ways an unwary soldier could be maimed or killed by carelessness in the field. He studied the body carefully, trying to block out the grisly reality and concentrate on the task as if it was just another Legion exercise. But it wasn't easy.

The body was a man's, eyes still wide open and staring at the smoke-filled sky. He had probably been killed by surprise, judging from the way his throat had been slit. The other wounds had apparently been inflicted later—the ears and nose had been cut off, and a deep gash in the shape of an inverted V had been cut in the stomach and chest, with the point over the breastbone. A glance left and right showed that all of the victims had that same incision no matter what other wounds showed.

"I've seen that work before," Legionnaire Yancey commented over the commlink. "It was rebels, all right. The damned savages like to leave us . . . messages like that."

"I see no signs of booby traps," Wolf said, trying to keep his voice even.

"You probably won't," Yancey replied. "Not when the

bodies are laid out like that. But be careful anyway, nube. There's always a first time.''

All of the bodies in both of the groups were much the same as the first one, but repetition didn't make the examinations any easier. Twelve men and four women had been treated the same way. Sergeant Baram reported finding three more bodies barricaded in one of the burnt-out buildings. From the signs, Baram said, the fires had been set during the fighting, and the humans had preferred to burn to death rather than fall into the hands of their assailants.

Baram and the recruits from Charlie Lance confirmed that the plantation was deserted. Returning to the APC, the sergeant spent ten long minutes in the driver's cab, putting in a call to higher authority at Fort Marchand. When he finally emerged, looking grim, he called them all together.

''This is a bad business,'' he began. ''The bastards that did this might be a few hundred meters away, or they might have magged out entirely. There's no way to be sure without searching this whole damned island, and two lances of nubes ain't my idea of a proper search party.''

''So what are we gonna do, Sarge?'' Yancey asked.

''First thing is to bury those poor devils we found, and smother the fires that are still smoldering. With one lance keeping watch while the other works that's going to use up most of the daylight we've got left.'' He frowned. ''Unfortunately they've had some other problems with rebels around Marchand today, and they won't be able to spare any more troops to check out this area until tomorrow. We've got orders to remain in place here until a regular patrol can relieve us.''

''What the hell is there to guard, for Christ's sake?'' Banda burst out.

The sergeant didn't react the way Wolf expected. Instead of a reprimand or a quick stroke of his stun baton, he simply shrugged. ''There's gear in the processing shed that's worth a lot of credits. Robotics. The rebels even left a couple of floatcars in the repbay. Ordinary marauders would leave that stuff if they were in a hurry, but they could just be waiting for a chance to bring a boat in and haul off everything that isn't nailed down. Anyway, even if there wasn't anything they wanted, they could still move in after we left and prepare a nasty reception for the next bunch that comes in. I've seen them do that a time or two . . . let an area be pronounced clear and then set up an ambush.''

''So we stick it out until tomorrow,'' Yancey said.

''That's the size of it. After we finish the burials we'll deploy remote sensors out in the jungle in a perimeter line to protect the clearing here. If they do try to pay us a visit they'll run into a hell of a lot of a firepower.'' He glared at the recruits. ''Think you nubes can handle it all?''

Myaighee replied before anyone else could respond. ''It doesn't sound like we are in that much danger, Sergeant,'' he said softly. ''It isn't that much different from an overnight route march.''

''Yeah . . . except for the fact that there are real hostiles out there somewhere,'' MacDuff added from the far edge of the semicircle of recruits. ''But aside from that little detail, it's just a bleeding picnic.''

There were a few laughs at that, but it was nervous, uneasy laughter.

Wolf, thinking about those mutilated bodies, didn't join in.

Chapter 16

You must never remain deaf to cries of "A MOI
LA LEGION."

—Momento du Legionnaire
Recruiting Pamphlet
French Foreign Legion, 1938

Mario Antonelli felt a trickle of sweat running down his
back and shifted uncomfortably. The sun had been down
for hours now, but the cloying jungle heat still smothered
the plantation clearing like a wet, heavy blanket.

His battledress fatigues were supposed to have built-in
climate controls to compensate for extremes of heat and
cold, but he'd been having trouble with the settings ever
since the platoon had landed at Fort Marchand. One more
thing, he thought bitterly, that he just couldn't manage to
do right. At least Sergeant Baram had allowed him to stand
his watch with a borrowed FEK and wearing his fatigues.
The onager with its heavy armored protective gear would
have been doubly uncomfortable tonight.

He fumbled with the studs on his wristpiece computer
to try to correct the settings, but he couldn't see what he
was doing. With his helmet faceplate set to receive sensor
readings from the perimeter he was working blind. Suddenly angry, he cursed and cut off the external feed, then
raised his faceplate and blinked a few times before he realized that the darkness around him was as thick and im-
penetrable as the jungle that lay only a few meters away.
Konrad had assigned him to sentry duty, monitoring the
perimeter sensor net, and after staring at the readout for
what seemed like hours on end Antonelli had forgotten
how black the nights in the Archipel d'Aurore could get.

Switching on a tiny light mounted on the side of his
helmet, Antonelli studied the 'piece. It was hooked di-

rectly into the uniform's climate-control system, and with a few quick touches he changed the settings that governed the environmental maintenance coils woven into the fabric of the battledress. He felt cooler almost at once.

Antonelli cut the light, but left his faceplate up for the moment. There was something almost comforting about the dark. The enveloping blackness hid the sight of the burnt-out plantation, though it couldn't blot out the memory of the grisly tableaux of mutilated bodies arranged in their neat rows in the clearing. That was a scene that would remain burned into his brain for a long time to come.

He'd been assigned to the burial detail in the afternoon, and almost inevitably the horror of the bodies, the heat and humidity made even worse by his onager armor and the swaying motion he'd endured for over an hour in the Sandray before they reached the plantation, and cumulative fatigue from too many nights without enough sleep had all come together to hit him at once. Right in the middle of the work Antonelli had been overcome by wave after wave of nausea. He had torn his helmet off and tossed it aside as he doubled over to throw up. Afterward Baram had worked him twice as hard, and of course he'd been singled out to take the first watch after the rest of the party had turned in for the night.

He wasn't sure how much more he could take. The extra training Vanyek had handed him, solo practice and tutoring from Kern, had helped him squeak through Weapons Training and was keeping him even with the rest of the lance now that they were at Fort Marchand, but it was grueling. On top of that he had the Christmas craft work Ortega had assigned, an hour or more each night, and it was a rare week that didn't see him pulling some kind of evening punishment duty as well.

Antonelli wasn't sure how much longer he could keep up with the physical pace the Legion was demanding of him. Sometimes he thought that was exactly why the instructors kept throwing more evening duty at him. After all, Vanyek had tried his best to convince him to accept failure as inevitable and resign . . . maybe they had decided to push him to the breaking point and force him out since he refused to accept the trip to the penal battalions gracefully.

He shook his head wearily. He didn't really think it was

any kind of deliberate plot. It was just that sometimes everything seemed stacked against him.

And he was just so damned tired all the time. . . .

He leaned his head back against the trunk of the *arbebaril* behind him and closed his eyes. Just for a moment, to help him clear his head before he went back to staring at the sensor readouts . . .

Just for a moment . . .

Movement close by brought Lisa Scott instantly awake. That was something she had lived with for five years, the hair-trigger sensitivity that made her react to the slightest hint of a disturbance anywhere around her. She sat up, eyes wide open, her hand instinctively wrapping around the hilt of the Legion-issue knife under her sleeping bag. It wasn't as good as the one that had been confiscated the first night of training, but it was good enough.

She relaxed as she saw Wolf crouching a few meters away, his back to her as he rolled up his sleeping bag. "Time for your watch already?" she asked softly, sliding the knife back into its accustomed place.

He glanced toward her. His face was hard to read in the soft illumination of one of the portable camp lights Baram had set up a few meters away, but she thought she could make out the mixture of bemusement and wariness that she'd come to expect from the aristo. He knew her foibles by now, and he went out of his way to keep his distance. That was fine by Lisa Scott. She knew in her mind that none of her lancemates, not even Antonelli, would do anything to hurt her now . . . but five years hadn't erased all the scars, and she didn't entirely trust herself if she was pushed too far or backed into a corner. Not even with someone like Wolf.

"Yeah," he replied quietly. "You'd think the Sarge could've split the watch schedule between us and Charlie Lance . . . but I guess that'd make too much sense."

" 'Ours not to reason why . . .' " she quoted.

"Ours but to do *and* die," he finished. "Just do me a favor and make sure Sleeping Beauty over there relieves me on time, okay?" He pointed toward Kern, who had spread his sleeping bag a few meters away from the rest of the lance. They were camped about halfway between the APC and the ruined plantation house, while Charlie

Lance had set up much closer to the vehicle. Baram had insisted in spreading the recruits out, just in case. Scott found herself hoping that the precaution would prove foolish in the morning light.

"I'm perfectly capable of waking myself up," Kern's voice cut in before she had a chance to reply. "Especially when other people make all this noise. So move out before I decide to test my night shooting skills."

Wolf chuckled and straightened up.

"Need a rifle?" she asked him. Since he was saddled with the rocket launcher, Wolf didn't have an FEK of his own.

He shook his head. "Antonelli'll turn his over to me. Thanks, anyway." Stiff-backed, he donned his combat helmet and started off. Outside the circle of light, he was quickly swallowed up by the darkness.

She stretched out on the ground again, but didn't close her eyes right away. The horrors of the afternoon were still too close, ready to spring unbidden from the dark recesses of memory. There had been clustered bodies the other time, too, five years ago, and one bad memory fed on the other.

Scott shut the thought out of her mind, just as she had during the burial earlier. She took a deep breath, going through the meditation technique she had originally learned to clear her mind in order to access the computer implant in her brain. Since the day the terrorists had kidnaped her from her father's estate she had found that the same formula could help her banish the nightmares . . . at least for a while.

Slowly she let herself slip into the darkness.

And suddenly she was fully awake once more as the commlink receivers in every helmet in the camp shrilled an alarm simultaneously. The standby communications setting was designed to attract attention to an emergency alert message from a distance when the helmets weren't being worn, and now they were doing just that as Wolf's voice, edged with an urgency that bordered on panic, boomed from the speakers.

"Alert! Alert! Movement outside the camp!"

"Antonelli! For God's sake, man, answer me!" Wolf resisted the urge to call out, either aloud or over the comm channel, and kept his voice to a hoarse stage whisper instead. He didn't want to get the younger recruit in trouble with Sergeant Baram by calling unnecessary attention to him . . . but the Italian's silence was exasperating. Where *was* he?

The image of the civilian with the slit throat rose unbidden in his mind, but Wolf thrust it away. "Antonelli!"

He had his combat helmet set for light intensification, and the faint starlight was enough to make the clearing look as if it was lit by floodlights on his faceplate. Wolf paused and took a careful look around, getting more concerned now. The Italian had been ordered to pay special attention to the southern perimeter, where the barrel trees were thickest and approached the plantation buildings most closely. Although he could have monitored the sensor net from almost anywhere, Antonelli had taken the orders literally and headed for that end of the compound at the start of his watch. The clearing, as defined by the five plantation buildings, formed a U shape with the open end facing south and the APC resting near the mouth, less than fifty meters from the treeline.

If Antonelli had done the sensible thing and set up his watch near the Sandray it would have saved a lot of trouble. As it was, Wolf couldn't very well relieve the kid unless he could find him first. And so far there was no sign of the Italian . . .

No, *there* he was. Wolf could see his legs past the squat trunk of an *arbebaril* at the very edge of the trees. The recruit was sitting with his back to the clearing. Still, he should have heard Wolf.

He cursed silently and unbuckled the strap on his pistol holster. It was his only weapon, since he would ordinarily have taken over the FEK Antonelli had borrowed. Wolf covered the distance to the tree quickly and dropped to one knee beside the Italian. He was sprawled against the trunk, head back, faceplate up. There was no sign of any injuries, and his breathing was deep and regular . . .

Antonelli was asleep.

Wolf prodded him. "Goddamn it, kid, wake up!" he whispered urgently.

The Italian straightened up, looking wild. "What? What is it?"

"What a *stupid* stunt to pull!" Wolf told him, still whispering. "If the Sarge had caught you . . ."

Antonelli flinched. "I didn't mean to, man. I . . . I only closed my eyes for a moment. I swear!"

"Yeah . . . well, now you can turn in for real. I'm supposed to be your relief. So get back to the camp and get some rest."

The younger recruit kept his eyes fixed on Wolf's face and didn't move. "Are you . . . are you going to report me?"

"Well . . . you only closed your eyes for a moment," Wolf told him with a half-smile. He knew he ought to do just that, but he wasn't willing to be the one who finally got poor Antonelli busted. The kid looked scared enough never to fall asleep on watch again. "No, I won't report you. Word of honor on that. But you know I could get a fast trip to Tophet myself for covering your ass. Keep it in mind, kid."

The Italian nodded and stood slowly.

"Okay, I relieve you. Let's see the perimeter . . ." He switched from LI to sensor feed, and his faceplate lit up with a dozen blinking red dots. The unexpected sight made him forget his Terranglic. *"Mein Gott!"*

Each one of those red lights was a sensor reporting movement by man-sized bodies pushing through the jungle. There might be a dozen moving targets out there . . . or perhaps many more.

Wolf hit his commlink button. "Alert! Alert! Movement outside the camp!" He didn't even have time to repeat the warning before the whine of kinetic energy rifles erupted from the brush. He grabbed Antonelli by the web gear and pulled him down on the ground beside him. "Keep your head down, kid!" he said harshly, switching his faceplate back to LI vision again before groping for his pistol. "And let 'em have it!"

A grenade went off behind them, near the heart of the camp, and half a dozen bulky figures burst out of the jungle howling and waving a weird assortment of weapons as they ran. Wolf drew a bead and squeezed off a round, but the shot was wide. "Lay down some autofire, Antonelli! Nail the bastards!"

Antonelli clutched his FEK, but made no move to use it. He lay where Wolf had pushed him, eyes wide, his mouth opening and closing but making no coherent sounds.

Wolf fired the pistol again, then rolled sideways as one of the rebels took aim with an antiquated-looking rifle. The crack and whistle of the shot was nothing like the sound of a kinetic energy rifle, but it made Wolf duck anyway. He'd heard of old-fashioned projectile weapons, and even though his battledress was reportedly adequate protection against typical longarms of that sort he had no desire to test those reports.

The bullet missed him by a safe margin, but the massive alien shouted and pointed, and more of its comrades turned to join the fight.

Now they knew exactly where the two recruits were, and with Antonelli paralyzed it would be an uneven match. . . .

Lisa Scott crawled on her belly up to the protective bulk of a log, braced her FEK across the top, and got off a long full-auto burst. It was just blind, random fire, but it elicited an unearthly scream that made her skin crawl. She fired again.

The camp was a scene of chaos. The attack had started hard on the heels of the first warning, and before anyone could react explosions and shouts were already filling the clearing. The first grenade had gone off close to the APC, where a couple of the Charlie Lance recruits, Owens and Banda, had bedded down. Peering over the top of the log, she could see one body sprawled there on the ground. It was too small to be Banda, so it was probably Volunteer Owens. Dead?

No . . . she could see the figure moving feebly. Beyond were the hulking shapes of Wynsarrysa rebels fanning out across the clearing, large, slow-moving, but relentless as so many juggernauts. One was heading straight for Owens, holding a massive sword and baring his teeth in a savage snarl.

She remembered the mutilated bodies and opened fire again, raking the ponderous form with a stream of needle projectiles that tore into the rebel's torso. With a screech like the one she'd heard before the alien toppled.

"Legionnaires! Hold 'em, legionnaires!" That was Yancey, the Sandray driver, waving a pistol as he ran toward the APC, heedless of the swarming hostiles.

Scott opened fire to cover him. If Yancey could make it to his armored vehicle, its kinetic energy cannon would make short work of the attackers.

But at that moment the driver's back exploded in a haze of blood. At least one of the savages had a captured FEK and knew how to use the 1cm grenades to good effect. She swallowed sour bile and squeezed the trigger again, feeling sick but refusing to give in to the nausea.

Where were the rest of the recruits? She couldn't see Antonelli or Wolf, but she noticed Kern crouching at the corner of the nearest building, the warehouse, off to the left. Myaighee had given his weapon to Antonelli when the latter had gone on watch, but the diminutive hannie was scrambling up a ladder on the outer wall of the warehouse, apparently oblivious to the shots the attackers were taking at him. She wasn't sure what he intended, but the roof would at least give him a good vantage point to act as a spotter for grenade fire.

As for Charlie Lance, she wasn't as clear. Owens was down, of course, but there was no sign of Volunteer Banda or the others. The fight had erupted so fast that she'd lost track of almost everyone.

"Come on! Hold them, damn it! Hold them!" Sergeant Baram's voice was familiar, at least, something to latch on to in the chaos. A moment later he appeared as if out of nowhere and dropped to one knee beside her. "Keep up the fire, Scott," he growled, spraying needle rounds at the closest clump of rebels as he spoke. "Yeh Chen! Banda! Report!"

There was a pause. Then the commlink crackled. "Yeh Chen's down, Sergeant," Banda said. "His arm's off at the elbow. I've got the bleeding stopped. . . ."

"Leave him! Get in the game, Banda! We need to get to that goddamned Sandray!"

"Y-yeah . . . yes, Sergeant! On my way!"

"Scott, MacDuff, maintain covering fire. Everyone else rushes the APC on my order!"

There was a chorus of acknowledgements. A moment later Baram was on his feet and crossing the clearing at a dead run, zigzagging, while Scott covered him with a sustained FEK burst. "Legionnaires!" Baram shouted. "Legionnaires, form on me! Nail the bastards!"

Out of the corner of her eye she saw Kern grappling with

a Wynsarrysa rebel who had sprung on him before he could get clear of the warehouse. Myaighee gave a blood-curdling, ululating screech and leapt from his perch to help the redhead.

Then her attention was wrenched away from that melee as Baram took a hit and stumbled. The black recruit, Banda, ran past him straight into a hail of needle rounds. He flopped backwards and lay still, and there was a long moment of stunned silence.

One of the rebels had an old-model FEK, and Karl Wolf scrambled over the uneven ground as needle rounds whispered just over his head. Reaching Antonelli, he pried the rifle out of the Italian recruit's trembling hands and flicked the selector switch to full automatic. Clamping his finger down on the trigger and aiming up from his prone position, he raked the four charging rebels with a steady stream of fire until all went down. Then he cautiously peered around the sheltering bulk of the *arbebaril*.

Light-intensification made the darkness look bright as a cloudy winter day, and it was easy enough to spot the rebels spreading out along the edge of the clearing between the two recruits and the APC. A few of them had fallen under fire from the camp, but there were still more of the hulking alien shapes moving than the entire two-lance Legion outfit . . . and there was no way of knowing, from here, how many of the legionnaires had been killed in the first rush.

His commlink didn't enlighten him much. There was a confused babble of orders and shouted warnings, but it didn't sound like Baram had established any kind of control over the firefight.

Or maybe Baram was dead already.

He decided against trying to break into the channel to ask for instructions. Even if there was anyone left to give them, it sounded as if everyone in the camp already had enough to worry about. Instead, Wolf shut off his commlink altogether and studied the scene spread out on the inside of his helmet visor.

Three of the raiders were crouched near the corner of the nearest building, the processing plant, and several more were visible clustered around the APC. The vehicle was the key to the whole situation, of course. That heavy turret gun would turn the tide in no time. No doubt there were others in the camp with the same idea, but the clearing would be an open killing ground, hard to cross without coming under concentrated fire from the rebels.

But the rebels weren't paying any attention to their flank or rear now, and that gave Wolf the edge.

He looked back at Antonelli. The young Italian was still on the ground, plainly terrified. His hands clenched tight around the FEK in frustration, but Wolf knew it was no use trying to goad the younger recruit into action. He'd have to behave as if Antonelli was out of the action entirely.

Wolf started to turn away, then had another thought. He belly-crawled to the cluster of rebels he'd killed before, grabbed the old FEK/24 one of them had dropped, and checked the magazine. It was still half full. Switching the selector switch to three-round autobursts, Wolf crawled back to Antonelli and thrust the antiquated weapon into his hands. The Italian stared at it uncomprehendingly.

"Use it to defend yourself, kid," Wolf hissed. "Just stay put here."

Somehow, Antonelli managed to nod acknowledgement. Wolf left him and went back to the *arbebaril*. Raising his borrowed FEK/27 carefully, he switched to the single-shot setting and took careful aim on the nearest of the three rebels by the corner of the processing building. He squeezed the trigger and saw his target collapse in a heap without attracting any attention from either of its partners.

With a quick movement he shifted his aim and fired again. This time, though, his aim was off and the rebel felt the breeze of the high-velocity needle whispering bare centimeters past what should have been its ears, if these ales had sported anything identifiable as external ears. The raider grabbed its friend by the arm, pulling it to one side and gesticulating wildly. The image would have been funny if the situation hadn't been so grim.

Wolf cursed. If he didn't move fast, those two would have the whole rebel force on top of him . . .

Chapter 17

Dying is what the Legion is all about.
> —Legionnaire William Brooks
> French Foreign Legion, 1978

Legionnaire Third Class Myaighee felt the battle lust overwhelming kys senses. A quick thrust of kys combat knife had killed one massive Wynsarrysa rebel, and Kern had brought down a second one with a quick burst of FEK fire, but more were pouring into the plantation clearing from the jungle behind the warehouse. The surroundings and the situation took ky back to the long retreat by Bravo Company through the jungles of Hanuman, when kys own people had been the enemy.

Ky didn't have a battle rifle, but one of the rebels had dropped a heavy autopistol of Gwyrran design, more like a submachinegun for Myaighee. Ky snatched it up and studied the awkward weapon. It wasn't far removed technologically from the weaponry ky had used in the militia back home, several long ages ago. The hannie crouched over the unmoving body and checked the creature's belt, coming up with a pair of extra clips.

"Look out!" Kern shouted, cutting loose with another burst of fire. Myaighee rolled sideways just as a pair of rebels opened fire. If not for the redheaded male-human's warning, the shots would have hit ky in the head.

Myaighee raised the pistol in a clumsy two-handed grip and returned fire. One of the bulky aliens threw up his arms and fell, screeching like an injured *zymlat*. Others kept coming, though. Ky could feel the surge of excitement in kys veins, the stirring of the neck ruff that signaled fury. Ky gibbered a challenge and blazed away into the dark.

"Myaighee!" Sergeant Baram's voice was weak, wavering, and Myaighee barely noticed it as a distraction in kys ear. "Myaighee . . . take charge! Get . . . to the Sandray . . ."

The hannie shouted again, fired again, and lunged forward to meet the oncoming foes. The sergeant's words meant nothing now next to the fight ky already was waging.

Lisa Scott ducked behind the barricade and bit her lip as another fusillade split the air overhead. The relief she'd felt on hearing Sergeant Baram, realizing he wasn't dead after all, had given way to doubt. Myaighee hadn't responded to Baram's order, and she wasn't sure what she should do. Should she try to help Baram, or get to the vehicle? Or stick to her position and hope she could keep the hostiles from getting any closer to the wavering human position?

As if reading her mind, Volunteer MacDuff spoke up on the comm channel. "Stay where you are, lass, and keep giving those bastards hell. Voskovich and I will make a try for the APC."

"Right," she said through clenched teeth. Her FEK chattered, its magazine exhausted. She switched to grenades and got off a quick three-round burst at the nearest group of rebels, then ejected her empty clip, fished a fresh magazine of caseless needle ammo from her pouch, and slapped it into the receiver. "Make your move, MacDuff!"

MacDuff and Voskovich advanced carefully, leapfrogging forward in the classic fire-and-movement pattern they'd been taught during weapons training. Moving from cover to cover, with one laying down suppression fire as the other ran, they worked their way up the right side of the clearing opposite the warehouse. The repbay with its three large, slightly recessed vehicle-sized doorways dominated that side of the compound and gave the two some shelter.

MacDuff had discarded his laser rifle for an FEK, probably Yeh Chen's, and he used it to deadly effect as they advanced. All it would take now was one rush from the corner of the repbay and the Caledonian would be at the APC. Scott switched back to grenades and laid down a heavy pattern. MacDuff gave her a cocky thumbs up and burst from cover, running at top speed. He moved with the sure grace of a cat, and in seconds he was at the driver's hatch of the APC, stabbing at the door controls.

A giant shape loomed out of the shadows. Before she could shout a warning Scott saw a blade flashing down, once, twice, a third time. With a gurgling cry MacDuff collapsed.

Half blinded by tears of rage and frustration, Lisa Scott was on her feet, sweeping her FEK back and forth as she ran. The alien who had struck down MacDuff fell over the body of his victim, but there were more of them out there. A rational part of her mind, detached and strangely calm, knew she would never make it to the Sandray. . . .

She kept running.

Wolf switched to full-auto and sprayed the enemy position. As he fired, he surged to his feet and ran toward the two aliens. The needle rounds shredded through flesh and bone, and by the time Wolf had reached the corner neither of the aliens was moving. In fact there wasn't much that was recognizable as a once-living creature left.

But the FEK was chattering on an empty clip now, and Wolf didn't have any fresh ammo, just a clip of minigrenades. Those would cause casualities, all right, but they would also draw too much attention to him . . . and could put other legionnaires at risk if he overshot his target. He gave another curse, softly, through clenched teeth, at his thoughtlessness. He should have taken Antonelli's extra magazine before leaving the Italian alone back there. Now it was too late. He was committed. Wolf slung the battle rifle over his shoulder and drew his pistol once more.

Without firepower there was no way he was going to make it to the APC from this position. There were half a dozen rebels right around the vehicle and several more further back, at the edge of the jungle, who would spot him if he made a move. What he needed was a diversion. . . .

He thought of the smoldering fires they'd put out during the daylight hours. The *arbebaril* sap was flammable, and in his mind's eye Wolf could picture the maze of pipes that carried the sap from the processing building to the next building down the line, the main warehouse. The pieces of the puzzle were starting to fit together.

Wolf sprinted toward the back of the building, hugging the wall and keeping low. It didn't take long to swing around the back. He dropped to one knee at the back corner, scanning the space between the two structures carefully. Two rebels were visible beyond the complex of pipes and conduits, both of them intent on the center of the clearing. More cautious than before, Wolf crept forward until he was among the pipes. He found a keyboard for a maintenance check-valve and bit back another curse. An old-fashioned manual valve would have been easier to deal with. He considered backing off and using a grenade, but there was no guarantee of success . . . and he'd only have the one chance. Discarding that notion, he pulled the interface wire from the side of his wristpiece computer, plugged into the keypad, and whispered orders to the 'piece. The self-programming chip inside quickly established the parameters of his command and began the code-breaking sequence to activate the keypad.

Precious seconds ticked by. One of the rebels near the APC fell, but more ran forward. Wolf had a glimpse of a dark-clad human figure running across his field of view, but saw nothing more of the human defenders. When there was no further change in the firefight in the clearing he couldn't help wondering who had made that desperate charge . . . and what had happened. It could have been Kern, or MacDuff then . . . even Lisa Scott, probably cut down by the rebels close to the APC. The thought made Wolf want to cry out and charge into the fighting, but he forced himself to stay put and wait for the computer to do its work.

At last a green light lit up on the keypad, and Wolf hit the control to open the valve. Thick, dark liquid oozed from the check pipe, like congealing blood. Wolf disconnected the interface and sprinted back the way he had come, leaving a pool of the viscous sludge spreading slowly under the pipes.

From the back corner he'd paused at before, Wolf waited and watched until he was sure enough sap was on the ground to give him the diversion he needed. He returned his pistol to his holster and unslung the FEK once again, checking the magazine out of habit even though he knew all too well what the indicators read. Then he carefully aimed the rifle and fired three 1cm grenades into the mid-

dle of the pool. Wolf was running by the time the first
explosion went off, racing for the spot where he had killed
the three ales. As he ran, the blasts went off in quick succession. Hoarse shouts from the clearing attested to the
attention he had drawn, and a cloud of thick, choking
smoke, black against the black night, roiled and twisted
from the burning inferno he had created.

He only hoped the surprise would last. . . .

Something tore the air close enough to Lisa Scott's faceplate to make her flinch. Her Legion training took over,
made her drop and roll away from the danger. Even as she
came up to one knee she was searching for the source of
the fusillade. She recognized the bulky shape near the rear
of the Sandray as an enemy and had her weapon up and
firing almost without thinking about it. Part of her was
smiling inwardly. Brutal and often senseless though it often seemed, her Legion education was certainly proving
effective tonight.

The alien was literally flung back against the hull of the
APC by the power of her full-auto blast. She surged to her
feet and started forward again, vaguely aware of Katrina
Voskovich shouting support and laying down suppressive
fire from off to her right.

She dodged around Baram's prone form, encouraged
when she saw the sergeant moving, trying to claw his way
forward to the shelter of a pile of debris left over from the
original sack of the plantation. For a moment she was
tempted to go to his assistance, but that would have been
a wasted effort at this point. Unless someone got to that
Sandray and brought its heavier weaponry into play, the
entire cadet patrol was liable to be swamped by superior
numbers, and there weren't enough legionnaires left on
their feet now for her to take herself out of the fight just
to help Baram.

The whole decision passed through her mind in an instant, and she barely broke her stride as she continued her
zigzag course toward the squat APC. Ahead, a pair of
rebels appeared at the door of the processing building,
opening fire with antiquated hunting rifles. A bullet hit her
squarely in the chest, splattering ineffectively on her
breastplate armor. The force made her stagger, but she
kept on running.

At that moment a fireball erupted from between the buildings to her right, with a flash so intense that it overloaded her LI gear. Panic gripped her for a moment. *I'm blind* she thought, stumbling over some obstacle and sprawling to the ground. She clawed at her helmet, then realized she was seeing again. The LI circuits were coming back on line, none the worse for wear.

She blinked a couple of times, then saw the two aliens gaping at the smoke and flame, her presence apparently forgotten. Groping for her discarded rifle, Lisa raised herself to her knees and cut loose with a spray of automatic fire.

The two rebels fell under the autofire, but she used up the rest of her magazine bringing them down. Grimly she ejected the spent clip and started to snap her last one into place in the FEK's receiver.

Another Wynsarrysa loomed up just in front of her, seemingly coming from nowhere. The sudden menace made her fumble with the magazine. Lisa Scott had grown up in an environment that didn't encourage foul language, but she yelled a lurid curse she had learned among the legionnaires when the clip spun out of her hand and into the mud.

The rebel's teeth were gleaming in the firelight as he raised his own FEK to finish the human off. . . .

Nothing happened.

The Wynsarrysa gaped uncomprehendingly for a long moment before he realized that his own magazine was empty. Then he surged forward, two meters of fang and muscle and fury, clubbing the rifle and drawing back to deliver a single skull-crushing blow. Lisa stumbled backward, trying to bring her weapon up to block the savage attack, but she knew her strength was no match for the nonhuman's.

The familiar *whoosh* of a rocket bullet split the night, clear despite the noise of battle and fire that filled the plantation clearing. The alien's chest erupted in a fine spray of blood and flesh. He stood transfixed for long seconds before finally toppling in a heap beside her.

And Karl Wolf was there, the PLF rocket pistol in one hand, his rifle clutched by the barrel in the other.

Myaighee's scavenged pistol was empty now, out of ammunition, and ky threw it at the face of the closest rebel.

The fight had carried the hannie, with Thomas Kern close behind, past the warehouse and almost to the jungle, rushing forward from cover to cover each time there was a brief let-up in the attack. The battle lust was starting to give way to fatigue now, and for the first time Myaighee became aware of Kern's voice shouting in his earphones.

"Damn it, Myaighee! What are you doing? Sarge said for you to take charge and get to the Sandray . . . !"

Ky gaped at Kern's tall, stocky form, not quite comprehending.

Then pain lanced through kys shoulder as a rebel's heavy sword slashed down, seemingly from out of nowhere. Kys battledress absorbed the worst of the shock, but Myaighee still felt the pain like fire in kys arm and upper chest.

Kern shot the Wynsarrysa rebel, and stood over the hannie. . . .

Then the night lit up with a string of explosions, and the rebels stopped in their tracks to stare at the fireball rising over the processing building on the other side of the compound. Kern grabbed Myaighee by kys webgear and sprinted back for the safety of the warehouse.

Myaighee passed out from shock and fatigue before they reached the building.

"Come on! While we've got an opening!" Wolf shouted and turned, sprinting for the Sandray, knowing Lisa Scott would follow him.

He hopped over one body, dodged another, and reached the corner of the vehicle. Four more aliens broke from the cover of the trees, heading his way, and he squeezed off two shots in quick succession before they ducked behind a half-ruined shed. In the next instant Lisa Scott was kneeling by his side, her FEK at the ready. She fired a three-round burst of minigrenades that finished the destruction of the shed. At least one of the aliens fell, sprawled under a collapsed wall. She switched to needle rounds and laid down a murderous stream of fire across the clearing, sweeping back and forth along the treeline to suppress the enemies still lurking there.

Wolf turned the corner with the pistol held high, but there were no living rebels there. Several dead bodies littered the ground nearby, including at least one shape that had to be human, not Wynsarrysa. He forced himself to ignore the casualties and rushed up the length of the Sandray. The driver's hatch was closed, electronically sealed, but the tiny transponder in his helmet would identify him to the onboard computer as a friend and release the locks when he hit the pressure pad beside the door.

Another ale popped out from behind the cover of the Sandray's blunt nose, and Wolf fired from point-blank range. The rocket bullet didn't have time to build up enough velocity to do much damage, and the rebel shrugged off the stinging hit in its shoulder and raised a massive, curved sword of native make.

But Lisa was right behind him, and her shots did more than just sting. The alien flopped on its back with its chest and throat shredded by the hail of needle rounds the woman had fired over Wolf's shoulder.

"I'm out of ammo," she said, throwing the FEK away. "Needles and grenades both."

He didn't answer. His fist rapped the door release, and with a hiss of escaping air the hatch swung up. He clambered in, then turned to help her climb up after him.

"Fire up the fans," he said. "I'll take the gun."

She nodded agreement and settled into the driver's seat as he scrambled to the other side of the cab and took the gunnery chair. The turret on top of the Sandray with its kinetic energy cannon was remotely operated in the APC, and in a pinch the driver could handle both jobs. But two were better, especially in a situation like this one.

The hatch sighed shut, and Wolf discarded his helmet, thankful to be rid of the clumsy thing. Soft red lights illuminated the compartment, and the monitor screens along the front of the cab lit up as Lisa ran her fingers over a bank of control switches. She had taken her helmet off as well, and even in the faint battle lights her face was pale and drawn, smudged with dirt and a large bruise on one cheek.

He checked the power supply for the turret and smiled. Now they had the edge they needed. . . .

Lisa Scott revved the fans, and the Sandray stirred ponderously from the ground on interlocking maglev fields. Wolf moved the joystick in front of him, lining up the glowing green crosshairs on his monitor with a clump of *arbebaril* trees where a trio of rebels had disappeared a moment earlier.

"Firing!" he shouted as he hit the trigger stud.

Lisa wasn't sufficiently familiar with the vehicle to completely compensate for the shot despite his warning, and the Sandray slid back and to one side, but the shell tore into the target. Wolf fired again, then a third time, as his lancemate steered the APC toward the jungle at a deliberate, menacing speed.

He wasn't sure how much longer they kept at it, but eventually it was over. The rebels were in full retreat, and Lisa Scott turned the Sandray back toward the plantation. The battle was won.

Now came the job of counting the cost of that bitter victory. . . .

Morning found the legionnaires back in the protective confines of the Sandray, speeding back across the open sea toward distant Fort Marchand. They had spent the remainder of the night huddled close to the APC, with one cadet constantly on watch in the vehicle's cab and two more walking the perimeter. Only six survivors had come out of the fighting more or less able to carry on, half the original contingent, and the new watch schedule had stretched their resources thin. Not that any of them thought much of sleep in the wake of the battle.

Soon after dawn they'd finally been relieved by a larger patrol in a trio of maglev vehicles, not cadets this time but crack veterans stationed at Fort Marchand for just this sort of work, responding to rebel attacks and tracking their enemies to their lairs in the wild. They were part of a larger force that was spreading across the district in search of the Wynsarrysa rebels who had survived the night's encounter.

Weary from their long night, the cadets had gratefully turned over the responsibility for the plantation to the new arrivals. Now they were safe aboard the Sandray, with a driver/gunner team assigned by the lieutenant in command of the patrol and a medic from his platoon to look after the wounded. In another hour, maybe less, they would be back at Fort Marchand, and the ordeal would be over.

Mario Antonelli wanted to believe that, but he knew that his problems were far from done.

He sat huddled in one corner of the rear compartment, hardly aware of his surroundings. It was a good place to be alone. The medic and his two seriously injured charges were the only other occupants, with the rest of the cadets in the middle chamber. Antonelli wanted to be alone right now. He couldn't face the others . . . not yet.

He couldn't remember much of what had happened in the night, beyond a feeling of paralyzing terror that had gripped him from the moment he and Wolf had first spotted the enemy, but he knew he hadn't taken part in any of the fighting that followed. Antonelli wasn't even entirely sure how he'd come back to the camp after it was all over, though he had a vague memory of Karl Wolf pushing him bodily out of the jungle with a look of utter contempt on his haughty, aristocratic features.

The cadet knew he merited that contempt several times over. He had fallen asleep on watch and allowed the rebels to get close to the camp . . . and when the battle started, he had been completely unable to force himself to do anything useful. From first to last, he had let everyone down, and as a result four men were dead and two more seriously injured. Sergeant Baram and Volunteer Yeh Chen would recover after a stint in the fort's hospital. The same couldn't be said for Corporal Yancey or the three volunteers from Charlie Lance, Banda, Owens, and MacDuff. They would be coming back in another Sandray, wrapped in body bags, making their final trip home.

"No," he muttered aloud. "It's not my fault. It's not."

"What was that, Cadet?" the medic, a corporal named Alvarez, looked up from the litter that held Sergeant Baram.

"Uh . . . nothing, Corporal," Antonelli said hastily. "Sorry."

It *wasn't* his fault, though, he told himself vehemently. Not entirely. Ordering a bunch of half-trained cadets to stand watch over the ruined plantation . . . expecting Antonelli to stay awake after the kind of grueling pace they'd been forcing on him for so many weeks . . . not posting other guards or a watch in the Sandray . . .

No, it wasn't all his fault. He had to believe it. The alternative, to accept responsibility for everything that had happened, was simply unthinkable.

Chapter 18

A lot of youngsters feel that by joining the Legion
they become men—but you don't become a man
overnight.

      —Corporal-chief James Campbell
      French Foreign Legion, 1984

"Ten-HUT!"

Wolf drew himself to attention as the door to the tiny
classroom opened to admit Commandant Akiyama and his
aide. The officer had been appointed to investigate the battle in the Archipel d'Aurore, and Wolf had already had
several interviews with him over the course of the past two
weeks. But this was the first time all of the survivors of
the fighting at Savary's plantation had been assembled together to meet with the commandant. Rumor had it that
today's session would be the last.

Even the battle hadn't been enough to halt the jugger-
naut of Legion training. The survivors of the battle at Savary's had been granted a day off to rest after their ordeal,
but after that it was back to the regular grind. The investigation into the night's events proceeded, but it wasn't
allowed to interfere with the ongoing classes at Fort Marchand. In due course the jungle warfare/reconnaissance
course was wrapped up, and Training Company Odintsev
moved on to the desert warfare training center at Fort
Souriban, located deep in the Great Desert that covered
half of Devereaux's primary continent. Akiyama's inquiry
went on after they settled in to the new post, with hearings
squeezed in to free periods or arranged to fit in with the
platoon's training schedule.

Wolf hadn't been surprised to see this further proof of
the Legion's single-minded determination. Nothing about
the Fifth Foreign Legion surprised him anymore.

"At ease," Akiyama said.

"Take your seats so we can get this thing started," Sergeant Baram growled. He waited as the recruits found places near the front of the classroom, then limped slowly to find a seat off to one side. His kneecap had been shattered in the battle, but after two days in Fort Marchand's hospital he had been returned to limited duty, his leg encased in a regen cast that supported the limb while regeneration stimulators encouraged the regrowth of bone and tissue. Wolf couldn't tell if the irritated expression on the sergeant's face arose from the continuing pain in his leg, or from the prospect of the hearing itself.

At least Baram was back on full duty. Volunteer Yeh Chen had lost an arm in the battle, and that was something the ordinary regeneration process couldn't cope with. He was slated for a medical discharge as soon as the investigation was closed out. The recruit hadn't said much about it, but Wolf knew he must feel cheated. The Legion hadn't even offered to fit him for an artificial limb. His enlistment would be marked as satisfactorily completed and given the customary H&F stamp, which would grant the wounded man the full privileges of Commonwealth Citizenship, but that was all. No accumulated bonus for years of service, and no help to a man who had sacrificed so much to the cause of the Legion. Just a Citizen's dole for the rest of his life . . . and the knowledge that he had been all but abandoned.

Commandant Akiyama and his aide sat at a desk at the front of the room. The investigating officer had a compboard, which he consulted at length before finally beginning to speak. "This inquiry has been convened to consider the events of the past 23 November, standard calendar," he said, matter-of-factly. "The fighting at Savary's in the Archipel d'Aurore, to be specific. It is based principally on the reports each of you has filed, in combination with findings made by other Legion troops on the scene after your patrol was relieved." He looked up from the compboard in front of him to study the recruits. "For the benefit of you trainees, we call an inquiry of this kind any time a Legion unit loses personnel in combat. It is not to be considered a military court . . . although it would be within my power to recommend a full court martial if I felt that events warranted one. As it happens, this matter has proven fairly straightforward, and all questions of punishment can be handled through ordinary administrative disciplinary channels.''

Akiyama looked down at the compboard again. ''Sergeant Menachem Baram . . . ?''

''Sir!'' the sergeant responded crisply. He rose awkwardly and stood at attention.

''Sergeant, I find that you showed poor judgment in your precautions against a possible night attack by the Wynsarrysa at Savary's. You should have been aware of the fact that the rebels frequently double back on targets they have previously attacked for the express purpose of ambushing our forces. Our records show that you chipped the appropriate intel bulletins prior to being authorized to lead recruit patrols in the field. Do you deny this?''

''No, sir,'' Baram said flatly.

''Are there any mitigating circumstances you feel should be taken into account in connection with this finding?''

''No, sir,'' the sergeant repeated. ''I should have posted more guards and kept someone in the APC. I badly underestimated the threat from the rebels, and accept full responsibility for the mistake.''

''Very well.'' Akiyama made a note on the computer's screen. ''Sergeant, you are sentenced to a reduction in grade and relief as a recruit instructor. You will be transferred to a line unit as soon as you are certified for a return to unrestricted duty and a vacancy becomes available. Is that clear?''

''Yes, sir,'' Baram said.

''Legionnaire Myaighee!''

The hannie stood and saluted smartly, none the worse for wear despite his injuries in the battle. A short set of regen treatments had been sufficient to deal with the wounds. ''Sir!'' Although Myaighee looked efficient enough, Wolf thought he could detect a note of concern in the alien's voice. The quills of the hannie's neck ruff were twitching.

''Myaighee, we expected good things from you as a recruit lance leader. After the death of Corporal Yancey, you were the most experienced legionnaire under Sergeant Baram's command and had the responsibility of taking command of the entire unit when your superior was incapacitated. The evidence we have gathered shows that you did not, and your own report indicates that you failed to live up to your responsibilities. Do you dispute these findings?''

"No, sir," the hannie replied. "I . . . allowed myself to become too involved in hand-to-hand fighting and was not fully aware of what was happening on the rest of the battlefield."

Akiyama nodded and jotted down another note. "The fact that you were engaged in combat at the time is certainly a mitigating circumstance. But you have demonstrated that you are ill-suited to a leadership position, and I will be recommending that you be relieved from your current position as Recruit Lance Leader."

"Yes, sir." The hannie didn't betray any more emotion in his voice, but the neck ruff remained in constant motion. Myaighee sat down again, and Akiyama consulted his notes once more.

"Now . . . Volunteer Mario Antonelli."

The Italian stood up slowly. "S-sir," he stammered.

"The reports filed by Sergeant Baram and Volunteer Wolf made it clear that you must bear much of the responsibility for the loss of life in the battle. The attack began as you were in the process of turning over your watch to Volunteer Wolf, but the proximity and number of the attackers suggests that they were able to get into position largely as a result of inattention on your part. Moreover, it is evident that you took no noticeable part in the actual fighting."

Antonelli was pale. "I . . . I . . ."

"Go ahead, Volunteer. What did you wish to say?"

He shook his head. "N-nothing, sir."

The captain regarded him for a long moment before continuing. "Your record has been rather spotty throughout training, Volunteer. Any form of poor performance or misconduct is certainly enough to justify terminating your service with the Legion . . . which could cause you to revert to the penal battalions for the duration of your enlistment, that being your only other option under the terms of your original court sentence. But I am recommending a further investigation of this case, specifically to discover if you might be guilty of gross negligence. If the deaths of your comrades are directly attributable to some failure on your part . . . sleeping on guard, for instance, or being unfit for duty as a result of intoxicant use . . . then you can expect to be sentenced to the penal battalions for an additional period of time to be determined by a court martial board.''

The Italian recruit looked stricken. He turned a mournful glance on Wolf, then stood straighter and met Akiyama's piercing stare. "I understand, Commandant," he said softly.

Wolf looked away from the tableau. He had been honest in his report regarding Antonelli's failure to join in the fighting, but had said nothing about finding him asleep. That had been a hard decision to make. His first impulse had been to bury the young Italian. It had been Antonelli's fault . . . and Robert Bruce MacDuff and the other casualties had paid the price for his lapse. But he had given his word of honor not to say anything about finding the kid asleep . . . and when the time came he hadn't been able to go back on that word. But now Antonelli would probably think he had been betrayed.

"Pending further investigation, you are relieved of all duties and placed on administrative restriction. That means you will drop out of your lance. Transient quarters will be provided. You have the run of the fort, but you will not leave without my express permission or orders from a higher authority. And you will make yourself available for detailed questioning until I am satisfied that I have reached the truth in this matter. Should I find sufficient evidence of negligence, I will order court martial proceedings. Is that clear to you, Mr. Antonelli?''

"Yes, sir," Antonelli said again. He sat down, his shoulders slumping in defeat. He was no longer Volunteer Antonelli . . . and because the courts had taken away his citizenship and wouldn't restore it unless he completed honorable service, he wasn't even Citizen Antonelli anymore. Wolf had never given the matter much thought before, but now he could see how much the honorific might mean to someone like the Italian.

"Now . . . last on the list. Volunteer Karl Wolf."

Wolf stood reluctantly, wondering why Akiyama was singling him out. Would he be held jointly responsible, with Antonelli, for failing to spot the rebels before the attack? Or had Antonelli lied about Wolf's part in the fighting in an effort to save his own skin?

"Volunteer Wolf, the attack began at a time when you were officially on guard duty, but it is the opinion of this investigation that you could not have issued a warning any earlier than you actually did. Therefore you are exonerated of any responsibility for the attack itself."

"Thank you, sir," Wolf said, relieved.

"All reports agree that it was your initiative and steady performance which was largely responsible for the retreat of the enemy force. The Legion demands obedience, but we also encourage initiative. You have been recommended for an Award of Valor, Second Class, and a copy of that recommendation has been placed in your permanent service file. If a Review Board finds in your favor, you will receive the decoration and a twenty-point boost in your recruit standings, which in your case, I believe, would place you near the top of your class."

Wolf didn't respond. He had been treated like a hero ever since the battle, but he still didn't feel much like a hero. He had done what he'd been trained to do, no more. And luck more than courage had carried him through the battle.

The real heroes were the ones who had died. Like Robert Bruce MacDuff, killed trying to reach the Sandray at the height of the fighting. MacDuff, who had been his first friend among the cadets.

"Additionally, Volunteer Wolf," Akiyama continued. "I am recommending that you be awarded the Lance Leader position which Legionnaire Third Class Myaighee previously held. Although Volunteer Kern's combat proficiency scores are higher than yours, your academic standings put you at the head of your lance . . . and I believe your performance at Savary's indicates that you have leadership potential we would be well advised to tap. Your platoon leader will have the final say, of course." The officer gave him a thin smile. "But it is very rare for a noncommissioned drill instructor to ignore the recommendations of an Investigating Officer."

"Y-yes . . . sir. Thank you." Wolf could hardly choke the words out. He had always hoped, secretly, that Myaighee would be relieved of the lance leader's position, but he had never thought they would give it to him instead. It should have been Kern. . . .

"Very good. This inquiry is adjourned. Carry out your orders."

Kern slapped Wolf on the back, grinning, and Lisa Scott pumped his hand, but he hardly heard their words of congratulation. His eyes were on Antonelli as the young Italian walked out of the room, no longer cocky or confident.

He had been angry at the kid for surviving when MacDuff died in the battle. His friend's bravery had stood out in sharp contrast to Antonelli's paralysis, and it just hadn't seemed right that the hero should die while the coward lived on. But this was no fair trade. Antonelli had tried hard and just couldn't measure up . . . but did he deserve an even longer stay than he was already guaranteed with the Colonial Army's infamous penal battalions?

Wolf was the only one who had seen Antonelli asleep that night. His word could condemn the Italian youth to an extra term of hard labor . . . at the cost of Karl Wolf's honor.

He shook his head slowly. Punishing Antonelli further wouldn't bring MacDuff or the others back. The best thing he could do, now, was to let Antonelli know that Akiyama had no evidence of negligence to go on, and wouldn't get any from Karl Wolf. It wouldn't save the kid's Legion career—that was gone, one way or another—and it wouldn't even save him from the penal battalions, since whatever original crime he had committed back on Terra had warranted the choice between the Legion or prison service. But at least Wolf's forbearance would leave him with a shred of dignity.

That was little enough, but it was all Wolf could give him.

The Great Desert was bleak, a seemingly unending expanse of rock and sand where Beau Soleil, the system's primary, beat down without mercy. Legionnaire Third Class Myaighee didn't mind the heat—the temperatures in the jungles of Hanuman soared higher even on a cool day. But ky wasn't accustomed to the parched atmosphere, the dryness so completely unlike anything ky had seen before. The fatigues ky wore, specially tailored for the hannie's small frame, contained climate control settings that adjusted to almost any extremes of temperature, but they weren't designed to deal with different levels of humidity.

Myaighee felt the effects of the desert much more than kys comrades, and needed to drink frequently to replenish precious body fluids.

The whole platoon was on the march, another exercise in desert warfare operations contrived by Platoon Sergeant Konrad less than an hour after the end of the hearing back at Fort Souriban. When they had mustered on the parade ground outside the block of classrooms where Akiyama had passed judgment on them, Konrad had already known the results. He had curtly informed Mario Antonelli that all his effects had been moved to transients' quarters during the hearing, and he had sent the young male-human away without a further word or thought. Katrina Voskovich, the only survivor of Charlie Lance able to return to duty, had been reassigned to Delta Lance in Antonelli's place.

And Karl Wolf had been confirmed as the new lance leader. Myaighee wasn't sure how to take that part of the hearing. Ky had never been happy at being a leader. On Hanuman, kys caste had been everything, and ky had always been a servant. In the Legion ky had found a measure of respect, but as junior member of a lance. The leadership role hadn't come naturally, and ky was relieved not to have to face the responsibility.

But to have Wolf in charge . . .

The male-human from Laut Besar hadn't displayed his contempt for Myaighee openly for a long time, but ky knew it was still lurking under the man's polished veneer. It rankled ky to have the male-human promoted in Myaighee's place . . . as if in confirmation of the man's arrogant claims of superiority.

If only ky had been able to stay in control during the battle at Savary's. In previous fights ky had seen some desperate moments, and the battle madness had helped ky survive. But this time had been different. Ky had paid the price for ignoring the rest of the battle.

It was a price ky was determined never to pay again.

Lisa Scott was grateful for the climate-control features of her uniform coverall. The heat of the Great Desert seemed to suck up every vestige of moisture, but the cooling coils woven into the fabric made it almost comfortable . . . which meant she could focus on a dozen other hardships instead. Her aching feet, for instance, sore after the long route march through the rocky desert. Or the outcome of the hearing, the end of Antonelli's long struggle to make good.

She had no high regard for Antonelli, but Scott couldn't help feeling disturbed by the whole thing. It was all so impersonal, not at all the way she had pictured the life of ordinary soldiers. There was the gigantic military bureaucracy at the top, of course, cold, heartless . . . all the things she associated with her father and his cronies. But she had imagined more sentiment, more of a feeling of fellowship, among the ordinary fighting men and women.

At least the inquiry was over. Now maybe they could put the past behind them. She hadn't known any of the dead recruits very well, but she knew MacDuff had been a good friend of Karl Wolf's. He had been distracted and withdrawn ever since the battle, and his mood had infected her of late. Today, though, Wolf had seemed more concerned with Antonelli's fate, and she didn't know what to make of that. There had been little love lost between the street kid and the aristocrat. . . .

Wolf still looked glum, plodding through the desert sands just ahead of her with his eyes fixed on some unknown point beyond the horizon. She'd expected him to be more pleased at his promotion—after all, he'd never been very happy at taking orders from Myaighee, Legion toleration lectures or no—and at the possibility of a medal. The recruit had certainly earned it, that night at Savary's. But he seemed equally oblivious to both . . . and indeed to the whole world around him.

The slightest of motions made her look down at Wolf's feet. She shouted a warning and lunged forward to push him out of the way. . . .

And felt a searing fire coil around her left ankle.

Wolf stumbled, barely keeping his balance after the unexpected shove from behind. A curse sprang to his lips, but died as he turned to see Lisa Scott falling heavily to the ground. She screamed once, a sound of sheer agony, as the muscles of her leg spasmed uncontrollably and she thrashed on the ground like a woman possessed.

He rushed to her side and started to kneel, one hand reaching for the first aid kit on his web gear. But Kern loomed up beside him and grabbed his shoulder roughly, pushing him back.

"Hold on, boyo," the redhead ordered, his voice harsh. "Sandray . . ."

The Devereaux sandray, which had lent its name to the Legion's primary APC, resembled nothing so much as a Terran manta ray adapted to the environment of the Great Desert. A burrowing predator, it hid under a thin layer of sand with only the tip of its long, flexible tail showing. The appendage contained a breathing tube, a motion-sensitive organ that detected the approach of prey, and a poison stinger. Any of the large animals that lived along the fringes of the Great Desert were prey for the sandray.

They didn't hunt Man by choice, but anyone foolish enough to wander the desert without precautions was likely to make a meal for one of them.

Kern rolled the stricken recruit clear of the sandray's hole with the butt of his FEK, and Myaighee, his own weapon unslung, fired a long, full-auto burst into the ground. The hannie only stopped when dark red blood soaked through the sand layer.

They didn't have much time. Sandray poison spread fast, causing the muscles to convulse and then go rigid. Already she was curling into a tight fetal position, arms wrapped around her stomach, still twitching horribly. Wolf knew that the sandray venom would stop her breathing and her heart within a minute unless she was given prompt first aid. . . .

Then Corporal Vanyek pushed past Wolf, his own first aid kit ready in his hand. "Take it easy, Scott," he said. "This is the antivenom patch." He was already positioning the adhesive pad over her carotid artery as he spoke. Then he produced a knife to cut away the leg of her coverall to put another patch over the wound itself.

The convulsions seemed to ease somewhat, but she was still curled up, her breathing shallow and ragged. She didn't seem aware of any of them.

Vanyek, though, appeared satisfied. "Wolf, Kern, monitor her vitals. I'll call for medevac. The rest of you straks keep your eyes open! This ain't some goddamned walk in the park!"

Wolf bent over her, shaken. It had all happened so quickly, but one fact stood out. She must have seen the questing tail as it moved to strike him, and in pushing him out of the way had taken the attack in his place.

She had saved his life.

"Thanks . . . no thanks are enough," he said quietly, not sure if she could even hear him. He produced his own medical kit and found a sedative patch to position on her wrist. "This'll relax you. Put you to sleep, maybe. You hang in there, Scott. Do you hear me? Hang in there. . . ."

Chapter 19

It is to the mystery of his origins that the legionnaire owes much of his character.
                    —Legionnaire Georges Manue
                       French Foreign Legion, 1929

"Mail call! Form up for mail call! Aiken!"
  "Here, Sergeant!"
  "Ambrose!"
  "Here!"
Wolf skirted the edge of the small cluster of recruits,
cocking his head to listen as the names were called. Mail
call was far from the minds of most of them. More than
half of them, after all, had joined the Legion to break their
ties with the past entirely, and even those who had signed
on with the knowledge of friends or family were unlikely
to start getting messages for some time to come. With
interstellar communications limited to the speed of the
fastest carriership, eight weeks was scant time for anyone
on a distant homeworld to have learned that a recruit had
actually been accepted, much less dispatch a holetter or
message chip.

But on this particular day a lighter had arrived from the
carriership METTERNICH, fresh in from the frontier
around Robespierre. Fort Hunter had forwarded the mail
to Fort Souriban promptly. That was one thing about the
Legion. They were always good about getting mail from
home into the proper hands. Mail call had sounded just as
the evening free period began.

"Antonelli!"
"Here," came the listless reply. Wolf started to angle
across the parade ground to intercept him. He hadn't been
able to talk to the Italian since the hearing had adjourned
the day before, and it was still important to him that he

let Antonelli know that Akiyama's comments hadn't been based on anything Wolf had reported. But by the time he reached the spot where he had last seen the failed recruit, close by Sergeant Konrad and his mail sack, Antonelli was nowhere to be seen. Wolf lingered for the rest of the mail call, just in case something might have arrived from Freidrich Doenitz von Pulau Irian, the consul-general who had befriended him on Robespierre.

As it happened, there was nothing for him, but when Sergeant Konrad noticed him waiting the NCO shoved a small package at him. "Something for one of your lancemates, nube," he growled. "Take care of it."

The address chip on the front responded to his touch with a voice that echoed deep in his mind. "Recruit L. Scott, Fifth Foreign Legion Training Center, Fort Hunter, Devereaux." Almost immediately it grew hot under his finger, and Wolf shifted his grasp on the packet at once. He'd heard of privacy chips before, but hadn't encountered one before. Only the intended recipient could order the chip to open the package. Anyone else who tried to tamper with it would get a nasty burn.

Its presence confirmed Wolf's opinion of Lisa Scott. Only someone very rich or very important was likely to seal correspondence with a privacy chip.

She was still in the fort's tiny hospital, after the Sandray attack the previous day. Luckily Vanyek's first aid had come fast enough, and the fort's medical warrant officer had been able to set her up on a full detox program as soon as the medical APC had brought her in from the field. Wolf was glad of an excuse to stop by and see her. Exercises had kept the recruits occupied almost constantly since the accident, and he still hadn't been able to stop in and thank her properly for what she had done. The thought of taking a dose of sandray venom made his skin crawl. . . .

The ward was small, and Lisa Scott was the only patient. She looked up as he came in, smiling.

"Package for you," Wolf announced, holding it out. "Maybe it'll take your mind off the hospital food for a few minutes." He grinned.

Her welcoming smile turned into a black frown. "Package. But who . . . how . . . ?"

She took it from him, held her fingers over the address chip for a moment. "No! God damn it all, no!" Lisa threw the package at the wall with savage fury. "I should have known he'd find me here!"

Wolf took a step toward her, then checked the movement and the question he had been about to ask. The Legion's no-questions-about-the-past policy was something none of the recruits was likely to violate anymore. Gunnery Sergeant Ortega had already made it clear that no one would enjoy going against that particular quaint tradition.

But she looked so miserable, lying there staring at the offending packet where it had landed beside the door. He struggled to find the right thing to say, then crossed over to the offending object, retrieved it, and raised one eyebrow. "This obviously doesn't belong here," he said lightly. "What should I do with it? Dump it in the fusion hopper? Or plant it out on the grenade range?"

That drew a reluctant smile. "Too easy," she said, her voice husky with suppressed emotion. "I'd want something more creative." She hesitated. "I guess I'd better take it until we come up with something." Another quick smile crossed her face, but her eyes were still bleak.

As she composed herself Wolf laid the packet on the table beside her bed. "At the risk of violating all sorts of Gunny Ogre's rules, is there anything I can do?" he asked quietly. "I've got a sympathetic ear, if you want one. And Lord knows I owe you."

She sat down with a sigh. "I don't know," she said slowly. There was a long pause. "Hell, if the message is what I think it is I won't be keeping secrets long here anyway. Dear Daddy will see to that."

"Daddy?"

She nodded slowly. "Next to the rest of you guys I don't have a very exciting past to run from. I mean, Antonelli's got . . . had . . . his criminal record, and Myaighee turned his back on his own kind to stay with the legionnaires, and whatever Big Red's hiding must be a really big deal. And you . . . the messtalk has it that you're on the run from the war on Laut Besar." She plunged on without waiting for a response. "I'm just a rich kid who got sick of being a prisoner in my own house. So I cut loose and joined the Legion, figuring I'd be safe even from Daddy's long arm. But he found me anyway."

"If what we were told is the truth," he said slowly, "I don't think his finding out is going to make any difference.

They claim the Legion looks after its own, no matter what.''

"Yeah, and I believe in the Milky Way Magician and all ninety-nine of the Ubrenfar hero-gods, too," she said bitterly. "My father's one man who can get his way, Legion or no Legion." She hesitated. "Senator Herbert T. Abercrombie sits on the Military Affairs Committee, after all. If he says he wants his daughter discharged, the Legion's not going to buck him on it."

He let out a long, low whistle. "Abercrombie . . . ?" Even on Laut Besar, where Commonwealth politics weren't of much interest, Abercrombie's name had been well known. The terrorist attack two years back that had killed the Senator's wife and left his only daughter wounded. . . .

His only daughter . . .

"You're Alyssa Abercrombie?" he went on, hardly believing it. "The one who—"

She nodded wearily. "Yes, the teenaged heroine who avenged her mother by killing a terrorist and making a daring escape from a hotel window." She recited it in a singsong voice. "God, you'd think the media would have got sick of it before the story made the interstellar circuit. They never bothered to cover the trial where the rest of the gang got off on some legal shortcut the compols took arresting them."

"That kind of attention . . . it must have been pretty tough."

"Yeah, and the Semti War was a mild disagreement between reasonable beings," she shot back. "First I was the famous heroine. And by the time the story finally started dying down Daddy was convinced I'd be a bigger target than ever, and that's when it really got bad."

"So you decided to strike out on your own."

"You sound like you really understand it," she said, a note of surprise in her voice. "Anyone I ever talked with before thought I was crazy for wanting a life of my own." She looked across at the unopened package on the table beside her. "Money and clout never seemed very important. I mean, it was nice to have, but I would have given it all up if it could have brought my mother back. And living for what everybody else wants . . . it's . . . I don't know. I can't really explain it right . . ."

He thought of his own life. His father was long dead,

but his uncle had expected young Wolf Hauser to be a good aristocrat. Those expectations had taken him to the Sky Guard Academy . . . to the fighting on Telok and the duel on Robespierre. "I hear you, Lisa. Alyssa, I mean . . ."

"It's Lisa here," she told him. "And . . . thanks. It's nice to know there's one person who doesn't think I'm just an ungrateful, spoiled little rich girl."

He gave a sour laugh. "Hell, you turned your back on it all to go after what you wanted. My family had money and political connections, too, and I spent my whole life doing exactly what I was told to do just because that's the price an aristo's supposed to pay. Noblesse oblige, and all that garbage."

"So what changed? How'd you end up here?" She raised an eyebrow. "If you don't mind my asking . . . at the risk of violating all sorts of Gunny Ogre's rules."

"The Ubrenfars took away my planet," he said bitterly. "And some of my own kind took away my honor. I decided that was one price I couldn't pay."

It was a letter, an old-fashioned scribed letter that had been dictated to a computer and printed on paper. His parents had never been able to afford a holorecorder.

Antonelli crumpled the paper in his hands, but the action couldn't erase the words that had burned into his mind. *What else can happen?* he asked himself bitterly. *Haven't enough things gone wrong already?*

He had been struggling to keep up with the other recruits, and had even started making some progress . . . right up until the battle at Savary's. That had ruined everything. The commandant's announcement that he would be headed for the penal battalions hadn't been much of a surprise. Antonelli had been prepared for that inevitable consequence of failure for a long time. But the possibility that he might be punished for his part in the battle was something else entirely. He'd never expected that. Never thought Wolf, for all his arrogance and superiority, would betray him.

And now his father was dead, and his mother was sick. Uncle Giuseppe's letter made it clear where the blame lay. Salvatore and Nunzio and some of the others from the old gang had started shooting their mouths off, and his father

had overheard them, learned about the court sentence. It
had been too much for the old man's heart to learn that
his son had dishonored the family, had lied about everything. All that pride gone in one moment, and nothing to
take its place but death . . .

Tears stung Antonelli's eyes, and he sat down heavily in
the single chair in his Spartan transients' quarters, still
clutching the letter in one fist. His parents' pride had been
all that had held him on course. Without it, what did he
have left?

The penal battalions would claim him now. After all his
efforts, all his struggles. They'd all been useless. . . .

Antonelli chucked the paper away. There was really only
one option open to him now, and he had to take it quickly,
before he lost the will to go through with it. . . .

Wolf paused outside the hospital door and checked his
wristpiece. The miniature computer was tied in to the fort's
much larger database, and it was easy to query the personnel files for a room assignment. After a few seconds
the screen displayed the information he'd asked for, and
Wolf gave an approving nod and set off across the compound.

It was high time he saw Antonelli. He'd put off the confrontation too long. Somehow the whole incident, from
the battle at Savary's right through the hearing and even
Lisa Scott's accident, had all made Wolf doubt his place
in the Legion more than ever. MacDuff had died, and Scott
had come close to it herself, and either one of them was
better Legion material than he was from start to finish.
And Mario Antonelli, though he wasn't much of a soldier,
had tried with all his will to make it and still failed. Wolf
hadn't put in one-tenth the effort to fit in. What right did
he have to succeed where the kid had failed?

And what guarantee was there that Wolf *would* succeed,
in the long run? Myaighee, who had the advantage of past
Legion experience, hadn't kept his lance leader's star. Even
if he kept his nose clean and did everything the Legion
demanded, a rebel bullet could still strike him down the
next time he had to fight. . . .

He had always understood the dangers of a soldier's life.
The possibility of death was something he'd accepted long
ago, even before the Ubrenfars attacked Laut Besar. But

he had come to terms with the problem by thinking of it in the traditional aristo fashion. He was an aristocrat, and it was his duty to fight, and if need be die, for his world. His honor and his family name demanded no less.

But what was he putting his life on the line for in the Legion? His name wasn't even his own. These weren't his own people, by any stretch of the imagination. Their customs and beliefs were like nothing he had been raised to revere . . . with these notions of species equality and all the rest of it. The Fifth Foreign Legion was nothing but a mercenary unit in thin disguise, fighting for money or personal glory or the sheer love of violence. Wolf found it hard to think of putting his life on the line for any of those things.

His mood was thoroughly black by the time he reached the transients' block. This Foreign Legion adventure had been a mistake, pure and simple. Wolf . . . *Hauser* knew that now. He should have taken his chances with Neubeck's family.

But he still had a duty to perform here and now. Wolf stood for a long moment outside the door of Antonelli's room, gathering his thoughts, trying to put aside his own problems and focus on the Italian instead. Perhaps he could tap Doenitz on Robespierre for a loan to help Antonelli out once his sentence was finished . . . ?

There was no answer when he pressed the intercom buzzer.

Wolf shrugged. Maybe Antonelli had heard about Volunteer Cromwell's secret still and was out drowning his sorrows. He would just have to keep trying.

As he passed the single tiny window next to the door, an odd flicker of motion caught his eye. Wolf looked into the room, curious.

The limp body of Mario Antonelli was swinging back and forth from a rope dangling from a light fixture on the ceiling. He was clearly dead.

Antonelli's funeral was quiet and subdued, with only a handful of the recruit's comrades and instructors in attendance. Wolf stood rigidly at attention between Kern and Volunteer Mayzar, convinced that Konrad and the other NCOs were keeping close watch on him.

It was a Catholic service, like the majority of religious

observances in the Legion. When Mankind reached out for
the stars it had been a largely European effort, with Catholic France in the vanguard of interstellar expansion, and
when France became an empire and dominated Terra and
the colonies the religion had taken firm root on dozens of
worlds. Perhaps as many as three-quarters of the people
who called the Legion home followed some version of the
faith.

But on Laut Besar it had been different. The Indomay
community followed Moslem, Hindu, or Buddhist beliefs
on the whole, with a sprinkling of Catholic and Christian
Protestant adherents, while the Uro upper classes who had
any religion at all were almost entirely Protestants who
had brought their faith with them from the German-settled
colony world of Lebensraum.

Wolf himself had grown up in a largely agnostic atmosphere, and tended to scoff at religious pomp and ceremony. But today, standing in the hot afternoon sun, there
was something comforting about Father Chavigny's solemn words.

The chaplain finished by making the sign of the Cross,
and Ortega nodded to Vanyek. The corporal stepped forward, and Wolf, Kern, and Mayzar followed. They lifted
the plain wood coffin and lowered it carefully into the
ground. As the four men stepped back, Chavigny sketched
the Cross again before turning away.

A work detail with shovels moved in to cover the coffin
with earth, and the funeral was over.

There would be no eulogy, no headstone, nothing but a
shallow, unmarked grave for Mario Antonelli. He hadn't
even died a legionnaire. Just a suicide who had found his
disgrace impossible to bear.

Wolf lingered, looking down at the grave as the others
left. He tried to analyze his feelings and found that he
could not. Antonelli hadn't been much of a lancemate, but
he had deserved better than this. It was typical of the Legion to ignore him in death after hounding him to the
breaking point in life.

Something stirred behind Wolf, and when he looked he
found Myaighee there beside him. The hannie hadn't been
told off as one of the pallbearers because of his small size,
but as one of Antonelli's few real friends the little alien
had come to the service, Wolf found himself wondering

what Myaighee thought of the human religious service, then realized that he had probably seen it many times before while serving in Fraser's Bravo Company.

The alien knelt beside the grave and fumbled with something at his throat. It was a small vial which hung from a chain, hidden by the neck ruff. Myaighee opened the vial and carefully added a few grains of sand from the earth the workers had used to fill in the grave to a layer of dirt inside the container. Then he sealed it up and returned the vial to its place.

"A custom from your planet?" Wolf asked the hannie.

"No," Myaighee said quietly. "A custom of the Legion. When a comrade falls, dirt from the grave is collected in one of these containers. I carry a reminder of all the friends I have lost, and of the worlds they fought for, wherever I go."

Wolf sniffed disdainfully. "Another Legion tradition. Wonderful."

"I have learned that there is great comfort in tradition, Wolf. It might help you, if you would only let it." The alien didn't wait for a reply. Myaighee turned away, leaving Wolf alone beside the grave.

He stood there for a long time, lost in thought. When he finally walked away, he saw Vanyek coming back into the quiet cemetery. Wolf stopped and watched the corporal from a distance and was surprised to see the man kneel and take a small sample of dirt from the grave.

Chapter 20

You're given a hard time and you can't relax. If you can't take it, you shouldn't have joined in the first place. I've changed a lot since I joined the Legion.

—an anonymous Legionnaire
French Foreign Legion, 1984

The sign over the bar door read THE WHITE KEPI, and the entrance was flanked by a pair of mannequins clad in Legion dress uniforms. It was a popular watering hole for legionnaires from Fort Hunter, located a block from the maglev terminal in the seedier side of Villastre known as Fortown. The owner, Jacques Souham, was an ex-Legion NCO who had chosen to invest his retirement money and Citizen's stipend to build a business on Devereaux, rather than migrating to some more popular world. That was how the Commonwealth did business. Citizens had power and prestige on frontier worlds like this one, and over the years their numbers grew until they could bring the planet painlessly into Terra's star-spanning empire.

Karl Wolf clutched the package in his hand a little more tightly and went inside. The bar was dimly lit and crowded, and though there were plenty of legionnaires within there were a fair number of civilians as well. He even noticed a table of Gwyrran-descended Wynsarrysa natives in one corner. Not all of the ales on Devereaux were rebels.

The smell of narcosticks and cheap synthol made him choke, and Wolf regretted agreeing to use the bar as a meeting place. He hadn't particularly wanted to come into Villastre in the first place, even though this was the first pass the recruits had been granted since the start of training. Since the training battalion had gathered back at Fort Hunter for the holiday break in their schedule, Wolf's idea of recreation had been to seek out some precious moments of privacy so he could think . . . and try to map out his future.

But Lisa Scott had wanted to do some Christmas shopping in town, and she had talked him into coming with her. They had split up at the maglev station, setting The White Kepi as their rendezvous point, and Wolf had dutifully battled the crowds in the city's commercial district in search of token gifts to give to the rest of his lance. He wasn't very satisfied with his purchases, but thought it was probably just his bad mood influencing his judgment.

He spotted her, sitting alone at a table near the Gwyrrans in the corner. She waved, and with a curt nod he pushed his way through the crowd to join her. When he reached the table he saw that she had turned to examine a display of knives on the wall above her. Her interest in them brought back a flash of memory, the sight of her that first night in the platoon shower room, her knife at the ready to hold off young Antonelli.

A lot had happened since then, he thought bitterly as he put his package on the table and sat down opposite her. More than he cared to think about, today.

"Glad to see the decor's to your taste," he said, trying to keep his tone cheerful and light. In the ten days since Antonelli's suicide he had been fighting hard to avoid letting his ill humor show, but it took an effort. Wolf had never been much interested in small talk, and it was harder than ever to keep from sitting and brooding when the people around him were enjoying themselves.

She smiled at him. "You bet. This guy Souham's got a great collection. So how did you make out? Find what you were looking for?"

A waitress in a tight-fitting, low-cut parody of Legion fatigues appeared to take their drink orders. He checked the chrono function of his wristpiece. Another maglev car would be leaving for the base in thirty minutes. Enough time for a beer, perhaps . . .

He ordered, then looked back across the table at Scott. This excursion had been her idea. Was she ready to head back yet?

"Find what you were looking for?" she asked again, seemingly ignoring his byplay with the 'piece.'

"Some," he said shortly. "But I still agree with what

my father told me when I was a kid. If we had been meant to mingle with crowds of shoppers, God never would have invented computer shopping networks.''

She laughed. ''That would take all the fun out of it,'' she told him. ''Anyway, you can't haggle over the price with a computer.''

''I wouldn't have imagined you as the haggling type,'' he said absently. ''Not much need to haggle when you've got money. . . . '' The words were already out by the time he realized what he had said. Since that day in the hospital at Fort Souriban he had been careful not to mention anything about her background.

But Lisa didn't seem put off by his comment. ''Where else do you want to try?'' she asked. ''We've got time.''

He sighed. ''Look, I think I'd rather head back to the tube station and catch the next car to Hunter. I've had about all the holiday shopping I can take.''

''If that's what you want,'' she said with a shrug. ''But if you still have stuff you need to pick up . . .''

''Hell, I don't even know what to buy,'' he told her. ''I mean, you and Kern are easy enough, but what the devil am I supposed to buy for an alien who never even heard of Christmas until he joined the Legion? What *do* you buy a hannie, anyway?''

She looked at him with a stern expression. ''You really don't like Myaighee much, do you?''

Wolf shrugged. ''I don't dislike him,'' he said defensively. ''It's just that nonhumans aren't real common back home, and I don't know how to deal with them.''

''Try treating them the way you would anybody else. As long as you keep thinking of every nonhuman you meet as something different, you'll always treat them as inferiors. Myaighee's a better person than a lot of humans I've met, and he doesn't deserve this human superiority act of yours.''

''Hey, I went along with him as lance leader. I took his orders when he bothered to give any.''

''Sure. but everyone could see that you resented it, Wolf. How would you like it now if one of us started acting that way toward you?''

He looked away. ''Doesn't matter much now,'' he said slowly.

''What are you talking about?''

"I don't think I'm going to Kessel next week," he said slowly. The thought had been nagging him for days, and he said the words with a feeling of making a decision at last. "I don't think I can make the grade in the Legion, Lisa. Maybe it's time I just admitted it and left the soldiering to the people who are qualified for it."

"Nonsense!" Now she looked angry. "You've got the highest score in the lance, and I heard Konrad telling Vanyek the other day that you're still in the top ten in the whole company. You can't just give up!"

"We're only partway through," he pointed out. "There's plenty of time for me to screw up yet . . . especially now that they gave me the lance. Look what happened to Antonelli. He was finally starting to show some progress. Then he screws up once and . . ." He trailed off, picturing the body swinging back and forth in the tiny barracks room back at Fort Souriban.

"Antonelli was a whole different case," she said. "Nobody knows the whole story. He did, but he'll never tell it now. He muddled through as long as he could, but you know how close he was to a downcheck the whole time. When they finally cut him, he couldn't take it. Pure and simple. So don't sit there and use Antonelli as an excuse. He didn't have what it takes. You do."

"Do I?" he asked. "Really? The only thing I had in common with the kid was not fitting in around here. I just can't buy into all the mystique. The traditions they try to foist off on everybody to turn us into obedient little drones. 'Honor and Fidelity' and 'the Legion takes care of its own' and all that drivel. They didn't take very good care of Antonelli when the chips were down . . . or even Yeh Chin, who couldn't help getting hit before the real fighting started."

He looked down at the table. "I didn't see anybody rallying around to help Antonelli when he got in trouble. Not the rest of our class, and certainly not the regular legionnaires. Do you know that when a lance came to take down the body and investigate his quarters they took the rope he'd used and cut it up to sell as *souvenirs?* Another of their damned traditions . . ."

"I know," she said. "It's supposed to be a good luck charm, or something. The superstition goes back to the very beginning of the Legion, back on Terra."

"My point is, they weren't worried about *him*. Just like most of the other recruits didn't even bother to come to the funeral." He thought about Myaighee and Vanyek taking dirt from the grave, but dismissed it. Just another superstition . . . it had nothing to do with their feelings about Antonelli himself. "So where do they get off preaching about camaraderie and dying for the Legion and all that garbage? You've got to believe if you expect to get anywhere in this outfit, and I just don't believe."

"Oh, come off it," Lisa said harshly. "You don't believe the advertising hype, and right away you think that makes you doomed to failure? That's ridiculous." She reached across the table and took both his hands in her own, fixing his eyes with her ice blue stare. "Yeah, the mystique can be pretty damned silly sometimes. But it isn't just empty words. If that was true, Banda would have left Yeh Chin to bleed to death when the fight started at Savary's. And your friend MacDuff wouldn't have rushed the Sandray trying to save the rest of us. Do you think he believed all the crap they've been feeding us about Camerone and Hunter and all the rest? I doubt it. But he thought enough of his duty . . . and of the rest of us . . . to put his life on the line when we were in trouble. As I recall, you were doing the same thing. But where was Antonelli? Crouching out in the woods somewhere, wasn't he? You never said so, but I saw the way you were looking at him later on. He was afraid, wasn't he? Don't compare yourself to him, Wolf. And don't try to make him a martyr. He killed himself, because he couldn't take the pressure."

"Yeah. Maybe." He nodded reluctantly. The scorn in her voice hammered at his newfound resolve, but deep down he wasn't convinced. And he was sure that Antonelli had taken his life largely because he believed Wolf had betrayed his trust, and that was a stain on Wolf's honor that couldn't just be dismissed as unimportant.

The waitress returned with their drinks before he could say anything more. He took a cautious sip of his beer and set it down with an expression as sour as the beverage tasted. Most of the crops grown on Devereaux picked up a tart flavor from the local soil. But all legionnaires professed to enjoy Devereaux products, and even though he had enough money in his ident disk to buy offworld imports he had decided long since that it was best to blend in as much as possible.

He was starting to think that protective coloration wasn't worth the assault on his taste buds. Beer had never been his favorite drink before signing up anyway, and this local brand . . .

Not that it mattered much anyway. If he went ahead and resigned, he wouldn't have to keep up the pretense much longer, and even though Lisa Scott had made some good points she hadn't really said anything to make him change his mind.

Lisa gave a sudden, mirthless laugh. "Wouldn't you know it," she said with a bitter smile. "You want out, but I'm the one who has a father pulling strings. And I'd give damn near anything to stay. . . ."

He couldn't find any way to answer that.

The silence went on, and deep in thought, Lisa Scott drank her beer without noticing its tart flavor.

She had joined the Legion with the firm intention of keeping others at arm's length. That was another legacy of the kidnapping and its aftermath, the reluctance to allow anyone to get close again. Long ago she had started dividing the universe up into three distinct groups—the masses of people who had nothing to do with her or hers, the ones who wanted something from her, and the few who were genuinely worth caring about. The latter category, she had found, were in danger of dying or being sent away. Alyssa Abercrombie had vowed that she wouldn't hurt—or be hurt by—anyone else again.

But Karl Wolf had gotten past her defenses somehow. She still wasn't sure how to define her feelings about him. There was some physical attraction there, but she thought of him more as a friend than as a potential romantic interest. Growing up as the Senator's only child, she could only imagine what a brother might have been like, and perhaps that was how she regarded Wolf. An older brother, someone who understood her, someone she could look up to . . .

But it was hard to reconcile the Wolf she was seeing today with the man who had turned the tide at Savary's. If he went through with this idea of resigning, it would be a terrible waste. Not that it could really matter to her. As she had expected, the package from her father had been one of his holocube lectures, ending with the promise that she would be out of the Legion just as soon as the paperwork was over and done with. Another week or two, at most. She wouldn't even get the chance to put on the white kepi.

It was ironic that Wolf wanted out even though he had everything going for him, while she wanted to stay in but couldn't escape her father's long arm. People adapted to the Foreign Legion at different rates, she decided, thinking back to a discussion in the lance's barracks at Fort Marchand a few nights before the battle at Savary's.

They had been comparing their views of the training process. Kern had talked about the main obstacle that every trainee had to overcome sooner or later, called "the Hump" by some, "the Wall" by others. Every military recruit, whether he served in the Legion or the Centauri Rangers or the Commonwealth Space Navy, found it hard to make the transition from civilian to soldier. In the Legion the pressure was particularly hard because the conditions were much harder than in ordinary services. The first goal of any Basic Training, according to Kern, was to break down the individuality of recruits so that they could learn to subordinate themselves to the army as a whole. In a state as diverse as the Commonwealth, and particularly in the polyglot Foreign Legion, harsh treatment was one way to encourage would-be soldiers to let go of that individuality. Not only were tongue-lashings and the occasional beating effective methods of getting a point across, but the recruits also tended to be drawn together by a common resentment toward their instructors. It was a tough process, and the only options open were to adapt or to fail. That was the real essence of the Hump.

Most Legion recruits just opted out, earned their downcheck and gave up all hope of a successful five-year hitch with a Citizen's benefits at the end of it all. But for some, the Hump was too much, especially when there were pressures from other directions that made failure as impossible to face as the training the recruit couldn't handle. When that happened, anything was possible. It was like cafarde, the classic Legion disease, starting with a little voice whispering the gospel of hopelessness and ending with madness, suicide, desertion . . . depending on the individual recruit, almost anything could happen.

It had happened to Antonelli, though he hadn't actually broken until after the Legion had ordered his discharge. But she had never expected to see it happen to Karl Wolf. And it worried her . . . in more ways than one. Why was she suddenly so concerned over how Wolf lived his life?

But whether she liked it or not she did care. But she didn't know how to reach him. Plainly he needed to cling to that sense of individuality the Legion was just as determined to squash. She could understand that much, at least. An aristocrat, accustomed to command, would find it hard to surrender the freedom that was an essential part of his makeup. It was easy enough for her to make it past the Hump, because compared with life with Senator Abercrombie the Legion for her was a genuine taste of freedom.

If only she could help make Wolf see that he could become a part of the Legion without giving up everything of himself . . .

"Well, fancy that," a voice said at her elbow. "A couple of genuine junior white-caps in for a look at the big city!"

She looked up. A trio of teenagers in motley civilian dress were looming over their table. The speaker was short and slender, and his cocky manner reminded her instantly of Mario Antonelli in the early days of training. His two friends were larger and seemed ready to take their lead from him.

"Hell, I guess we're lookin' at the future of our fair planet," one of them rumbled. "The next generation of protection from the lokes and the ales, huh?"

Neither recruit answered. Lisa took another drink and studied the display of knives on the wall.

"Hey, junior white-caps," the leader persisted. "Maybe you can tell us why your Legion won't let us change things around here. We're ready here for Membership . . . but it's you white-caps who won't let us have it. Isn't that right? Explain it to me, why don't you?"

She looked him over slowly, coldly. "I'm not up on local politics," she said in a quiet, reasonable voice. "We're just marchmen signed up for a hitch."

The political situation on Devereaux was a complicated

powderkeg with twists and turns she was only vaguely aware of. The planet's human population had once been ruled by the Semti Conclave, but the Terran Commonwealth had liberated the world and made it a Trust. In the usual course of things a slowly expanding Citizen base would eventually have been able to form a government able to apply for full Membership, with votes in the Grand Senate and a voice in the administration of the Commonwealth as a whole. But conditions weren't that straightforward. There was the ongoing problem of the Wynsarrysa rebels, for one thing. And there was also the problem of the Fifth Foreign Legion.

Devereaux was the official home of the Legion. It had been built on the ruins of the Fourth Foreign Legion that had died defending the world in the Semti Wars, and for over a hundred years it had been home to the current outfit. But unlike other units of Terra's Colonial Army, the Legion was not permitted to be directly tied to any one Member of the Commonwealth. Individual worlds fielded military forces that served in the Colonial Army—the Black Watch from Caledon, for instance—but by statute the Legion was drawn from all parts of the Commonwealth and even from worlds outside the Terran sphere. If Devereaux became a Member-world, the Legion's connections would have to be severed, and that was something most legionnaires found unthinkable.

There are inevitably rumors that the Legion had blocked every attempt to gain Devereaux a better place in the Commonwealth, even accusations that the Legion was secretly fostering the Wynsarrysa risings in order to make itself seem indispensable for the planet's defense. And there was a vocal body of human colonists who were calling for the expulsion of the Legion. . . .

"C'mon," the agitator insisted, getting louder. "You come here to our planet to perpetuate your Legion rule . . . but you don't want to own up to it, do you? Afraid people will learn the truth about you? We're sick of having the scum of the galaxy calling this their home. So why don't you leave and find some place that wants you?"

A few of the other civilians applauded. The other legionnaires, though, had gone silent. The atmosphere was suddenly tense.

Wolf stood, a smooth, fluid motion. "Why don't you

go peddle your politics to someone who cares, Citizen?''
he said, soft-voiced.

"Citizen!'' The agitator hooted. "You think me and
mine have a chance to be Citizens? Hah! The only way we
get to be "Citizens'' is if we go out and take what should
be ours! Like this!''

His fist lashed out at Wolf, but the aristo parried the
blow easily. Then one of the toughs grabbed him from
behind, and the other reached for Lisa Scott. . . .

She ducked and pushed back her chair, bringing her foot
up in a roundhouse kick in the same motion. Her boot
caught him in the kneecap, and he fell heavily. Wolf elbowed his attacker in the stomach and pulled free. They
were back to back now, facing the two remaining rabble-
rousers. A few other civilians were starting to move toward
the fight, as if to join in. . . .

Until the legionnaires scattered around the bar surged
forward.

There was a long moment of deadly silence. Then a loud
humming broke the quiet. A scarred man wearing an apron
over old Legion fatigues with the name "Souham'' prominent on the right breast stepped onto the floor, a stun
baton in each hand. From the pitch of the hum they were
both set on full power. "Break it up, you scum,'' the man
growled. "Take your politics out of here and leave my
comrades-in-arms alone!''

For emphasis he lashed out at the leader of the toughs.
The young man screamed and backed away, clutching at
the livid welt on his bare arm.

As suddenly as it had started, the fight was over. Civilians and legionnaires alike drifted back to their tables and
started drinking and talking again. But a couple of noncoms stopped to clap Wolf on the back, and Souham ordered another round for the two recruits, on the house. He
shook Wolf's hand before retreating behind the bar again.

Sitting down opposite Wolf again, Lisa Scott smiled.
"Looks like you've got to take back a few of the things
you were saying before, Wolf,'' she said.

He raised an eyebrow. "Such as?''

"Well, if you don't call that rallying around a fellow
legionnaire, I don't know what would qualify.''

Wolf looked thoughtful as he took another swig of beer.

Chapter 21

I started out a soldier of this Foreign Legion, and
now that we are reunited once more I know that
nothing can defeat us.
> —Marshal F'Rujukh's Order of the Day
> Battle of Frenchport, Ganymede
> Third Foreign Legion, 2419

A holiday air filled the familiar confines of the mess hall.
According to the intricate conversion of the standard Terran calendar and clock to local Devereaux time, Christmas
Eve had started at 0934, and had run for over twenty hours
now. Legion tradition guided the celebration of the holiday
as it did so many other things, and according to that tradition four training companies and the entire staff of Fort
Hunter had gathered in the mess hall at 2630 hours local—
about 1700 hours GMT, Christmas Eve, according to Terrestrial timekeeping—to start an ongoing round of eating,
drinking, and partying punctuated from time to time by
more serious or ceremonial moments. This was the Christmas vigil, and everyone not on duty was expected to attend.

Wolf sat in a dim corner of the hall, feeling out of place
amid the merrymakers. At the far end of the huge room a
space had been cleared. At "midnight" an improvised al-
tar would be moved into place so that Father Chavigny
could hold mass. For now, though, the area was a stage
where groups of recruits were putting on skits or singing
Christmas carols to entertain the audience. Right now six
recruits and Corporal Vanyek were singing a haunting holiday song that had originated with the noncom's Slavic
ancestors. Another group was huddled to one side hastily
improvising the skit they were supposed to do next.

He took a long swig of punch and set the empty cup on

the table beside him. Ever since the excursion with Lisa Scott he hadn't been able to put his feelings in order. Part of him still wanted to make it through Legion training, to prove that he really did have what it took . . . but he was growing more aware each day of his inadequacies as a soldier. A very basic part of him resisted the entire process of giving up his individuality. He wasn't sure he'd ever be a cog in the Legion machine.

On the maglev tube car heading back from Villastre he'd asked Lisa for advice. Somehow she seemed able to deal with the situation even though her background, like his, had been one of privilege and ease.

"It's all a matter of giving them what they want," she said with a shrug. "I got used to that from years of pleasing my father. It isn't an all-or-nothing proposition, Karl. You can bury your individuality far enough to please the powers that be without losing sight of who you are entirely."

Watching the other recruits mingling amid the Christmas festivities, he wondered again if he'd ever be able to strike that balance.

"You're quiet tonight," her voice broke in on his sour thoughts. He looked up to see her standing behind his chair, sipping a glass of wine and watching him through thoughtful eyes.

"Yeah. Still a lot on my mind."

Lisa smiled. "The least you could do is let down for Christmas! What's it take to put a smile on that face, anyway?" She didn't wait for an answer. "Did you see the cribs? They're really incredible!"

Each company had entered one Nativity crib in competition, and the four entries were lined up along one wall. Wolf had been drafted into the work party Sergeant Ortega had put together to set them up. "Yeah," he said slowly. "Er, they're not . . . not exactly in the holiday spirit, some of them."

She flashed another smile. "I'll say. Especially ours."

Training Company Odintsev had submitted a crib that showed three bearded legionnaires abseiling from a hovering transport lighter into the midst of a typical Nativity scene. Volunteer Hosni Mayzar, who'd been in charge of the project, had entitled the composition "The Hostage Rescue of the Magi." No one was entirely sure if the Moslem recruit was having his own little joke at the expense of his Christian comrades. . . .

But it was eye-catching, intricately detailed, and Vanyek thought it stood a good chance of winning Father Chavigny's First Prize award despite—or perhaps because of—the unusual blend of theology and small unit tactics.

The thought made Wolf smile despite himself. Mayzar, at least, had kept part of his own individuality intact. And Antonelli had played a big part in the design and execution of the crib before his untimely end. Maybe Lisa had been right after all.

"Did you see the one Schiller's bunch did?" he began, trying to keep up this end of the conversation. "It's—"

He was interrupted by a disturbance at the double doors ten meters away, where a cluster of officers and noncoms had suddenly stopped comparing notes on the training program so they could greet a new arrival. Wolf had to strain to see through the throng.

The object of all the attention was an unprepossessing sight, a frail, white-haired woman in a life-support chair. Her legs and lower torso were completely enclosed by the chair's mechanism, but she wore a Legion uniform jacket. The rank device was like a sergeant-major's, but with an extra rocker and a black star added, and a long strip of chevrons denoting her time in service. Wolf wasn't familiar with any such insignia, but plainly the legionnaires around her, even the officers, were treating the old woman with considerable deference and respect.

She had a right to respect, Wolf thought, just on the basis of age. Regen therapy could extend life by a fair number of years, and bionic and geriatric medicine could do even more. But sooner or later—say after a hundred and twenty five or so—the human body just couldn't keep repairing itself no matter how much artificial assistance the high-tech doctors could bring to bear. At that point, full-support wheelchairs or beds were the only way to keep the aging body alive. More often than not the mind went first, though.

But this woman's eyes were sharp, almost supernaturally alert and bright. And, frail though she looked in that chair, it was plain that she wasn't ready to give up the fight for life just yet.

"Who the hell is she?" Wolf asked aloud. Beside him, Lisa shrugged.

"Keep your voice down, nube," another voice countered in a hoarse stage whisper. It was Sergeant Konrad, leaning against the wall nearby. He moved forward and took a seat beside Wolf. The platoon NCO had plainly been drinking and looked as unsteady as he sounded. "Show some respect. That's Aunt Mandy."

"Aunt?" Wolf asked, raising an eyebrow. "Whose aunt?"

Konrad looked disgusted. "That's what we call her in the Legion. That's Amanda Hunter, for God's sake."

Hunter . . . "You mean, as in *Fort* Hunter?" Lisa asked, echoing Wolf's thought.

The sergeant nodded curtly. "Of course. Commandant Thomas Hunter's wife. She was hiding out up in the hills of the Nordemont range when her husband died in the attack on Villastre."

"That was a hundred and twenty years ago. . . ." Wolf said softly. "That means she must be . . . what? A hundred and fifty?"

"One hundred fifty-three last month," Konrad said with an air of pride. "She's the last surviving member of the Hunter family. And the only living link to the Fourth Legion. When they ordered the Fifth established, she was given the honorary rank of chief-sergeant-major. When she finally dies it will really be the end of an era."

"But what's she doing here?" Wolf pressed. "A woman with her name could have her pick of the high society balls on Devereaux. Age and an historical name are always a sure route to invitations."

"She's here, nube, because this is where she wants to be," Konrad hissed. "Every year since the Fifth Legion was formed she's attended one of the Legion Christmas vigils at Fort Hunter. This year she chose the Training Battalion. You should count yourself lucky, nube. Aunt Mandy might not be around too many years longer." The tough sergeant looked like he was about to break down and cry at the thought.

Gunnery Sergeant Ortega got behind her chair and helped guide the old lady toward the front of the mess hall. Vanyek and the other carolers had finished, and the recruits preparing for the next skit looked relieved at the interruption.

Long minutes went by as the officers and NCOs arranged themselves around the life-support chair. Then an officer, resplendent in dress uniform and heavy braid, stepped forward and nodded to the legionnaire at the sound systems panel. The technician adjusted the directional sound pickup, and the officer cleared his throat.

"Good evening and Merry Christmas," he said. His voice was clear throughout the mess hall, but didn't sound distorted or amplified. "Many of you don't know me by sight, but you've cursed my name often enough. I'm Commandant Stathopoulos, commander of the Training Battalion here at Fort Hunter. Tonight we have been honored by a visit from a very special lady we fondly call Aunt Mandy. Every year she picks out one unit at the base to share Christmas with. This year it's our turn, and as usual Aunt Mandy has picked out some presents for all of you here. When you hear your name called, come up to the front and take your gift."

A sergeant took over, bawling out a name at a volume louder than any technical augmentation would have allowed. Wolf tuned out the proceedings and muttered an excuse to get away from Sergeant Konrad. The NCO was fearsome on the parade ground. Half drunk and maudlin he represented an entirely different set of problems.

Lisa Scott followed him to the door. "You're not leaving, are you?" she asked. "You'll be in trouble if they call you up and find out you wandered off."

He shrugged and sat on the floor beside the open doorway. A cool breeze was coming off the desert, and it felt good after the heat of the crowded mess hall. "More of their precious tradition," he said gruffly. "They trundle this woman in here and get her to hand out little trinkets to make the recruits think somebody really cares." He shook his head sadly. "They fall for it, too."

Lisa slipped her hand inside her uniform jacket and drew out a flat package. "Well, here's one trinket that comes from somebody who does care," she said. "Go ahead . . . open it."

The plain wrapping paper covered a plastic case. Inside rested a silver medallion. He drew it out and squinted at it in the poor light.

On one side the medallion bore the tricolor-and-V of the Fifth Foreign Legion. On the other . . .

"How in the name of God did you find this?" he demanded. The reverse side bore the stylized coat of arms of the Hauser family. "I never even told you my name . . . !"

"No," she admitted. "But you had that crest stamped on the inside of your wristpiece. I . . . er . . . exercised my reconnaissance skills one night when you were showering, and a craft house in Villastre did the rest."

"It's . . . great." Words weren't adequate.

"When you look at it, think of it as the balance you've been looking for, Karl." She smiled. "I just hope you don't opt out now. Not after I had them put the Legion emblem on it."

He swallowed. "I'll have to keep that in mind. Thanks, Lisa." He smiled at her. "Alyssa. I don't feel right thanking someone who doesn't really exist, you know."

Wolf spotted a silver chain coiled in the box and went through the motions of attaching the medallion to it. With Lisa's help he settled it in place around his neck and tucked it under his uniform shirt.

"I bought you a present, too, but I'm afraid I can't give it to you for a few weeks," he told her.

"What is it?"

He grinned. "A knife, to replace the one our beloved corporal took that first night."

"A knife. Now there's a fine present to give at Christmas!"

"Well, if you don't want it . . . I mean, it's just a Novykiev Spring Knife, no big deal."

"A Novykiev . . ." Her eyes were wide with surprise. "How did you lay your hands on one of those?"

The lineal descendent of a weapon first used on Terra before starflight was born, the spring knife combined a fine hand-to-hand edged weapon with a powerful spring mechanism that could propel the blade thirty meters or more with deadly accuracy. The best were made on the colony world of Novykiev, where they had enjoyed considerable vogue as a hunting weapon for a time. Since the Riots of 2839 and the imposition of martial law, though, Novykiev Spring Knives had become scarce as hens' teeth.

"Found an old legionnaire who'd picked up a couple as

souvenirs back in thirty-nine,'' Wolf said with a smile. "He decided he could afford to part with one."

He didn't mention the fact that it had taken most of the credit in his ident disk to buy the weapon from old Corporal Souham in town. He had gone back to the bar the day after the fight specifically to get the weapon for her. The cost hadn't seemed important even though he had nothing left now but his meager Legion salary . . . and if he ended up resigning he wouldn't even have that.

But he owed this woman his life . . . and more. The knife was perfect for Lisa Scott.

"I—I don't know what to say," Lisa told him. "You shouldn't have gone to that kind of trouble. . . ."

He touched his jacket where the medallion lay. "I thought it was the best way I could pay you back after you helped me start to sort things out the other day. Among other things. And whether you stay in the Legion or your father pulls you out, you'll need the extra edge. A very sharp one."

Lisa made a face at the pun. Before she could reply, Kern's gentle voice interrupted her. "They're going through the gifts up front by units," he said quietly. "Our platoon is up next, and it might be a good idea if we were ready for it. If it wouldn't be interruptin' anything important here, that is." Wolf looked up to see the big redhead favoring them with a suggestive leer.

There was a line of recruits moving past the officers and NCOs by Aunt Mandy's life-support chair. Lisa and Wolf joined the line.

They moved forward slowly, but eventually they approached the old woman. Wolf couldn't hear what was said to Myaighee or Kern, but as Lisa's turn came he heard Gunnery Sergeant Ortega say her name and saw Amanda Hunter nod. She looked up at Lisa and held her eyes for a long moment before speaking.

"Captain Odintsev tells me there has been a request for a certain Lisa Scott to be released from her provisional contract immediately," she said in a dry but surprisingly firm voice. "From what I hear there is quite a lot of pressure being applied from a very high level indeed."

He could see Lisa's shoulders slump in defeat. The old woman gave a dry chuckle, and it was all he could do to keep from stepping forward and shouting at her. Why had she ruined Lisa's Christmas this way?

Then he caught a glint of gold in her hand as she held something out to Lisa. "My gift to you is a choice, my dear. The ident disk you're wearing is about to be updated with new orders requiring your discharge. This one, on the other hand . . ." She chuckled again. "The Lisa Scott this one describes has a different serial number, a whole different background. We don't often change a legionnaire's identity again so soon after starting Basic, but if you don't want to leave the Legion . . . Well, by the time anyone found out and started searching for you again, you'll have the white kepi, and no one can make you leave then, my dear. No one."

For the second time that night Wolf saw Lisa speechless. She took the gleaming ident disk and finally managed to stammer out an awkward thanks.

Then it was his turn.

"Volunteer Karl Wolf," Ortega said. At Amanda Hunter's gesture he backed away out of earshot.

When the old woman looked up at him, Wolf could see her eyes glittering with something that might have been amusement . . . or understanding. She nodded slowly. "I've seen your file," she said. "Your real one, not Karl Wolf's recruit file. I like to know a little something about the people I give gifts to, you see, and I'm old enough and respected enough to get my way."

She held out a flattened box, an adchip module. "You've come to the Foreign Legion from a culture that's quite different from your own, Wolfgang Alaric Hauser von Semenanjung Burat," she went on. "Not as different as some alien ones, admittedly, but still . . ." She seemed to pause to gather her thoughts. "It may seem like you're facing pressures no one else has ever had to meet. When my husband was alive . . . but that's a different story. The fact is, the path you're on now has been well trodden over the centuries, young man. You might benefit from seeing how one of the ones who went before walked that path. A merry Christmas to you . . . Karl Wolf."

He smiled and nodded and mumbled something he hoped was appropriate and moved on, surprised at what she knew about him and hardly aware of the gift in his hand. The old lady had put a lot of thought and effort into these gifts, more than he would have believed reasonable. Earlier he had sneered about the Legion snaring foolish recruits with worthless trinkets. Now he knew better.

Wolf found a chair and touched the chip module to the side of his head, just behind and below his left ear. The chip clung there after he released it from the module. He closed his eyes and triggered it with a thought.

For a moment he was far from Devereaux, on an empty, airless plain below a cluster of half-ruined domes. Without being told he knew this was Ganymede, a colony known as Frenchport, and the end of the French interstellar empire was drawing near.

A figure was visible in the scene, only vaguely humanoid with four arms and a low, domed sense-organ cluster instead of a head. Even clad in an old-fashioned vacuum suit the alien seemed to exude an air of authority and competence.

"In 2419 A.D. the only nonhuman ever to hold the rank of Marshal of France faced his last and greatest challenge," a voice only Wolf could hear said deep in his mind. "Marshal F'Rujukh, outnumbered, outgunned, without hope of retreat or relief, led a mixed army of Imperial forces into combat in a campaign that would cost him his life. But in the process he earned a place few can match in the annals of military history."

There was a fanfare of music. "F'Rujukh ended his life a Marshal of Imperial France, but his beginnings were by no means so auspicious. Forced to flee his homeworld of Qwar'khwe when the planet fell under the sway of a military dictatorship, F'Rujukh entered the Third Foreign Legion as a common soldier. Years later he lived up to an ancient Legion saying: 'The only way for us foreigners to repay our debt to France is to die for her.'

"Though not of Terra, he shed his blood for Mankind's sake."

Wolf terminated the biochip and returned from Dreamland bemused. A few weeks before he would never have thought that he could be interested in the career of an alien, no matter how distinguished his place in history.

Now he was looking forward to studying that career in the hopes that it might help him shape his own.

Chapter 22

To be a good soldier, one has to leave his personality at the barracks gate, become wax which receives all impressions, put his tongue in his pocket, hide the resentment in his eyes . . . and despite all that display everywhere a finesse and a superior intelligence.

—Legionnaire Charles des Eccores
French Foreign Legion, 1873

The Christmas holiday was over, and the training had moved into a new phase which Gunnery Sergeant Ortega had promised would be at a more intense level than ever before. Where the specialty work before the break had focused primarily on honing specific skills, the new round of instruction was supposed to bring everything the recruits had assimilated before together into a single, unified approach to soldiering.

The recruits had been given passes into town for Christmas afternoon, and the following day was one of light duty. At morning assembly on the parade ground a new set of reorganizations had been announced, abolishing the training company's fourth platoon entirely and absorbing the lances from that outfit to fill in vacancies in the other lances. It still left Wolf's platoon, the Second, understrength, with only four lances instead of six. Charlie Lance had ceased to exist as a result of the casualties taken at Savary's, and Foxtrot Lance was now broken up to fill in other vacancies in the TO&E. Any further losses, they were told, wouldn't result in further changes in the company's organization.

Wolf's lance was unchanged by the reshuffling of other units, to his relief. The problems of trying to lead a lance were daunting enough when he knew most of his troops from their weeks of shared training. Katrina Voskovich was already an unknown quantity, and he was happy there would be no others to deal with.

Somewhere between the Christmas Eve vigil and that first postholiday assembly the idea of Wolf's resigning had faded away. He wasn't sure what had turned the tide. Aunt Mandy's presents, both to him and to Lisa Scott, had made him reexamine his image of the Legion . . . but the medallion his lancemate had given him was like a talisman. It seemed to symbolize what was possible, and he was unwilling to put it aside. Unwilling, also, to let her down after she had shown confidence in his ability to continue.

He wasn't sure if he had actually found his way over the infamous Hump during the holiday, but at least Wolf had found a new resolve to keep on trying, whatever might happen.

Now they were on the move again, heading for a new base of operations near Fort Kessel in the rugged Nordemont region a few hundred kilometers north of Villastre and Fort Hunter. Unlike their previous training assignments, this time around they would be spending the whole two-week period in the wilderness, conducting full-company exercises in competition with some of their opposite numbers from one of the other training companies. They might go the entire time without ever seeing Fort Kessel, sleeping in field habitats or under the open sky.

As with the previous changes of base, they were ferried into the mountains aboard a Pegasus transport carrying all the troops and equipment assigned to the platoon. This time they weren't to have any vehicles, which meant they would have to hump their gear over rough terrain on their backs. Still, Wolf told himself, it was probably better to handle this part of the training in the Nordemont than, say, in the Archipel d'Aurore. Long marches with full field packs in those dense jungles, and with the threat of Wynsarrysa rebels lurking behind every tree . . . he was definitely glad they had done their vehicle patrol exercises at Fort Marchand. First Platoon had drawn field exercises there, and he didn't envy Suartana and the others in that outfit.

The Nordemont mountains were a startling change from the other regions where the Legion carried out training exercises. They were well to the north of the subtropical

zone around Villastre, and latitude combined with altitude
to make the area considerably cooler than the more heavily
settled areas of Devereaux. The climate was still largely
arid, and the mountains, though far from barren, were clad
in a sparse scrubby growth. Down in the valleys there were
lush forests, but so far these had gone largely unexploited
by the human colonists. Large bands of Wynsarrysa were
reputed to roam those valleys, some hostile, some merely
hoping to be left alone. Few were ever seen along the
higher slopes.

Their transport's landing site commanded a particularly
spectacular view, and even hard-bitten noncoms like Konrad and Vanyek were drawn to the edge of the plateau
where the platoon had been instructed to set up camp to
look down into the deep, narrow confines of Mistfloor
Gorge. The Blanc River, the largest on the continent, had
carved a deep canyon through this part of the mountains.
Dropping over a magnificent waterfall, the river vanished
below a perpetual cloud of mist at the valley floor.

According to Wolf's chipped briefing, the Mistfloor
Gorge was also the termination of the annual migration
route of the nasty little animal native to Devereaux known
as the strak. Combining the worst features of several Terrestrial species, including the rat, the lemming, and the
cockroach, straks traveled in huge bands from their breed-
ing grounds in the northern wastelands, dying by the thou-
sands here at the Mistfloor Gorge every year. It was little
wonder that their name had passed into the Legion lexicon
as a sort of all-purpose swear-word that could refer to appearance, uncleanliness, stupidity, sexual obsession, or any
of a number of other bad qualities commonly attributed to
the disgusting little creatures.

And the gorge held a special significance for the Legion,
as so many things did. Somewhere on the far side of the
canyon a network of caves had been used by the Fourth
Legion as a base during the guerrilla campaign against the
Semti, and later as a refuge by Amanda Hunter and other
family members after the legionnaires had doubled back
into the inhabited regions along the edge of the Great Desert.

Looking down into the tumult of white froth deep in the
canyon, Wolf thought he could understand why the Legion

would esteem this place. It was the sort of landmark around which legends were bound to be built.

"What's the matter, you straks?" Vanyek's voice broke into his reverie. "Want to follow your kin and take a jump? Well, go ahead . . . or else get back to work!"

The spell was broken. Wolf turned away from the vista and concerned himself with the practical problems of helping Kern and Myaighee set up Delta Lance's field habitat.

Six days of arduous marching and mock fights that were difficult to distinguish from the real thing had confirmed the promise of harder work in this new phase of training. They never remained in the same camp for more than a few scant hours, rising well before the local dawn each day to pack up their gear and set out through the wilderness for a new position. These forced marches made Wolf long for the routine twenty-kilometer hikes of days gone by, and they were usually punctuated by skirmishes with Training Company Hamilton either en route or at the end of the day's journey.

They fought their battles using modified FEKs and support weapons fitted with low-powered training lasers that registered hits by interacting with the microcircuitry in their fatigues. A hit would cause the chameleon cloth to turn a lurid red, making it quite clear when a recruit had become a casualty. By the fifth day Wolf was becoming quite used to being seen in red . . . and to the inevitable dressing-down Vanyek or Konrad would give him and the other simulated casualties for allowing themselves to become targets in the first place.

Tonight, though, the lecture he was receiving was of a different kind.

"If your lance had been in its proper position, nube, the ambush would have gone perfectly." Vanyek jabbed him in the chest with two fingers, but Wolf stayed at attention. "As it was, your little band of nightslugs was twenty minutes late showing up, and you came in from the northeast instead of the east. That gave the enemy just the kind of opening they needed."

The exercise had been an elaborate battle of maneuver, with the four lances of Konrad's platoon each taking a different route through the hill country to converge on a command post in a centrally located valley. Delta Lance had set out at the same time as the other units, but Katrina Voskovich, who had been rotated to duty as the lance's pointman for the day, had managed to take the wrong path halfway through the march. By the time anyone had realized it, they'd been committed to the new route, which led to a point near their target but took them over much rougher terrain.

Wolf fought down the impulse to respond to Vanyek, and the corporal jabbed him again, harder this time. "If it hadn't been for Mayzar, those reinforcements coming in from the east would've cut up our assault faster than you could say 'dishonorable discharge.' In a *real* fight, nube, you can bet we'd be licking our wounds now, all because you decided to take the scenic route instead of following orders!"

Again he held back. His instant reaction was to defend himself from Vanyek's charges. He wouldn't have picked Voskovich for the point position in the first place, but she had been foisted on him by Vanyek's own rotation schedule. Kern wouldn't have made a mistake like that . . . even Myaighee would have done better. Although Voskovich, like the hannie, had seen action with Fraser's famous Bravo Company, she had been a civilian electronics technician who had been forced by circumstances to fight alongside the Legion, and her experience had been minimal. She still didn't have very good combat instincts despite her training, and though she had been brave enough at Savary's her contribution there hadn't proved very helpful overall.

And the whole mess had been her doing from first to last. That, to Wolf, made the corporal's tirade doubly bad. Wolf had done his best to redeem the situation. . . .

But he held his silence. The Legion's creed held that the unit was supposed to look after its own, and Delta Lance was Wolf's outfit. The leader had to take responsibility for what all of his charges did . . . and there was no point in complicating the situation by trying to make Voskovich share the blame.

Vanyek's eyes bored into his own for a long moment. Finally the corporal stepped back. "All right, nube," he said. "Your lance pulls the mule duty for the rest of the week. And you . . . I want you on guard tonight. All night. You get me?"

"Yes, Corporal," Wolf responded.

"All right. Free time for two hours. Fall out!"

Fuming inwardly, Wolf headed across the platoon's campsite until he found Kern and Myaighee putting the finishing touches on their field habitat, or fab as it was commonly called, the portable, inflatable hut that could hold a five-member lance with minimal discomfort. Lisa Scott handed him a ra-pack and a mug of thick Devereaux coffee fresh off the fire, and Wolf sat down on a log to eat and sip and think.

He had learned, these last few months, that legionnaires looked out for one another, and that a leader should always accept responsibility for the actions of the soldiers in his command. But he had learned something else from the Legion as well. No mistake ever went unpunished. Sooner or later, any error had to be redeemed by proper action. In the case of Katrina Voskovich, the punishment for her inattention at point would be shared with the whole lance when they had to undertake mule duty, carrying all the excess baggage of their section on future forced marches. Each lance was responsible for personal and lance gear, but there were always extras that had to be carried— medical supplies, demolitions gear, spare ammo for the heavy weapons, and so on. When there were no vehicles on hand, some legionnaires had to be told off to carry this additional baggage, and it was a common form of punishment to assign the duty to individuals or lances who were under a cloud.

So Voskovich would not face any specific penalty to encourage her to think twice the next time she tried to read an electronic map at a crucial fork in the road. Not unless Wolf himself handed down that punishment . . .

He had seen lance leaders in the company teach an errant recruit a lesson by tying them inside a sack and getting the rest of the outfit to kick and punch the helpless target. That kind of brutality repelled him, but it was all too common in the Legion's ranks.

Wolf looked up from his steaming mug to see Vanyek watching him from the far side of the camp. Something in the corporal's expression told him that Vanyek was expecting him to take some sort of further action. If he didn't, he was all but inviting trouble. The corporal could give Wolf low marks if he didn't handle the situation right . . .

or he might step in and start handing out fresh punishments that were a lot less pleasant than mule duty.

Voskovich couldn't be allowed to escape punishment completely, so it was up to Wolf to handle it in such a way that it didn't go further than Delta Lance.

On Laut Besar, Uro women were cherished and protected. That had been part of what made Lisa Scott interesting, her independence and ability to look after herself. But it was hard for Wolf to even consider meting out punishment to a woman like Voskovich . . . harder than he would ever have imagined. Despite all the Legion training, there was still a lot of the Uro aristocrat in him. But something had to be done, and as he finished his drink and his evening rations he thought he had a way to handle the problem.

"Listen up, people," he said, hardening his resolve. "We've got some time to ourselves here. I think we could put it to good use brushing up on unarmed combat techniques."

"Unarmed combat?" Kern said, an eyebrow raised in curiosity. "Any particular reason, boyo?"

"Yeah," he said. He motioned Kern closer and then gave him a quick jab to the ribs. "Yeah. Because I say so, that's why. Any problem?"

The blow hadn't been a hard one, and the big redhead could have come back and flattened him. But the punch and cuff were the accepted signals in Legion ranks that a superior intended an order to be carried out, and Kern just grinned and nodded. "Unarmed combat it is," he said cheerfully.

He led them away from camp to a clearing screened from view by a line of trees and set them to work. Each recruit in turn took on Katrina Voskovich in one-on-one combat. The attackers could rest while a comrade took her on, but Voskovich herself had to keep on fighting. By the time it was all over, two grueling hours without rest had taken a toll on Voskovich and left her with a set of bruises to remember it by. Nonetheless, the violence had been controlled throughout.

Wolf felt smug as he led them back to their fab afterward. Perhaps he was finally getting the hang of leadership after all.

And Stefan Vanyek, watching the proceedings from the cover of the trees, nodded approval as Delta Lance left the field. For a time, Volunteer Wolf hadn't been considered good Legion material. He was too independent, too conscious of his own privileges, to be a legionnaire, no matter how well he performed academically.

But Vanyek had always believed there was a capable legionnaire somewhere inside the pampered aristocrat, and now he knew he had been right.

Wolf would make it after all.

After the end of the Nordemont training, the company was reassigned to Fort Gsell, the Legion's orbital facility positioned in a synchronous orbit over Fort Hunter, for the final phase of their instruction. The other companies in their training battalion shared this duty, uniting the entire recruit force for the first time since the beginning of the process three months earlier. Things would have seemed crowded, but Fort Gsell was a large station, and in zero-G, space utilization was far more efficient than anything possible on the ground, so the quarters and training areas allocated to the platoon were actually roomy.

The focus of the training in the orbital station was on zero-gravity and zero-pressure combat, learning to convert ordinary battledress fatigues into space suits. Wolf was in his element now, for the Sky Guard training he had received back on Laut Besar had included extensive training in these areas, and he had practical experience as well.

In fact, the training was an unpleasant echo of the last fight for Telok. He woke up several nights running from a nightmare replay of the battle, thrashing against the tether cord that held him in place while he slept in zero gravity. A medical warrant officer prescribed a sleeping patch which helped some. So did a long talk, off duty, with Lisa Scott. It helped to tell her about the fight on Telok, and afterward the dreams weren't quite so vivid or terrifying.

The most notable event of their stay was the arrival of fresh news from the Republic Trisystem. The Ubrenfar leadership had rejected a Commonwealth demand for the evacuation of Laut Besar, and the CSNS *Genghis Khan* had been attacked by a small squadron of Ubrenfar patrol ships inside the orbit of Danton. The Warlord-class cruiser had driven her assailants off, destroying two and forcing a third to surrender. According to unconfirmed reports leaking from the Commonwealth news media, the attacking Ubrenfar ships had belonged to a different warclan from that which had staged the original occupation, suggesting that the confrontation was now widening on both sides of the frontier.

The batch of letters and messages accompanying the news had included a brief holo from Consul-General Doenitz. Wolf had holoed him a few times during training, but this was the first message back. The old diplomat congratulated him on his progress in the Legion, and mentioned in passing that the Free Besaran units Neubeck had been mustering were now on Danton, preparing for the expected push to reclaim Laut Besar from the invaders. Viewing the holetter, Wolf felt a twinge of regret. He had been questioning his reasons for serving with the Legion, when there were reasons aplenty for him to be part of that army confronting the Ubrenfars. His mistakes dealing with the Neubecks had barred him from taking part in the only military career that would have been truly worth his support. . . .

He didn't send a reply right away. The holo had raised new questions in his mind, and Wolf wasn't sure how to deal with them. It was pretty much accepted that he would pass Legion training with flying colors, and on one hand the thought of overcoming all the obstacles he had faced along the way was encouraging. But the knowledge of past failures diminished the achievement in his mind.

The zero-G portion of the training proved relatively easy overall, though the company suffered four men killed in the company from suit accidents over the course of the first week. Then they moved into more complex operations, practicing high-altitude atmospheric insertions in Legion transport lighters. The drills taught the recruits the basics of High-Altitude/High-Opening parawing operations, so that the legionnaires could jump from a ship high in the atmosphere and have a fair chance of reaching the ground in one piece. There were three more deaths in that stage, and Lisa Scott came out of the training with a regen cast on one leg but an unyielding determination to pass the final test that would determine which of the recruits had the honor to don the white kepi at last.

Wolf knew that test would be a tough one . . . but he also knew that he could pass it. He could be—*would* be— a legionnaire.

Chapter 23

I figure it's like this: being a civilian is easy; being a legionnaire is easy; but the difficulty is the change.

—an anonymous legionnaire
French Foreign Legion, 1984

"Five minutes! Five minutes to drop coordinates!"

The interior lights of the assault shuttle switched to red, and recruits began checking each other's gear one last time. They had done this plenty of times during the last week at Fort Gsell, but Wolf could feel the difference in the air, in the purposeful movements of his comrades . . . and most of all in himself. This assault jump was unlike any they had practiced before. This time he and his lancemates would be on their own from start to finish.

Sixty-eight recruits had finished the orbital operations course at Gsell with high enough marks to move into the last phase of their training—the two-week cross-country endurance test which was the final challenge for every legionnaire. They were to be dropped high above the Nordemont wilderness, descending by parawing. Each lance was supposed to come down, assemble, and then make their way overland with minimal equipment, ending up at Fort Hunter. The lances that made it through would pass the training. Those which didn't . . . some might be picked up by Search and Rescue craft later. But the drill instructors had made it clear that no recruit class ever underwent the final test without suffering casualties.

The fact that he was aboard the shuttle today was proof that Wolf really did have what it took to be a legionnaire. In fact he was number six in the training company, a respectable score indeed. But even the best of them could still wash out in this course.

"Three minutes! Delta Lance, on the line!" Gunnery Sergeant Ortega was serving as Jump Master today, checking to make sure each recruit was fully prepared when he leapt from the hatch. After that, the sergeant's responsibility ended. Tomorrow, in fact, he would be working against them, leading a small force of legionnaires and instructors into the wilderness in search of the recruits. Ortega's troops were one extra hazard to be overcome. Anyone captured by the patrols would get an automatic downcheck.

The five recruits made their way to the rear of the fast-flying shuttle, weighed down by their field packs and the bulky parawings strapped to their backs. Wolf looked them over one last time. He knew that Ortega was doing the same, but this was too important to leave to anyone else. The arrangement of personnel and equipment for the drop might be absolutely crucial to their survival.

Kern would jump first. The big redhead was the strongest member of the lance, and he was weighed down by more than his fair share of the equipment. Myaighee was too small to carry a full load, so Kern had to hump the hannie's share of the communal load. The little ale would be following Kern down, ready to assist him on the ground. Voskovich, and then Lisa Scott, would go next, with Wolf jumping last. He hoped he could coordinate the descent so they wouldn't become too badly separated on the way down. . . .

They looked ready. Wolf gave a tight nod and turned to face Ortega. "Delta Lance, ready, Sergeant," he reported crisply.

The Hispanic noncom pointed to the hatch. "Coming up on one minute," he growled. "Get ready."

Ortega moved down the line, starting with Wolf, checking parawing packs and other fittings. He tapped Wolf on the top of his combat helmet before moving on to Scott.

Finally he reached the head of the little line, finished inspecting Kern, and slapped the switch beside the hatch. It swung open, and air whipped around them like a small hurricane. Wolf was glad for the safety line that held them together until the moment came to jump.

"Ten seconds!" Ortega called, reading off the numbers displayed over the hatch. "Five . . . four . . . three . . . two . . . one Go! Go! Go!"

One after another the recruits jumped. As Wolf reached the head of the line his eyes met Ortega's, and the sergeant gave him a brief smile. Wolf dropped his faceplate down and stepped through the hatchway.

The wind tore at him like an animal, and for a moment he was back in the freefall conditions he'd become so familiar with from all the practice at Fort Gsell. Wolf closed his eyes, and the image of the fight in the warehouse on Telok flooded into his mind unbidden. The same thing had happened every time he'd practiced, a few seconds of near panic, disorienting, almost paralyzing, until he could force himself past the memory.

When he finally opened his eyes he could see two parawings open far below and off to the left. Kern and Myaighee, probably . . . Wolf adjusted the image intensifier setting of his faceplate and nodded. The redhead and the alien had their wings extended to ride the air currents all the way down. A flashing sequence on his helmet's HUD display counted down the seconds before his own parawing would unfold.

The number hit zero, but nothing happened. . . .

Malfunction! Wolf fought back another tide of panic and groped for the manual release. His fingers found the control at his belt and tightened around the trigger grip. An instant later he felt the straps around his chest and shoulders dig into his flesh as the wing opened up and checked his plummeting descent. His sigh of relief was almost audible over the rushing of the air past his helmet.

The parawing was a lineal descendent of the old-style parachutes of ancient Terra. Constructed of extremely lightweight materials, it could be stored in a small backpack, but unfolded into a small glider which gave the rider excellent maneuverability in the air. The wings were independently managed by a small computer which could alter their configuration to get the best possible lift and control in any situation. The descent could be left entirely to the computer's discretion, or modified as necessary by simple commands entered through the belt control box.

Wolf called up a descent profile on his combat helmet's faceplate. The miniature computer's projection said he was right on target for the preselected LZ, so he let go of the belt control and let the parawing do its work unattended.

Instead he concentrated on making sure the rest of the lance was also going in according to plan.

He had checked each of his lancemates in turn when he lost sight of Kern's parawing. Even though he'd been expecting it, Wolf went through a moment's fear before he reminded himself it was all part of the program. The parawings were made of the same sort of chameleon cloth that was woven into Legion battledress. The helmet chip, tied into sensors in the fatigues, picked up surrounding light waves, analyzed them, and altered the reflective value of the fabric to duplicate the background shades as closely as possible. From above, the parawing tended to blend in with the greens, browns, and grays of the planet's surface below, while an observer on the ground would have trouble telling the wing apart from clouds and blue sky. A quick change of his faceplate setting called up flashing symbols that identified the location of each member of Delta Lance, and he was able to relax again. Everyone was on target. . . .

Long minutes later, with the ground perceptibly closer, Wolf switched from computer to manual control of his parawing, using the air flow to bank in a long slow circle over the LZ. From this vantage point he could scout out their surroundings and make sure Ortega hadn't arranged any special surprises to complicate the landing exercise. Finally he keyed in his commlink.

"Delta One to all Deltas. Lima Zulu is clear. Repeat, Lima Zulu is clear."

"Delta Three, acknowledging," Kern responded. "Commencing final approach . . . now."

Each recruit glided in to the narrow clearing Wolf and Kern had selected as the landing zone during their pretest planning. Although the instructors knew the general area, even Ortega himself didn't know the exact spot where the lance was landing, a clearing along the banks of a stream that fed into the Blanc River just above the Mistfloor Gorge. They had covered this ground thoroughly during the Nordemont training exercises. There was a route down from the plateau into the lower land below the gorge, and their plan called for a stealthy overland move to another tributary of the Blanc to the south. There they could build a small raft that could take them downriver quickly and in comparative comfort. By moving only at night, and concealing themselves along the bank in daytime, Kern had figured they could make it to Fort Hunter in a week. That would give them an ample cushion in case they encountered unexpected difficulties along the way.

Wolf came down last, a little clumsy despite all the practice they had put in. He overshot the clearing and ended up touching down in shallow water, much to the amusement of Kern and Lisa Scott.

But in this test style didn't count. They had made the drop successfully, and that was what was important. Now all they had to do was elude the hunters and reach their destination. . . .

Myaighee moved through the brush silent and unseen, like one of the phantoms of kys homeworld's rich tradition of myth and legend. Twenty-eight hours had passed since the lance had touched down, and they were still working their way through the rugged hills toward the mouth of the Mistfloor Gorge. The terrain was supposed to be familiar from the training exercises they had gone through prior to the tour at Fort Gsell, but familiarity didn't help that much. It was still a confused tangle of trails and tracks. Ky remembered the time Katrina Voskovich had misdirected them, and was doubly wary as a result. Wolf had assigned the hannie point duty, and ky was determined to come through for the lance. The memory of Savary's, and the shame of being replaced by the male-human aristo, were both burning reminders that ky needed to do the best possible job on this test, no matter what.

And today's reconnaissance was absolutely vital to their march. This section of the Nordemont range was well guarded by the Legion against the possibility of a Wynsarrysa incursion. Several hostile tribes lived to the north of the so-called Hunter Line of fortifications and outposts, and the Legion's main function was to keep those potential foes from penetrating this perimeter and threatening the settled lands to the south, especially the city of Villastre. Checkpoint Tatiana, a permanent outpost manned by a reinforced section of Legion infantry, was perfectly placed to interdict the route the recruits wanted to take down to the Blanc River, and it was vital that they work their way past the position without being noticed. Right now Myaighee's job was to determine just how tough a job they faced, and ky was determined to do the job quickly and well.

It wouldn't be easy, though. Ky had already spotted several areas covered by a mixture of remote motion sensors and clusters of Galahad antipersonnel mines. The latter, fortunately, were on stand-by mode. In a combat situation the Galahad could be set up for any of a number of trigger systems, including a recognition-friend-or-foe setting which would set the weapon off the first time anything of roughly human size moved into the lethal radius without a working combat helmet broadcasting an acceptable identification code. But that was impractical for permanent defenses, and Myaighee had determined that these mines were all controlled from the checkpoint itself by remote detonators.

The sensors were another problem. But Myaighee's size made ky the ideal scout in this situation. Like the Galahad recognition system, the sensors were set to pick up certain types of body heat, sound, or moving objects of a roughly human-sized mass. Ky was small enough to move in among the sensors. Those which threatened the unit's safe progress could be temporarily disrupted with the right equipment from Myaighee's small field pack.

Ky could hear the sound of running water nearby. That would be the Sinueux River. Checkpoint Tatiana should lay on the far bank, beyond the bulk of the low, hump-backed hill ahead. . . .

Myaighee sniffed the air. Something was wrong . . . a smell that didn't belong . . .

The smell of fire. Of scorched wood and charred vegetation. Of burnt flesh.

Ky flipped up the visor of kys combat helmet for a better look. The late afternoon sun was dipping low beyond the hills to the west, but there was plenty of light to see by. And the coil of smoke rising from the direction of the checkpoint confirmed Myaighee's first fears.

It took five more minutes to reach the bank of the river beyond the projecting ridge line. Crouching in dense brush, Myaighee studied the far bank with a sinking feeling gnawing at kys stomach.

A long time later, ky departed as cautiously as ky had approached, heading back along the path in search of the others. They had to be told.

The exercise had just turned deadly.

* * *

Checkpoint Tatiana was still smoldering.

The five recruits had reached the outpost well after dark, but their LI gear made the nightmarish scene all too visible as they crossed the narrow foot bridge and passed through a gap in the surrounding duracrete berm. Wolf couldn't help but remember Savary's as he surveyed the damage here. There had been no ritual mutilations here, but the attackers had sacked the place even more thoroughly than the Wynsarrysa had at the plantation. And there were plenty of bodies in evidence.

The post wasn't large, just a low berm enclosing a few buildings, a landing area large enough for a Pegasus transport craft, and a reinforced command bunker near the center of the installation. Four of the buildings were little more than permanent fabs, one for each lance normally stationed there. A fifth structure had served as a storehouse and armory, but there wasn't much left there now. The attackers had ransacked the place first, then burned everything they didn't want or couldn't carry off.

The attackers had been Wynsarrysa tribesmen, apparently, if the scattering of Gwyrran bodies around the perimeter was any indication. The defenders hadn't taken very many foes with them, which Kern claimed probably meant a surprise assault. There were mysteries which needed to be cleared up, such as how the attackers had penetrated the sensor and mine nets in the first place. There were also three bodies which didn't belong at all . . . humans in civilian garb, all apparently cut down by FEK fire just outside the command bunker. Who they were and what they were doing in the outpost, were questions Wolf had to put off answering, though. They had other work to do.

It was plain the perimeter line had been breached. A body of rebels that got past Checkpoint Tatiana was well placed either to strike toward the inhabited zone between the mountains and the Great Desert, or to turn northeast and overpower Fort Gsell from the rear. And the garrison at Kessel had been reduced to provide Ortega's roving patrols for the training exercise.

The Legion had to be warned. But how?

"The command bunker's a wreck," Katrina Voskovich reported as Wolf finished his examination of the three unknown humans. "An explosion went off inside. Knocked out the commlink, the whole C-cubed set-up . . . the remote detonators for the minefields, too."

"So there's no transmitter," he said quietly.

"Nothing. And you can bet we'd have heard them on the air if they'd been able to get off a message before the place was hit. They're in the dark back at Kessel."

"How about our helmet commlinks?" Wolf asked.

It was Kern who shook his head. "In these hills? Forget it. No way we can reach Kessel. Maybe—*maybe* we could get lucky and raise a patrol or some of the other recruits, but I doubt it. The drop zones were scattered pretty wide, and it would be one chance in a hundred."

"So what's the answer?" Wolf asked, looking from Voskovich to Kern and back again. He felt helpless, boxed in by events he couldn't control. The recruits had to do something . . . but it looked like all his options were closed off.

Voskovich rubbed her chin. "There's one thing we could try. . . ."

"Shoot. I'll take anything."

"I might be able to rig up something makeshift. Hook a helmet commlink into the outpost antenna, maybe get the kind of range we need. I don't guarantee anything. . . ."

"Do it," Wolf said. "I want it yesterday."

"You'll have it in six hours . . . if you get it at all. Can I use Myaighee to help me?"

"Myaighee? Is he the right one for high-tech work? I thought his race was pretty backward."

She looked disgusted. "He's been in the Legion for two years, Wolf. He probably knows more about field maintenance on a commlink than you do."

"Sorry I asked," he said curtly.

She looked like she was ready to say more, but just then Lisa Scott appeared, breathless from a run across the compound. "You'd better come, Wolf," she said. "I found a survivor."

"Take it easy, Corporal," Lisa Scott said. "You've lost a lot of blood."

That was an understatement if ever she'd made one. By rights the man should be dead, but somehow the corporal had lived through the battle and hours of unattended misery. He had been hit by FEK slivers that had pierced his battledress fatigues and cut up his left side, and a pair of deep slash wounds across his chest looked like the products of an attack by one of the heavy Wynsarrysa scimitar-type swords. She had seen plenty of suffering these last few years . . . her mother, the terrorists she had shot, the casualties at Savary's. But seeing the corporal now was worse than anything she'd been forced to look at before.

"Drink this," Wolf added. "It's a stim pill in water."

"Wolf," she said softly. "In his condition . . . a stim pill . . ."

"I know," he said harshly. "But we need him at himself to answer some questions."

The corporal took a long drink, then dropped the cup. "The kid's right," he said, his voice labored. "I'm for the Last March anyway . . . got to do something worthwhile before God starts calling the muster." He tried to sit up, but Wolf pushed him back gently.

"Lie easy, Corporal," he said. "Just tell us what happened here."

"Civilians . . . said they needed help. First aid. We spotted them on sensors downriver and sent a patrol . . . found one of them shot. They said . . . hunting accident. So we brought 'em back."

"How many?" Wolf urged.

"Six. Guess we . . . didn't pay enough attention to the ones who weren't hurt. One of 'em . . . tossed a grenade into the bunker. Whole damn thing went up . . ."

"Why? Why would humans want to knock out the defenses?"

"Separatists . . ."

Scott remembered the three young thugs in the bar in Villastre. It was hard to picture them involved in something like this.

"Separatists," the corporal repeated, gasping for breath. "Some kind of deal with the rebels, I guess. They took out the defenses . . . next thing we knew, those screaming devils were all over the wall. Too damned many to fight . . ."

"They've moved on into the lowlands, haven't they?" Wolf asked.

The corporal shook his head. "I heard . . . I heard them

talking. They'll hit Kessel. The armory there . . . enough
to give them some real firepower. Unless they're stopped."
He closed his eyes.

Wolf straightened up slowly. "Make him as comfortable
as you can, Lisa," he said. "Find out anything else you
can. If he's right about an alliance between the Wynsarrysa
and the separatists, getting through to Fort Kessel's more
important than ever."

She nodded grimly and bent over the injured man, too
worried now to notice the horror of his wounds.

Chapter 24

"Delta One, this is Kessel Command. Wait one." The
voice was thin against the static, and Wolf had to strain to
hear it. The commlink Voskovich had cobbled together
from damaged gear and her helmet system left a lot to be
desired. It hissed and crackled like frying bacon, and the
signal was apt to fade without warning or reason, but it
worked. Fort Kessel had answered his desperate calls at
last.

He only hoped it wasn't too late.

Wolf drummed his fingers on the lowest girder of the
antenna assembly in growing exasperation. *We don't have
time for this waiting!* he thought bitterly. Voskovich had
finished in just under five hours instead of the six she'd
promised, but in that time the rebels would have covered
a lot of ground. He had already repeated his story three
times, to three different people on the other end of the
commlink, and it was starting to seem like he would never
convince them of the danger in time.

"Delta One, this is Ogre," Gunnery Sergeant Ortega's
voice suddenly crackled over the commlink. Despite his
anxieties, or maybe even because of them, Wolf had to
fight back the urge to laugh at the drill instructor's use of
his training company nickname as a call sign. "Wolf, if
this is some kind of stunt . . ."

"Everything in the report is accurate, Sergeant," he

said, irritated. "Corporal Gallagher passed most of it on to us . . . before he died. An hour ago."

There was a short silence. "Gallagher . . . we were on Gwyn together." The gunnery sergeant, usually so gruff, sounded genuinely disturbed. But the moment passed. "We've confirmed parts of your report, Delta One. We diverted a Pegasus when your call came in, and we've spotted your rebels. Commandant Czernak has already started coordinating an operational plan to deal with them."

Wolf breathed out a relieved sigh. "Thank God. I wasn't sure if we'd be able to get through in time."

"Don't bring God into it just yet, Delta One," the sergeant told him. "Not until you hear what's in store for you next. The commandant's plan requires a unit to block the rebel retreat route up the Sinueux, and you're the only ones in position. It won't be easy, Wolf, but we need you. . . ."

He listened in growing horror as Ortega began spelling out the plan.

"Fight? That's a laugh. Every rebel in this district is out there, Wolf. How are we supposed to fight them all?"

Wolf studied Katrina Voskovich for a long moment, then shrugged. "They've left it to us," he said. "If we can't do anything, we're to head up into the hills and try to avoid contact. But if that happens, the rebels will just escape. If we could do something to slow them down, maybe the people who died here won't have died completely in vain."

He wasn't convinced himself, so there wasn't much reason to expect as much from the other four recruits gathered around the base of the antenna array. Ortega and Commandant Czernak had outlined a plan to counter the rebel attack, but it sounded like nothing short of suicide for Delta Lance.

Czernak was calling in all the patrols and as many recruits as they could assemble to bolster the strength at Fort Kessel, while a fast-moving rapid response force would drive north from Fort Hunter to catch the rebels in a pincer. It was a classic military operation, lacking only one thing to make it foolproof.

The missing ingredient was a way to slam the back door on them. Right now Delta Lance was the only group in a position to even try. Ortega had promised to send more men into Checkpoint Tatiana as soon as possible, but it still might take hours. Those men were needed everywhere, and prying enough legionnaires and equipment loose in time to do any good was easier to promise than to deliver.

And Wolf knew as well as Ortega did that it was poor policy to reinforce a forlorn hope when other forces needed the manpower more. . . .

It reminded Wolf all too vividly of Erich Neubeck's orders on Telok. Wolf was supposed to hold the enemy as long as possible, with a vague promise of help to sustain him. In the fight with the Ubrenfars he had tried to hold, but superior numbers had quickly overcome his ramshackle outfit. The reinforcements had never arrived, and good men had died before he had the chance to extricate the handful of survivors from disaster.

His initial reaction to Czernak's plan had been a mixture of horror and disbelief. He couldn't face a replay of Telok. And he couldn't try to lead his lance to certain death. These people were his comrades . . . his friends. Their deaths would hurt even worse than the ones he'd caused on Telok that day.

But he had listened to Ortega without comment, and gravely promised to see if there was any action Delta Lance could take to block the retreat route, at least for a few hours. On the surface it sounded impossible, but the situation Wolfgang Alaric Hauser would have found impossible, Karl Wolf, soldier of the Fifth Foreign Legion, was willing to examine. He couldn't do less.

For too long Wolf had been on the run. He had failed at Telok and run. That had led him to the duel with Neubeck, and he had run again, his honor further stained. He had nearly run from the Legion when the going got tough, but Lisa Scott and the woman called Aunt Mandy had convinced him to stick it out.

He had discovered something these past weeks with the Legion. Honor, reputation, even life itself weren't worth anything unless they were backed up by a genuine commitment. It could be to family or to country or to some cause, but without commitment there was nothing else.

It had taken him a long time to find what a legionnaire was committed to, but Wolf thought he understood it now.

Legio Patria Nostra . . . the Legion is our Fatherland. They had sounded like empty words before, but he knew better now. A legionnaire was committed to the most important cause, the greatest of fatherlands . . . the Legion itself.

Wolfgang Hauser had failed to uphold his honor, his family, his reputation, and his planet, and that failure had led him from aristocracy to this last asylum of misfortune. But Karl Wolf wasn't going to fail again.

"I'm not much on suicide missions, boyo," Kern said, managing to sound cheerful. "Just because we're on Devereaux 'tis no good reason to *do* a Devereaux like our esteemed predecessor, Commandant Hunter. At least not for an empty gesture. Do they really think five people can make a difference against a few hundred?"

"If the minefields could still be switched to active, the rebels wouldn't have much chance of getting away," Lisa Scott observed. "But with the command bunker smashed . . ."

He looked across at Voskovich. "You were able to rig the commlink. What about the mines?"

She looked thoughtful. "It might be done. But anything we rig will be vulnerable. I can't keep them from shutting everything down if they get to the controls we rig here."

"That means defending the place," Kern said slowly. "It still leaves us with the original problem. Five against hundreds . . ."

"Corporal Gallagher told me there was a hidden ammo stock under one of the huts that the rebels didn't get," Scott said. "The sergeant in charge didn't like keeping all his eggs in one basket. That gives us something better than our exercise load to play with."

"Thank God for small favors," Kern said with a grin. The recruits were carrying FEKs, but the only ammo they had been issued consisted of riot control munitions, smoke grenades, and anesthetic needle rounds. With some real ammunition they had a chance.

"We'll have the edge on them in firepower," Wolf said. "Except for what they looted here, they probably aren't all that well equipped, and they won't be all that familiar with what they have picked up."

"Don't make the mistake of underestimating them," Myaighee warned. "Some of them have been fighting for a long time."

"And a club can kill you just as dead as a grenade if you don't watch out," Kern added. "But I'll agree with you on this much, boyo. We can make the bastards know we're here."

"It's damned slim," Wolf said. "If you want to opt out, now's the time. I know you can't run a military unit like a democracy, but I'm not going to decide for the rest of you. Anyone who wants to run for the hills has my blessing. And Gunny Ogre's, too, if that makes any difference. He said to make sure you know this is strictly for volunteers."

"Well," Katrina Voskovich said. "You aren't going to get those mines back on line unless I stay. So I guess I'd better get to work. What about you, Myaighee?"

The hannie's neck ruff twitched. "I let everyone down before, at Savary's. I will not do so again."

"Good enough," the woman said. "What say we tackle the job together, then? With your permission, oh great lance leader . . ."

"Ah . . ." Wolf hesitated. It was hard to bring himself to actually speak the words he needed to say now. "Myaighee, you're still a Legionnaire Third Class, not just a recruit like the rest of us. You've had more experience in real combat situations. I think . . . I think you should take back command of Delta Lance for the duration."

Myaighee crossed his arms, the hannie gesture of denial. "No. No, I was not suited to leadership. I am content to take your orders, Wolf." He paused. "But thank you. This was . . . a gesture I will not forget."

Wolf looked away, uncomfortably aware of the new respect, not just in Myaighee's eyes but in Voskovich and Kern's as well. The hannie and the electronics expert stood up and turned toward the command bunker, already starting to talk over ideas.

"What about you, Tom?" Wolf asked.

The big redhead didn't answer right away. When he finally spoke, his look was focused far away, and he might have been talking to himself. "I joined the Legion because there was nothing for me in civilian life," he said softly. "I ruined a good career with the Marines. Killed a recruit by accident, then skipped out instead of taking my term in the penal battalions. But I didn't fit in anywhere, Wolf.

The only life I was any good at was the Service. So I decided I'd finish out in the Legion. I intend to die fighting, and whether it's today or ten years down the line . . . well, it doesn't really matter that much. I've got no reason to run.''

He stood up. ''I'll walk the perimeter, make sure everything's in order.'' Then he was gone.

Wolf looked across at Scott. She cut him off before he could say anything. ''Let me ask the question,'' she said. ''What are *you* planning? Once upon a time you didn't think Legion traditions meant anything. It must be strange for you, thinking about the oldest tradition of all.''

''I'll fight,'' he said. ''Not because of any Legion tradition about lost causes, though. Because we really can make a difference here. And we might be able to give some meaning to the sacrifice the garrison already made. I won't believe Gallagher held on all that time, gave us that information, to no purpose at all.''

''Noblesse oblige?'' she asked with a faint smile.

He shook his head. ''The Legion takes care of its own.''

Karl Wolf peered over the top of the low berm and studied the valley below Checkpoint Tatiana with growing dismay. The longer he waited and watched, the more his doubts gnawed away within. How could five Legion recruits even consider stirring up a hornet's nest of over two hundred armed rebels? The odds against them were more than just numeric. These Wynsarrysa were tough, fanatic outlaws, well used to fighting as a way of life. Like the Ubrenfars who had overwhelmed his troops on Telok . . .

He tried to ignore the memory and concentrate on the problem at hand, but it was hard to separate past and present.

Dawn would be breaking over the mountains soon. They had spent a long night getting ready, but now the time for waiting was almost at an end. Somehow Katrina Voskovich had managed to rig up a control for the Galahads, using a mine recovered from the field by Myaighee, components from her wristpiece computer, and odds and ends scavenged from damaged equipment in the bunker. The mines were no longer on standby. From here on out, anything the size of a man that moved through a minefield would set off the devices.

In fact, they had already seen them working. The rebels had started drifting back up the river valley soon after planetary midnight. Evidently the assault had run into the first Commonwealth resistance, and this unexpected loss of surprise had been enough to persuade some of the faint-hearted to turn in search of a retreat route. A small party had run straight into a minefield. None of them had survived.

But the next group had spotted the casualties and guessed the truth. Wolf had tried to confuse them by having the recruits launch some of their stock of smoke grenades into the woods on the other side of the refugees. Some, apparently convinced the Legion was close at hand, tried to break through the mines, with the same results as their late friends. The rest withdrew back down the valley in haste.

That had been an hour back. Since then the rebels had been gathering in the valley, gradually marshaling themselves for a concerted effort. Someone down there, perhaps one of the human separatists, had realized that the key to escape lay in retaking the outpost and shutting down those mines. Otherwise the Wynsarrysa wouldn't win free before the main body of legionnaires caught up with them. The Galahads had been carefully positioned over many years by legionnaires thoroughly familiar with their business, and the antipersonnel mines were designed to flip an explosive charge into the air each time the device was triggered. With multiple warheads, Galahads could be lethal again and again before they finally ran dry, and that made them doubly effective at barring escape through any of the narrow valleys that opened up around Tatiana.

So the only way out for the rebels lay through the heart of the outpost. And five would-be legionnaires stood ready to defend the position.

Movement caught his eye. The LI setting on his faceplate showed the rebel force clearly even in the predawn darkness. He zoomed in on the enemy and studied them for a moment.

"They're coming!" he shouted, bracing his FEK on the wall of the berm. The wall would have been a substantial barrier if the power cells in the central bunker hadn't been thoroughly wrecked by the explosion there. Topped with electrified wires, the berm could have held up an assault for a long time if the defenders had been able to tap into a generator, but they'd have to do without that defense now.

Kern dropped to one knee at the other end of the east wall, his own weapon held at the ready. This time they had full combat loads, grenades and needle rounds. The other three recruits were posted behind Wolf and Kern, defending a slit trench the redhead had dug overnight. It made the ideal fall-back position, halfway between wall and bunker. Wolf expected the three of them to be quite a surprise for the rebels to meet once they overcame the wall itself.

They waited. Slowly, the enemy advance gathered strength, surging up the valley. Wolf estimated there were forty or fifty of them, waving an assortment of weapons and shouting hoarse cries exhorting one another to glory.

The two recruits opened up.

With no restrictions on their fields of fire, they used their 1cm minigrenades first. Explosion after explosion burst amid the enemy force, and even those that did little damage contributed to the morale loss of the Wynsarrysa vanguard. After less than a minute of sustained fire the rebels wavered, crumbled.

And the waiting began again.

Lisa Scott and Legionnaire Myaighee were on the firing line when the second serious attack developed. Kern and Wolf had run through nearly half of their meager stock of live minigrenades, so the fresh magazines had been moved forward. Kneeling at the berm with the enemy main body in the crosshairs of her faceplate target display, Scott wondered what Senator Abercrombie would think if he knew what his daughter was doing. For years he had treated her like a possession, not a person. Now she felt free for the first time. . . .

Perhaps it would also be the last.

The rangefinder showed they were coming close enough to be hit hard, and Scott began firing. Across the compound, at his post overlooking the riverbank, Myaighee did the same.

It was just as Wolf had described it, more like a dreamchip game than a real battle. She fired, and kept firing as long as there were targets in her sights. As before, the rebels broke long before they were a threat to the berm, and there was little return fire.

Maybe, she told herself, the odds weren't as overwhelming as they had seemed after all. . . .

"Fafnir! Fafnir to the front! Hurry!" Myaighee's shout was almost gibberish, but somehow the words penetrated her brain and Lisa Scott cut back the magnification on her image intensifiers to get a panoramic view of the battlefield.

That was when she saw them. A pair of flattened turtle shapes, hovering a few scant centimeters off the ground with the morning sun glinting off gleaming armor. She blanked her mind to access her computer implant, and almost instantly her mind was filled with the information she had asked for. They were Sandrat APCs, the predecessors of the Legion's Sandrays. Many had found their way into civilian use after being phased out of the Legion . . . and it seemed that these two, at least, were still doing duty with an army after all these years.

Two armored magrep vehicles, even if they didn't mount any heavy firepower, would be proof against the firepower available to the recruit defenders. Except, of course, for the Fafnir. The missile launcher was an easy match for any APC.

But the hidden military stores at Checkpoint Tatiana had contained only one missile for the launcher, and there were two enemy vehicles out there.

"Go! Go!" Wolf shouted the order and practically lifted Katrina Voskovich out of the trench. The dark-haired, stocky woman sprinted for the berm, clutching the Fafnir tight in her hands.

He had considered taking the weapon himself. Through most of the training he had been assigned as the Fafnir gunner for heavy weapons drills, and he'd slowly developed an affinity for it. But Voskovich had scored better marks with the launcher . . . and a gunner rarely had the luxury to oversee a whole battle the way an ordinary rifleman could. That was why the typical lance in the Fifth Foreign Legion didn't burden the lance leader with any specialty work, though of course there were frequent exceptions.

She ran for the berm, and Wolf cursed under his breath.

He hadn't expected vehicles. Most of the Wynsarrysa were primmies, living from hand to mouth, unable to survive except on what they scavenged. Who would have thought they could have kept the APCs in working order?

Wolf vowed not to underestimate his opponents again. If he lived to profit from the lesson. . . .

Voskovich reached the wall and steadied the Fafnir. An instant later, the APC was on top of them, turbofans whining as it picked up speed. At that moment something flashed from the top of the vehicle. For a moment Wolf thought they were using a weapon mounted in a small remote turret, but then he realized it was a Gwyrran with a heavy rocket launcher lying on top of the vehicle.

The rocket streaked toward the wall. Toward Voskovich.

The explosion tore a hole in the berm twice the width of the vehicle, sending chunks of duracrete spinning in all directions. Wolf saw Voskovich fall, the unfired Fafnir rolling from her arms as she clutched at her stomach.

He was out of the trench in an instant, racing toward the discarded launcher. Wolf barely had time to throw himself sideways and scoop it up as the armored monster drifted almost casually, arrogantly, through the gap. The rocket gunner was sitting up now. So was another rebel, this one with a heavy machine pistol.

The second one was raising his massive weapon slowly, training it on Karl Wolf. . . .

Chapter 25

Are you worthy to be a legionnaire?
—Sergeant Georges Manue
French Foreign Legion, 1941

The Sandrat was less than ten meters from Wolf, floating on its magnetic cushion with the turbofans cut back to a dead idle. With the vehicle dominating this side of the compound, the rebels could advance unhindered, supported by their comrades on top of the APC and their weaponry. Wolf knew, though he couldn't see directly, that the second Sandrat was closing fast.

Time seemed to move in slow motion, and every thought, every action, had a crystal clarity about it unlike anything Wolf had ever experienced before. He could see the muzzle of the machine pistol coming into line with him, and could feel the soft stirring of the air kicked out by the slow-burning fans. Behind him he could hear someone shouting his name. . . .

Then, like the breaking of a dam, time returned to normal. Something struck him in the back just as the machine pistol spat, and a slug tore through the battledress fatigues just above his elbow. If it had not been for the shove Lisa Scott had given him, the bullet would have taken him square in the chest. As it was, fire burned in his arm, and it was all Wolf could do to keep from dropping the Fafnir.

Lisa hit the ground and rolled, coming up with her FEK whining on full-auto. The rebels on top of the APC both rolled back and off the vehicle under the intense impact of the high-velocity needle rounds.

He struggled to his feet and fumbled with the rocket launcher, cursing his throbbing arm. At point-blank range, the computer targeting system was as useless as it was unnecessary, and Wolf had to override the settings and aim and fire strictly by sight. The Fafnir roared from its tube and streaked to the APC, striking it squarely above the driver's hatch. The missile penetrated before it exploded, and the clang of debris ricocheting around the interior was audible where Wolf stood.

Slowly, painfully, the vehicle settled to the ground as the magrep fields collapsed. The fans continued their slow, rhythmic beating, but the APC was too heavy for fans alone to lift.

Wolf staggered, caught himself before he fell, and tossed the empty launcher aside. Kern sprinted past and knelt by the wall, FEK blazing away at full automatic. The missile shot had knocked out one target, but there was still a battle out there.

Wolf kneeled beside the bloodstained form of Katrina Voskovich. Lisa appeared beside him, but he angrily waved her back to the wall. "I'll take care of her," he said. "Pour on the fire! Go!"

The injured woman stirred at the sound of his voice. Ignoring the pain in his arm, Wolf half carried, half dragged her back to the slit trench. At least she would be out of the line of fire there. Dropping into the bottom of the trench beside her, he opened his first aid kit and put painkiller patches on her carotid artery and over the worst wound, a deep gash in her upper leg dangerously close to the femoral artery. Then he dug into the kit again for the roll of sterilite cloth. Working quickly, he wound it around and around the leg, finally cutting it off with his combat knife. As the woman's body heat interacted with the bandage, it would tighten to conform with the shape of her leg, hopefully stanching the flow of blood.

He waited for a long moment, looking down at her. They had never been close, not since the day he had first met her back in the Legion bunkroom on Robespierre. But she was part of his lance, and it had been his decision to let her have the Fafnir that had led to this. His decision . . .

Then he shook off the mood. Wolf returned the knife to its sheath in the top of his boot and clambered awkwardly out of the trench. The rest of the lance was still in the fight. His duty was to them now.

The second Sandrat closed more slowly than the first, but the lower speed allowed a trio of rebels on the hull to maintain a steady fire as the APC approached. Needle rounds chewed at the berm just to the left of Myaighee's position, and ky flinched once as tiny shards of duracrete rattled off kys faceplate.

Myaighee could feel the battle lust stirring once again, just as it had back at Savary's. Ky had started out a servant, not a warrior, but each time ky had gone into battle ky had lost control that much more easily. The lance couldn't afford having one of their number out of control, but Myaighee wasn't sure ky knew how to keep from becoming lost in sheer savage fury.

Maybe the male-human Wolf was right after all. Perhaps the *kyendyp* race really was closer to its animal roots, its barbaric heritage. Ky had seen humans go berserk at the height of a fight, but somehow they seemed to channel it better. For all of kys progress these last two years, ky still hadn't adapted to this strange world of gods and demons and forces beyond the comprehension of kys own kind.

Like Oomour . . .

Out in the valley the rebels were shouting epithets and curses as they ran, waving their weapons overhead. The protective fire from the Sandrat was making the defenders keep their heads down more often than they could shoot, and the mass of the enemy force was pressing forward unchecked. This time they might carry the wall. When that happened, the battle would be over.

Ky fired again, trying to pick off the passengers on the hull of the APC, but the shot didn't have any apparent effect. Myaighee swore, a human curse of the kind favored by Corporal Rostov back in Bravo Company. Nearby Kern was trying to lay down a sustained blanket of fire, but the big male-human was drawing unwelcome attention from the enemy. Myaighee lifted kys weapon again.

The second Sandrat put on a burst of speed, leaping straight for the gap the first one had opened up. It slammed into the grounded hull of the first APC and hovered for long seconds, as if the driver had been stunned by the collision.

Then Myaighee realized the real reason it had stopped. The rear door was dropping, and ky could see hulking shapes pushing toward the ramp. . . .

Ky hardly thought, letting instinct take over entirely.

Swarming over a pile of rubble, ky leapt for the top of the APC, a motion kys tree-climbing ancestors would have been proud to witness. Myaighee jabbed the muzzle of kys gun into the opening hatchway and squeezed the autogrenade launcher's trigger tight. Round after round pumped into the rear of the vehicle, and the whole APC seemed to shudder as explosions ripped through it.

But at least half of the passengers had already dived out the back as they realized what the hannie was doing. One of them, an oversized Wynsarrysa with a string of human ears around his neck and a huge scimitar in one hand, swept his blade in an upward cut. The massive sword caught Myaighee in the stomach, and the force of the blow knocked ky off the vehicle.

Legionnaire Third Class Myaighee lay still on a mound of debris, staring at the open sky. Kys last thought before death claimed ky for its own was the knowledge that ky need worry no more about civilization or savagery, whether ky was bound for the Afterlife among the Blessed Sky Gods kys own people believed in, or the Heaven the chaplains preached about in the human Legion.

The long struggle was over.

"Fall back! Fall back!" Wolf shouted the order as Myaighee went down. The unexpected enemy APCs had wrecked his careful planning, drawing the recruits out of their prepared position at just the moment when the full shock of the rebel attack was sweeping toward them. Instead of a withering fire from the trench, the rebels would encounter nothing but disjointed, individual resistance.

The little hannie's leap to the top of the Sandrat, and his grenade attack on the vulnerable interior, had been the acts of a real hero, but he—ky—had died nonetheless. So it would be with all of them. They could fight on with all the courage they could muster, but in the end Wolf's faulty plan would bring them all down.

"Fall back!" he shouted again.

Kern had clubbed his FEK and was wading through a crowd of Gwyrrans. More were swarming over the berm, too. Wolf lost sight of Lisa Scott entirely. . . .

The high-pitched whine of another battle rifle took Wolf by surprise. He fired again, heard the loading mechanism chatter as his magazine ran dry. As he discarded the FEK,

Wolf realized that the new firing was coming from the slit trench.

From Katrina Voskovich. Seriously wounded, she had still dragged herself upright. Now she was leaning against the lip of trench, clutching her battle rifle like a talisman to ward off the pain and the terror and pouring autofire into the enemy ranks. As the rebels recoiled, Wolf ran for the trench. Kern followed, and after a moment Lisa Scott appeared, bleeding freely from a gash in her forehead but wielding a long, slightly curved sword like an outsized dueling saber and waving a Gwyrran pistol in the other hand.

"We've got to get back to the bunker," Wolf panted. "We can block the door . . . try to hold the bastards a little while longer . . ."

"Somebody has to stay and lay down cover," Kern said. "So you three mag it out of here."

Voskovich shook her head. The effort seemed to cost her most of her remaining strength. "I can't run anyway. And I'd slow you down if you tried to carry me. I'm the one to stay." As if for emphasis, she turned away from them and started firing again, cool, calculating. But Wolf could see the sweat on her forehead, the lines of pain around her eyes and mouth. It was a miracle she was still standing at all.

But she was right.

"Do what you can," he said softly. "What you have to." Wolf pushed Lisa out the rear of the trench. "Mag it! Go! Go!"

Bullets plucked at his uniform as he ran for the command bunker, but the only one that hit was almost spent. Beside him, Kern wasn't as lucky. A bullet slammed into the redhead's back. The big man stumbled and fell. Wolf threw himself down beside Kern, checking his back. There was no blood, no sign of penetration. The duraweave had saved his life.

"I can make it!" Kern snapped, rising unsteadily and plunging on. Wolf was right on his heels.

They had just reached the bunker when the firing slackened by the trench. Voskovich was out of the action. Dead? Or just exhausted at last, overwhelmed by shock and blood loss and the painkillers in her veins, lying in a heap at the bottom of the trench? It didn't matter much now.

They closed the door and barred it, but there wasn't much they could do now to defend themselves. The bunker hadn't been designed to defend against a sustained attack . . . and they were down to their knives, a captured pistol and a bloodstained saber for weapons. The Wynsarrysa still outnumbered them despite the heavy casualties they had suffered in the attacks.

Now it was just a matter of time. . . .

Something thumped against the door, once, twice, and again.

"They won't use explosives," Kern said. "The bastards don't know what our set-up is in here. Probably figure wrecking our new controls will keep the mines active."

"Will it?" Wolf asked.

The big man gave a curt nod. "The way they're set now they'll go off no matter who goes through there. No recognition function." His eyes met Wolf's. "I know what you're thinking, but we can't wreck them ourselves. Our own people will be driving into those mines soon."

"They don't know that," Scott pointed out. "Maybe we can cut some kind of deal. . . ."

Kern shook his head this time. "They won't keep it. No honor. We'd be better off going out still fighting. If we're captured . . . it wouldn't be pretty."

The blonde shuddered. Outside, the thumping continued, louder now. The door bucked and strained under the blows.

Wolf took the sword from her. "Then let's do it."

The door splintered. Wolf shouted a Germanic oath and leapt forward, blade slashing fiercely. The attackers gave ground, and he was suddenly outside again. The large Gwyrran who had killed Myaighee loomed in front of him, his scimitar a menacing gleam in the morning sunlight.

The other rebels were jeering and shouting, but none made a move against Wolf. The swordsman stepped closer, turning a casual-seeming move into a sudden blurring attack. Wolf's blade flashed up to meet the sweeping cut. In the same motion Wolf pressed forward. Surprised, the Gwyrran gave ground, defending himself from Wolf's sudden follow-up lunge. His left-handed attack seemed to have his opponent off-balance.

In Wolf's mind he saw the duel with Neubeck again. He pushed the image away, launched a slashing attack that drew blood from the Gwyrran's right shoulder. But the wound didn't seem to bother the other at all. He counterattacked, a vicious, savage attack that pushed Wolf back step by step toward the door to the bunker. The Wynsarrysa was bigger, stronger, with a better weapon. He had all the advantages.

Just like Erich Neubeck . . .

Then the alien slashed again and wrenched the saber from Wolf's grasp. It spun, end over end, catching the sunlight. The crowd was silent for the first time.

"The loss is disgrace," the Gwyrran rumbled in broken Terranglic. "In defeat . . . death." He gestured arrogantly to a pair of rebels close by. "The human is taken. Bind him. The sport comes later."

Wolf flinched as the Gwyrrans closed in, then staggered and dropped to his knees. In a single lightning motion he drew his combat knife and threw it. It sank into the Gwyrran's back, just below the neck, and the rebel collapsed in a heap. There was a long, stunned moment when nobody moved.

Suddenly shots rang out as Lisa Scott came out of the door with the machine pistol blazing. The silence ended in shouts and screams, chaos. It was only a temporary respite, but Wolf smiled faintly anyway.

It had been like living through the fight with Neubeck all over again, but this time Wolf felt no guilt over lost honor. This time he hadn't given in to hatred or instinct. He had done as he had been taught, and he thought his Legion teachers would approve.

The legionnaire fought to win, not merely to score points or prove superiority. And even if he died in the next instant, Wolf knew now that he had truly become a legionnaire. . . .

"Bank left! Over there!" Gunnery Sergeant Ortega tapped the pilot of the Pegasus on the arm and pointed, and the corporal nodded and followed his order.

The transport shuttle stooped low over Checkpoint Tatiana. The cluster of rebels around the command bunker had already started to break up, and the sudden appearance of the Legion craft, twin Gatling guns hammering into the crowd without mercy, was enough to keep them on the run. Two more shuttles swept over the humpbacked hill on the far side of the river, their own guns raking the enemy, to finish the job.

As they passed over Tatiana, Ortega saw the three ragged figures by the door. Delta Lance had done everything they had been asked to do, and more. Soon the main body of Czernak's legionnaires would come up and round up the rebels who had fled.

A notable victory . . . won by a lance of recruits.

Ortega smiled. That was a story that would be told to future recruit classes . . . perhaps for as long as Mankind fielded a legion of foreigners.

They buried Myaighee at Checkpoint Tatiana, alongside the legionnaires who had died in the first surprise attack. He was the only one of the lance dead, though Katrina Voskovich's fate still was far from sure despite the high-tech miracles of Commonwealth medicine. Wolf, Kern, and Lisa Scott had all been wounded in the fighting, but they were in attendance alongside the veteran legionnaires of Czernak's strike column and an assortment of their fellow recruits who had been pulled in from the field when the exercise had turned real. The regen cast on his arm was an inconvenience, but Wolf steeled himself to keep from trying to scratch at the healing flesh encased in the cylinder.

Father Chavigny, as the Training Company's chaplain, had been flown out to conduct the ceremony. He read the burial service in slow, measured tones, and Wolf found himself making all the appropriate responses right along with the others.

As Father Chavigny finished the service and put away his prayer book, Wolf couldn't help but think of the funeral they had held for Antonelli. These honored dead were heroes of the Legion, and treated as such. He knew the difference now.

It was old Legion tradition for the lancemates of a dead legionnaire to divide up his personal effects among themselves. Kern had taken a length of rope Myaighee had claimed was used by another alien legionnaire to commit suicide, but Wolf had been interested in only one item the hannie had left behind.

As the service broke up he produced Myaighee's tiny vial from under his shirt and took it off its thin chain. Wolf kneeled by the open graves, and put a tiny quantity of soft earth inside. He straightened up and drew out the medallion Lisa had given him. It had helped him find the balance in his life at a time when he had needed it, but in the past days he had learned that the true source of that balance was within.

He weighed the medallion in his hand for a moment, then tossed it into Myaighee's grave. It was the last honor he could pay to a better soldier, a better legionnaire, than he would ever be.

EPILOGUE

> The training affects people in different ways. Yes,
> there were times when it was rough, but I survived.
>
> —A legionnaire of the 13th DBLE
> French Foreign Legion, 1984

Dusk was gathering over Fort Hunter.

It was an evening just like any other, but for Karl Wolf and fifty other recruits from Training Company Odintsev it was anything but ordinary. The shrunken company stood in ranks on the parade ground with an air of anticipation and excitement, waiting for the officers and noncoms to settle into place on the reviewing stand in front of them with ill-disguised impatience.

Tonight was the ceremony of the *kepi blanc*. After this, the training would end. They would be legionnaires.

Gunnery Sergeant Ortega made a curt gesture, and a line of Legion security troops ignited their hand-held torches in unison. The flickering light of the flames highlighted fifty-one drawn but happy faces.

Standing at attention in full dress uniform with his white kepi held behind his back, Wolf thought back over the weeks of training and wondered how he had made it through. The battles had tested them to the limit. . . . but the calculated training of the Legion's noncoms had prepared them well for those fights by pushing them beyond their limits.

Now the survivors of that difficult process of molding and tempering were about to be accepted into the ranks of the Fifth Foreign Legion.

From his position in the first line, between Kern and Scott, Karl Wolf couldn't see many of the other recruits, but he knew them like brothers and sisters now. Hosni

Mayzar, the fiendish Arabic lance leader . . . Soak Burundai, who had overcome his poor start to stand here tonight . . . Lauriston, MacDuff's friend . . . Radiah Suartana, whose path had rarely crossed Wolf's during training, but who remained as faithful now as when they had signed up together.

And Katrina Voskovich. She was out of danger but facing a long recovery period. Alone of the training company she had already received her orders back to Colin Fraser's Bravo Company, still stationed in the Trisystem facing the Ubrenfar invaders. The long trip back would be time enough for her to heal from the physical wounds. Other scars might run deeper, Wolf thought. But if anyone could overcome those, it was Katrina Voskovich.

Wolf jerked his attention back to the ceremony. There was a galaxy of important people in attendance, including Aunt Mandy and Corporal Souham, the barkeeper who was also president of the Legion Veterans Association. Captain Odintsev and Commandant Stathopoulos, commander of the Training Battalion, had already given their speeches, laying emphasis on the fine work and bright prospects of the recruits now that basic training was over. But the third officer to speak held Wolf's complete attention.

"For over a thousand years the white kepi has been the symbol of the legionnaire," Colonel Jason Carr, the commanding officer of Fort Hunter, said in solemn, measured tones. "Through the centuries the units which have taken the name and symbolism of the Foreign Legion have carried the kepi in victory and in defeat, fighting for the good causes and the bad. We legionnaires are a strange breed, true not so much to the colors that fly above us as we are to ourselves and our traditions. There are those who call us mercenaries, others who call us scum . . . but we shall always know that we are first and foremost *legionnaires,* bearers of the sacred white kepi. And it is for the honor of our comrades, of our Legion, and of our sacred kepi that we make the pledge of honor and fidelity. The day may come when you must emulate the heroes of Camerone or Devereaux or a thousand other desperate battles." He glanced toward Delta Lance, and Wolf drew himself up a little straighter. "In fact, some of you already have. If and when that day comes, I know each of you will remember your pledge and redeem it with the heroism that is the essence of the legionnaire.''

He nodded sharply, and his C3 technician touched a key on the reviewing stand's sound board. The slow, stately notes of "Le Boudin" the ancient marching song of the Legion, filled the air.

The music had been passed down over hundreds of years almost unchanged, but the words went back only a century or so to the formation of the Fifth Foreign Legion. Wolf was surprised to find himself joining in with the rest of the recruits as enthusiasm and a stirring feeling of belonging welled up inside him.

> Under strange skies so unfamiliar,
> By the light of a distant sun,
> Stands the sentinel, the warrior,
> Of the Fifth Foreign Legion.
>
> To die with honor is our wish,
> For the Glory of past Legions;
> We shall all know how to perish,
> Following old traditions.
>
> One world's unnumbered blood was shed,
> For Honor and Fidelity,
> Heroes of war, our hallowed deed,
> We know you shall judge us worthy.

As the final words of the song rang out, Captain Odintsev gestured to Gunnery Sergeant Ortega, whose swarthy face managed to look stern and proud under the flickering torch light. Ortega nodded, and with the last trumpet flourish all fifty-one men and women in the recruit company donned their kepis as one.

It was done.

There were more speeches, but the magical moment was over. They held the rank of Legionnaire Third Class now, and their five-year contracts had gone into effect the moment the ancient kepis had touched their heads.

Wolf listened to the speeches with a sense of unreality. It was hard, now, to think of life outside of Fort Hunter. The recruits would be moving on, to advanced training or to assignments in the field. There was even word that drafts of reinforcements would soon be on the way to the Republic Trisystem as the confrontation over Laut Besar continued to escalate.

And Karl Wolf had made a decision. He would be there. He had been forced to abandon his home, and then the cause itself. And even though he had found a new place here among these legionnaires, he knew he would never be truly free of his past until he laid his ghosts to rest.

After the ceremony, he and Lisa Scott walked across the grounds, past the Monument aux Morts and toward the tube station. It was quiet now, the perfect night for a walk and a chance to talk about the future. He valued Lisa's advice over all others, and he thought she would approve of his choice.

As they talked, the gates to the tube station swung open and a trio of noncoms led a ragged line of mismatched civilians through. They looked young, for the most part, baffled, awed, scared. . . .

Fresh recruits . . . for Fort Hunter to turn into legionnaires.

GLOSSARY

adchip: short for "adhesive chip", any of the button-sized minicomputers designed to hook directly into the human nervous system for total sensory interaction. A cheap alternative to computer implants.

ale: slang for *alien;* applied to any nonhuman.

anfangen: German (Laut Besar Uro dialect) for "begin." Used to order the start of a fencing engagement.

anteilzucht: German (Laut Besar Uro dialect) for "part-breed," a child of mixed Uro and Indomay blood.

arbebaril: French (Devereaux dialect) for "barrel tree," the multitrunked tree cultivated in the Archipel d'Aurore for its sap.

aristo: slang for "aristocrat." On Laut Besar, a complimentary term. In the Legion, it generally denotes one too soft and pampered to have much future with the Legion.

battledress: the combat uniform of the twenty-ninth century soldier. The typical battledress uniform, as worn by the Foreign Legion, consists of a duraweave coverall, boots, and a combat helmet. The coverall is not only resistant to shrapnel and small arms fire, but also contains a net of microcircuits which provide environmental control, plus a "chameleon cloth" weave which detects patterns and shades of light and matches the uniform to various backgrounds. Web gear may be worn to hold a variety of items, and a backpack may be provided for extended marches. Many soldiers augment the basic uniforms with plasteel armor segments covering chest and back, arms, or legs; there is little uniformity in the extent and use of armor. Onager gunners wear full body armor over their regular battledress. Light gloves and a hostile environment version of the combat helmet may convert the outfit into a lightweight spacesuit, and other adaptations allow it to be used in a variety of environs.

Batu: outer satellite of Laut Besar, a planetoid holding a small astronomical observatory but no other facilities. The name means "Rock" in Indomay.

binatanganas: "wildbeast," a savage predator native to wilderness regions of Laut Besar.

C3: Command, Control, Communications. (1) the science of military command-control. (2) the backpack computer/commo system issued to Commonwealth forces on a platoon level. (3) the headquarters of a combat unit, often "c-cubed."

cafarde: originally a French term (literally: "the cockroach") with close associations with the Legion. "The bug" is the madness caused by boredom and stress common to Legion forces on garrison duty.

cargomod: "cargo module," a standard shipping container used for transporting shipboard cargoes. Also slang, the equivalent of "crate."

carriership: generic term for the multimillion-ton FTL ships used by the Commonwealth, so-called because they are used to carry large numbers of interplanetary vessels from one system to another. Requiring the computing power of a full artificially intelligent computer to handle interstellar navigation, carrierships are imbued with distinctive personalities. These carry the names of famous philosophers or wise counselors from history and mythology. Breaking with usual navy traditions, the computers and the ships are both referred to using masculine pronouns.

C-cubed: the C3 center of an HQ or vehicle.

chief sergeant: NCO equivalent in rank to U.S.A. master sergeant; found as battalion-level NCO.

Citizen: anyone with Commonwealth citizenship; this

includes virtually everyone born on Terra. Citizenship is highly prized off-planet, but regarded as essentially trivial on Earth. The honorific "Citizen" is frequently used in the Colonies as a token of respect.

Commandant: Fifth Foreign Legion military officer commanding a battalion; equivalent to the rank of major.

commlink: standard personal or vehicular communications system used by the Commonwealth armed forces.

compboard: a portable computer terminal, roughly the size and shape of a clipboard or legal pad.

compols: short for "Commonwealth Police", the chief law enforcement arm of the Terran Commonwealth.

CSN: Commonwealth Space Navy, the arm of the Commonwealth armed forces charged with interplanetary and interstellar transport and combat missions.

Fafnir: man-portable rocket launcher issued on a section level to the Fifth Foreign Legion. The Fafnir uses a rocket that is "smart" (able to discriminate various target silhouettes preprogrammed by the operator). It is equally proficient in antitank and air defense roles.

FE-FEK/24 (Fusil d'énergie Kinetique Model 24): kinetic energy rifle manufactured by Fabrique Europa, now considered obsolete but still found in local militias, security forces, and private collections. The model lacks the grenade launcher found on the FEK/27.

FE-FEK/27 (Fusil d'énergie Kinetique Model 27): kinetic energy rifle manufactured by Fabrique Europa, standard longarm issued to the Fifth Foreign Legion.

FE-MEK/15 (Mitrailleuse d'énergie Kinetique Model 15): kinetic energy assault gun manufactured by Fabrique Europa, the standard lance-level support weapon used by the Fifth Foreign Legion.

FE-PLF (Pistolet Lance-Fusee): 10mm rocket pistol manufactured by Fabrique Europa.

FLB: Free Laut Besar; the designation of the Besaran forces who fled the planet after the Ubrenfar invasion and accompanied the Commonwealth counterattack.

floatcar: an unarmored magrep vehicle, used in both civilian and military roles.

Freiheit Stern: German for "Liberty Star," the Germanic version of Soleil Liberté. Also a liner of Laut Besaran registry.

Freiherr: honorific on Laut Besar between Uro aristocrats.

FTL: Faster-Than-Light. The term has entered slang usage as an expression describing any sort of great speed.

fusion airjets: propulsion system used in magrep and other vehicle types. Air is superheated and expelled by small fusion reactors in the system's intake ducts. The Commonwealth prefers turbofans when vehicles are to be used in conjunction with troops due to safety considerations, but other races, notably the Ubrenfars, are less fussy.

Graff: a major landholder on Laut Besar.

gunnery sergeant: NCO in Commonwealth forces, equivalent in rank to a U.S. Army staff sergeant. Employed as a company-level NCO. Frequently addressed as "Gunny."

Gwyrran: Native of Gwyrr (Lywstryn IV) or any of the colonies planted under the auspices of the Semti. The typical Gwyrran is a bipedal, furred, homeothermic sophont standing roughly 1.9 meters in height. Their culture is highly feudalistic, with similarities to that of Medieval Japan on Terra. Humans and Gwyrrans find it very hard to understand one another's languages and underlying philosophies even with the aid of the adchip instruction.

The Gwyrrans, like the Ubrenfars, were favored by the Semti Conclave as soldiers, but Gwyrr never chose to rebel from Conclave rule.

H & F stamp: Legion slang for an honorable discharge, derived from the phrase "Served with Honor and Fidelity" stamped on the discharge papers of the legionnaire.

hauptmann: rank in the Army of Laut Besar corresponding to Commonwealth captain.

holetter: message using a holocube to send 3D sound-and-video data.

holo: slang for a holographic image.

holocube: a small, flat projector which can store and image 3D still or moving pictures. Very inexpensive models simply project an unmoving, silent image. Advanced types can carry up to half an hour or more of sound and video.

holopic: a holographic image in a wall or frame mount, the lineal descendent of a painting, poster, or photograph.

holovid: a 3D holographic projection using full sight, sound, and motion.

HUD: Heads Up Display. Found in many vehicles and craft, this type of display system is also used in combat helmets by individual infantrymen.

ident disk: a derivative of chip technology worn by most people within the Commonwealth and associated regions. The ident disk contains retinal scan and DNA trace for unique identification of the owner. It also contains a record of professional, financial, educational, and other background. The ident disk is considered the most reliable method of recording information available, and is an individual's most important single possession.

Indomay: person of Indonesian/Malaysian descent; member of Laut Besar's lower class.

kajudjati: a dark hardwood grown on Laut Besar.

kapitan: rank and position in the Navy of Laut Besar, usually denoting the commanding officer of a ship.

kepi: the traditional headgear of the Foreign Legion dress uniform. Enlisted personnel wear a white kepi, officers black. Much mystique is built around the award of the kepi to the Legion trainee.

kopral: rank in the Army of Laut Besar corresponding to the Commonwealth's corporal.

lance: the Commonwealth's basic military unit, either five infantrymen or a single tank or aircraft. On Laut Besar the unit is known as a squad or trupp.

Lebensraum Bergbau und Ingenieurwesen Korporation: Lebensraum Mining and Engineering Corporation, a now-defunct resource exploitation firm originally based on the colony world of Lebensraum which provided the first Uro technical experts who took over economic and later political control of Laut Besar shortly before the Semti War.

legionnaire: loosely, a member of the Fifth Foreign Legion (or any other "Legion" in the Army, past or present). Specifically, an enlisted soldier holding the rank of Legionnaire First Class, Legionnaire Second Class, or Legionnaire Third Class. Non-Legion units use the designation "soldier" instead of Legionnaire.

leutnant: rank in the Army of Laut Besar corresponding to the Commonwealth rank of subaltern.

life-support chair: powered wheelchair used for extreme injuries and geriatric cases who no longer respond to regen or bionic therapy. The chair is enclosed around the legs and lower torso, and houses a variety of life support equipment. It is powered and can be steered by voice command or keyboard input.

linnax: naval or planetary defense gun; the name derives from "linear accelerator." It fires projectiles at very high velocities, using the same principles as the kinetic energy rifle but on a much larger scale.

loke: slang for "local"; applied to any native, human or nonhuman.

mag: slang for "move," as in "Mag it!" or "Mag out!" The word derives from the magrep vehicles used by the Terran military.

maglev tube: fixed transport system commonly used around large Commonwealth cities and installations. By mounting magrep modules in the tubes themselves and in the cars traversing them, manipulation of magnetic fields allows high speeds to be reached. The tubes are in a vacuum to reduce friction problems.

magrep: slang for magnetic repulsion, used to refer to vehicles riding on a magnetic suspension cushion.

magrep module: small semihemispherical projection unit (linked to a generator) which produces a magnetic suspension cushion.

Magnetic Suspension Vehicle (MSV): official designation of any vehicle operating on a magnetic suspension cushion.

major: rank in the Army of Laut Besar corresponding to the Commonwealth ranks of commandant or major. It is pronounced "maiyor" when used by or for Besarans.

marchman: Legion slang for the common soldier; doughboy; grognard; grunt.

messtalk: slang for rumor or scuttlebutt.

Milky Way Magician: figure from a popular children's entertainment series of the Reclamation Era. The Milky Way Magician stories have become classics in the past two hundred years. "I believe in the Milky Way Magician" is on par with belief in Santa Claus or the Easter Bunny.

narcostick: a nonaddictive, mildly narcotic cigarette.

nube: slang for a newcomer or recruit in the Legion. Used with extreme scorn.

oberleutnant: rank in the Army of Laut Besar corresponding to the Commonwealth rank of lieutenant.

oberst: rank in the Army of Laut Besar corresponding to the Commonwealth rank of colonel.

onager (*fusil d'onage;* storm rifle: plasma gun, originally invented during the French Imperial period (hence the French-derived name). The onager is one of the standard section-level heavy weapons used by the Fifth Foreign Legion (the other is the Fafnir rocket launcher). Onagers require soldiers to wear fairly cumbersome body armor to protect them from heat effects, but are devastatingly powerful on the battlefield.

onnesium: a trans-100 element existing in an "island of stability" beyond the short-lived radioactives on the periodic table. Onnesium is used to plate field coils in Reynier-Kessler FTL drive units. It is rare and extremely valuable, both monetarily and strategically.

Ortwaffen: German (Laut Besaran Uro dialect) for "Place of Arms," a training area devoted to weapons practice found in institutions and some private homes.

Pegasus (TH-39): hypersonic shuttle used by the Commonwealth military for rapid deployment of small units over continental distances or to and from orbit.

penal battalions: auxiliary units of the Colonial Army, employed for dirty jobs involving heavy labor, including construction, colonization projects, Terraforming preparation, and similar tasks. The penal battalions are filled by criminals facing short-term punishment, often as an alternative to regular military service.

platoon sergeant: NCO rank equivalent to the contemporary rank of staff sergeant. Serves as Platoon XO.

regen therapy: advanced Commonwealth medical technique that regrows damaged tissue.

rembot: labor-saving device, a robot controlled by a master computer system in a household, factory, etc. This approach to robotics was found to be far more efficient than the use of numerous independent machines.

repbay: maintenance and storage facility for vehicles, aircraft, and so forth. A hangar or garage.

Republic Trisystem: name given by Captain Francois Robespierre of the ISS TALLEYRAND to the loose trinary system surveyed by his expedition in 2362 A.D. The three stars he dubbed Liberté, Egalité, and Fraternité in honor of the French Revolution, which was an especial interest of his due to his famous name. The Trisystem was never settled as a single entity. The planet bearing Robespierre's name was colonized by Imperial France, while Laut Besar was settled under the Clearance Edicts by Indomalaysian troublemakers; it later became an unaligned neutral outside the Commonwealth. Two planets orbiting Soleil Fraternité were claimed by the Ubrenfars during the Shadow Centuries.

Reynier-Kessler Drive: the Terran stardrive, named for its two inventors, Jules Reynier and Erich Kessler.

rezplex: residential complex, a self-contained arcology-style community containing housing, services, etc.

Sandray: (1) The M-786 standard maglev APC in use by the Fifth Foreign Legion, with several distinct variants filling different military functions. (2) (s-) life-form native to the Great Desert of Devereaux, a burrowing carnivore trapper which subdues its prey with a muscle-paralyzing poison.

section: an infantry unit containing three lances.

Semti: alien race, formerly rulers of the Semti Conclave but now subject (for the most part) to the Terran Commonwealth. Their ruthless pragmatism brought them into direct conflict with Terra during the Semti War, in which they lost control of the two-hundred-world empire known as the Semti Conclave.

Semti War: conflict fought between the Terran Commonwealth and the Semti Conclave (2725–2745 AD). The initial Semti penetration of Terran space was slowed down by the Fourth Foreign Legion's heroic stand on Devereaux, giving the unprepared Commonwealth time to gather military forces and make several crucial diplomatic alliances with other interstellar powers bordering on the Conclave. The final Terran offensive deep into Conclave space ended with the surrender of the last Semti military forces in 2745.

serdadu: rank in the Army of Laut Besar corresponding to the Commonwealth ranks of legionnaire or soldier.

sersan: rank in the Army of Laut Besar corresponding to the Commonwealth rank of sergeant.

sersan peloten: rank in the Army of Laut Besar corresponding to the Commonwealth rank of platoon sergeant.

Shadow Centuries, the: term applied to the period of 2425–2590 AD, a period of anarchy on Terra. The Shadow Centuries were marked by a lapse of some Terran technologies. Although existing carrierships continued to operate on an irregular basis, there was no new ship construction and no organized effort to stay in touch with the bulk of the human colony worlds. Mankind's return to interstellar space was put on hold until Terrestrial affairs could be set in order, leaving the colonial worlds to survive—or perish—on their own.

Sky Guard: military organization on Laut Besar. A largely ceremonial formation.

softsnake: a large but primitive animal native to Laut Besar, snakelike in appearance but lacking an endoskeleton and possessing many characteristics of Terran gastropods.

sol: basic unit of Commonwealth currency, buying power roughly equivalent to one dollar in 1990 U.S. funds.

Soleil Egalité: G3V star, part of the "Republic Trisystem." Robespierre, a Commonwealth colony world, circles this star.

Soleil Fraternité: F8V star, part of the "Republic Trisystem." The system's two habitable planets are controlled by the Ubrenfars.

Soleil Liberté: K2V star, part of the "Republic Trisystem." The system supports two habitable planets, Laut Besar (I) and Danton (Vb).

strak: (1) a small, nasty, ill-tempered, rodentlike species native to Devereaux which congregates in large swarms. They are smelly, dirty, stupid beasts that combine the worst behavioral characteristics of rats, cockroaches, and lemmings. (2) swear word, derived from the creature. The word has entered the language, especially in the Legion, in a number of ways: as a noun, "you filthy strak" (very insulting); as a verb, "strakking" (i.e. behaving like a strak), etc.

synthol: a synthetic alcohol beverage much favored in the Legion.

systerm: "system terminal," the major port facilities used by carrierships near the fringe of a star system.

Systerm Liberty: name of the system terminal in the Laut Besaran system, administered by Commonwealth authorities.

tacdata: tactical database. Before a mission or during transport, all soldiers are given a tacdata feed from HQ or vehicle computers to their individual wristpieces or other personal computers. Tacdata includes maps, last known dispositions of friendly and enemy units, radio frequencies, mission profiles, etc.

Telok: inner satellite of Laut Besar, housing planetary port facilities and a military installation. The word, in Indomay, means "port."

Terran Commonwealth: the human interstellar state which fields the Fifth Foreign Legion. Formed near the end of the Shadow Centuries, the Terran Commonwealth led the way toward unified global government and the return to space known as the Reclamation. Following the Semti War, the Commonwealth acquired virtual control over most of the Conclave Sphere, and thus became a colonial power in the old (nineteenth Century) sense of the term.

Terranglic: the common tongue of modern humanity,

especially the Commonwealth, derived from English with many borrowings from other tongues, especially French.

Tophet: Alpha Crucis V, a marginally habitable world in the Terran Commonwealth owned and exploited by Interstellar Metals, Limited (Instelmet). The hellish conditions of the planet prompted the earliest explorers to bestow the name, an old synonym for the Underworld. It has since entered the lexicon as an epithet.

Tuan: Indomay term of respect, the equivalent of "sir" or "my lord," usually (but not always) reserved for Uros.

Ubrenfars: alien starfaring race, a serious rival with the Terran Commonwealth for interstellar power. The typical Ubrenfar is a two-meter tall, warm-blooded biped with a powerful tail, highly mobile and expressive ear-folds, and thick scales. The gross appearance suggests a Terran dinosaur, but the actual biology is totally alien. They are known pejoratively among humans as "scalies."

The Ubrenfars, like Mankind, were involved in hostilities against the Semti when the Conclave collapsed, and indeed were perceived by the Semti as the more dangerous opponent. They are aggressive, territorial, and warlike.

Uro: person of Germanic/European descent; member of Laut Besar's upper class.

vidmag: entertainment medium common in human space for infotainment purposes. The vidmag is a cheap alternative to adchips, worn like glasses and providing direct trideo images to the viewer. They are most frequently used for periodicals and other material with a short span of interest to consumers.

Whitney-Sykes HPLR-55 (High-Power Laser Rifle Mark 55): laser rifle manufactured by the Australian small arms company Whitney-Sykes, commonly used as a sniper's rifle by the Fifth Foreign Legion.

wristpiece: computer terminal worn on the wrist and forearm. The wristpiece is now becoming largely obsolete on Terra (where computer implants are the cutting edge of technology), but are still quite common off Terra. They can perform virtually all of the functions of a contemporary PC, including calculation, data storage/retrieval, translation, and other jobs. Some are designed to link to implants or adchips worn by the operator, while others are voice-activated with a remote radio receiver worn behind the ear. It is commonly known as a "piece."

Wynsarrysa: "the Lost," descendants of the original Gwyrran colonists on Devereaux, or, more specifically, those who have not been assimilated into colonial life. They are regarded as brigands and rebels.